UNDER LOCKE

MARIANA ZAPATA

This book is a work of fiction. While reference might be made to actual historical events or existing locations, the names, characters, places and incidents are either the product of the author's imagination or are used fictitiously, and any resemblance to actual persons, living or dead, business establishments, events, or locales is entirely coincidental.

ISBN: 978-0-9904292-0-3

Book Cover Design by Jasmine Green *http://jasminegreen.net*
Interior Design by Kassi Cooper of Kassi's Kandids Formatting

DEDICATION

I know this doesn't cut it,
but I hope you understand
that an infinite amount of gratitude still wouldn't
be enough.
Amanda, Grace, and Dell—thank you for putting
up with me through this.

CONTENTS

CHAPTER ONE

Pins and Needles.

The business sign loomed ahead of me. Ominous. Foreboding.

Crap. Crap. *Crap.*

I was going to puke.

And it wasn't going to be a pretty puke like when you're a baby and even farting can be considered cute. It was going to be nasty. Nasty, projectile vomiting straight out of a horror movie.

And if that wasn't bad enough, immediately after throwing up all over the dashboard of my twelve-year-old Ford Focus, I was going to burst into tears. And exactly like my puking, it was going to be nasty. It wasn't going to be classy or snot-less, and I'd probably sound like a wheezing baboon.

The white number on my dashboard clicked to 3:55.

Holy moly.

My stomach churned at the same time nervous tears threatened to well up in my eyes.

What in the hell were you thinking, Iris?

Leaving the only home I'd ever known. Moving to Austin. Staying with Sonny.

Being broke had made me desperate. The knowledge that my bank account was bleeding a slow death had wrung me dry. It'd stripped me of what made me up; pride, perseverance, and apparently, the ability to make good choices.

Because someone who made good choices wouldn't be taking a job from a man like Dex Locke.

3:56 flickered into place on the clock.

With trembling fingers, I took the keys out of the ignition and slipped out of my car. Luckily I'd found a spot in the lot adjacent to the trendy shopping center the business was found in. With its terra cotta roofing and white stonewashed walls, it seemed so at odds with the reputation a biker-owned tattoo shop should have, especially since it was located smack in the middle of a real estate agency and deli.

I mean, shouldn't it be right by a strip club and some massage place that promised a happy ending?

I shouldn't and couldn't complain. I knew that. There wasn't a reason why I should even think about being anything less than grateful that Sonny had found me this job when I'd gone more than six months unemployed. You had no idea what desperation was until there was less than a hundred bucks left in your bank account and no job prospects.

I guess that was the problem with an associate of arts degree in community college. Too educated for minimum wage and not educated enough for a good paying job unless you were lucky.

And lucky, I was not.

Crap luck was why I found myself hustling across the street to Pins and Needles, eyeing the satin black Harley Dyna parked directly in front of the shop. With the exception of the color, the frame was the exact same as Sonny's. A young cousin of the bike my dad had owned once upon a time.

Which was a route I wasn't going to go down. No, siree.

Big, classic bold font illustrated the name of the shop as I came up to the tinted glass door.

I gagged.

God, my mom would be rolling in her grave if she knew what the hell I was doing.

Sonny had called me two hours before, given me an address and told me to be there at four. I'd scraped through my suitcase looking for work clothes and grabbed the first shirt, pants, and cardigan I found that weren't too wrinkled. I wasn't sure how long it would take me to get to the business he was sending me to and getting places late was a huge pet peeve of mine, so I hurried the hell up to get ready. After slumming it for so long, I couldn't help but think his call was kind of a miracle.

Until he threw in Dex's name.

But what other choice did I have? This was why I'd come to Austin.

Now, I wasn't expecting anything amazing and really, I didn't need anything great from a job. I'd been perfectly happy answering phones all day and scheduling other people's dream vacations at the cruise line. It was slow but whatever. A very long time ago, I'd told myself that I wouldn't complain about inconsequential things and I wasn't planning on starting now.

I mean, boring and monotonous was safe.

I'd done boring and monotonous since the moment I turned sixteen by working at a real estate agency, then a discount bookstore, followed by sales for a weight loss pill, dog sitting, watching over kids at a daycare center, and filing at a medical practice. I did what I had to do to pay the bills. So as long as I wasn't prostituting or having to make collection calls, I'd pretty much take whatever I could get.

Only I hadn't anticipated a job with the infamous Dex. A man that I'd heard enough of in ten minutes to know that I wasn't exactly going to be working for the Pope.

Notorious, yes. Bad, yes. Reformed like they made it seem? I doubted it.

We'd thought my dad had been "reformed" and that didn't exactly work out.

Screw it. What was the worse that was going to happen? I'd grown up around a felon. A biker. I'd loved that felon biker for longer than he'd deserved.

My half-brother was a biker but not a felon. And I loved that moron, too.

I knew something much scarier than a big, bad biker with a record. A new job would be nothing in comparison, right?

Right.

"*Cajones*, Iris," *yia-yia* would have said in terrible Greek-accented Spanish. So I pushed open that shiny heavy door, ready for whatever was waiting for me on the other side.

What hit me immediately inside was all the natural light in the place. The orange-yellow light streaming in set off the dozens of framed newspaper and magazine articles mounted on the tinted blue wall. One magazine article immediately caught my attention with its glassy, red font proclaiming "Ink of the Year."

Two black leather love seats were angled against the entrance window with a black lacquered coffee table directly between them. Across from the seating was a flat, very long and modern looking desk that matched the coffee table with a computer in one corner. I'd barely started taking in two tattoo stations directly behind the waiting area when a male voice hollered, "Hold on a sec!"

I looked around as quickly as I could, noticing two more identical stations to the left.

Another article titled "Up and Coming Sensations: Locke and Company," was framed right in my peripheral vision.

Could I work at a tattoo parlor?

I thought for a second about the only other place I'd gotten an email back from and the cocktail waitress position at the strip club wasn't exactly appealing. I had a friend who had worked in a salon waxing people's private parts. What's been seen cannot be unseen, she'd told me once.

So, yeah. I could. I didn't have a choice.

"You Sonny's girl?" the deep baritone voice asked from down the hall, in time with the low squeaking thud of boots on tile.

It kind of happened in slow motion. Turning around. Coming face to face with him.

It should be said that the first—and only—time I saw Dex Locke had been the week before at Mayhem.

Sonny had dragged me to the bar by sheer manipulation. I'd just gotten to Austin not even two hours before.

And it probably didn't help that I'd just kind of... dropped in.

It'd been a last minute trip. Up until the moment I turned in the keys to my apartment, I hadn't been sure what exactly I was doing. Not that there were many options. I could either drive to Sonny's place in Texas or go up and crash on Lanie's couch in Cleveland. After living with Lanie for a year and knowing that I'd be staying with her and her parents, going to Sonny's hadn't really seemed like much of a decision.

It was inevitable.

But then again, Mom and Dad had kept me on the east coast for a reason. A reason I was clearly dumping into the garbage and possibly setting on fire.

"It'll be fun," he'd said at first.

"A lot of people remember you when you were a kid," he'd kept going, knowing I was a sucker for him.

Sonny wanted to make a point because he kept babbling. "Just because you lived in Florida doesn't mean you weren't born into this."

Like a fool, and because I loved Will and I loved Sonny just as much, even if he wasn't my full-blooded brother, I fell for it. We'd dragged ourselves to Mayhem so he could welcome me into my estranged family.

During the drive, all I thought of was my mom. It was a blessing she wasn't around to strangle me with her bare hands, smiling throughout the process of her choking the life out of me.

Surprisingly, it'd been fine.

Mayhem was smoky and smelled faintly of piss and not so faintly of beer. The place was old, with stained bars and scuffed hardwood floors that had seen better decades. Pool tables were set up on the far side of the bar that smelled like... yep, that was pot. I was pretty sure—only about ninety-nine percent sure—smoking was illegal inside but I definitely wasn't going to complain to the abundance of tattooed and leather-vested men that mobbed the floor.

Like a proud peacock, Sonny had walked me around the floor, through crowds of people that bordered on inebriation and did the splits on the ridiculous. Loud, outgoing, boisterous, young, old, hairy, not-so-hairy, tattooed, not-so-burly. The factors that made up the WMC members varied across the spectrum.

Having been steered toward a stool in the middle of the bar, Sonny and his very blonde, very flirtatious, very bearded friend, Trip, flanked me.

It was a little weird, I guess. Growing up, it'd just been Will and me. Being the oldest, I'd always been the one watching out for my younger brother; the person to threaten to rip organs out of orifices if he wasn't left alone. I'd been the protector. The one who cleaned his butt when he was too little to do it himself without smearing more poop than he actually wiped.

So having Sonny around, worrying about his friends getting too close or giving me looks that he didn't like, was strangely nice.

I'd barely been sitting there a minute, an entire, lonely, miniscule minute in a bar that had been so heavily smoked in over the years that the scent seeped from the wood like sweat on a professional athlete. A bar that was owned by a group of people that my parents hadn't wanted to raise me around. A total of sixty seconds before the noisy crowd burst into loud jeers right by the door.

Trip had groaned, shooting Sonny a side glance, shaking his head like whatever was going on was old news. "Somebody's on his damn rag."

"Quit being all dramatic, he's not always PMSing." He cut me a glance. "No offense."

I held up my hands and shrugged. "Eh." I'd be a hypocrite if I said that I didn't turn into a moody zombie on my period.

Trip rolled his eyes at my brother's comment. "I"m just sayin', Son, you'd figure he'd have his shit together by now. Don't they teach better tips than counting to ten in those classes he had to take?" he snickered, glancing over my shoulder. "Dumbass."

My inner nosey hooker perked up at all the clues they were dropping. Anger management classes? "What happened?" I asked in a conspiratorial whisper.

"It's cool, Ris." Sonny shot Trip an aggravated look. "He got in trouble for assault a long time ago. He's fine now."

"I don't know who you're talking about." It wasn't like whatever man they were referring to had 'Anger Issues' tattooed on his forehead. I hadn't even seen him yet.

"Dex."

I blinked at Trip's explanation.

"Locke?" he offered like that would mean something to me. It didn't.

Sonny grabbed the top of my head and shook it. "Don't worry about it, kid. I'm sure I'll introduce you sooner or later."

At that time I thought to myself that it wasn't like I really cared whether or not I met someone that was constantly pissed off.

Shoulders and chest.

The guy was somehow all elegant trapezius muscles and pectorals when I first saw him up close. A tight, black v-neck stretched over broad shoulders, barely hiding two bold tattoo sleeves that ran up from the wrist and disappeared underneath the fitted shirt.

That alone made me go a little brain dead though I should have known better than to let my hormones run rampant. I'd never really had much of an opinion on whether I thought tattoos were that much of a deal breaker when ogling a guy but…from the heat that had flamed up my neck, I was a fan. A big, season ticket holding fan.

I kept looking at him while he closed the distance between us, a portfolio shoved under one long, muscular arm that drew my attention to the inches of colorful red skin the cut of his shirt showed tattooed on his chest. I'd been too far away at

Mayhem to see more than just splotches of heavy color on his skin.

Holy crap.

I should have been glad the cap had hidden his facial features at the bar, so I had time to take in the magnificence that was his tattooed upper body without the added distraction of a face that made my ovaries scream glory hallelujah. His wide shoulders and thickly veined forearms were more than enough to make a girl stare. Because his face… Jesus, shit. *Jesus. Shit.*

I was going to ask Santa for his good identical twin for Christmas.

"Hi," I squeaked out. Hot men went on my list of people who made me nervous and therefore had me acting like more of an idiot than usual. Like if knowing I'd be working for a man who had been to jail for assault wasn't nerve-wrecking enough. "I'm his sister, Iris," I corrected him. My smile was wonky for sure. "Half-sister to be specific."

The guy with the most striking face ever created blinked at me.

Oh boy he was friggin' hot in a very masculine, raw way. Not like the men I saw so often back home who used more skin products than I did. High, angular cheekbones that looked sharp enough to cut granite were crafted alongside a hard, square jaw that had needed a shave yesterday. The purest and bluest eyes I'd ever seen were deep set above a nose that was just short of straight, and ohmigod lips that I knew had to have been used thousands of times—it'd be a shame if they weren't. The guy had the most flawless male bone structure I'd ever seen.

Those blue eyes locked on my face, unblinking and expressionless.

Had I done something wrong?

I looked down at what I was wearing: a tan cardigan went over my short-sleeved light pink button-up shirt that was miraculously missing wrinkles—thank goodness—and dark brown work pants. It was something I'd wear to one of my old jobs. I looked closer to make sure that my clothes weren't stained.

They weren't.

Still he stared right at me looking completely indifferent. So absolutely different from the scowling, bleeding man I'd seen tugging a petite blonde behind him as he left Mayhem last week. There was only a small crusty fleck on the edge of his eyebrow that served as a reminder of that night.

"You're late."

Uhh, what?

I glanced down at my cheap, electric blue watch to see it was four in the afternoon on the dot. "Oh. I thought I was supposed to be here at four."

Wasn't that what Sonny had said? I thought back on the call. There was no way I'd heard differently.

He looked at me, his expression unmoving. That handsome, hard face was a block of stubbled concrete. "I have a business to run, girl. I'm doin' Son a favor by hirin' you. The least you could do is show up on time."

Cue my mouth gaping wide.

Was this guy insane?

"I'm sorry," I told the man, eyeing the blue-black hair that went in ten different directions, only slightly tamed by the cap on his head. There was no way I got the time wrong, I knew it, but what was the point in arguing with him? I needed the job. "I really thought he said four." I flashed him a careful, wary smile. "It won't happen again."

He didn't even bother responding. Flicking two tattooed fingers at me, he waved me forward. Leading me toward a life I wasn't so sure I'd been destined for. "C'mon, I don't have all day to show you how to do shit."'

CHAPTER TWO

"I need you to update this every Friday. Got it?"

Got it? *Got it?*

Ef me. No, I didn't have it.

How the heck does someone go through the inner workings of QuickBooks in less than twenty minutes? I was going to need someone to explain to me how that was possible because I had no clue.

I wasn't an idiot, or slow by any measure—or so I liked to think—but he'd blown through the program with mouse clicks quicker than my poor eyes could keep up with. One minute he was explaining something about expenses and the next he'd started babbling about saving the files into a specific folder. I'd caught onto...maybe half.

Okay, realistically, more like a quarter of it.

For a brief moment, when I was looking down at the legal pad he'd slid across the desk when I'd followed in after him, I thought about asking him to show me one more time so I could write better notes. Because that wasn't uncalled for, right? I mean, who learned things perfectly the first go around? It'd taken me at least three tries to figure out how to use the cubed ice feature on Sonny's refrigerator correctly.

And then I glanced up at him, Dex Locke. His big body leaned over the edge of the dark brown desk, a red tattoo peeped out at the world over the collar of his shirt, the side of his surprisingly full mouth twisted just barely to the side...and I balked.

"Got it."

What. A. Liar.

A little coward of a liar. Pathetic.

He nodded at me briskly and started pulling up a file on his desktop that said 'Waivers' on it. We were off again.

Curt words. Brisk nods. All business.

At one point, he got up to "go take a piss" and I took the opportunity to look around for the first time after following behind him like a lost puppy. When I'd come in, those hard, pure blue eyes were some form of impatient so I focused in on sitting at the chair he'd dragged over around the desk, and followed along. My chance to snoop had finally presented itself.

The office wasn't at all what I would have expected. The walls were a plain bright white, nearly empty with the exception of two framed pieces and… were those television screens mounted in the corner? Maybe. He didn't seem like the type to watch daytime soaps though.

The colorful art was the first one to catch my eye. An angry, flaming red octopus looped across the paper in what looked like oils. Tentacles swirled and curled in bisecting lines. Bright and full of so much life, it seemed strange to be held captive on paper.

The other frame, directly next to the octopus, was done in black ink. Black ink that sketched out an immaculate replica of the Widowmakers' Motorcycle Club insignia. The one I'd seen bearing down on my father's bicep for years. The one that up until coming to stay with Sonny had only been a sign of the supposedly terrible things I'd been shielded from.

Bad things my mom had told me about to keep me fearful but I pushed that thought away and kept looking around. My mom's memory was meant for a different time. She already took up so much room in that designated little area I let her memory rest in. A place that I didn't want to get sucked into.

The rest of the small office consisted of the large desk, two matching padded chairs, and a cabinet that crowded the corner. It was almost immaculately clean. There was also a hint of cigarette smoke that clung to the air.

Huh.

"It smell in here or somethin'?" that deep, husky voice I'd heard for the last hour asked from the door.

I looked up at him and smiled. Did he smile in return? No. But I brushed it off and lifted a shoulder. "Do you smoke?"

Dex took a breath so deep and long that it seemed to last a solid minute in length. "When I want."

I almost scrunched up my nose. *Almost.* Because I hated cigarettes though I doubted the barely-there trace would bother me. I nodded at him again, taking in the dark Rangers cap he had pulled down tight over his head, the ends of his raven hair peeping out in tufts. Realizing that my hands were still damp, they hadn't stopped sweating from the moment I'd been in the car, I wiped them over my pants.

He blinked, breaking the silence. "You got legal ID?"

There were illegal IDs? Yeah, I wasn't going to ask for clarification.

I left Pins and Needles at seven that night. In a little more than three hours, we'd crammed a tutorial on how to use the appointment log and calendar on the computer by communicating via two-word groupings of instructions and grunts after our marathon accounting overview and paperwork for payroll. Dex had then pointed at a digital camera sitting on the edge of his desk and said I needed to upload pictures onto the computer and hard drive daily.

Did I ask where to upload the files? One look at that twist of his mouth had me agreeing to the job. Nope.

I learned where everything was hidden in the studio by watching where he pointed: inks, needles, gloves, water bottles, paper towels, disinfectant, cleaning supplies, everything. Dex briefly explained how to time appointments. How to handle walk-ins in every situation. What to say and not to say to clients. He mentioned that there were four tattoo artists that worked in the studio including himself. The only other person I got to meet was a nice bald man named Blake, who had a double piercing through thick black eyebrows and multicolored tattoos that went up to his jaw.

Everything seemed easy enough.

I still couldn't get a solid feeling about the job and much less Dex since he hadn't so much as smiled once, but oh well. The job wasn't worth jumping for joy over but I wasn't exactly dreading the idea of going back. And it wasn't like I had any other option after looking at my bank statement.

I'd take what I could get, damn it.

Plus there was something about the shop that called to me. Maybe it was because I'd been expecting some seedy place with customers that were stinky, old men that got into fights over old ladies, and had more body hair than I had on my head.

Then again, was Sonny what I'd imagined a biker to be? Sonny with his gaming system obsession. Sonny who I'd caught watering his potted plants one morning. Sonny who made me tofu recipes without batting an eyelash.

No. He wasn't.

So I tried to push my worries to the back of my brain, accepting the fact that maybe I'd been wrong to be worried. Maybe.

Sonny's bike, a sleek deep red Harley that cost as much as my car, was in the driveway when I parked in front of his house a few minutes later. Sonny's bungalow was small and located in an old, lower middle class neighborhood. Families and young couples populated the homes up and down the block, loud and constantly in motion.

It was nice and I liked it. After living in an apartment where the walls were so thin I could hear every television show my neighbor watched, his place was friggin' great. The house was painted a deep tan with a front yard that would've been nice if he mowed it more often than every leap year, and comfortable. It wasn't exactly what I'd envisioned him living in before I'd punched his address into my GPS. While he wasn't necessarily neat, it wasn't a pig-sty but it was nicer after I'd spent two days cleaning the floors for what seemed like the first time since he'd bought it seven years before.

I whipped out the key he'd given me the day I showed up, and let myself in. The television blared from the other side of the wall.

Sitting on his favorite recliner, Sonny grinned at me the minute I closed the door. He leaned forward, clutching the remote to his PS3 in one hand. "You survived, Ris?" he asked, his grin widening so much it made his thick, auburn beard twitch with the movement of his facial muscles.

The resemblance slapped me out of the blue. When had he started looking so much like our dad? Not that I would ever ask that out loud while he was around unless I was in the mood to get pinched.

Instead I smirked, plopping down on the couch perpendicular to him. "Barely."

He laughed, loud and deep. Curt Taylor all over again. I wonder if he even knew how much alike they were? Probably not. I'd only gotten ten years out of the old man before he'd taken off, and that was ten more years than Sonny had gotten. And while I wasn't exactly our dad's biggest fan anymore, Sonny had fallen out of love with him a lot sooner than I had. A shitty father who only showed up once a year wasn't going to win any awards, much less one that disappeared out of the blue leaving a wife and two kids behind.

As much as I wanted to, I had to beat back calling him an asshole even in my head. I'd promised myself I wouldn't do that anymore. Another promise I'd lined up neatly in a row along the way.

"That's just the way he is," *yia-yia* had said time and time again despite how much mom and I had wanted to fight his true nature.

So, so ignorant to the fact that you can't fight a person's instincts even if they were awful, even if they caused bad and painful things to those they should have cared about.

"I knew you'd be the one to make it through the whole day," Sonny claimed in his own individual voice that resembled nothing like our dad's gravelly draw. Thank God.

Wait a second though.

"What do you mean?" I suddenly had a feeling that my brother had fed me to the heavily tattooed wolves—well, one wolf in particular. On friggin' purpose.

Sonny looked at me, his hazel eyes—the color that we'd both inherited from our sperm donor—narrowed. And then he coughed. "There were a few people before you, kid."

He'd been calling me kid for so long that it didn't even faze me anymore. Even if it did, he'd probably call me that more often. What did faze me was the gnawing feeling he was hiding something. "And?"

"Most of them didn't last past the introduction. Much less a couple hours." He flashed that lazy grin again. "I knew you would though."

It was my turn to narrow my eyes at him. Sonny had never lied to me before. He was unapologetic about everything he did. If anything, it'd been me who had kept things from him until the absolute last minute. Even past the last minute, and yet, he'd always forgiven me for lying. At least eventually he did. I wasn't going to think that he'd start spouting crap now.

"I don't think that he likes anything very much."

Sonny snorted. "Last I heard from Trip, he'd called six people into the shop to get interviewed for that job."

Six people? Oh boy.

Before I could focus on the idea of six individuals before me getting the boot, he thrust a game controller into my hand and tilted his head toward the massive flat screen mounted to the wall. If it was strange that he was changing the subject so abruptly, I didn't catch onto it. "You can survive anything, kid, right?"

Damn him. Those were the same words I'd thrown back at him each time the rabbit hole had seemed to pop out of nowhere.

CHAPTER THREE

"So you just moved from Florida?"

I smiled out of the corner of my eye at Blake, who was sprawled out on the empty couch by the reception desk, casually.

It was only my second day at Pins and Needles. Dex had already been waiting when I'd shown up ten minutes until four. Under the natural sunlight, his tattoos seemed to pop out even more starkly against the smooth, lightly tanned skin beneath the ink. Blues and reds and blacks fought a battle I didn't think any of them were capable of winning on the majestic scale.

Especially not when they were stamped onto the nearly flawless, somewhere around six foot three form.

Why couldn't he have been ugly at least? For some reason, dealing with an impatient, unattractive person seemed easier to swallow than a smoking hot one.

He was standing outside of the building—why, I didn't have a clue. He had a key, he could have gone in but I wasn't going to bother asking. The less interaction we had the better, it seemed.

His fit frame leaned against the stonewashed walls that separated Pins from the real estate agency. He had a cigarette nestled between two fingers, taking deep drags as he faced forward. Just like the day before, his black t-shirt stretched across his chest and arms, the only light color on him was the faded denim jeans that molded to his legs.

Nice legs. Thick thighs. But most importantly, the thighs of a jerk.

"Good afternoon." The words had barely left my mouth and I was cringing. Had I really just said good afternoon? *Awkward, so friggin' awkward, Iris.* I had to shake myself out of thinking about his thighs and how uncomfortable I'd made myself feel as I pulled my purse closer to my chest and forced a tight smile on my face.

The moment I was close enough to him, he flickered his gaze over in my direction and glanced at his watch. "I don't like waitin' around." Dex took another pull from the cigarette before dropping it on the ground, crushing it with the sole of his motorcycle boot.

What?

For a split second, I got the urge to check my watch but I didn't. I knew what time would be on the face. Three-fifty. Not four o'clock. Three-fifty. What in the heck was this psycho babbling about?

"I'm ten minutes early," I told him, standing five feet away so that I wouldn't come in contact with the fumes from his smoking.

Dex raised an eyebrow. "Yeah, and I've been here for ten minutes."

Something mean tickled my lips, teasing me to take the bait and be as callous with him as he was with me. I couldn't do it though. I couldn't risk pissing off a man with very little patience that I needed a paycheck from. So I swallowed hard and in the blink of an eye, hoped that he'd get explosive diarrhea at some point in the near future.

"Okay."

God, I was such a friggin' pushover.

Dipping a hand into the front pocket of his jeans, he pulled out his keys, giving me a once over before tilting his head up. "And quit wearin' that fancy shit. I know you ain't got any ink but you don't need to look like some sorority girl either."

Fancy? I bought most of my clothes from the clearance rack at Target.

By the time his words—insulting my clothes—settled into my brain, Dex had already unlocked the front door and let himself in.

Maybe it should have bothered me that he told me to change the casual work clothes, but it didn't. The thing was, I couldn't get that pissed off. I felt resigned and annoyed.

Halfway down the hall by the time I came in, Dex called out on his path toward his office. "There's a week's worth of pictures to upload."

Did I have a clue what I was doing? Nope. I connected the camera to the computer anyway and thanks to my investigative skills—and the search option on the operating system—found where I needed to dump and arrange the thirty five pictures.

That's exactly what I was in the middle of doing when Blake strolled in, plopping onto the couch like they were old friends.

I nodded at his question, not wondering once how he'd found out where I lived before. "Yep. Near Miami, well, really Fort Lauderdale. Miami's way too expensive." It was. It totally was. Completely out of the price range of a customer service employee. Astronomically out of the price range for two unemployed girls, which only reminded me that I should check in with Lanie at some point.

He made a whistling sound. "Always wanted to go to Miami. Why the hell would you move here?"

At the risk of not wanting to be rude, I didn't laugh. "My old job had a lot of cutbacks. Since I was one of the newest hires, they let me go first. I couldn't find another job, one thing led to another, and I thought it'd be best to—," come mooch off my brother? "Come here. Mr. Locke knows my brother."

Blake laughed, loud. "Mr. Locke?" He laughed again. "Call him Dex. Please."

I smiled at him and shrugged. It wasn't like he'd told me what to call him. Plus, with as quiet as he seemed to be, the last thing I wanted to do was piss him off and call him something that he didn't approve of. My last boss had lost his mind if he wasn't referred to as a sir.

Which I figured completely merited the fact that we called him an asshole when he wasn't listening.

"I heard Sonny's sister or something was visiting the last time I went to Mayhem," he threw in.

"Are you... a member of the Widows?"

"No," he answered instantly, his face flushing out of what I could assume to be embarrassment for shooting down the idea so quickly. "I've known Dex for a long time. That's it. I know all those guys." Then he plunged in the knife. "Only heard of your dad though, never met him."

It took such a small part of me to smile like what he said wasn't a big deal, when it still was. Which was stupid. I was too old to still let him bother me. I'd been through too much to care about where he was and who he'd kept in touch with, when he hadn't kept in touch with his own kids.

But it did.

I'd gone from thinking about him once a year to all-of-a-sudden getting constantly bombarded with reminders of something—someone—I'd rather forget.

And it must have been noticeable on my face because Blake had a guilty expression on his.

"I'm gonna get a pop, you want one?" he asked, already pushing himself off of the couch he was on.

Avoiding the awkwardness? I think I liked Blake already.

"No thanks."

He shrugged and was around the desk a moment later, his Meshuggah t-shirt draped loosely around his shoulders, faded jeans sagging, before he was out of my line of vision. It kind of made me feel like an old grandma, dressed in black work pants and an elbow-length lavender blouse that covered all my fleshly valuables.

I just didn't feel like explaining my arm. Everything always changed after The Arm Conversation.

As long as I could keep wearing my longer sleeved shirts, I could put that bomb off for a while.

I'd been staring at the screen for the last hour. The notes that Dex had set down almost two hours ago seemed to be mocking me in mute delight.

What I should have done was ask him the day before to explain to me one more time how to work the program.

Half of it had been more than easy enough. Memos, dates, all that stuff I could guess. But I'd already gone through the same spreadsheet twice, and I swear two of the numbers on the balance were different than they had been originally.

Holy crap.

I had two options. I could go ask Dex for help. The other would be that I could look up instructional videos on how to use the accounting program because the Help button wasn't as helpful as I'd hoped.

In hindsight, I'm really not sure why I chose to ask Dex instead of suffering through a thirty minute long video.

But I got up and headed toward his office, feeling that same urge to gag as the day before, creep up my throat.

Crap. Crap. Crap.

The folder clung to my fingertips as I paused right outside of the opened office door. Dex was behind his desk, a sheet of paper spread out where the keyboard had been yesterday. A pencil bobbed back and forth as he stared at the sheet, two fingers pinched the bridge of his nose.

Deep down I knew I was going to regret this. I really, really did.

"Hey Dex?"

Those two Crayola Blue eyes shifted up to look at me. Emotionless. Impassive. "Yeah?"

I had to swallow back the urge to gag as I lifted the blue folder for him to see. My mouth, the traitor, lifted up into a nervous smile. "I'm having some trouble with that program you showed me yesterday, and I was wondering if you could show me how to use it one more time?"

He didn't say anything. That concentrated, undiluted gaze stayed on me indefinitely.

And the babbling kept spewing out of me. "I just don't want to mess it up any more."

Dex's blink was so slow it could have lasted a day. The hand that had been up shielding his mouth while his fingertips pinched the bridge of his nose, dropped. He let out a deep, deep sigh straight from the monstrous caverns hidden beneath his chest and flat abs. "You already fucked it up?"

Triple crap.

I'd smiled at things worse than Dex, so the fact that my nervous smile stayed on my face wasn't a surprise. "I may have messed it up, but I haven't saved my work yet. That's why I was hoping you could help me."

He looked up at the ceiling and closed those brilliant eyes. "Fuck me. Fuck me."

Quadruple crap.

Maybe I should have told him I was sorry for bothering him, but I wasn't. I really didn't know very well what I was doing, and I figured that I was saving him time now by asking for clarification and not waiting till later and causing a bigger mess. Right?

"I already showed you how to do this shit yesterday, girl. I don't have time to hold your fuckin' hand through this, got it?"

What. The. Hell?

Something that wasn't exactly shame or humiliation rushed through me. I wasn't sure what exactly the emotion was, but it left this terrible, sticky layer over my skin.

"I'll show you one more time, but if you can't handle somethin' as easy as that program then I don't think you have any business workin' for me. I need help around here. I don't have time to be helpin' the help, make sense?" he asked in that clipped, sharp tone that could saw off pieces of lumber.

My fingers curled into themselves on their own just as something knotted in my throat. I was a spineless little wuss. Where had this person come from?

I was pretty passive. Okay, extremely passive, but I could hold my own. I knew when to say no. I knew when people took advantage of me. Yet, there I was. Letting my boss get mad because I hadn't mastered how to do something on the first try.

A spineless little wuss that went and sat right next to Dex, the wielder of the verbal whip, and let him show me how to use the damn computer program one more time.

It seemed like the words went in one ear and settled gracefully deep in my memory. I'd just nodded through the entire fifteen minute demonstration, keeping my eyes directly on the screen and avoiding all forms of communication with him.

By the time the impromptu tutorial was over, I high-tailed it back to the front desk to start the spreadsheet all over again. I mumbled out my thanks and tucked my tail between my legs. Embarrassed and a little pissed off weren't exactly my favorite emotions. I hadn't even been able to look him in the eye.

I kept myself busy after that by asking Blake if there was anything I could help him with when he was free. He showed me how to sterilize the bottles they used to rinse off ink. He showed me where all the artists kept their business cards. How to use the thermal fax in the break room. Where the catalogues were for ordering supplies—I told him I didn't know how to do that yet and he grinned, promising that I'd learn soon.

It was close to eight and the shop was dead, Dex still hadn't come out from his office and Blake had disappeared a few minutes before, when the urge to pee struck. I beelined toward the restroom, ignoring the open call of Dex's office as I did my business and closed the door on my way out, thinking of when I could ask Dex at what time I could take a break. I'd brought a peanut butter and jelly sandwich in my purse and—

"Even a fuckin' idiot can figure out how to do it."

The tile floors carried the not-so-quiet conversation down the hall. I recognized the deep baritone voice as Dex's and my stomach revolted.

There was a laugh. His. "I don't give a shit if she's hot. I'm not lookin' to get my dick wet. I need to get shit done around the shop that I don't like doin'," he snickered. "How hard is it to find a reliable bitch to help out around here?"

I froze for a split second right there in the hallway. The words seeped into my pores, rejuvenating my blood cells and apparently my tear ducts as well.

He thought I was a fucking idiot? All because I asked him a simple question?

I wasn't stupid. I knew that. Knew it without a doubt. I hadn't gone to school anymore because I couldn't afford it, not because I wasn't smart enough. And while I'd worked for a boss that was an asshole back at the cruise line, he wasn't an unfair asshole. He was simply an overzealous, hardworking asshole.

He'd never upset me though, and here I was. Standing like a pathetic fool that wanted to cry. Then again, I always wanted to cry. I cried when I was happy, sad, excited, and frustrated with life. And I hated it. Especially now.

Because I shouldn't let shit like Dex's skewed opinion bother me. I needed a paycheck like I needed my next breath. I shouldn't care what one delinquent biker thought about me as long as he paid me, right?

Right. Why did it feel like I'd gotten stabbed in the gut, though?

CHAPTER FOUR

I checked my bank account at least three times after overhearing Dex's one-sided conversation. Unfortunately, the amount that showed up on my screen stayed the same each time.

Seventy-eight dollars and thirty-nine cents cemented my fate.

I needed gas, I wanted to buy some groceries so that Sonny wouldn't have to buy them again, and I had to pay my cell phone bill in two weeks. None of that was even including the credit card I'd run up on the drive over to Texas when I'd stopped for gas. Did I have a choice? Not really.

The only option I had was to bite back the ugly feeling that continually swam up the back of my throat when I thought of Dex's harsh words. Was this what I'd sunk to? I mean, the universe couldn't be that cruel.

It couldn't be. There was no way that a handful of surgeries had led me to work for a man that called me a fucking idiot. I wasn't even going to touch his use of the word 'bitch'.

Don't cry, Iris.

Sacrifices were necessary sometimes, I knew that. After Dad had left, we'd moved from a house into an apartment. Downgraded the car. Quit going out to eat. And that was all before the universe and all its assurances of having a happily-ever-after went supernova on me. Life was hard sometimes and there was no book or movie that could prepare you for how harsh it could be.

Except maybe that zombie television show where everyone died. That was pretty accurate.

If it were Will who had found me the job, I wouldn't have a problem shooting the finger at this place and walking out. I knew he'd forgive me if I made him look like a douche bag. He owed me for busting my butt to feed him and keep him clothed for years. But Sonny? God.

I wanted to leave. Whether it was Pins and Needles, or Austin altogether at that point, I wasn't sure, but the urge to flee was right on the horizon. Why hadn't I just gone up to Cleveland with Lanie?

This terrible feeling of embarrassment didn't work for me. Then again, I'd made the commitment to work here, and I really needed the money. Like so badly I was desperate to see just one more digit in my bank account balance.

My pride wasn't going to pay my bills.

But finding another job would.

"What's up, new girl?"

I looked up to see Blake coming into the shop with a brown paper bag in one hand.

I'm sure my smile was shaky because my hands were still trembling. I was nauseous too, and I was still seriously considering bolting. Knowing that Sonny worked around the corner if I needed anything, and that I needed a paycheck badly, were the only things that kept me in my seat. "Hey, Blake."

"You got some lunch in?" he asked, coming to stand right in front of the desk.

Lying, I nodded because it was all I had in me. The peanut butter and grape jelly sandwich I'd made that afternoon was still sitting in my purse.

Blake's sky blue gaze narrowed a tiny bit as he slid them over what I could assume were my wet, traitorous eyes. "Dex piss you off?" he wondered in a quiet voice.

I had to keep from sucking in a ragged breath because that would definitely set off an alarm, and shook my head weakly. If I would have been paying attention, I would have taken in the fact that he suspected Dex was capable of doing something to upset me. Like making girls cry wasn't out of the ordinary for that jerk.

But Blake's eyes were too perceptive. He opened his mouth to speak but his eyes slid passed my seat and he tilted his head up in the direction of the door.

"Sup," Blake called out, still keeping his spot directly in front of me.

"Slim called in. You mind stayin' late?" Dex. The smooth, rich, melodic voiced dick-face spoke.

"Whatever." My bald coworker shrugged and slid his eyes over to me discreetly, tapping his fingertips on the desk. "You want something to drink?" I kind of loved him for ignoring the jerk that had just made me feel like I was the dumbest person alive.

I did want a drink but since I wasn't sure what the hell was about to happen with Dex, I didn't want to take the chance that I'd be mooching off a soda and have to walk my shamed hide back across the street, so I shook my head.

Blake shrugged and walked around the desk to head toward the back.

From my peripheral vision, I could tell Dex was standing just to my right a few feet away by that point. His black shirted blur told me so. Every instinct in me wanted to walk out, but I wouldn't until he, the mean jerk, said something.

Some small, sadistic part of me wanted to look in his direction, but I didn't.

Will had always told me I wore my emotions on my sleeve. I was a terrible liar because of it. I was wary of looking people in the face when feeling crappy came more naturally than being in a good mood. It wasn't a shock Blake could tell something was up, but he wouldn't know what since he'd walked in after the unintentional verbal beat down had finished.

"Hey—," the good-looking ass started to say before Blake saved me from further humiliation by calling out Dex's name a moment later.

The last thing I wanted to do was stay. I didn't want them to keep me either. I'd been someone's charity case for half of my life, and I sure as hell didn't want it to multiply now. I'd told myself I was staying because it wasn't just a matter of wanting a job. It was a necessity. Plus, Sonny was friends with these people, and I didn't want to embarrass him. Maybe if I could suck it up a couple weeks, and then put in my notice it wouldn't be as bad as just walking out. Just two weeks.

I could do two weeks.

I'd lived for years not knowing whether I'd even be alive to turn twenty. Two weeks of dealing with an asshole couldn't be worse than a million other scenarios I'd already lived through.

So even though everything in my heart screamed at staying and battled against my pride, I was going to stay, regretting with every inch of me ever having walked into the damn building to begin with.

It was close to midnight when the second to last customer, an older man that Dex had worked on for well over two hours, made his way out with a wink and a "Goodnight, sweetheart," in my direction. Blake still had a young girl spread out on his chair with her pants down to her crack as he tattooed a Monarch butterfly on the top corner of her butt cheek.

I'd spoken to Dex twice throughout the last few hours. Each time went along the lines of, "Dex, so-and-so is here for their session." In reality, I wanted to ask him if he'd sold his soul or if he'd never had one to begin with.

But the minute the dollar signs popped up in my head, I forced myself to say what I needed.

I was surprised by how consistent business was. Most of the customers were scheduled in advance but one had been a walk-in.

A brief conversation with Blake had explained more of the things I'd be responsible for. Shop manager duties mainly consisted of reordering supplies—like inks, gloves, jewelry, etc.—filing expenses, paying utilities. Easy things. Dex handled everything else, any cash deposits at the bank, and settled accounts with the company they used for debit card usage.

He and Blake had been busy, and I'd been busy talking to customers about random stuff while they waited. I was surprised by how nice everyone had been—with the exception of Dex's dumb face.

There hadn't been a single biker in the shop either. Weird.

All of this assured me that I'd avoided having to interact much with my boss. The owner. The bleeding mouth sore.

The snot-faced asshole that I only kind-of, sort-of hoped came down with an infectious illness in his private parts. But you know, something he could get medicine for.

I tried my best to keep from replaying the scenario in the office but it was impossible. It wasn't his tone but the words that had seared me.

And each time, it made me want to cry. It didn't get any easier or any less painful. How the hell could someone be so rude? I didn't understand and I couldn't get over it.

Every cycle had me coming up with different things to call him. A dick. A slimy bastard. A slimy, small-dicked bastard. Right? Maybe he wouldn't be so mad at the world if his pubic hair wasn't longer than his full-blown erection. God, I felt awkward thinking about what he had under his clothes but it was the best insult I could come up with.

I didn't normally hold grudges. If something upset me, I'd get over it quickly. Being pissed off took way too much effort and stressed me out, and I had no business stressing if I could avoid it. Plus, there weren't that many things in life really worth being mad about.

Until today.

After cleaning up my desk and logging off the computer, I wiped off the coffee table, and put the magazines and binders of photographed tattoos back where they belonged. I swept the floor by the front just in case I was supposed to and started spraying the frames on the wall because I'd seen people touching the glass several times throughout the day. Up close, I saw that each frame held articles, clippings, or mentions of Pins and Needles, or Dex Locke's work.

Certain phrases caught my eye even when I wasn't trying to read the writing. The ridiculously large fonts made it impossible for me not to catch the highlighted statements.

"Art was the only class I never skipped in high school." The caption was directly below a picture of Dex standing in front of the shop with his arms crossed over his chest. Typical.

"It's an addiction," another article screamed.

Then there was the one that had me rolling my eyes. *"Can't get arrested for it anymore."*

Blah. Blah. Blah.

I was in the middle of cleaning off one of them when I heard, "Ritz."

I knew it was Dex speaking. His voice was its own unique drawl of deep and rich. All baritone and rasp. On anyone else, I would've liked to hear them talk all day but Dex? I'd be perfectly fine not hearing him talk for, oh, let's say, the rest of my life.

"Ritz."

Now he wanted to talk? Ha. I sprayed the glass and quickly wiped it down, ignoring him.

"Babe."

Jerk. I scooted over and sprayed the next frame.

"Babe, I'm talkin' to you. Quit sprayin' for a sec," he said, the quick irritation in his tone hinting at the fact this man wasn't used to repeating himself.

As much as I didn't want to, I stopped what I was doing and turned to look at him. He was standing just to the side of the desk, hands shoved into his front pockets.

"Yes?" I asked, keeping my gaze locked only as high as his bare neck.

"Ritz," he repeated the name he'd used at first.

"My name's—," I started to say before he cut me off.

"Would you look at me?"

No.

Was there a treatment for gonorrhea already?

I clenched my teeth together. "You didn't tell me what you wanted me to do until you guys were done, so I figured I'd clean up. Blake said you would put up the—," I started to tell his neck in a surprisingly even voice. You couldn't even tell I'd been fighting back tears the majority of the day.

"Look at me," Dex interrupted in a low voice.

Slowly, fighting everything in me that ached from his shitty words, I dragged my eyes up to his.

"Yes?" It was like the words were pulled from my throat with rusty tweezers.

Some indecipherable emotion reflected back at me from his true blue eyes as I grudgingly held his gaze for all of ten seconds before turning back to finish cleaning the frames.

Dex exhaled. It sounded like he rubbed his palms together before speaking. "You gotta toughen up," he gritted.

Oh my God. The first person in my life who I had the urge to punch in the face was a six-foot-three-ish biker that I assumed beat the living crap out of someone and went to jail for it. Of all the people in the world smaller than me that I could have chosen, and this was who I wanted to nail right in the testicles? Not Sonny, or even Trip who hadn't given me the impression he'd try to murder me?

I bristled and like clockwork, my molars ground together.

I need the job.

I need the job.

I need the job.

"Wipe down the counters for me," he added in a low voice that seemed to go immediately against the harsh, no-nonsense tone he'd used a moment before. How was this man even capable of speaking in that kind of tone after the daggers he'd been spitting out earlier?

I nodded and swallowed back that gross feeling in my throat again. "Okay."

"Yeah?"

I held back my long sigh, keeping my eyes on the title, "Ink Me!" on the mounted magazine while I wiped streaks across the glass. I wasn't going to argue with him, I wasn't going to care enough about the fact he didn't remember my name, and I definitely wasn't going to let him know how shitty he'd made me feel. In all actuality, this just made it easier for me to want to find another job. "Yup."

My pride won out because I didn't turn back to look at him while he stood in place another minute, and when Blake walked with me to my car twenty minutes later after closing, I didn't look at Dex again then either.

Fuck him. Not screw him, or damn him. Fuck him. He deserved the f-bomb for being such a dick and heaven knows I saved that word for special occasions.

Just because I let my conscience guide me into keeping the job out of respect for Sonny—and my need for some cash—didn't mean I had to like my boss. It didn't mean I had to let what happened go and get over the fire he'd breathed for no reason.

Friggin' asshole.

"What's wrong?"

Sonny was going to blow a gasket. There was going to be smoke coming out of his ass and ears. I just knew it.

I'd underestimated him my entire life. When I was a kid, I'd thought he hated me because Will and I had lived with our dad and he hadn't, except for yearly visits that lasted until Son was old enough to tell him to screw off. As a teenager, I thought he wouldn't care too much about the disasters that had stockpiled in my life.

But the fact was, he had. As an adult, Sonny had become the most solid figure in my life even if he lived over a thousand miles away.

We hadn't been raised together, obviously. Sonny had lived in Austin with his mom, where I'd grown up with mine in Florida nine years later. We'd settled for seeing each other once a year when I was younger, when my dad would take Will and I to Austin to see Sonny. So I'd never had that typical overprotective older brother situation as a kid until he got old enough to drive himself, and by that time, Dad was long gone.

Sonny Taylor, whose mom hated Curt Taylor with a magnitude that led her to move out of state the moment Son graduated high school, did care for me. He loved me in his own way, and he knew my facial expressions.

So when I walked into his house, still more hurt than pissed off over what I'd overheard that afternoon, he'd caught onto the clues like Sherlock Holmes.

And now I was a little worried to tell him because I'd promised to quit lying. Apparently, I'd run out of get-out-of-lying passes when I didn't tell him they'd found more cells in my arm.

"Iris, tell me," he insisted.

Crap. He never called me by my first name.

I blurted the tiny story out, feeling like a kid again who wanted her mom or dad to make things better.

The words rode a boomerang in my head over and over again. The moment I'd gotten to Sonny's house, it all hit me straight in the solar plexus.

The guy was just a dick. An ass who didn't know how to get past the things that made us all up—the good and the bad.

When I was in the hospital, any of the times—all of the times—I'd met so many people who just couldn't let go of the anger. The resentment. Frustration with the hand they got dealt. I mean, I got it. I did. If anyone understood what it was like to think that life was unfair, I'd probably won the award a few years in a row.

But at some point, you had to get over it. I didn't want to be a bitter old lady the rest of my life.

Now I was stuck working for a bitter, mean, happiness-sucking leech.

"It's not a big deal, Son. Whatever. I don't care what he thinks."

Liar. Liar. Big, fat liar.

Sonny's lips twisted in a way I'd only seen once before. Barely restrained anger hid beneath the thick layer of his red-brown beard. "That fucking dumbass," he ground out. He cocked his head to one side, and then the other. A deep breath blew out from between his lips. "I'm gonna knock his teeth in."

He was being completely serious. So, so serious about defending my honor, I couldn't help it.

I started laughing.

"It's fine." I snorted. "Son, it's really fine. Knock his teeth in another day." I laughed again. "Or maybe once I find another job, okay? Then you can bust all his teeth and his kneecaps for all I care."

Those hazel eyes that were an exact replica of mine, narrowed. And then he quirked a little smile. "His kneecaps too?"

I shrugged. "Why not? Call him a friggin' idiot while you do it."

Sonny shook his head, full out grinning by that point. "To think I used to call you a good girl. My little sis telling me to break someone's kneecaps. You might make me cry, Ris." He leaned forward across the armchair I was sitting in and ruffled my hair. "Thatta girl."

I snorted and batted his hand away.

His face sobered a moment later, his gaze serious. "Nobody talks to you like that, you hear me? I don't care if it's another member of the MC or some asshole on the street. If somebody takes their anger out on you, I'll beat the shit out of them."

Lord. Where had he been when I was fifteen and got made fun of? I pushed the thought out of my mind and nodded, settling in just to make him feel better.

"Yes, father." I gave him a little smile. "Quit stressing, would you?"

By the way his jaw clenched, you could tell he wasn't exactly happy with staying quiet but he didn't argue against me.

"Fine, but wear whatever the fuck you want, kid. Wear a three-piece suit just to piss him off," he grunted. Sonny leaned forward again to mess with my hair until I swatted at him.

He stood up, grabbed his phone out of his pocket and disappeared down the hall that led toward his bedroom, silently.

Wait...

Sonny wasn't the silent type.

"What are you doing?" I yelled out after him.

His answer, "*Nothing*!"

A minute later, from the confines of his bedroom, he started yelling.

What did I do? I tip-toed into the hallway that led toward his bedroom and tried to listen in. Just for a minute. That was it.

"—the fuck is wrong with you?...She's shy with strangers, Dex. Shy. You think your attitude helps that any?....No. No. Imagine if she was your sister. How the hell would you feel if somebody called her a bitch....Well, that's Lisa. That's not Ris. Imagine if it was Marie...Did you hear me? What if—no. Fuck you, Dex. If something crawls up your ass, don't take it out on her. You act like a bitch—"

I might have smiled. Big.

CHAPTER FIVE

I wore my usual clothes the next day. Khaki pants and a white, long-sleeved button-up shirt were my big "fuck you" to Dex. Throwing all those "fuck you" comments around sort of made me feel empowered. Just a little, at least.

He'd taken a long look at me when I showed up at the door fifteen minutes until four and didn't say anything. Neither did I.

My silent treatment—and eye aversion—lasted exactly eight work hours. For eight hours, I managed to dodge Dex during business hours by bothering Blake. We'd only spoken when he needed me to schedule something and when a customer came in for him.

Each and every single time, I'd feel this incredibly nauseating pressure on my neck. It was my body's wordless reminder of how carelessly mean he'd been, and how he'd made me feel like I needed a tetanus shot afterward. I'd stayed up the night before wondering why it bothered me so much that he thought I was stupid. It was really his fault I didn't understand what I was supposed to do, wasn't it?

Such a beautiful man, and he was a complete friggin' asshole. Go figure.

Only a very small part of me wanted to drop the issue. Pretend that he hadn't lost his mind briefly and said something that I'm sure Sonny and the rest of the Widowmakers more than likely said casually. But I couldn't. I just couldn't. When had I become the type of person who couldn't let things go, I had no idea.

Even when Lanie had taken my car without permission and wrecked it, I hadn't stayed mad for more than a couple of hours.

When Will lost my cell phone, I think I'd gotten mad for all of an hour. And when I'd gotten fired, I'd been more sad than mad. Stuff was replaceable, so I didn't bother holding onto my frustrations.

Except every time I saw him, Dex, something ugly churned inside my chest.

I only let myself look at him below the face when he'd walk by, and by that I mean that regardless of whether he was a dick or not, I considered looking at his tattoos—and body—as a lesson in learning about body ink. You know, occupational research and all. After occasional and close observation, I was able to figure out that his sleeves were complete opposites.

His right arm was a matting of solid black ink, broken up by a spiral of rectangular tiles surrounded by an inch of the most beautiful black, gray, and skin tone flower outlines. Outside of the flowers it was flat, almost shiny black ink that made my arm hurt to look at.

Dex's other arm was as colorful as I figured a guy who wore black shirts three days in a row could be. Trying to be discreet wasn't exactly a strength of mine, so what I was able to distinguish were the tracings of what seemed to be a black wing that wrapped around his bicep and the upper part of his forearm, with the brightest red, blue, and gray triangles that clustered together at the shoulder and eventually faded out toward his wrist.

I'm not going to lie. The tattoos on his arms, the only ones I was able to see but had a feeling were only the beginning, were really hot. And I mean really hot.

But it didn't matter how attractive his ink was or how corded and ripped his biceps were when he had his tattoo gun to someone's flesh, or even when he was just standing with his arms over his chest while I tried my best to ignore him—Dex, my boss, was a prick. And I wasn't going to pretend like his douche-baggery didn't bother me. I hadn't seen him crack a single smile or say something nice to anyone but his clients. It was like Blake and I didn't exist, but me especially.

In front of clients, he was relaxed and easygoing. A completely different person. If I wouldn't have been on such a one-way track with thinking I disliked everything about him, the things he said randomly would have made me laugh.

But I didn't let myself.

So in my head it made sense that my work day had been spent A) ignoring Dex, B) avoiding Dex, and C) getting to know my coworkers slowly.

On the brief occasion that we'd speak to each other, I'd look at his right ear. Another time I looked at his left. Then I'd focus on the tiny, barely noticeable scab he had on his eyebrow, because I couldn't bear to look at his face without my heartbeat accelerating. The traitor.

I blamed my period. It was coming and it made my hormones get all out of whack. It's true. It had nothing to do with his jaw or the fact that I could see the outline of his lateral muscles through his t-shirt when he bent over my desk to type something on the computer. It was my crazy ass hormones. I swear.

Maybe it was childish, but I couldn't help it. I had hope that in time, I'd forget what I overheard. But obviously, it was going to take some time to let it go and I wasn't in the mood to rush things with my PMS on the way and all.

And by some time, I estimated it would probably be closer to my retirement age before I purged that moment from my brain.

Instead, I focused on trying to find another job. Which had been useless. Everything I found was too far away or didn't pay enough. All that meant was that I needed to look harder to find somewhere else to work.

What I didn't expect was how much I liked the two other tattoo artists that worked alongside Blake and The Dick. Slim was a cute, lanky, tall redhead who greeted me warmly. He seemed super sweet and outgoing. Blue, the other artist, was a woman a few years older than me with pink-highlighted hair, so soft spoken I had a feeling I was going to learn to read lips before I quit to understand what she was saying.

The only thing I let myself stew on was Dex The Dick and the fact that I was bumbling around trying to figure things out so that I wouldn't ask him for help.

Friggin' asswipe.

It was easy to pretend he didn't exist during the day before work. I'd kept busy cleaning up Sonny's house slowly, carefully and thoroughly. I think the last time someone had dusted his place had been before he bought it. The dust, unorganized DVDs, and randomly strewn laundry nipped at my borderline obsessive cleaning tendencies.

My day at Pins had at least, while embarrassing the shit out of me, warmed me up to the people I'd be working with until I found another job. Slim had finished up with a customer and sat down on the edge of my desk, crossing one leg over the other like I'd seen him do while sitting at his station alone. I liked this crossing-his-leg thing he had going on.

"Iris, right?" he asked.

I nodded, smiling just a little. "Yeah."

"First time working at a tattoo place?" He'd smoothed his hand over the longish red hair that curled at the ends.

For some strange reason, I felt comfortable around this guy from the get-go and it might have been his crazy natural red hair, the Harry Potter lightning bolt he had tattooed right smack behind his ear, or the fact that he crossed his legs, but I'm not positive so I blabbed. "My fourth time in a tattoo parlor, but don't tell anyone." I bugged my eyes out.

He sucked in a sharp intake of breath and if it wouldn't have been for the amused grin on his face, I would've worried he thought I sucked as a human being or something. "No shit?"

"No shit."

Slim had shifted his hips to face me more comfortably, one leg still tossed over the other, the coy fish tattoo on his forearm right in front of my face. "No tats?"

I shook my head, a little embarrassed.

"Piercings?"

My face flamed, but I shook my head anyway. "Do my earlobes and cartilage count?"

The grin on his face spread so wide I thought it'd be painful. "You're kidding."

"I'm not." The infectious grin contaminated me. "How many do you have?"

"Not that many." Slim pointed at the wide gauges stretching his earlobes. "Two." He stuck his tongue out. "Three." Luckily, he just pointed at the right side of his chest. "Four."

My eyes went wide.

"Blake! How many piercings do you have?" he yelled, trying to get Blake's attention from the other side of the divider.

"Seven!"

Slim nodded. "Blue doesn't count because she has at least ten, and I think Dex only has three now." He tipped his chin up, giving me a teasing smile. "You should think about getting one." He paused. "Or three."

I put my palms up and shrugged. "Maybe." I almost told him I had been thinking about getting something, but I kept my mouth closed.

He slowly got to his feet, patting around his back pocket. "I'm gonna go get a sub from the deli next door. Want something?"

"No thanks." What a nice guy.

"Blake, you want something from Sal's?" he asked.

"Six inches," was his initial reply before adding something like "salami" at the end of his request.

I didn't hear that though because that was when I did it.

I shouldn't have been surprised. I had the worst habit in the universe of just blurting shit out of my mouth without thinking. I liked to blame the fact that my mom, brother, and yia-yia were the same way. Hell, even Sonny said whatever came to mind and he wasn't even on the right side of the family.

Some families passed on traits like bad eyesight, receding hair lines, stuff like that. My mom's side of the family passed on diarrhea of the mouth. Add that onto the fact that Will and I used to catch each other with the same joke every chance we had, and it was inevitable.

So I blurted out the dumbest crap I could have said in a mix of a snicker and an amused laugh that everyone in the parlor could hear. It was instinct.

"That's what she said."

Silence.

Friggin' silence followed.

Three seconds of quiet time filled the shop. Even the low buzzing noise of the gun was strangely absent in my words' wake.

And then they all—Slim, Blake, Blue, and the customer at Blue's station—burst out laughing and howling. Laughing and howling at the same time.

Crap.

Blake pressed his forehead against the divider while his shoulders shook. Meanwhile, Slim covered his face with both of his slender artist hands as his chest vibrated.

"Did that really come out of your mouth or am I imagining it?"

I face-planted the desk. "Oh God, I'm sorry, Blake." I'd muttered. "It just...came out."

"She got you good," one of them barked out loudly before making a noise that sounded like a cry right as it dissolved into a cackle.

"What the fuck are you guys laughin' at?" that melodic voice asked from somewhere behind me.

I didn't have it in me to look up because I was mortified.

Mortified because I was A) an idiot, B) an idiot, and C) an idiot. I didn't know these guys and that was rude, wasn't it?

Luckily Slim managed to get something out when Blake started laughing even louder. "Blake—Iris—six inches," he gasped.

I tilted my head over to shoot Slim the most withering look in the world. I probably looked more constipated than mad. "I said I was sorry."

"What?" Dex asked again.

Someone patted my head, which was still friendly with the lacquered black wood beneath me.

"Tell him what you said," Slim urged me. "It's funnier if you say it."

I groaned.

"One of you just tell me what's so fuckin' funny. I don't need to hear your life story," The Dick groaned.

With a long, amused sigh, Slim repeated the incident, snickering his way through the beginning of the six inch request.

The original four started laughing really loudly again, which made me start laughing again too because what the hell was I going to do? Cry? Maybe.

By that time, Slim and Blake were wheezing even as I heard the steady hum of the tattoo gun start up again.

"Ritz? What'd you say?" Dex asked in an exasperated tone that sounded exactly like the one he'd used when I had asked him for help my second day.

The reminder of his words the day before cooled me down insta-friggin'-ly. I was sober in seconds, blinking away the embarrassed tears that had come up when I started laughing at my dumbass comment.

"It was inappropriate, I'm sorry for saying it," I told my boss, averting my eyes to Slim's still covered face.

"Just tell me what you fuckin' said. I'm dyin' here," he cursed, the tips of his words sounding more curious than angry.

Well, screw it. If he was going to fire me for making a that's-what-she-said joke, then so be it. If I needed to make dumb jokes to get The Dick to cut me loose from this job, then that was a loss I'd take for Team Iris. I'd just been hoping to have another job before then.

My eyes went up to land on the short, dark scruff on his jawline. From those two seconds I was staring at his face, I'd deduced that his facial hair was the same inky black as his head. Which was nice, until you figured out he was a huge asswad.

"I told Blake that's what she said." He blinked. "You know, about wanting six inches." I breathed out, darting my eyes back over to my redheaded coworker for throwing me under the bus and making me talk to my arch nemesis.

But Dex didn't say anything in response.

Of course he didn't have a sense of humor. I guess you couldn't have a sense of humor if you were missing a soul. The thought almost made me laugh.

He just stared at me for the longest moment, his gaze intense and disarming. Those blue eyes lingered over my face before he told Slim to go clean up his station so we could get the hell out of there as soon as possible. The minute those words were out of his mouth, I sensed that Blake had walked away too.

Since that little chat, he hadn't ventured further than four words at a time with me until Friday.

It was a little after five o'clock and the shop was dead. There weren't any appointments scheduled until eight so I wasn't expecting any customers to walk in until much later. I started going through the catalogues I'd found in the desk drawers, trying to get familiar with equipment. Who did show up instead, were two bikers that pulled up to the street parking like they owned the boulevard the building was on. Wearing heavily patched-up black leather vests, maybe in their mid-thirties or early forties, and each sporting some serious facial hair, they prowled in through the door looking around immediately.

WMC members.

"Hi," I called out to them.

One of them, the older looking of the two with a belly that had a monogamous relationship with six-packs of beer, tilted his chin up at me. "Dex here?"

I nodded.

The other biker guy, pretty attractive in his own way with his dark hair pulled back in a short ponytail, winked at me. I had a feeling he was the same guy that Dex had been arguing with at the bar my first day in town. "Get him for us, sweetie?"

I wished that it wasn't The Dick of all people they were asking for, but I nodded anyway and headed down the hall. When Dex was in, I stuck to the front desk so he could use the office. It was only when he wasn't around or if he was busy with a customer that I slunk in to do whatever was needed that day in peace and quiet. Meaning that I had no clue what the hell I was doing and tried figuring everything out on the go.

Luckily, Dex was stepping out of his office before I made it all the way.

My focus zoned in on his so-black-it-almost-looked-blue hair that flopped out from beneath the rim of the Rangers cap on his head. "There are two people asking for you in the front."

"I saw 'em in the camera," he informed me. I didn't even know there was a camera out front. Dex handed me a big manila envelope he had under his arm. "Do me a favor. Walk this over to the body shop around the corner, will ya?"

Sonny! I still hadn't dropped by, then again, neither had he. But it didn't matter. He still texted me at least once a day to make sure I was alive and hadn't gotten lost or abducted in my new city.

I must have thought too long about going over to the body shop because Dex cleared his throat, raising a heavy eyebrow. This guy really thought I was an imbecile.

I wasn't about to let him know I was excited to see Sonny by running the errand, so I nodded at his hair instead. "Sure."

"You know where it's at?" he asked me.

Anger rose up the vertical muscles in my throat. "Yeah, I know." And then I muttered, "I'm not completely stupid."

He didn't say anything as I took the package from his hand, keeping my eyes everywhere but on his face. Not bothering to say anything else to him, I turned around to walk down the hall.

"Make sure Luther gets it, babe," he called out after me.

Babe. Guh.

It was something so far I'd only heard him call me when he wasn't referring to me as Ritz. In the last two days he'd helped other women who came in but he strictly referred to them by their first name or "sweetheart." Under normal circumstances, I would have thought that was cute but this was Dex The Dick, so it automatically defaulted to douche-bag language.

Either way, he could shove his pleasantry up his pie hole while I went across the street. I had no idea who the heck Luther was but Sonny would.

Dex walked just a few feet behind me, his heavy footfalls—from the black motorcycle boots I noticed he wore daily—echoed on the tiled floor where my flat ballet shoes didn't make a sound.

Dirty Biker Guy winked at me as I walked passed him. I flushed just a little but winked back and was out the door, making it through before the two men began speaking with The Dick.

It was pretty impossible not to feel relieved to see my only real friend—slash sibling—in Austin during the day. I'd been getting off work so late we only got to talk for a few minutes before he'd pass out on the couch or bid me goodnight if he didn't stay up watching television while I ate. I had no idea what time he got up, and to be honest, I figured it was pretty early even though he went to bed a lot later than I would have if the tables were turned.

I'd been parking in the lot for days now, but I hadn't paid enough attention to see just how large the shop was. Which would've been my sign, as I walked up to the body shop, on how big the property was. The ratio was about five to one.

And it was owned by a member of the MC, Sonny had explained in the past.

The garage itself could house eight cars. There was another building adjacent to it. One that looked exactly like the main one minus the bays, probably an office and reception area.

As soon as I stepped onto the lot, I saw Sonny standing in the third open bay from the gate. Hauling my butt over in his direction, he attention darted over to me at the same time I saw a couple of guys in the same jumper suit he had on looking over.

I gave him the "princess wave"—a cupped hand that rotated at the wrist—before yelling, "Hey!"

But Sonny, who had rightfully given me the impression he didn't give a shit what anyone else thought when I saw him walk outside the house in only his boxers one morning when I got up to pee, smiled at me this quick, open grin before walking in my direction too. "Ris, what are you doing here?"

"I have to give this to someone named Luther." I held the envelope up to his face. "Not that it's not nice to see you, or that I haven't been planning on coming to visit you since we work like right next door."

He shot me an easy smile before gazing down at the package. "This from Dex?"

"He asked me to drop it off," I informed him, proud of myself for not calling Dex a dick when I had the chance.

"Is he still giving you shit?"

I shook my head. "He just pretends I don't exist and I mess stuff up because I don't ask."

He snorted. "Good girl." Sonny looked over his shoulder, scanning the remaining open bays down the side of the building after he'd glared at some of the employees looking in our direction. "Look for Trip. He's probably down at the last lift with him."

I thanked him before remembering what I'd been putting off for days. "I keep forgetting to ask you, do you know where I can get an oil change for pretty cheap?"

Those light brown eyes went blank. "You're serious?"

"No, you know I just like cracking jokes about car repair."

"You're a pain in the ass, kid." He let out a deep sigh, placing a hand on top of my head and shaking it. "Ris, I'm a mechanic." I knew this but it didn't mean I wanted to take advantage of him by asking. "We'll come in the morning and I'll do it for you tomorrow."

"Here?"

"Here," he confirmed. "Your tires need to be rotated while we're at it. I can do it faster here."

I grinned at him. "Deal. I owe you." For a bunch of things but I didn't have a doubt he was absolutely not keeping track of.

With a light smack to his shoulder blade, I told Sonny I'd see him later and made my way across the forecourt to the last open bay. There were two Harleys parked inside with Trip and an older looking man with what had once been brown hair that was now streaked with gray, standing together and talking in low tones.

Settling on being rude over being nosey, I cleared my throat and forced a grin on my face. "Sorry," I called out over to them.

Trip turned around, his expression smothered in frustration and what I thought could be anger at first before he spotted me. "Hey beautiful," he murmured with a head nod as the older man turned his attention to me as well.

The man looked to be in his late fifties, face weathered, expression telling me he wasn't much of a grinner unlike his younger companion. He had on grease stained jeans, a t-shirt that had once been white, and a distressed leather vest with multiple patches. The Widowmakers' vest—or cut, as Sonny had corrected me back at Mayhem my first night.

I figured I probably shouldn't waste his time based on the fact that he didn't look happy to see me and probably didn't look happy to see anyone, period. Ever. Moving my focus back and forth between Trip and the man I assumed to be Luther, I raised the envelope up.

"I'm looking for Luther."

The old guy took three steps toward me, reached for the envelope with a grunt of a "Thanks" and turned around to open it, shielding me from its contents.

Trip and I both looked at each other and shrugged.

"I'll see you later," I told Trip, who looked even more attractive during the day than he had when I saw him at night the week before. In the natural light, my guess was that he was probably a handful of years older than my twenty-four. He had on the same thing that Luther and the other two guys back at the parlor except his t-shirt was black and his jeans looked pretty new.

Trip was pretty friggin' handsome. Long legs. Nice yellow blonde goatee. Easy smile.

So I knew right then that I really needed to get my ass back to work before I thought any longer about how nice and handsome Trip was. Because it then reminded me how hot and asshole-ish my boss was, and I knew that would only make me bitter.

No thanks.

"You comin' to the party tomorrow, gorgeous?" he asked when I took a step back.

"There's a party?"

He nodded.

"Well, this is awkward." Both of my eyebrows shot up. I whispered, "I wasn't invited."

Trip laughed. "You're invited. Sonny only parties in one place, and that's with the Club." He crossed his arms over his chest and lifted his chin. "You hafta come. You got it in your blood."

Sonny had used those same exact words to con me into going to Mayhem with him last week. You got it in your blood. Then why the heck had my parents taken me to Florida?

"Me and your boy won't let anybody mess with you," he offered. "You'll come?"

Oh, what the hell. I hadn't been out in almost a year with the exception of the last trip to Mayhem. "Yeah, sure."

Trip grinned.

Glancing down at my watch, I sighed. It'd been twenty minutes since I left the shop and the last thing I wanted was to get in trouble when I got back. "See you tomorrow?"

He nodded, still grinning. "Sure will."

Waving at Trip, I kept taking steps backward. "Bye, Trip." He winked at me right before I waved once more and speed-walked down the forecourt.

I spotted Sonny bent at the hips with his entire upper body suspended over the motor of a Chevy and since I didn't see Luther—more than likely the boss— around, I yelled at him. "See ya, Sonny!"

He didn't move but I heard him call out after me, "Later, Ris!"

It might have been because Trip was a handsome flirty bastard, or it might have been because Sonny went above and beyond the call of being a half-brother who had spent less than a year of his total life with me, but I smiled the entire—short—walk to work.

"You ever thought about getting a tattoo?" Slim asked me.

It was a little after ten. Blake was working on the same piece he'd been going at for two hours and Blue had just gotten saddled with piercing a cute but barely legal girl's tongue. I had a feeling she was going to regret that thing tomorrow, but I kept my mouth closed.

Rule number one in working at a tattoo parlor according to Blake—don't talk customers out of services unless they were a really, really bad idea. Which meant I really, really needed to find out what they thought a bad idea was. Maybe a facial tattoo?

Slim and I had just given each other bug eyes when Blue walked off with the nervous girl and we'd followed after them with our eyes until they disappeared into one of the private rooms. Earlier, a woman well into her thirties had come in requesting to get one nipple pierced. Blue had been in the room with her for ten minutes when a scream pierced through the parlor, scaring the crap out of all of us. It was a miracle that Dex hadn't messed up the tattoo he'd been working on because I'd whacked the computer mouse across the room in response.

I was fondly starting to call the private room the "torture chamber" in my head.

I nodded my head at Slim. "I wanted to get a tattoo on my lower back when I was eighteen."

He raised an incredulous eyebrow. "A tramp stamp?"

The guy enunciated the words a little too carefully. Smart ass.

For that, he earned a smirk. "For the record, I didn't know they were called tramp stamps before I wanted to get one," I gave him a flat look. "I just thought they were kind of cool."

"Cool?" He smiled, still enunciating slowly.

I repeated myself with a smirk.

"But…?" Slim trailed off, fishing for an explanation.

"But I couldn't think of anything I liked enough to get tattooed on me for the rest of my life, you know?" And I'd found out two weeks later that I was going to need another surgery, but I kept that tidbit to myself.

Slim, who from what I'd seen over the last few days, was tattooed from ears to toes, nodded in understanding. "They're addicting. I was only going to get one when I turned eighteen, and then one turned into two, and two into three—"

"And three into—," I fanned out my fingers and wiggled them, "Everything?"

He snorted. "Exactly."

I got it.

Pretty much ninety percent of the clientele I'd seen over the week were repeat customers. They'd mostly all been familiar with one or all of the guys working, and while not everyone had the amount of ink coverage that the artists had, two tattoos was more than my whopping zero.

And they were cool. Almost all of the work that wasn't walk-in was original, hand-drawn and transferred. They really were pieces of art or at least pieces of art in the making.

From what I'd seen in such a short amount of time, the tattoos weren't just random crap people would regret when they were elderly. The pieces clients got seemed to be so much more than that. They were memorials and declarations. They were outpourings of love and pain. Letters and images, icons and symbolism, personal and eternal.

It was eye-opening for me. The art that they created were badges of honor. It was impossible not to get sucked into the emotion that went behind the artwork.

Well, at least that was the case with most of them. I'd already seen a sketch for a flaming penis that made me cringe.

"You have great skin. It'd be a perfect canvas." He lifted both of his eyebrows before looking up abruptly and lifting his chin, still grinning but past me. "Done hibernating?"

I tensed up.

"Done with three hours of Club financial shit," that grumbly, deep voice that I'd learned to associate with Dex's cool mood answered from what felt like just a few feet behind me.

"Bummer." Slim made a face.

"I don't see us gettin' any more business. Ritz, you're free to go home whenever you're ready, and Slim, clean up, yeah?" Dex said.

Slim nodded, hopped off the edge of my desk and walked toward the back. I heard the soft sound of Dex's motorcycle boots lumber off, and I got up. I'd already cleaned everything about thirty minutes before. The frames, the coffee table, all the free surfaces. My stuff for the day was done.

Blake happened to look over when he took a mini break as I was throwing my purse over my shoulder, so waved at him and mouthed, "See you tomorrow." He closed both his eyes and nodded before I walked out of the shop.

The street, usually heavy with pedestrian and automotive traffic during the day, was eerily quiet. There weren't any cars besides the two Pins clients' and it freaked me the hell out. It was like one of those scary movie scenes before the heroine gets chased by some psychopath serial killer but manages to survive. Survive half-naked, whatever.

Instantly, I regretted not asking one of the guys to walk out with me, but I didn't want to ask them for favors. I didn't need to get babysat and plus, I didn't like being that needy girl. I'd been on my own for years. I could walk to my car by myself.

Sucking in a breath, my feet were brave enough to make their way down the strip, passing the real estate agency while I talked myself out of looking in. The last thing I needed or wanted was to see some masked face staring back at me from the other side.

I'd barely made it to the end of the street when someone yelled out, "Yo!"

Under normal circumstances, if I thought it might have been a stranger instead of someone from the shop calling out after me, I'd start running. But it wasn't. It took me a second out on that empty street to realize it was Dex's deep voice yelling.

"Hold up!"

I forced myself to turn around and see him jogging over. "Yes?"

He cut the distance between us to stop just two feet away. "What the fuck are you doin'?"

I blinked. What? "You told me I could leave when I was ready." I blinked again. "I was ready."

Dex's amazing eyes, even under the dim streetlight that cast shadows in the shadows, looked incredulous. "Girl, I said you could leave when you were ready but not by your fuckin' self. You can't be walkin' around this side of town all alone so late."

Did this man just... scold me?

And what the hell did he mean this side of town? This side of town seemed safe enough.

"My car's just right there," I told him, pointing in the general direction of the nearby lot.

Dex shrugged. "You gotta have some self-preservation or somethin', babe. Can't be walkin' around here by yourself."

"It's right there," I repeated, pointing again. It was seriously thirty steps away.

"I don't give a fuck," he pointed out. "C'mon, I got a business to close. Last thing I need is your goddamn bro callin' me, bustin' my balls over somethin' happenin' to you." Dex wrapped his fingers—long, not too slim but most, most, most definitely manly—around my forearm and pulled me across the street.

I wiggled my arm in his grasp a little, pointing at my car with my free hand. "You can let go of my arm." I jerked it again futilely, thankful he'd grabbed the good one. "I don't need a babysitter, but I appreciate the gesture," I groaned under my breath, shaking my arm in his grasp once more.

"Obviously you need a babysitter if you're walkin' around shitty ass Austin alone this late, babe." He shook his head, yanking me not so gently around Blake's white Nissan Frontier and toward my old Ford. "So fuckin' stupid," he hissed under his breath.

Jerk. Total jerk.

"I'm not stupid and I'm not a friggin' idiot," I snapped, wiggling my arm again but he didn't let go.

He also didn't say anything. The only noise that came out of his body was a sharp inhale that was impossible to miss.

"Can you please let go of my arm now?" Why the hell was I saying please? I tried jerking out of his grasp, feeling like an idiot for asking permission to get control back of my body. I should have just… demanded it, damn it.

"No."

His simple, curt answer grated on me.

"Not till you're in the car," Dex explained.

I pulled at his hold. "Let. Go. Of. My. Arm." I lowered my voice into a whisper. "Or else."

He didn't need to know that the *or else* depended on me slapping his tiny nuts with the back of my hand.

Dex didn't respond and he didn't say anything either as he pulled us to a stop in front of my Focus. I was fishing through my purse the minute my arm was free.

"Thanks for walking me over," I murmured to him, still indignant. Still pissed. Still keeping my eyes a million miles away from Dex The Dick's face.

You need the job.

You need the job.

You need the job.

But that didn't mean I completely shut up. My dumb mouth kept going. "I'm not stupid enough to not pay attention to my surroundings, by the way."

Well, that could have been a lot worse.

Normally, I would have been shocked by how angry I felt all of a sudden. It was as if the two days of working with this asshole and the last ten years of my life had suddenly joined together in a tsunami of pissed-offness that threatened to drown everything in the world. Normal Iris would have and should have just continued to ignore Dex Locke. Pretend like his words hadn't bothered me but that Iris was a victim of the tsunami, apparently.

He didn't say anything for a long minute, an ink covered hand pulled at the sleeve of his crew neck shirt. His tight gray crewneck shirt. Guh. It seemed so friggin' unfair. It should be a standard that attractive men be just as nice on the inside as they were on the outside. But they weren't and it sucked big time.

"Ritz?" he asked in a softer tone than I'd ever imagined hearing from him. The dry, bored tone seemed to be a staple in his vocal cord usage.

I groaned. "My name's—"

"Ritz."

"No," I told him—well, his neck.

"Look at me," he said but it sounded more like an order.

I didn't want to, and I knew he knew it too.

"Babe, look at me," he repeated the command, still in that lax, casual voice.

Slowly, like a snail making a long trek, I rolled my eyes over to his face, taking in the flawless bone structure staring back at me from over demon flesh incarnate.

When my eyes landed on his bluest of blues, he frowned. That handsome, angled face shifted in uncomfortable displeasure. Should it have been a surprise that a look that resembled guilt seemed so foreign to him? No. "Chill out, yeah?"

I forced that same look he'd copyrighted onto my face. Flat, plain, and emotionless. "Sure."

He blinked. "You're lyin'."

I tried to take a step back. "Goodnight."

Dex's hand whipped forward to grab the hem of my shirt, stopping me. "Ritz." His tone was insistent.

"That's not my name."

He chose to ignore that. "Will you look at me?" he growled, exasperation dripping from his words. That soft voice disappearing in an instant.

I looked at him but felt a million miles away.

Dex cut the distance between us, towering over me. His brilliant eyes searched over my face, resting on my mouth for a brief moment before looping back up to my eyes. "Son already bitched me out."

I tugged on my arm. "Goodnight."

"Babe," he said, tugging on my button-down. "I got a bad temper and that was a crap day for me. I say shitty things when I'm pissed."

Sure, because it was that friggin' easy. He had a shitty day so he could call me names behind my back. Right. Made total sense. *Not.*

Dick.

I just stared back at him.

"Just let it go, 'kay? It drives me fuckin' crazy you won't look me in the eye," he breathed. "I don't do this awkward shit, babe."

"If I look at you from now on will you leave me alone?" I asked him in a whisper.

Something shuttered across his eyes. "You're not gonna let this go?"

My chest flared with white hot anger. Getting fired would be better than quitting if I was standing up for myself, wouldn't it? Sonny was my brother, he'd understand in a heartbeat if I explained. Then afterward, some kneecaps would be busted.

There was always the job at the damn strip club. Lord.

Schooling my features, I leaned forward to close the short distance between us to a microscopic one despite the near foot in height difference.

"It's not every day someone I don't know calls me a fucking idiot, then insults my clothes and my time management." I looked him right in the eye, not caring that he winced. "I'd say I'm sorry that I had to ask you for help, and that I can't pretend you didn't hurt my feelings, but I won't. If you would've showed me what to do slower or not rolled your eyes each time I wrote something down in my notebook, I wouldn't have had to. I'm not stupid or an idiot or a moron or whatever else you've called me." In all honesty, I hadn't intended to tell him he'd hurt my feelings but once the words were out in the universe it was a done deal. Whatever. I couldn't take them back so I had to stand by them. "And now, I'm just pissed off, and I want to go home."

And Dex, Dex just looked at me with those irises the same shade as a crayon. "You don't know what it's like to have a shit day, princess?"

Princess?

Princess?

This dickwad had no clue.

I sucked in another breath, steeling myself. I wasn't going to be a pushover again. No. Friggin'. Way. I was done. If I could get fired, it'd be better than leaving on my own. So I laid it out on him as politely as I could. "When I have bad days, princess," I whispered, opting at the last minute to leave out the Duke Dickface teasing my tongue, "I cry. I read. I clean. I eat crappy things. I swim or do the yard. I don't make people feel like crap, your royal highness."

CHAPTER SIX

"Are you sure this won't get you into trouble?"

Sonny's upper body had disappeared beneath the car minutes ago with tools and a pan. I plopped down on top of a tire that was sitting off to the side of the bay at the body shop he worked at, watching him because I had no idea how to help. "It's fine, Ris. Trust me."

Well, shit.

The shop was closed on Saturdays; there was a very clear sign by the gate that we'd come through. Personally, I'd rather not get arrested for trespassing but Sonny didn't look worried even a hundredth of a fraction. Plus, I'd spotted three bikes and two cars parked alongside the big adjacent building to the bays, so I figured we either weren't alone or somebody was using the space as a parking lot.

Only I wasn't sure whether that was a good thing or not.

"You trust me, don't you?" he asked in a teasing voice when I didn't respond.

"No." I extended my leg out to nudge his knee with my toes. "Yes."

Because I did. A lot. Sonny had never let me down when he knew I needed him.

Regardless, I still didn't want to risk him losing his job all because I couldn't change my own oil. "You're positive?"

A dirty blue rag went airborne and smacked me in the face. "Quit asking."

"Sheesh," I muttered but made a face and picked the rag up with my index finger and thumb before tossing it back at him.

He worked quietly for a few minutes, the sound of metal on metal and *drip, drip, drip* filling the silence before he spoke again. "Wasn't your mom's anniversary last month?" he asked in a muffled voice.

I froze, sucked into the fact he remembered the date.

But just as quickly as my appreciation for him flared, a distant but familiar feeling that was both pressing and heavy swam around in my stomach. It was awkward and irregular shaped, but after a second it went away like it always did in the past. I licked my lips and focused on answering him. "Yeah. It was." Eight years had passed since my mom had died and it'd felt like something that happened two lifetimes ago instead. Which was a good thing, I thought. Will and *yia-yia* would agree, too.

It'd taken me years to get over my dad leaving. Years of crying and suffering and feeling like the hole his absence left in my life would never go away. At ten, it's unfathomable that the father you love and adore would just... leave. By the time he showed up again when my Mom got sick, I'd gone from being upset to downright pissed.

When I'd needed him before, he'd fallen off the face of the planet. Not even Sonny had seen or heard from him.

I'd even blamed him for a while for what happened to Mom. Maybe if she wouldn't have loved him as much as she did, and then been left alone with two kids, juggling two jobs, she might have been fine.

But she hadn't been. She died and left us with my crazy ass *yia-yia* that made the most amazing *baklava...* for breakfast.

Dad was alive but he'd become a long lost dream. A long lost dream that withered into smoke and ash right after Mom was buried.

Will was there though. And without Will, who needed me to keep going, I wouldn't have gotten through those floating, disaster months that ruined any chance of me making grades that were good enough to get scholarships. Scholarships that I should have been shoo-ed into if I'd played up The Arm

Situation, but not even that could make up for my crap, quarter-hearted grades.

"The older you get, the more you start to look just like her," Sonny noted, pulling me out of my thoughts.

Yia-yia and Will had both said the same thing. "Yeah, it's kind of creepy." Mom and I had the same black hair. We had the same normal nose, the same small mouth and slightly fuller bottom lip. Our build was the same too from what I could remember. Mom had been long and lean, and while I wasn't as long as she was, at five-seven I wasn't exactly short either.

I was my mother's daughter. The looks, the impulsiveness, the temper, almost everything. My brother, like Sonny, was a mirror image of our dad, where I was our mom's doppelganger.

Sonny slid out from beneath my car, wiping his hands on the rag I'd thrown back at him. He reached over and patted the top of my running shoe, his eyes warm. "It's a good thing. I take more after my mom, too." He closed his eyes and let out a long breath. "Thank fucking God."

That was a blatant lie. He looked just like our dad but I wasn't about to ruin the mood by stating what seemed so obvious to me.

"You do have those girlish features," I told him with a grin, wanting to pull away from the talk of my mom.

Sonny snickered and sat up. "Stupid." With a shake of his head, something behind me caught his attention making his eyes narrow. And because I'm nosey, I turned around to see what he was looking at.

Dex.

Walking onto the lot, his short black hair went in ten different directions. Wrinkled jeans and an equally wrinkled blue t-shirt finished off his obviously bedhead ensemble. But what caught my attention, and what might have also caught Sonny's, was the blonde woman he was walking beside. A blonde woman in a very wrinkled dress that screamed she wasn't opposed to public fondling. And it wasn't the same woman I'd seen him with two weeks ago.

Dex stopped just a few feet shy of a Hyundai parked in front of the office. It was a magnetic pull that kept me watching him drop a quick kiss on her mouth before slapping her ass as she crossed the distance toward her car and got in.

Pig.

"That motherfucker," Sonny murmured, shaking his head in a disbelieving fashion.

My eyes went from my brother to my boss, who stood with his back to his lady friend, completely disinterested. Sonny didn't look mad, but he looked annoyed and that alarmed me. "Please tell me that wasn't your girlfriend."

His light brown eyes met mine, wide with amusement. "Hell no. I don't even think Becky knows how to spell the word girlfriend, Ris." Sonny looked past me again. "But that motherfucker's always talking shit about how he wouldn't fu—do her because she's been with half the club."

"Oh." He didn't strike me as the picky type, but then again, I guess he really wasn't if he couldn't hold his own word.

I looked back over my shoulder to see that the Hyundai was gone and surprise! Dex was walking over in the direction of the open bay we were in. Obviously. It was the only one open. I ignored the weird feeling in my chest I got from seeing him taking those lengthy strides toward us. "Well, you know I don't know how to kick anyone's ass but I'd try my best if she was being a cheatin' ho-bag."

Sonny threw his head back and snorted. "It's the thought that counts."

I grinned at him, extending my legs out in front of me again to kick his shoe.

He chuckled again but this time kept his gaze on Dex's approaching figure. "Well if it isn't my favorite hypocrite," Sonny greeted my boss.

"Fuck off," Dex snapped from feet away.

"Becky?" Sonny shook his head. "Outta all the pu—" he eyed me, "—women at the bar, you took fucking *Becky* upstairs?"

I was surprised my boss didn't give him the middle finger, instead he settled for a look that could only be described as withering and absolutely not amused. "I can't remember shit from last night," Dex explained in a voice that somehow managed to be both gruff and scratchy.

An attractive man that drank so much he slept with people he didn't like, and then couldn't remember? Absolutely excellent. My opinion of him was just getting better.

Was it unfair to judge him when the majority of single men did the same thing? Yes. Did I care about being fair? No.

Sonny looked down at me, raising his eyebrows in disbelief. "Sure."

"I'm fuckin' serious, man. Buck had me try his home brew to celebrate, and I don't remember a single goddamn thing after my third one." Two boot clad feet landed right next to me, and I angled my face upward to take in the long length of Dex's legs and torso, only to find him looking down at me in return. His expression was tight. "Hi."

I breathed out a "Morning" back that was buried beneath Sonny's reply.

"You know better than to drink anything Buck makes. His shit puts moonshine to shame." There was some type of hesitation in my brother's voice that I didn't understand, like something was bothering him. "I forgot to tell you congrats," Sonny said, completely oblivious to the stare down his friend and I were having. "Me and Ris stayed home last night otherwise I would've met up with you for a drink. Congrats, man."

Dex's bright blue eyes slid away from my face and out toward my legs, lingering on them so long it made me self-conscious of how small my shorts were.

"Thanks," he replied, detaching his gaze from my direction and back toward Son. "Feels good."

"Well, you deserve it, fucker," Sonny noted.

When had he started speaking so much? I hadn't heard him string together so many words in three days total.

And what were they talking about?

Dex shrugged, glancing back down. His mouth was set in a fine line, something in his expression telling me that there was something he wanted to say but nothing came out. Just like nothing had come out of his mouth the night before after I'd told him he hurt my feelings in the parking lot.

Which was right before I called him a princess.

A-w-k-w-a-r-d.

Finally, he looked over at Sonny instead. "I'll let you get back to what you two were doin'. See you at the shop later," he spoke to me, glancing down at my legs one last time before nodding a goodbye at Sonny and making his way back to the building he'd come out from.

The moment he was out of earshot I asked, "What was he celebrating?" I didn't care, I swear, but I was nosey.

"He just paid off the loan Luther gave him to set up Pins."

I focused on big, bad Dex paying off the money he'd been loaned to set up his tattoo shop. "Huh." I'd spent my entire adult life trying to balance just having a lease, medical bills, cell phone, and random things to pay for; I couldn't imagine the responsibility of having a business to worry about on top of that when I could barely afford my minute sized expenses.

"Is it always that awkward between you two?" my brother asked.

Crap, was it that obvious? "Always." I made a face. "I probably made it worse when I called him a princess last night."

He busted out a laugh that had me giggling at the absurdity of what I'd done.

"Goddamn, kid."

"He made me mad and it just...came out." I didn't bother telling him Dex had called me a princess first. The phone conversation I'd overheard two days ago was still fresh in my mind. No need to fuel that fire, right?

Sonny nodded, dropping to his butt in front of my car before sliding back underneath it. "You sure you don't want me to have a talk with him?"

The sneaky turd. I didn't even need to think about it. "You already had a talk with him."

Sonny snickered but didn't apologize or make any excuses for the conversation he'd had following the fit he'd thrown in his bedroom.

"I do want to look for another job though if you know anyone else, " I offered him up. "Preferably one with someone who reminds you of unicorns and rainbows."

I heard him laugh from beneath the car. "Kid, I don't think anybody in the club would remind me of unicorns and rainbows," he replied, still laughing.

"Glitter and tutus?"

He snorted. "Hell no." Thinking better of it, he added, "Maybe Trip."

I was bored out of my friggin' mind.

Thirty minutes in, and I was ready to get the heck home.

Sonny had finally told me about the "party"—it really just seemed like an excuse to go to the bar—and on top of that, I'd found out that the guys from the shop were going to be there, I'd been relieved. While hanging out in places where I didn't know anyone usually freaked me out a bit, I'd mentally prepared myself for the fact that I was practically starting my life over. New city, new job, new home, new friends.

New, new, new, new, new.

I'd decided a few days ago that all this new stuff needed a solid commitment from me if I wanted to make it work long term. My hermit days of working to scrape by needed a positive boost. Plus, Sonny wouldn't let me get away with the same stuff that Lanie had. Like staying in, eating Ramen noodles, and watching PBS on Friday nights because we couldn't afford cable.

So I'd thrown a tough smile on my face and driven to the bar after work. Pins wasn't set to close until one but business was slow, and I'd already clocked in over eight hours, Slim had told me to go ahead and go. Was I going to argue with him about staying? No way.

Things all day had been awkward. Dex The Dick had been in a surprisingly good mood with everyone. He wasn't grumpy or aloof like usual, and I wasn't sure whether to thank the fact that he paid off his loan or the fact that he'd gotten laid—gag—last night, for it.

The thing that got to me, though, was that not once had I heard any of the guys complain about his previous shit-titude. Back at my old job, if my boss was having a bad day and was on an ass-ripping mission from hell, we'd all talk about him the moment we had the chance. Or at least I'd roll my eyes.

But did anyone say anything about Dex?

Nope.

I had no one to roll my eyes with. No one who understood my resentment for the jerk who had made me feel like I had no business breathing the same air as him just because he was supposedly having a bad day. I could only come up with the conclusion that while Slim, Blue, and Blake were friendly, they hadn't completely let me into the ranks yet.

Having someone else call him a dick wasn't too much to ask for, was it?

When Slim gave me the chance to get out of there so I could avoid being in Dex The Dick's general vicinity, I took it. I changed as quickly as I could—because you don't go to a bar owned by bikers wearing business casual.

Now that I was more familiarized with the area, I realized the bar was just two blocks down from Pins and the body shop Sonny worked at. It seemed like the entire city mile was Widowmakers' territory. There were a handful loitering around outside with my brother in their midst.

Old, still smelling strongly of cigarettes, pee, and beer, Mayhem had new upgrades like flat screen televisions mounted on the wall and new pool tables lined up far from the entrance that clashed with the old bar. The lights were dim, the place was as loud and crowded as it'd been two weeks before. And for some strange reason, I didn't feel completely awkward there like I usually did when I'd gone to bars with Lanie.

This in itself said something because in the first five minutes I was inside, someone had broken off a bottle against the edge of the counter and held it up to someone else's throat before two Club members split them up.

Sonny and I walked around the floor. I smiled and waved at some of the people he'd introduced me to the last time. People who knew the complicated web of our lives thanks to an irresponsible former Widow.

And apparently, because I was getting so chummy with strangers who were a little interested to meet a former member's daughter, Sonny thought it'd be fine to leave me.

The horny bastard said he'd be right back, and thirty minutes later, he wasn't. I'd seen him spying some brunette across the bar before pulling a Las Vegas magic show act on me and disappearing.

What was a girl who didn't really know anyone supposed to do? Sit her ass at the bar, watch, and wait.

And watch and wait was what I did. About a quarter of the people boozing and being really friggin' loud were dressed like Luther and Trip: jeans, a t-shirt, and a black leather vest with multitudes of patches. And so many tattoos I didn't know where to begin looking. I could still remember the WMC insignia my dad had worn proudly until he'd gotten it covered up one day randomly. I was never sure what had officially cut his affiliations with the Club after nearly a decade of living away from Austin but honestly, I didn't give a crap.

Not a single one.

The other half of the people milling around Mayhem doing shots, yelling, laughing, and smoking something I had a feeling wasn't legal in the corner, were still pretty rough looking.

Glancing around, I'd never seen so many tattoos, leather, and facial hair in my life—and that was just the men.

The women were all around mid-to-late twenties and older. Their skin and hair colors ranged across the color spectrum. Clothes were obviously optional after I'd seen a couple women flash their boobs just for the hell of it.

It totally made sense to me right then why my mom had hightailed it back to Florida when she found out she was pregnant with me. In the ten minutes that followed the first broken-bottle-to-the-throat incident, someone got socked in the face. What did I do? I sat there and watched.

Maybe I should have felt awkward and out of place. I was used to being alone and I didn't mind it. But even though the men were loud, burly, and kind of intimidating and overbearing, I liked listening to their laughs and voices.

I found myself alone, nursing a glass of orange juice Sonny had ordered for me, and people-watching. It was like my senior prom all over again minus the fancy dress, orange juice, and smoking.

The guys from the shop hadn't shown up yet, and at that point, I was desperate enough to attach myself at the hip to any of them. Well, with the exception of Dex.

"Iris."

I whipped around to spot Trip making his way toward the part of the bar I was at, dressed in a nearly identical outfit as the one from the day before. He was also either on his way to Shit-Facedville based on the glazed look in his eyes, or already there.

"What are you doin' here all by yourself, pretty Iris?" he drawled lazily, stopping to the side of me.

"Waiting on Sonny," I told him with a smile, but really, I was making sure he wasn't a belligerent drunk. Or worse, someone with a weak stomach. He hadn't been last time we stopped in but you could never be too sure. Getting thrown up on wasn't on my list of things I'd like to suffer through any time soon.

He tisked. "Saw him go off with Tiff. Might be awhile."

I made a face because seriously, that was gross. "Well, I'll wait for him a little bit longer."

Trip backed up to sit on top of empty stool to my left. "Not much of a party girl, eh?"

"Not really." I never had been. When I turned twenty-one, Lanie and I had bought a bottle of boxed wine to celebrate an age I wasn't sure I'd make it to. So it wasn't a surprise that we'd celebrated way too much. The next morning, when I was hunched over the toilet seat puking my guts out, I swore I'd never do it again. Three years later, I'd kept my word. On the rare occasion I'd drink half a beer or maybe a glass of wine.

Party animal, I know.

His fingers swept over the sides of his mouth, brushing the yellowish hair of his goatee. The look on his face was pure sin. "I'll keep you company then."

"Why thank you." I shot him a smile, still keeping an eye on his mouth's movement to catch any gag reflexes though I was grateful to have someone to talk to. "If I start to bore you, feel free to go hang out with other people."

Trip rolled his eyes and pressed the bottle to his mouth for a long drink. "Whatever you say, baby." He smirked. "You likin' the new job?"

Not wanting to be rude but also not wanting to lie, I shrugged a shoulder. "It's coming along, but I'm still looking for another one."

He leaned toward me. His face serious. "Dex bein' a dick?"

I didn't mean to do it but the laugh just kind of burst out of my chest. Wasn't Dex the first person Blake thought of when he saw someone had upset me? That should have been a sign of what I was getting myself into. If Trip immediately guessed, I could only imagine what that guy must have done to earn a reputation of pissing people off.

"Why you laughin'? I'm right, aren't I?" Trip grinned.

I had a record for putting my foot in my mouth so I shrugged instead, still laughing just a little bit.

It was Trip's turn to shrug. "He's as moody as can fuckin' be, baby. Always got somethin' up his ass."

So, so true. But I wouldn't admit it outright like that. They were friends, after all. It would be like me hearing someone call Lanie a bitch. I could call her a bitch but no one else could. "He definitely had something living up there a few days ago."

Blonde brows rose. "Was it his dad's shit?"

"I have no idea." But I wondered for all of a second what had been the cause. Then I realized I didn't give care because it didn't matter. A dick is a dick.

"You tell me if he's givin' you a hard time," Trip said. "I'll beat the dumbfuck out of him." His blue eyes flicked to the side. "He's got so much in him, it'll take a while."

Something really reassuring settled in my chest at his offer. I couldn't help but nod and pat his arm. "Sonny called his kneecaps, you can have the rest of him."

He chuckled. His eyes had drifted down to where my hand rested on his forearm, his gaze sliding up and over my elbow, stopping on my bicep. My sleeve had rode up my arm at some point. Out of the corner of my eye, I saw his hand clench open and close. His baby blue eyes flicked up to mine, his expression confused and curious.

Trip's lips parted for a moment before closing. Once, twice, three times.

I'd done this enough times to know what he wanted. Where his confusion stemmed from. Extending my arm out so he could take a better look at the scarring, he winced and instinctively reached out to touch it. It wasn't a good-looking scar. The flesh looked gnarled and silver-white against my healthy skin. After four different surgeries, I'd stopped caring what it looked like. Seeing it in the mirror didn't bother me anymore but I hated the looks I'd get from people.

Like I was broken.

Like there was something wrong with me.

I lost the name my mom had so carefully chosen and became a medical term.

A hand came down to smack Trip's fingers away. "What the hell are you doing?" Sonny asked, pushing himself between our two stools, his amber eyes going back and forth between Trip and I.

Trip didn't even seem bothered by Sonny's reaction. The look on his face was a little relaxed and a little more confused. "Hangin' out," he answered vaguely, keeping his gaze on Sonny.

Sonny narrowed his light colored eyes at his friend before turning his attention to me and pulling down my shirt sleeve as if it were a second thought. There were times when I'd catch him looking at my arm with an expression of pure, painful remorse. Like it'd been his fault that I'd gotten sick. Or maybe it hurt him to see it. I didn't know and I wouldn't ask. If I didn't make a big deal out of it—AKA pretend there was nothing different—no one else would either.

"Ris, I'm going out for a minute with a friend," he whispered into my ear, putting both hands on my shoulders and squeezing.

A minute? Ha.

I tilted my gaze up to look at him over my shoulder. There was a pretty brunette standing just behind him, a possessive hand clasped on his arm. Interesting. "Okay. Is it fine if I go home or do you want me to hang out here awhile?"

He smirked and squeezed his grip. "You can go home. I'll be there later." The gross ass smirked again. "Way later."

I faked a shudder.

With more pressure to my shoulder, I saw him reach out to slap Trip on the back. He gave him a hard look that I didn't understand before disappearing into the crowd behind us.

A woman squeal loudly to my right and I found Luther leaning against a high countertop table with a young—probably around my age—girl tucked on his lap.

Gross.

Trip must have recognized the look in my eye because he laughed, either forgetting all about what he'd seen or choosing to push his question aside. "You get used to it."

Not trying to be rude because obviously Trip knew Luther, I covered my dry gag by looking at him out of the corner of my eye. "But she's… young enough to be his daughter."

"She's younger than his son, baby."

I sucked in a breath way too loudly that made Trip smile wide. "But… but… how? Why?" Luther wasn't going to win any awards in the beauty department. He wasn't one of those men who had gotten better with age, or even aged gracefully. He was okay looking but that was as far as I'd compliment him.

Trip looked at me with a straight face and laughed, his beer bottle shaking in his hand. Once he settled down, he shook his head. "Because some girls don't care if a man's old enough to be their daddy as long as he's the Prez."

"The Prez?"

Trip nodded.

What the hell was the Prez? Even if he was the President of the United States, I'd have to get paid at least a few grand to go anywhere near his lap. Yuck.

"The Widows?"

Trip slapped a hand over the right side of his leather vest over where the white patch was stitched. "What else would he be the president of?"

I ignored his smart ass comment and focused on the men hustling around, messing with each other. "There's a lot of you guys."

"We got chapters all over Texas and the Southwest."

Hmm. I still didn't have a single clue what exactly it meant to be in a motorcycle club besides what I saw on television, or hell, the stuff my mom had told me about years ago when the club was mixed up in drug running. She hadn't told me much but it was enough to know that twenty-five years ago, the WMC wasn't a group of people that valued family and community service.

Though now, even after Sonny had explained that the Widowmakers had changed their ways, they probably still didn't hold bake sales but whatever.

As nice as Trip seemed, I figured I should probably hold most of my questions for Sonny. If anyone was going to laugh at me for asking dumb things, I'd rather it be him than someone else.

"If you would've gotten here last month you could've gone to our rally," he mentioned.

"What do you at a rally? Get together?"

Trip nodded, clinking his bottle against mine. "We all drive down to Galveston and," he smiled wickedly, "party for a couple of days."

It was impossible not to miss the implication in his face. He had trouble written all over him, making me snort. "I bet you guys just *party*."

"We do," he insisted with another grin, his fingers inching up his neck to scratch at a two-inch scar that scissored his skin. "Now. Ten years ago... that'd be a different story."

That was something to think about and ask Sonny about later. I shoved that plan into the back of my head and raised my eyebrow at Trip instead, just as the same girl squealed once more. We both looked back at Luther and the twenty-something who had her face buried in his neck.

Sheesh. That was disturbing. I was pretty sure that Luther was definitely older than my dad. Yuck.

There were plenty of other men scattered around, some in their forties and younger who weren't unattractive, sure they were kind of hairy and had tattoos that would probably give me nightmares, but they weren't eyesores. So I didn't understand why the girl was hanging all over Luther of all people. There was something really hard about his face that made me a little wary and added to the comment Trip had made about the club's activities ten years ago. If anyone had a face of a lifetime worth of doing risky things, it was Luther.

If Trip was right—and I knew he was—then the girl was just like any other little gold digger. Or groupie! She wanted the top dog even if he was in his fifties or sixties. And not so attractive. And more than likely had wrinkly balls, which I couldn't even figure out why I would think about to begin with.

Gag.

We talked a few more minutes about some of the people around us. Trip pointed out those who were native to Austin and his club.

I looked back over at Trip and raised my eyebrows, sliding the glass of juice I'd been holding away from me. "I guess I'm going to go home."

"Want me to walk you to your car?"

The incident the night before flashed through my brain. Friggin' Dex. "Nah. I parked close by."

"You sure? Son might kill me if something happens to you."

I snorted. Total Sonny. Threatening people left and right. "It's fine. He's a pussy cat."

"Are we talkin' about the same person?" Trip laughed. "The day you showed up, he said he'd break both my legs if I tried anythin' with you."

"Aren't you his best friend?"

He scrunched up his face, making the harsh lines of blonde facial hair seem pretty darn cute. "And?" Trip leaned back, shaking his head.

The mental picture of my half-brother breaking someone's legs made me grin. "It's really okay." He didn't need to know my car was back at the shop's lot. I mean, it was close by. Squeezing his forearm, I smiled at him. "Thanks for keeping me company."

"Baby, trust me, it's a pleasure."

I gave him a lopsided smile. "Bye, Trip."

Wiggling my fingers at him in goodbye, I hopped off the barstool and shimmied my way through the thick crowd of strangers. I'd barely pushed through the doors when the loud roar that could have only come from a group of motorcycles filled the air. The small group of people hanging outside smoking cigarettes were murmuring, but the louder the roar got, the louder their voices did too.

Six or seven bikers slowed their motorcycles to a crawl in front of the bar as I made my way down the block. Someone close by started yelling, but I wasn't paying attention to what was being said as I kept my eyes on the bikers. They weren't wearing leather vests like the rest of the WMC. They also didn't look relaxed and ready to have a good time like everyone else did either. Instead, their faces were pulled tight as they drove by. Bodies stiff with something that was the opposite of friendly.

And that was my mistake of the day.

I should have gone back inside and asked Trip to walk me out. I should have, but I didn't.

And that was my second mistake. I should have just looked at the bikers, and then hauled my ass as quickly as possible to my car. But I didn't do that either.

I moseyed because I was tired. It was then, in my nosey nature and slow feet that two of the men in the street turned to look at me in a way that wasn't a warm, appreciative gaze. It was a look that took in as much appreciation as a lion held for a gazelle before slaughter. It was a calculated thing.

But I'm an idiot and by that time, though it was too late, I walked faster down the sidewalk to the annex parking lot; Dex and Slim appeared from up ahead. They stalked down the block, keeping their eyes locked on the group parked behind me. Only when they saw me hopping over wide jagged cracks in the pavement, tugging my short, white shorts down my legs, did Dex veer in my direction.

Crap!

His dark eyes were locked on me. Raking me. Grazing me. Swallowing me. But whether it was in approval or just plain annoyance, I had no idea. To be honest, I didn't care. Dex was a dick. A good-looking dick—a very good-looking dick—but a dick nonetheless.

And he. Looked. Pissed. Well, more pissed than usual and that was saying something.

"What in the fuck are you doin' walkin' to your goddamn car alone again?" he growled, swear to God, *growled* as he cut the distance between us. "Didn't we just talk about this yesterday?"

It was my hormones. The hormones that raged through my body right before I started my period made me insane. I know it. Every girl knows it.

So obviously, they made me stupid. Because I looked behind me before slowly turning around to face my boss, taking in the angry, pulsing vein lining his neck. "Me?"

Slim paused midstride, looked between the two of us and kept walking toward the bar, throwing up a peace sign at me on the way.

Wuss.

"Who the hell else would I be talkin' to, babe? You're the only goddamn person walkin' to their car at night *by her fuckin' self*." He put way too much emphasis on the last two words.

I whipped the keys out of my front pocket and spun them around my index finger, talking myself back from losing my temper because that was clearly the road I was going down. What I really wanted to do was throw the keys at his face but that wouldn't exactly be the smartest thing to do. "You don't have to talk to me like that." I added a mental 'asshole' in my head.

Dex was in my face the second the words were out of my mouth, so close I could feel the heat from his skin. "We just had this talk yesterday. No more walkin' to your car alone. You hear me? I know you're still pissed off but it ain't that big of a deal, babe. I already told you I say and do stupid shit when I'm pissed and you were in the wrong fuckin' place at the wrong time. It ain't much to get over."

Maybe throwing the keys wouldn't be that stupid if it was either that or clipping him with my car's bumper.

"Did you or did you not call me a fucking idiot?" The strained silence he answered with was enough to confirm what I was already sure of. Thank you very much. "Being in a better place at a better time, boss, you still would've said what you did only I wouldn't have heard you." I ground out. "That doesn't make it better. I haven't done anything to you, and you act like… like I stole your Christmas presents as a kid."

His right eye started twitching but he didn't deny the thought.

So I shrugged at him. What else was I supposed to do? "Tell me what I did."

The pause was dramatic before he huffed out, "No." Dex's lips tightened in a hard line, not saying a word to argue with the fact that I was right. "You didn't do nothin'."

"What is it then? Because I'm not from here? Did I breathe too loud? Or because —"

"None of that. I already told you, you need to learn to grow a thicker skin, babe. Shrug it off, it ain't that big of a deal."

Someone was going to get stabbed, and that person was named Dex.

Unfortunately the same person that needed to get stabbed was the same one who would sign my paychecks. I had to grit my teeth. I wasn't going to apologize for not having a thick skin, as he put it. "I can't shrug off you being a jerk," I snapped. "Obviously, you don't really like me and that's fine. You're pissed right now again for some reason, so I'm going to leave," in hindsight, I should have ended the sentence right then. But I didn't. "Before you make me cry, your perfect highness."

Two things happened to Dex's hard face. I could see him physically flinch at the same time he sucked in a low, barely audible breath. Then he just stared at me. Eye to eye. Me having to look up at him because while I wasn't short, he still towered over me.

Dex lifted a hand to press his fingertips to his upper lip. Silent. His odd shade of blue eyes were penetrating mine, probably hoping that I'd go back to my state of being a quiet, avoiding wuss. "Look...I'm sorry."

Did he say he was sorry?

"I can be a fuckin' asshole sometimes," he kept going.

Well, I wasn't going to argue with him on that point, though I wasn't exactly positive why he felt obligated to care whether or not he'd hurt my feelings. Probably because of Sonny. I could only imagine what he'd threatened him with.

"You're impatient and you're mean," I corrected him, not bothering to admit that I'd called him an asshole in my head at least a dozen times. A dozen times an hour that is. "You're rude—and forgive me for saying it, but you make some dumb friggin' decisions. And you think I'm stupid? Why the hell would you risk hurting your hand by getting into fights with people? *That's* stupid." Should I have stopped? Yes. Did I? No. "What do you have to be so pissed off about anyway?"

It took me a second before what I said really hit me. What had I just done?

Stood up for myself. Sort of. It wasn't like I could take it back either.

Dex's nostrils flared, his face still impassive. "Said I didn't mean it," he repeated in a crisp tone.

"It's not that easy." I stood there, waiting for something I wasn't even sure of.

"Yeah it is. I said sorry, now you can quit bein' pissed," he said the words like a command.

Oh my God. "No." I narrowed my eyes at him. "It doesn't mean anything if Sonny had to threaten you to be nice."

That same muscle in his neck quivered again as he stared back at me. "Look…" That burning blue gaze made a slow trek from my face down my body and up again. Slow, slow, slow.

Under the thick black stubble of his neck, his throat bobbed. The texture of his voice got rougher. "I'm sorry, all right? Ain't that enough?"

This was pointless. I loved words. I'd always loved words. I loved the freedom you could find in them. I loved manipulating them. I loved the way they sounded and the power they held.

But sometimes, *sometimes*, they weren't enough.

Sometimes strings of letters were meaningless in comparison to actions. Actions held the power of a choir versus the strength of a solitary singer. My bones recognized that this was all I would get, this one person a cappella.

"Be the bigger person," my mom would have said. I didn't really want to but I lifted a shoulder anyway. My breath came out shaky. "Saying that you're sorry doesn't take back what's been done, at least in my book. I can't just forget it overnight."

Dex's throat bobbed again, those eyes beamed a hot line straight into me. "I wanna ask if you're bein' serious, but I think you are."

When I didn't say anything in return, he licked his bottom lip, looking down my length one more time.

"Say somethin'."

I didn't.

He stared at me for a minute, the tension in his shoulders tightening before he let out a whoosh of air. Pure exasperation. "C'mon."

Was I that resentful that he could see that I wasn't happy with him? That I'd rather sit in a portable toilet than next to him? I'd spent the last few years trying my best not to stress about things, trying to take care of myself, and the first time someone was genuinely mean to me–upset me—I crumbled?

I could still be hurt, but I didn't want to let that linger in me too long. Not anymore.

"Ritz?" he asked in a low voice.

I shrugged. God. There really wasn't a point in being bitter forever. Constantly raging against him went against the majority of the cells in my body. "Forget it. Apology accepted. I won't say anything to Sonny again." Words, words, and more empty words. I wasn't lying, I was going to find another job and never say a word about Dex again.

Beeping the doors unlocked with the key fob, I lowered my eyes to his throat, noticing for the first time that Dex had put on his Widowmakers vest at some point.

I cleared my throat and eyed his Adam's apple. "See you Tuesday."

Dex didn't say a word as I got into my car. He only took a step back when I turned the ignition.

When I glanced back in the rearview mirror after pulling out of the lot, he was still exactly where I'd left him.

CHAPTER SEVEN

"Son, on a scale from one to ten, how mad would you be if I quit my job?" I asked over breakfast.

And by breakfast I meant we'd both gotten up well after noon, but since it was the first meal of the day, I figured it was still considered breakfast. Wouldn't it? I didn't have a clue what time he'd finally gotten home. I was in bed by three and promptly passed out before the backlight on my cell phone was out.

Sonny made a noise that sounded like a muted chuckle in his throat before peering up at me, chewing on a piece of bacon while raising a tired auburn eyebrow. "More trouble in paradise?"

I scoffed. "Dex is kind of an asshole."

Sonny's nostrils flared and his lips twitched. The doofus was trying his best not to laugh. "Kid, tell me something I don't know."

The second person I was going to beat after Dex was my brother. "You sent me to work with him," I might have hissed out.

"Because I know you can handle it."

Handling Dex Locke would be like handling a scorpion. You were gonna get that poisonous sting at some point. Unfortunately for me, that sting had a taste for Iris Taylor. The urge to babble to him that Dex had gotten an attitude with me in the parking lot was right on the tip of my tongue. But... I'd just told Dex that I wouldn't keep going to Sonny and whining.

Damn.

"Right?" he egged on, taunting me.

I had to settle for grumbling. "Yeah."

He lifted that dark eyebrow. "I told you I'd knock his teeth down his throat."

"Don't forget his kneecaps." I kicked his shin underneath the kitchen table.

Sonny laughed before shoving another piece of charred bacon into his mouth.

"No, it's fine I guess I'm just not used to his type of personality You know—bossy and brooding." By bossy I meant jerk. Because that was the question. He was good-looking—very good-looking—and he had a successful business, what could really be that bad that sent him into such a crash?

He smirked. "Ris, you just described all my friends," he chuckled. "But I get it. He's not so bad, kid. I promise I wouldn't have sent you over there if he was a bad guy. He's a loner," he paused, thinking about what he said before adding, "usually an asshole, too, but he won't do a thing to you. He's got sisters, he knows how to behave around Widows' family."

Besides make me cry and yell. No big deal.

"But why?"

Sonny looked at me long and hard, his mouth twitching with indecision. He finally sighed. "Same reason we all have issues."

Because of other people?

What a lame excuse. There was more to that story but whatever he wanted to say, whatever he should have said, he wouldn't.

"If you really hate it, we can find you something else. The bar always needs help, but I don't know about you being around the MC constantly."

"Maybe. You're not a dick, and Trip is really nice," I tried to explain to him.

"I'm not a dick *to you*, and Trip's nice because he likes you," Sonny said.

I sighed and cut into my not-fully-cooked pancake.

"Look, Ris, I'd rather you not quit since you're right around the corner from me. But you're a big girl. You've been on your own forever now. I can spot you on money, no problem." He shot me a pointed look. "It's up to you."

Damn it, I hated it when reasonable people had reasonable points. Did I really want to ask him for money?

No.

So I blew out a long breath from my lips. "I'll try my best to put up with him, but if I get arrested for assault, you're bailing me out of jail. I wouldn't cut it in the pen."

My half-brother grinned wide. "Doubt that, but I'll bail you out if it happens. If he acts up again, treat him like you would Will if Will were tripping out."

Like my little brother? My reply was a silent expression that reeked of confusion. I'd pinch Will's nipples if he did something so thoughtless and stupid. The end.

"If he was being a dumbass, you'd give him hell, wouldn't you?"

"Well, yeah." Someone had to.

Sonny raised his eyebrows up and down. "Just don't let him get away with all the shit he does. I know Dex. You make him see what he's done and he'll react. He's not a total shit. He's got a big mouth and a short temper."

I thought about the night before and how he'd asked me for forgiveness. Forgiveness that I only half-assed gave him. Hmm.

Sonny's words, along with my insistence that I really didn't care too much about staying in my boss's good graces, swept over me in understanding and approval. I was already looking for another job, though that search wasn't going successfully. What was Dex going to do if I was being honest with him? Fire me? Like I friggin' cared by that point.

That was a lie, I did care. At least until I found another job, I'd care. There was always that back-up plan in the form of trampling over what remained of my pride and asking Son for money.

"I can do that," I told him honestly.

He nodded slowly. "I know you can, Ris."

With my game plan in mind, I smiled. "You got plans for the day?"

"What do you want to do?"

I batted my eyelashes, which I'm pretty sure still had clumps of mascara on them from the night before, and grinned. "Want to clean out your garage?"

We spent that Sunday afternoon going through Sonny's dusty, filled-with-crap garage.

At least five times I heard him muttering, "Only for you, Ris. Only for you." We managed to go through half of it, quitting only when the mosquitoes got so bad I was whacking a body part every other second.

By the time I came out of the shower, Sonny was dressed and stated that he had "club business"—whatever that meant—to attend to and that he'd be back later.

I made dinner for two, ate my share, and then molded my ass to the couch to watch television for a little bit. A little bit turned into hours, hours that added to my relaxation with rerun after rerun. The last thing I remembered before passing out a little after midnight was thinking that I should have moved to Vegas to get a job with the guys at Pawn Stars instead of Pins.

"Just leave her on the couch."

"Bro, that's fuckin' uncomfortable."

Someone sighed but I was still in my loopy, I'm-fighting-to-stay-asleep-world while the two voices spoke from what seemed like dimensions away. My dreamscape, a place that looked just like the park my dad had taken me to every week when he'd been a permanent fixture, was tilting on its axis as the voices outside got louder.

"You're right. Let me go take a piss, and then I'll get her up," someone said.

The silence that followed should have made it easier for me to slip back into my dream, but the depression of the cushion under me did the opposite. Two arms slipped beneath me, one spanning the width of my shoulder blades and the other hooking under both knees. Then I was up and against something warm and solid, something specifically that smelled like a hint of exhaust over clean laundry detergent. It was good. Even my half asleep dream-ass knew it.

My eyes cracked open to see that I was being carried down the hallway of Sonny's house. My face rocked against a chest, my nose pressed to a man's throat. And I knew, instinctively, that it wasn't Sonny's. That chump would have made me walk to my room.

I tilted my head up, blinking slowly to take in the person carrying me. Hair so dark it that couldn't be Trip. But the high cheekbones and hard angle of a jaw were all I needed to realize that it was Dex.

Dex!

"What are you—," I started to yawn, fighting the closing pull of my eyes.

"Go back to sleep," he murmured under his breath without even moving his lips.

He didn't look down at me when he stopped at the closed bedroom door or when he opened it by putting my butt on what I imagined was a raised knee. Dex finally looked down when he was setting me on the mattress gently. He didn't smile or wait for me to ask why he was putting me to bed.

He took a step back in my super dark room and whispered, "Night, Ritz," before closing the door and leaving me in there alone.

If I would have been less tired, I probably would have wondered what the hell was going on instead of falling right back asleep, but I wasn't, and trying to figure out Dex's actions wasn't something a half-asleep brain, much less a fully competent one, could handle.

CHAPTER EIGHT

When I got up the next morning, I was seriously asking myself what the hell had happened the night before.

I knew it couldn't have been a dream. Dex The Dick carrying me to my room had happened.

It. Had. Happened.

And I couldn't understand for the life of me why A) he'd been at Sonny's house so late. B) Why he'd taken it upon himself to get me to my bedroom. C) Was a repeat of A and B.

I could have walked or at least stumbled my way to bed.

It being Monday, my brother was at work by the time I woke up. Dinner from the night before had mysteriously disappeared and the dishes had been washed.

Hallelujah.

Limited by the lack of funds in my account until payday, I had to settle for the free things life had to offer. Like laying around the house, watching television, going through catalogues Sonny had on the kitchen table. Basically, I was a lazy ass the first half of the day.

In the middle of it, I sent Will another email. It'd been more than a month since the last time I'd talked to him but that wasn't completely unheard of. In the past year, I'd only gotten to see him a total of a week's worth. I should have been a seasoned professional at keeping calm when I didn't get anything from him but the fact was, I worried about Will every day.

He was my little brother. The boy I'd cared for like he was mine, before and after our mom had died. He was the reason why I learned what working a double was, the reason why I'd worked two jobs even while I was sick, and the reason for so many other things I learned.

A lot of times I felt like I was alive just for him. And then he'd joined the Army and left me in Florida. I mean, he was happy and that's what mattered but it still didn't fix the fact that I missed him.

That was life, wasn't it? Losing and regaining?

By mid-afternoon, I started to get cabin fever and walked out of the house to see if there was anything to do outside. There was. Sonny had weeds coming out every square inch around his bushes and lawn. Under normal circumstances, I probably would have pretended like there was nothing to do, but that's just how bored I was and how badly I wanted my mind on other things.

I found a pair of thick gloves in Sonny's garage that were way too big, pulled a long sleeve shirt on to avoid getting burned and went to work.

An hour and a half later, when my back was aching and I felt a warm tingle on my neck that screamed sunburn, I stuffed all the weeds into a trash bag and stood in the middle of the lawn, exhausted. The loud purr of multiple motorcycles echoed through the neighborhood. It being after work hours, a lot of people had pulled into their homes so I wasn't really planning to go out of my way to look and see where the bikes were coming from. It was second nature. A bike was a bike, wasn't it?

In the middle of hoisting a bag over my head to throw into the trash, two bikers with buzz cuts and hard glares drove by slowly. Their eyes were on me and the house. They didn't stop, but as soon as they'd crossed the driveway, they picked up speed and zoomed out of the neighborhood.

Weird.

The worst part of going to work on Tuesday was not knowing how to act around Dex. It shouldn't surprise me that he was hanging out with Sonny if they were in the same club, but still. Sonny was warm and sweet—though he had been specific and said it was only to me—while Dex was a temperamental bag of beaver dung. Maybe it was that whole "opposites attract" thing they had going on.

Maybe.

Luckily, it was Blake that came in and opened, leaving me to wonder where The Dick was. I sure as hell wasn't going to ask Blake or anyone, but I let myself think about it in my head. It was like mentally preparing myself for an incoming hurricane.

Business was pretty steady right from doors opening when Slim showed up. There was tattoo after tattoo for the first couple of hours, then a nipple piercing—which made my own nipples hurt—and a guy who wanted an eyebrow pierced. It was closer to eight at night when Dex finally showed up, looking mildly annoyed as usual, and striding directly to the back without a wave or a nod to anyone.

Once again, no one said anything. Blake and Slim didn't even look at each other. I didn't understand that at all because I was annoyed when he walked in.

In hindsight, I should have just gone to the back and lived with a tongue lashing from Dex for simply living so that I could order supplies for the month instead of staying in the front, talking to a customer's girlfriend about getting her nose pierced. But I didn't. In my quest to keep being a bitch because my feelings had been hurt, I stayed up front.

Mistake? Uh, yeah.

"Sweetie."

I looked over at the man standing in front of the reception desk. A man with a full beard and glassy, red-rimmed eyes, who smelled like rubbing alcohol. It was disgusting and it made my nose burn.

But this was my job and everyone had been nice up until then, so I didn't think anything of it. "Yes?"

"Need to get a tat."

I gave him a little smile without looking at the appointment log. Even if both Slim and Blake weren't busy and Dex had come out from the back, he still couldn't get tattooed. Whoops. "I'm sorry, but we can't help you if you've been drinking."

"Sweetie, I need a tat. Now," the guy slurred, smacking his lips so roughly spittle flew out.

Gross. The smell of alcohol got even stronger. Yuck.

I cringed a little. "I'm sorry but we really can't—," I tried to explain to him.

Alcohol Cologne grunted. "Get Dex."

"Dex isn't scheduled right now."

"Sweetie, get Dex."

Oh boy.

I took a deep breath and nodded, pushing away from my chair. "Let me see if I can get him." Years of mottos that highlighted "The customer is always right" was engraved into me. The music was so loud it wasn't a surprise that Blake and Slim didn't hear what was going on. They blasted it. Metal and heavy rock pounded through the speakers most nights after seven.

The office door was closed when I came up to it, but I couldn't hear anything from inside. I knocked a couple of times but there was no response. The light from the bathroom was on, and I wasn't about to go bother a man when he was on the toilet regardless of whether it was my asshole boss or not. Toilet time was personal time, I thought.

"Dex isn't available right now," I started to tell the guy who, with another look over confirmed that he was blitzed out of his mind. "But if you wait a few minutes, I'll try to get him to talk—"

He snapped.

I wasn't a drinker, and the couple of friends I'd had in passing weren't much either. They were occasional drunks. Funny drunks. Silly drunks. Loving drunks. I was okay with that. But a mean drunk was something I couldn't handle at all.

"Look, bitch, I don't have time! Get fucking Dex right now before I—"

The arm swiped at my waist from out of nowhere. Way too distracted, I realized it was Dex who had an arm wrapped around me, pulling me to his side. His fingers clenched the material of my cardigan.

I couldn't see his face but I didn't need to.

Dex The Dick was pissed. Enraged. I half expected him to shed his clothes and turn into a green skinned monster ten times his current—already tall and broad—size.

His wide shoulders were tense and the big man, well over six feet tall, seemed even more intimidating then. I think everyone could sense that unsettling dangerous mist of pissed off biker in their bones.

"Rick," was the only thing he grunted out.

Alcohol Cologne sensed that raw, crazy energy too because he took a step back. His face, as red as a lobster's cooked shell when he'd been yelling, blanched.

"I was looking for you, bro," the man exhaled.

Dex pinched my cardigan between his fingers. "Get out."

"Dex—"

His shoulders stiffened beneath the bright white t-shirt he had on. "Rick. Get. The. Fuck. Out."

"But—"

His hand squeezed my shirt so tightly it made me lean forward as he yelled, "Get the fuck out! Now!"

Holy shit.

Rick took on a shade of white formerly only seen on a sheet of college ruled paper, throwing up both his hands. "Dex—"

Dex let go of my sweater taking a step toward the drunken fart. "You know damn well you don't come into my shop demandin' shit, callin' my girl a bitch."

In the words of a rap song my neighbor used to play on his boombox when I was a kid: *Hold up, wait a minute.*

He closed the distance between them, making me ignore the fact he'd just called me his girl. I swear Dex grew three inches taller as he lifted his hands and pressed them to the drunk guy's chest. "Get the fuck out before I do something you're gonna regret," Dex notified him, shoving the man back so hard I'm surprised he didn't hit the glass.

The guy stumbled, righting himself slowly after one last withered plea. "Dex."

All he got in return was silence. Heavy, electric silence.

Rick opened his mouth to say something else before thinking twice and turning around to walk out. As soon as the door swung shut, it was like a rubber band of intensity snapped in the room. My heart was pounding from the sheer volume of the words that were tossed around.

I was so stuck in my own little world that I didn't sense Dex's presence inches away from me until his fingertips were on my chin, tilting my face up.

"You okay?" he whispered, so close I could feel his warm breath on my nose.

My hands shook. I swallowed hard and nodded a partial lie. "Yeah."

Dex's gaze flickered over my eyes, nose, mouth, and even throat. His expression was soft. He reached up to circle one of my free hands in his, his features tightening as my fingers trembled in his palm. "Your pulse is poundin', babe."

"I'm fine." Being freaked out fell into the same category as being fine. As long as I hadn't peed on myself, then I could still be fine.

He didn't speak as he pulled on the hand he was then holding, leading me toward the hallway. In a daze, I noticed that Blake and Slim looked worried as I passed by them, and I tried my best to give them a smile but it was shaky. It felt like I'd just gotten off a roller coaster.

Dex shook his head on the walk passed his office, passed the private rooms, clasping my hand even tighter as he pulled us into the break room.

"Come here, Ritz," he ordered, stopping us right next to the kitchen counter. Before I realized what was happening, his hands were on my hips and he was settling me on top of the counter. Dex's palms grazed my knees as he stepped back to the soda vending machine in the corner. "Wait a sec."

Like I could go anywhere, but I sat there silently, sliding my hands under my thighs so that I wouldn't feel them twitching anymore. He pulled out a bill from his wallet and put the money into the machine, getting a Coke in return. Holding it in one hand, he moved to the opposite end of the long counter and started fishing through the overhead cabinets. He pulled out a loaf of bread, withdrawing two slices before retying the knot and stashing it back into its hiding spot.

I wasn't sure what the heck was going on. I couldn't help watching him tenderly hold the slices in one hand and the Coke can in the other as he walked toward me, stopping so close his hip brushed against the side of my thigh.

"Here." Dex tried to hand me one of the slices, setting the soda down between us.

"What?" I was looking at the seeds in the bread.

"Eat it, babe." He held the piece of bread up higher.

I shook my head, darting my eyes back up to his. "I'm not hungry."

Dex lifted the slice even higher so that it was in line with my mouth. "I don't care if you're not hungry. It'll calm you down."

The urge to argue with him was *right there* but by the look he gave me, a hard, uncompromising glare, I figured it was useless. That wasn't the right moment to pick a fight with him. I plucked the bread from his hand and ate it slowly, watching him out of the corner of my eye the entire time. As soon as I finished, he was handing me the second slice. I gave him another look but got the same no-nonsense glare in return.

So I ate it because otherwise, he'd probably shove it down my throat by force.

He watched until I had about a quarter of it left, when he then popped the lid on the soda and handed it to me the minute I swallowed the last bite of nutty bread.

"I should've kicked his fuckin' ass for talkin' to you like that," he murmured when I was taking my first sip of Coke.

It was a miracle I didn't cough it up. Hadn't he talked to me like I was stupid at least three times before this moment? I know that I must have had a what-the-hell face plastered because the expression on his face darkened.

All right, maybe I wouldn't point out how much of a hypocrite he was.

Even if Sonny had said he was harmless, that didn't mean his words were anything that resembled soft and caring. He was probably just dealing with me out of guilt. Whatever.

"It's okay," I warbled out.

"No, it's not." He ducked his head close, eyes searching mine again. "He scare you?"

I sucked in a ragged breath, sensing for the first time that my heart wasn't pounding as forcefully as it had been at first. "He caught me off guard," I breathed out. Two men making me feel like a piece of crap in less than a week must have been a world record.

Dex tensed up before shifting his body over so that he stood in front of me, placing his hands on either side of my legs. He stayed quiet for the longest, his eyes flashing a multitude of emotions I couldn't recognize under a tightly controlled mask. For a split second I wished I would have known him better to understand what was going through his brain, but as quickly as the urge came, it left.

Breathing in through his nose and out through his mouth consciously the entire time until he scratched the tip of his nose. "It won't happen again."

There was no way he could promise that to me. No way. But that magnetic, hot violence was still rolling off his shoulders and chest, caging me in even more so than his upper body physically was.

"I'll talk to Rick, have him apologize, babe. I don't need you bein' scared. He's a lousy drunk."

I gave him a slow one-shouldered shrug, looking away. His breathing was noisy as I thought about how nice he'd just been, standing in front of me when his friend started yelling, trying to get me to calm down. But I didn't get it. Just days ago, he was losing his flipping mind. Last week he'd been trying to kick me out. I didn't get it and it made me feel uncomfortable and confused.

"I'm okay now," I whispered.

He didn't move or say anything.

I shifted forward on the counter, wiggling my bottom so that it was teetering over the edge but Dex was too close, and I couldn't hop off completely without pressing myself fully against him. "I want to get down now."

Of course he didn't move. "Sit a little longer."

"I'm fine," I insisted, fighting the urge to look up at his face.

One of his hands slid onto my knee. Even over the thick material of my brown pants, it was searing hot. Or at least it was like my blood flow had redirected itself to that one point under my skin. *Damn you, traitorous body.* "Iris, why won't you look at me?"

Oh hell.

His voice took on that milky, smooth, deep tone that made me feel like a book of matches had been lit inside my gut, and the way he said my name… Ef. Me. I didn't even think he knew my name. He hadn't used it once the entire time I'd been working at Pins.

"I just want to get down," I told him, glancing down at his hand.

Dex squeezed my thigh. "You can get down after you tell me why you still won't look me in the face."

I insisted. "Please."

"No."

"I want to get down."

He squeezed me again. "No."

"Let me down."

"No."

Oh shit. Annoyed as hell, I tilted my head up at him. "One minute you're kind of a fucking jerk—," did I just drop the f-bomb again? Why, yes, yes, I had. "Then the next minute you're carrying me to my room and sharing your secret stash of bread with me. It doesn't make sense," I said honestly. "I don't want to look at you because you hurt my feelings, okay? I don't know what to think."

And he just blinked. "That it?"

My head dropped back so I could look at the ceiling. Was this guy for real?

"Ritz, c'mon. That's why you won't look at me? 'Cause I talk outta my ass?" The questions were so casual it was like he was asking whether I wanted ranch dressing on my salad or Italian. So annoying.

"That's not enough?" I might have wailed my words a little.

This asshole started chuckling. "Don't get so pissed." The pads of his fingers brushed a line from my thigh down to my knee in an intimate, delicate gesture that was at odds with the man I'd met a week ago. "I told you it was a mistake. How many more times do you want me to say I'm sorry?"

I gave him a flat look which he returned to me with round, curious eyes. "I know. But you called me an idiot all because I asked you for help on my second day. Who does that?" The truth was, maybe I was an idiot. Because a smart person would have shut their mouth and accepted the forced apology, but there I was, my mouth still running. "The last time anyone called me a *fucking-something* was three years ago when I bought the last television on sale at Walmart on Black Friday for my little brother. But you know what? I didn't care then." The *but I care now* was implied in spades.

Dex's thick lashes fluttered closed as he let out a whoosh of air from his lungs. He looked pained. Dex didn't seem like the type of man who was used to apologizing to anyone. The expression seemed so rough and foreign coming from him, it was like trying to shove a square shaped object through a round hole. "Babe, I'm sorry." Those pretty blue eyes opened, focusing on mine. "I just...say shit."

"You just say shit?" I repeated.

Oh boy.

I blinked in his features. His long, dark eyelashes, deep set eyes, magnificent square jaw, that nearly perfect nose—Dex The Dick was unbelievably handsome. And I was making him feel like shit for not forgiving him when it truly seemed like he was remorseful. In what might be the first time in his life with the way he expressed it.

"Yeah." It was a statement, a fact. "You're MC, you gotta have thicker skin than that to survive here, you hear me?"

God, grant me strength.

"My dad was a Widow. Sonny's a Widow. I'm not," I explained to him calmly. "I can't just grow a thick skin overnight."

It was his turn to blink. "Yeah, you can." He blinked again. "Who gives a fuck what I say? Tell me if you got a problem. Don't run off and tell Son that I'm treatin' you like shit, and hide your fuckin' face from me because you're hurt over me bein' a dumbass. *Tell me*. Maybe you don't have a thick skin but I do. I can take it."

Like it was that easy.

I sighed and closed both of my eyes, annoyed with myself for having kept the job when I didn't really want to, all because of circumstances. Circumstances that, as always, revolved around money. Crap.

I sighed again.

Wasn't it easy to just be nice out of the kindness of his heart instead of bullied into it?

I almost laughed. Like Dex could be bullied into something. I'd known him a few days and I already knew he was immovable.

"Don't get all emo on my ass." He nudged my knee with his hip. "Tell me you got a problem."

I couldn't. I just couldn't.

The risk of losing this friggin' job that I wasn't even that fond of yet was too high. If he got pissed off about me asking for help, how pissed would he be if I told him to quit being a dick? Despite the fact that my brother had told me to do the same thing Dex was implying...I wasn't positive that I really had it in me.

"Babe, I'm not gonna have an issue tellin' somebody that they're pissin' me off," he stated.

No shit.

He nudged my knee with his hip again. "Say it."

"Say what?" I asked slowly.

"Say what you're thinkin'," Dex explained.

I shook my head.

His eyebrows knit together in exasperated patience. "Call me a dick. An asshole. A shit. Whatever you want, just get it out, Ritz."

The look on my face was probably half horrified, half nervous that he'd said the one nickname I usually called him in my head. "No."

"Why not?"

"Because that's rude."

It was Dex's turn to blink slowly. "There's a difference between sayin' it out loud and sayin' it in your head?"

Damn it. He had a point.

But before we could go any further, someone in the front yelled Dex's name loud enough that it was heard through the music playing. With a low grunt, he shifted so that his hip contact turned into the long length of his thigh pressing into my knee and shin. "I'll try not to take my shit out on you again but if I do, say somethin'. I'm not gonna bite your head off for bein' honest with me, all right?"

I gave him a dubious look because seriously? Did he really expect me to think he'd take me calling him an ugly name well? Oh please. But okay, whatever made him sleep better at night.

I was tired of being so angry. I could try to be a bigger person and wash my hands of this. It would be impossible to say that Dex wasn't trying to fix this muck in his own brutal way. He deserved points for effort.

Okay, not really but still. *Move past it. Forget it.*

"Look, I'm gonna hope you forget what I said or forgive me sooner than later because I'm not a fan of this shit right now. I'm sorry and that's the damn truth. But I want you to open that little mouth and say whatever's botherin' you from now on, all right?"

I didn't say anything in response because I didn't think he needed an answer.

He kept looking at me with those high intensity eyes until I realized he did want a confirmation. "Okay."

Dex ducked his head in to catch my eyes more fully.

This guy. God. I raised my voice and repeated myself. "Fine, I'll say something from now on."

With a single pat to my knee, he was gone a moment later.

And I sat there wondering what the hell had just happened.

CHAPTER NINE

The days seemed to pass by in a blur of work, Sonny, his home, getting paid, and my new favorite place—the Austin Public Library branch right by the shop. I registered for my card before work one day, since I figured that with my starving bank account I wouldn't be able to afford buying any books in the near future. And to be honest, once I got my card and settled into my routine, it was good—comfortable. I'd even applied for a couple of full-time jobs and that made me excited.

Hell, everything was pretty nice. Including the tension at work.

Dex had been in and out of the shop and when he was in, he was just kind of aloof unless he had to make deposits at the bank during the day.

Even though I'd pretty much—but not completely—gotten over our initial meeting disaster, I still didn't feel completely comfortable around him. The tension between us had gone from strained to…weird after the incident with the drunk guy. The same drunk guy who came in sober and holding a daisy the day afterward, apologizing for calling me a bitch. There wasn't a doubt in my mind that the The Dick had been behind the visit. With the exception of Dex's bad moment, I usually didn't hold grudges because they weren't worth the effort and I let Rick off the hook.

Work was easy but it seemed even easier when Dex wasn't within thirty feet. I managed to read my books in peace during my lunch break and got to know my coworkers when there was downtime. I couldn't really ask for much more.

So it was completely unexpected on Friday afternoon to be sitting in the back during my break, reading the book I'd picked up the day before, and hear, "What are you readin'?" coming from the doorway.

I looked up to see Dex standing there, hands shoved into his pockets, black hair going in a million different directions without his ball cap on. My eyes went from the text below me and back to him a couple of times before I answered vaguely. "A book from the library." It was a historical romance novel, so I'd rather tell him that in detail in oh, a million years.

Right then, in that moment, Dex The Dick grinned. Grinned. And sweet mother of God, it was devastating. So completely catastrophic I just stood there and absorbed the nuclear bomb going off in front of me, defenseless.

His eyes glittered at the same time his eyebrows shot up. "The library?"

I liked the way he drew out the pronunciation, so I nodded.

"The public library?" he asked slowly.

"Yes," I drew out the consonant.

His lips quirked on the corners. "They still have those?"

"They still have those," I confirmed, glancing back down at my book, shutting it carefully after memorizing the page number. I swallowed hard and reminded myself to let my old resentment finish trickling away. Dex was obviously trying, so I could too.

"And you go to libraries?" he asked just as slow as he had a moment before.

Was he antagonizing me? I didn't think so. The up-tilt of his lips made it seem like he was more entertained and curious than just simply being a cruel jerk.

I held up the back cover of the novel I'd just been reading since there wasn't a picture on it. "I like free stuff."

Dex grinned wide again.

Holy crap. Those were rare.

"Babe, I can't even remember the last time I read a book that wasn't for school, much less the last time I went into a library without my ma forcin' me," he admitted.

For some reason, the image of a Baby Dex with super blue eyes and crazy black hair pitching a fit as he was carried into the library by his mom, flashed through my head and it made me snort. That was probably the last time someone had forced him to do anything.

"Maybe you should go to the library then," I told him. "They have all kinds of stuff you can check out." Something nudged at me right then. It was the indulgent smile he gave me when I first told him about where I'd gotten the novel. Smart ass. I smiled slowly, feeling that familiar verbal geyser of crap ready to sprout out of my mouth and unable to control it. "Like picture books if the ones with words don't work for you."

Silence.

And then Dex tilted his head back and laughed so loud it made me smile even though I didn't think he would appreciate it. To be honest, I was surprised that the tease came out of my mouth. Unintentional and all, but still, it was like tap dancing on ice with him. How thin was the ice? I'd never know. "All right, I probably deserved that, Ritz."

Score one for Team Iris. If I could high-fived myself without looking crazy, I would have .

But luckily for both Dex and I, he started speaking again. "Come up front. We're pullin' straws."

"For what?" I asked him carefully. The last thing I needed or wanted was to pull straws to see who had to clean a backed up toilet.

He waved me forward, waiting until I was off my chair and at his side before explaining. "I didn't tell you about the conventions we go to?"

Pssh. I could have pointed out that he didn't really tell me anything period but I kept the comment to myself. "Nope," I replied.

Dex shrugged like the absence of information wasn't a big deal. "We hit up tattoo expos a couple times a year, and the next one is two weeks away in Houston." He shot me a look as we walked down the hall toward the empty reception area. "We're pullin' straws to see who's goin' this time."

That didn't exactly sound like a bad thing. "But I just work the front desk," I told him like he didn't already know that.

Slim, who had wheeled his chair to sit in the middle of the shop like usual, was being nosey—also as usual—and listening in on our conversation. "Consider it a learning experience," he claimed. "We always need help doing other stuff anyway."

I thought about it for a second, and then shrugged. It's not like I had anything else to do and if it was technically a part of my job, a job that I might not have for too much longer, then it'd be fine. "All right then."

Dex took a handful of straws out of his pocket, covering them with his hand as he arranged, and then presented them to me. "Ladies first."

I couldn't help but glance up at his dark blue eyes for a split second before I pulled a straw right in the middle of the four. Dex went ahead and held out the collection to Blue next before letting Blake and Slim grab the last pieces.

"Wait a sec, you okay sharin' a room?"

"Sharing a room with you guys?" I repeated the question right back to him, to make sure I understood correctly.

"Yeah, sharin' a room. You okay with that?" he asked.

I looked over at the three men I worked with slowly. "No one's going to tattoo a peen on my forehead when I'm sleeping, right?"

They all looked at me straight for a minute before starting to laugh, even Blue, who only laughed at me when I said something exceptionally stupid.

"I'll take that as a no," I shot Slim a nasty look. "In that case, no, I don't care." Though I'd prefer it not be Dex, I wasn't going to say that out loud. "As long as you don't do gross stuff in the shower, I'm fine."

Slim snorted. "Blake, that's all you man."

"I told you I didn't do it," he retorted, his face reddening as the words flew out of his mouth.

"Right. You didn't do it when you were the only one who took a shower that morning—"

Dex cleared his throat, biting back a smile. "Okay, okay, let's see who the hell is goin' before we argue over who jacked off in Seattle."

That was my cue to laugh. By myself. Awkward!

After comparing straws, it looked like Blue and I were the losers with the short ones. Based on the looks we shot each other—she wasn't much of a talker and I liked to make facial expressions that she seemed to understand—neither one of us was too heartbroken.

"Feel free to do whatever the heck you want to do in the shower since I'm not going," I blurted out, already taking a step back to head into the kitchen. My book and lunch were calling my name.

Blake's eyes cut over to Slim's accusingly. "I didn't fucking do it, man!"

Right.

"Someone left a voicemail for you, kid," Sonny noted, his gaze locked on the epic gun battle going on in the television screen.

I'd just come in from work, dropping my purse onto the couch that I'd rightfully claimed over the course of the last month and let myself get excited for a brief moment. "Who?"

He made a humming noise in his throat. "Umm, someone named Gladys or something from a place with a stupid name. There were a bunch of Rugrats screaming in the background."

It had to be one of the daycare centers I'd applied to.

"Yes!"

Two minutes later, I'd written down Gladys Ortega's phone number and high-fived Sonny for finally getting a callback.

"I don't get why you're so excited. The idea of working with a bunch of kids sounds like hell," he murmured.

The last time I'd worked at a daycare center, I'd been twenty and fresh out of radiation therapy. At that point, nothing could have brought me down. But now that I really thought about it...*crap*. I liked kids but did I like them that much? The better question was, did I dislike Dex enough to sacrifice one moody devil for a bunch of innocent demons?

The answer didn't come as easily as I would have expected.

"I can just see what they have to offer."

He shrugged and it made me narrow my eyes.

I didn't understand what was going on with him, but every time I asked, he always answered the same way.

He was fine. Always fine.

And he was completely full of shit.

"What's wrong with you?"

For the last two days, Sonny had been acting really erratic. One of the most laid-back people I'd ever met in my life, he wasn't the type to sit back and let things bother him. He was an advocate of either ignoring things or dealing with them head on. Preferably with his fists it seemed, when he came home two nights ago with a busted lip and refused to tell me what happened.

I made sure he was okay, and then changed the subject. The problem was, he was still acting weird. Something was bothering him and it was nipping at him, over and over again. He still smiled but it was shadowed and guarded.

I finally had it though. Only one of us could be a moody shit, and that would be me.

"What's wrong?" I asked him again when he didn't answer.

Those hazel-brown eyes slid over to me, a small smile lifting up one corner of his mouth but it didn't do anything. My beloved half-brother was missing. "I'm fine, kid."

"Bull."

He cracked a little smile. "My innocent little Ris."

Innocent, maybe a little. But really, he knew as well as I did, that I just wasn't used to cussing. At least on his level, much less the rest of his friends'.

"Just tell me what happened," I insisted.

Sonny looked at me for a long moment, blowing air out of his mouth before letting his head drop back dramatically onto the couch. "Can we talk about it later?"

I poked him in the thigh. "I'd rather not."

He sighed again, still looking up at the ceiling.

His silence was killing me. The longer he went with hesitating to tell me, the worse it made me feel.

"Please?"

Sonny grunted. "Our sperm donor came by."

And... that was absolutely not what I was expecting to hear.

"Are you joking?" Of course he was serious, but I was an idiot and what he'd said seemed so ridiculous he wouldn't be making it up.

He kept his eyes trained on the ceiling. "Nope," was his brilliant, detailed response.

"Why?"

I don't know why I asked. What I was expecting. There couldn't be anything for me to expect. He'd known where *yia-yia*, Will, and I had lived for those years after Mom died. He'd always known where Sonny lived. And in almost ten years, neither one of us had seen him. Now all of a sudden—

"Money, kid." I looked up to see him scrub a hand down his face. "He drove all the way over here to ask for fucking money."

"Did you give it to him?" I asked the question slowly.

"Kid."

Maybe it was wrong of me to hope that Sonny hadn't because he was my dad after all, but I couldn't find it in me to be mature about it. "Son."

He tilted his head down, his lips drooped into a scowl. "Fuck no," he confirmed. "I know he asked Luther after I shot him down though."

"And he said yes?"

Sonny shrugged. "I don't know."

I narrowed my eyes at his face, taking in the cut that split this upper lip. "Oh."

"Kid, I don't support a man that can't support himself. It's embarrassing that he crawls back here to mooch off other people—," I winced because *hello*. Hadn't I just done the same thing? Come crawling to my half-brother? I felt like a schmuck. Sonny must have read it on my face because he rolled his eyes.

"Your situation is completely fucking different. Don't give me that face. You're not mooching off me. You got a job you don't like. You're trying to get yourself together and I've already offered to give you money. You didn't take it, Ris. You're not like that piece of shit in any way, you hear me?"

Crap, I loved this guy.

"I don't want anything to do with him," he stated with so much conviction in his tone.

I didn't either but apparently my brain wasn't working properly because I asked something I shouldn't have. "Did he ask about us?"

Sonny gave me a look I hadn't seen since I was nineteen and been told I needed to have another biopsy. It was filled with a dreadful kind of remorse.

And it projected the answer like a beacon in the sky.

CHAPTER TEN

"How long you been here now?"

I looked up to see my redheaded buddy, Slim, plopping onto the couch across from me. It was Tuesday, almost a month since I started at Pins and Needles and to be honest, it'd gone by really quickly and mostly painlessly.

I'd fallen into a comfortable routine. During the day, I'd hang out at Sonny's house, cleaning and cooking when I wasn't going to the rare job interview—the one and only one had taken place the week before but I hadn't heard back from them—and applying for places online. Occasionally, I'd let myself think about Dad coming into town to ask Sonny for money but it was rare. The man didn't deserve my annoyance. At night, I'd go home and half of the time Sonny would be up and we'd talk or watch television until he went to bed.

How he made it to work at nine in the morning was beyond me, but I didn't ask.

The other half of the time, he was gone and I'd go to bed before he showed up again. In the days after he told me about our sperm donor coming into town, his mood had gradually improved so I didn't ask where he went unless he told me. More often than not, he didn't. But when Sonny was around, I always had a smile on my face though he was still acting a little strange since his unexpected visit. He was just like Will, whom I hadn't heard back from yet either, but I didn't let myself focus on that. I'd sent him weekly emails consisting of a short updates that confirmed I was alive, still with Sonny, still working at the tattoo parlor, and that I had a library card. No surprise there.

The mirror to my Sonny was Dex, who'd been in and out of the shop for days. Half the time, something was eating his butt cheek and he'd go into the shop and head directly into the office, leaving me to have to sneak in randomly to get my work done. On the occasion that he was in a good mood, he'd smiled at me exactly three times—and God, it was a smile—and once he touched my hand when he walked by.

Not that I was counting or anything.

My days off were spent driving around Austin. I visited the Capitol, walked down Sixth Street during the day, which completely turned me off almost immediately when some douche bag started following me around. Sonny took me to a swimming hole one Sunday. We visited Trip's apartment another day. We went to the movies together a few times. After my second paycheck, I signed up for the closest YMCA to the house—because I'd seen quite a bit of apartments close to Sonny for when I moved in the hopefully near future—and started spending a quarter of each day swimming and exercising there.

It was good. I was happy with my quiet, little life.

Including when I found myself back at Pins, with Slim asking me how long I'd been working with him.

"A month."

He sounded out the words slowly. "I think you've been here long enough."

This was suspicious. "For what?"

Slim grinned. "To break in that canvas, Iris."

I'd thought about getting a tattoo nearly every day but I still hadn't talked myself into it. "But I don't want to get one unless I'm sure I like what I'm getting."

"Then get a piercing on the house. Me or Blue can do it."

"Iris, you getting a tattoo?" Blake called out from his spot at his station, hunched over a customer's bare back.

I shot Slim a funny look. "No, but Slim's trying to talk me into getting a piercing."

"Do it," he egged on.

A piercing. A piercing? Hmm. I could live with a piercing. It wasn't permanent, and after seeing how many women and men came in to get various parts of their body pierced, it couldn't have been that bad. Plus I couldn't say I hadn't gotten a little envious when I'd seen someone walk out feeling like a million bucks after spending time in the torture chamber. What was the worst that could happen? I'd take it out if I hated it?

Plus, needles and I were old friends. Not necessarily best friends, but I wasn't afraid of getting poked and prodded.

My facial expression must have given away my thoughts because the redhead started nodding. "C'mon," Slim pressured.

"But where?" I looked down at my hands like there would be some magical map leading me to the best spot on my body to get violated with by a needle.

"Nose!" Blake called out. How the hell he still clearly heard our conversation from all the way over at his station with Mastodon playing was beyond me.

I shook my head, imagining myself with a nose piercing. While there was nothing wrong with it—there was nothing special or messed up with my nose—I couldn't see myself with one. "Nah."

"Your eyebrow?" Slim suggested.

I thought about it. "No. I'm not cool enough to pull it off. Or tough." Just yesterday, I screamed when a flying roach made its way into the parlor.

The two guys, and possibly even the customer, laughed.

"Get your tongue pierced," Blake threw out.

No. Hell no.

When I was seventeen, my best friend at the time snuck off and got his tongue pierced behind his parents' backs. A week later, he had a knot the size of a golf ball in his mouth, and ended up unable to eat solid food for months. That thing was traumatizing, and I liked food too much to risk it.

"No. I like to eat, and that'll make guys think I like to give hugs with my mouth, you know what I mean?" I stated, matter-of-factly.

"What the fuck?" someone asked from behind me. That someone specifically being Dex.

Kill me. Kill me now.

My face flamed up like a tomato when I turned around to see him smirking, holding a bottle of chocolate Nesquik in his hand. "Uhh… I meant—"

Dex burst out laughing. His head was tipped back and he was laughing his ass off, this deep, throaty sound that made me smile even though I felt like an idiot for what I'd said.

"I'm gonna have to use that one day," Slim grinned, shaking his head. "Hey girl, wanna give me a hug with that sweet mouth?"

I groaned through my smirk. "Please don't."

Dex, who couldn't contain his laughter, focused in on me. "What the hell are you talkin' about?"

Slim hooked a thumb in my direction. "We're trying to talk Iris into getting a piercing as her rite of passage to Pins."

Well shit. Before there was medical insurance, there was a piercing.

Dex looked over, sized me from the waist up since I was sitting down, and hummed.

"What about your—," Blake started before Dex shot him a pointed look.

"Not happenin', bro."

Whatever he was going to say I had a feeling wouldn't be something I really wanted to know about, so I didn't bother asking him to finish his sentence.

Dex focused in on me again, blue eyes bright against the tan skin of his face. "Belly button, babe."

My belly button.

It wasn't on my face. No one would see it unless I showed it to them, and if I took it out, the scarring would be so small no one would notice it.

But still. "Does it hurt?"

Dex seriously bit his lip but it was pointless. His mouth started curling upward in amusement. "I don't think any of us would know from personal experience."

I made a face. Smart ass again. "I'd hope not."

"Every girl I've ever pierced hasn't complained too much, Iris. I think your cartilage was more painful," Slim explained. "Now if you were getting your nipple," he bugged his eyes out,

"Or something like your hood pierced, then I'd probably tell you not to do it until you did something easier first."

"Uhh...where exactly does a hood piercing go?" I asked slowly, feeling naïve as I clenched my thighs together in perceived fear. I'd seen pictures of some non-traditional piercings and read things in novels that made me debate whether to grin or blush, but… I thought that was pretty rare.

His lazy grin was my answer. "Let's look it up," he suggested.

I shouldn't have done it. I shouldn't have been curious enough to look, but I did. Slim leaned over the computer, quickly typing in a search that brought up page after page of different types of piercings.

The first few pictures were pretty PG. A single eyebrow, double eyebrow like Blake's, nose, tongue, labret, snake bites, the septum, nose bridge! The more Slim clicked through, the more I started to wonder whether I should be looking or running. There were nipple piercings on men and women, and then I saw the vagina.

A hood piercing. A vertical one, horizontal one, a deep one...I shuddered and like an idiot, put my finger over Slim's to go to the next page.

Penis!

A dick popped out at me from the screen. A hard dick with a piercing that curled from the urethra through the head.

"Holy shit," I whispered, looking at the damn picture longer than I should have, crossing the line between appreciation and staring.

But it wasn't over. I glanced at the picture right below it and saw rows of penises.

I gulped.

A long, incredibly thick one with a piercing straight through the head. Top to bottom. In print on the lower half it had "Apadravya" labeling it. One penis after another popped up on the screen. Pictures with words like frenum, dydoe, lorum, and pubic slapped me in the face—visually, not physically.

Unfortunately, I would say since they were all impressive...could an erection be pretty?

Not that I had much experience to go off of but whatever.

My thighs clenched together, and I'm sure my eyes were nearly the size of the sun. I started huffing, a sign that I was going to regret the nervous words that were going to spill out of me. Words that cemented I was lonely in not just an emotional sense. "Do those help the man or the woman?"

"What do you think?" Dex asked a little too quickly.

I stuttered, entranced with the image on the screen. I should have been grateful I didn't reach up to stroke the screen, that would have been horrible. Not that staring was any better.

"Dex has one," Slim spit out in a laugh.

My gaze stayed forward. "Pardon?" I coughed.

Slim shook his head, grinning wide. "Dex? Am I lying?"

My focus slid over to the man in question. The man in question who had his eyes locked on me, bleeding me out with the focus of his gaze. And it was with that same confidence, that complete concentration that he shook his head slow, slow, slowly. Grinning just like a man with no shame at all. "You ain't lyin'."

A volcano erupted on my face with his answer. I opened my mouth, unable to say anything. *Whaaaat?* So I did the only thing that could remotely save my honor.

I face-planted the desk.

And then started mumbling, "Way too much information." They might have been laughing but I was too humiliated by the fact that I'd been ogling a stranger's penis—and requesting one just like it from Santa—when the man behind me had what I was sitting there admiring. And the man behind me being Dex. If it would have been Blake, I might have grimaced but…

"C'mon, Iris, it's cool," Slim chuckled, gesturing toward the screen. "You'd be surprised how many guys get them."

He was full of shit and I knew it.

I didn't bother looking up and settled for closing my eyes, but all I could do then was imagine that big, pierced cock on Dex's body. Holy moly.

"I can't—I mean—that looks really painful." I mumbled against the table in a strained whisper that sounded almost like a whine.

No one denied the fact that getting your genitals pierced was painful. Screw that.

"I hope they're worth it."

"You wanna find out?" Dex teased.

What in the hell?

Everything below my neck flushed at his question, but I steered away from it. There was no denying the hint of flirtation in his tone. Then again, I hadn't seen him with any other women since that morning at the auto shop. Though I doubted he was suffering from deprivation, you never know. Maybe he was.

But probably not.

"Babe, go choose a belly button ring," Dex murmured at the same time fingertips brushed across the back of my neck.

Glancing back at the screen, my belly fluttered.

Friggin' hell, those pictures were going to be burned into the back of my eyelids forever. If I ever got desperate for Spank Bank material, penis piercings were the thing to search for.

"Come on, I hid some of the cool rings we got in the last shipment," Slim urged.

I sighed, focusing on the gangly redhead instead of the beast on the computer screen. The picture with the monstrous thing. Gah! I needed to pull it together.

"If my belly button gets infected or the piercing is crooked, I'm going to give all your appointments to Blue from now on," I failed epically at joking from the chair in one of the private rooms.

Slim had showed me some of the new navel rings they'd gotten right before I was hired. I settled on a white gold piece—my ears swelled up if I put anything in them that wasn't gold or hypoallergenic—with a pretty, round, green crystal. To be honest, I was pretty excited to do it since I loved the jewelry.

"You'll be fine," he assured me, pulling out the sterilized equipment he'd need from the autoclave. A particularly large and thicker than normal needle made its way into his grip. Slim caught my eyes and grinned. "Needles freak you out?"

I snorted. Yeah right. "Not at all."

"Good."

He had already talked me through the procedure and all he needed to do by that point was wipe some orange stuff followed by marking two places where the needle needed to go through.

"Let's just get it over with. I'm getting anxious," I groaned, leaning back so that I was face-up on the chair, rolling my head to the side where the door was to find Dex standing just outside of it, looking in.

"I'll do it, Slim," he said, taking a step forward.

Slim shrugged without bothering to turn around and look at our boss. "Go for it. Everything's ready."

I thought it was weird that Dex offered to do it for me because I hadn't seen him do any piercings in the time I'd been there. "I don't mean to be rude, but do you know what you're doing?"

He turned to look at me over his shoulder and simply scowled. Slim snickered.

All right then.

There was the snapping and popping of gloves being put on, and the next thing I knew, Dex was rolling my shirt up over my chest. The fingers on one of his hands rested directly over my navel for a second before he swiped me with a cool towelette that stained my skin a dark orange.

He worked silently, making thoughtful faces as he leaned over with a marker in his hand dotting two spots. One directly on my belly and one out of view. He pulled a mirror off the counter to show me what he'd marked.

"Symmetrical, yeah?" he asked me like I could really tell if it was even or not when his big body loomed over mine with the apadravya piercing still so fresh in my mind.

My nod was slow. "Yeah."

He flashed me a little grin, another rarity, before murmuring as he used surgical-type clamps to pinch together the skin, "I'm gonna to tell you when to hold your breath, and when to let it out, all right? It's just a pinch."

The transfer from needle to jewelry was so quick, if it wasn't for the awkward burning sensation that happened after he pushed the needle through me and transferred the jewelry, I wouldn't have winced or anything.

Dex took a step back, admiring his work with a watchful eye. "Perfect."

I sat up on my elbows and looked down at my new piercing. It *was* pretty awesome. "Nice," I whispered, sitting up completely. I touched the top of it gingerly with my index finger before pulling my shirt down and over it with a grin. "Thanks, guys."

Slim nodded, his eyes focused in on Dex. "Dude, when was the last time you did a piercing? I can't remember."

"I need a drink." Dex announced, setting the alarm at Pins. It wasn't even midnight but the shop was dead and we all agreed it was pointless to stay open. "I'm buyin'."

Blake let out a howl of approval that was a perfect companion for Slim's whistle.

The loud beeping drowned out the slight murmur of whatever Blue said but based on the nod she was sharing, I figured she was excited about free drinks too. It wasn't until we were outside and I was trying to inch my way toward my car when Dex turned to look at me.

"You comin'?"

I hesitated.

"You're comin'," he said it as a statement instead of a question that time.

I blinked at him standing there with his arms at his sides. "I don't really drink." The same way I didn't eat fried foods, white bread, or meat. Plenty of people didn't like alcohol. But plenty of people also liked to tease me about being a goody two shoes when that wasn't the case at all.

"You don't really drink?" He repeated it just like I had when he'd asked me about my visit to the library.

I shook my head.

"No beer?"

"I drank half of one a few weeks ago," I offered.

"Cute girly drink?"

I smiled but shook my head. "Hardly ever."

Dex's lips quirked up at the corners again. "Straight vodka, babe?"

I snorted. "The day you get your belly button pierced."

And I waited. I waited for one of them to say some sort of smartass comment like the majority of people did when I told them. Most people made it seem like there was something wrong with me for not liking the taste of alcohol or beer and especially disliking the one and only time I got drunk. Going into an explanation why I didn't drink was unnecessary.

But none of them laughed. None of them did more than look mildly amused.

Dex finally smiled, gesturing toward his bike with a tilt of his head. "I'll get you a root beer then."

Well that wasn't at all what I expected.

There were a lot of things that bothered me about Dex. He was moody, bossy, and overbearing. He could be thoughtless—though to be fair it had only been our initial meeting that demonstrated this. And he was hot.

Not just attractive.

For all of the things about him I disliked that he could fix with a different attitude, the man breathed in oxygen and breathed out sexual masculinity at its finest when he was being a dick and even more when he wasn't. It was everything from the way he walked, to the way he clipped his words, ignored his messy hair, and wore the ink on his skin, that screamed at that primal part deep in me.

So it didn't help that all those things that irritated the shit out of me on a regular basis were displaced and replaced the minute we stepped into the bar.

Charles Dexter Locke—I'd found out his full name after spotting a bill with it on there and got a good snort—was easygoing then. Smooth, bossy even toward people he didn't employ, but he did it in a way that didn't scream needy or annoying, but rather confidence. The moment we'd sat down at a booth, a waitress was literally right there with a tray of beers on hand. Dex had cut her a quick glance, said the words, "Root beer for the girl, please," and when the bottled drink was set in front of me, another slice of eyes to the waitress at Mayhem with a low, "Thanks, Rach," and I swear to God the poor lady swooned.

The look in her eyes was almost comical. Keyword: almost.

I didn't know how to react around this talkative, casual man who laughed at a story Blake had about his son getting detention in school for cussing.

And his friggin' laugh.

Damn it. *Damn. It.*

I had to force myself to remember that this was the man who had made me almost cry. The man who had called me a bitch and called me an idiot behind my back. The same man who had made me think about leaving the only place I really had left.

But he'd apologized. Genuinely apologized and seemed like he regretted what had happened. Whether it was because he was really guilty or if he'd been bullied into it, it didn't matter. Ever since our little show down in the parking lot, he'd been distant, cordial, and concerned in a mix. Though I got to know the rest of the guys, Dex was still a volatile enigma.

As hot and smooth and relaxed as he was being, that wasn't the usual guy that I knew. But then again, what did I know about running my own business and having to balance work and personal relationships with employees? Absolutely nothing besides the fact that Sonny, who I trusted and loved, somehow managed to be friends with him. That had to count for something.

"Iris," Blake called out from across the booth we were in.

I tilted my head up at him, smiling. We'd only been there about thirty minutes and I'd been awfully quiet, more so than normal, soaking in their familiar conversations. "Yes?"

He smoothed a hand over his bare head, holding his beer close to his mouth with the other. "You old enough to drink?"

My mouth flattened. "Yes."

"When did you turn twenty-one? This year?"

I rolled my eyes at him. "Three years ago. I'm twenty-four going on fifty."

Blake made a face. "You're a damn baby."

"Maybe compared to your old butt." I laughed. Just last week he'd turned thirty-six. No one had bought him a cake or anything, but he'd mentioned it to me in passing. Obligation had me going to the deli next door to buy him a cookie in celebration.

"Where'd you live at before?"

It was Dex who'd asked the question. Dex who suddenly looked very intent across the table, an unlit cigarette nestled between his fingers mindlessly. And Dex who hadn't paid any attention to the paperwork I'd filled out when he'd given me the job. Of course.

"Fort Lauderdale."

"And you drove all the way over here by yourself?" he asked in that low drawl.

Oh God. "Yes."

"Babe, that's fuckin' stupid. Why?"

I thought for a moment about giving them some vague reason, but what was the point? "I couldn't find another job after I got laid off and my lease had ended."

"Your other family?" Dex asked, leaning forward in his seat as he planted his elbows on the table.

My non-WMC family, he meant. I guess. A certain part of me wasn't surprised he didn't know the answer though he was friends with Sonny.

"My little brother's in the Army. He's stationed in Japan."

My boss did that slow blink again, those eyes sucking me forward like a vortex. He looked from one side to the other, as if he was thinking about whether or not to ask the next question. "Your ma?"

The iceberg that lived permanently in my chest moved an inch. Shouldn't he know that by now? There were times when I went to Mayhem with Sonny that made me feel like everyone in the club knew all of my history. Then again, why would Dex care enough to wonder and ask? Or heck, even listen if someone mentioned it. Half the time he was wrapped up in his own lonesome world.

My voice was lower than usual, tender tissue paper in a wind storm. "She passed away a few years ago."

Slim, who had talked to me and asked me things, didn't know that specifically, so I wasn't surprised when he reached over and patted my hand. "Sorry, Iris."

Dex did this gradual nod in agreement. There was something about his face that looked stricken. Maybe I was imagining it though. "Sorry to hear about your ma, babe."

I did what I always did when someone found out about her, I shrugged. Not that I told very many people because I didn't. Over the years, I'd only met a handful that I had any reason to share that information with. Most never asked because so many people took their families for granted, but these guys had. "It happened a while ago but thank you."

The silence that followed was a little too thick. A little too long. It made me a little too uncomfortable.

"So…" I forced a smile onto my face. "Who really spilled the mayonnaise in Seattle?"

"I did not!"

Slim had his forehead to the table. "Yeah, yeah, you did."

"You're such a liar."

Dex was sitting directly across from me and on his fourth or fifth beer, I'd lost count after the awkward second one, and he was laughing. Laughing from deep within his chest, the richness of it vibrating from every pore in a way that had me swinging my eyes to him each chance I got. This Dex, the one who had been joking around with our group, messing with the guys was just… a completely different person from the one I'd seen at Pins night after night.

The good mood in the booth was so contagious, I couldn't find it in me to be the quiet vibe kill. They'd pulled me out of the normally reserved nature I had around them, and had me relaxed. I felt like normal Iris—the Iris I was around Sonny, Will, and Lanie—for once while in Pins' shadowy hands.

"You were, Ritz," he agreed with Slim. "I thought you were gonna pass out."

I guffawed, tossing back the Shirley Temple he'd ordered for me on the waitress' last trip. "My face turned red, but I didn't friggin' gasp when I saw it." We were referring to the penis piercing incident earlier. The incident that pulled us through the last topic the guys had been laughing at: the customers who cried or screamed when they got something pierced.

Blake shook his head in denial. "No, ma'am. Your face went red right after you gasped. I thought for sure you were gonna faint."

"Whatever," I scowled at all of them except Blue who was sitting back smiling. "I don't even understand why the hell you guys would show me that. You did it on purpose to embarrass me."

None of them denied it, confirming that I was right.

"My virgin eyes are scarred for life," I added. Why? Because I was a moron.

Also because I was an idiot, I glanced over in Dex's direction immediately after the words came out of my mouth.

"You serious?" And of course, he would say something now of all times.

I flashed a grin. "Just joking." Liar, liar, pants on fire. God, Austin was ruining me.

He raised a thick, black eyebrow but the look in his eyes made me feel like he could smell my lies a mile away.

"You're blushing," Blake chuckled. "Blue, why don't you ever blush?"

Blue, who was sitting on the same seat as me, shrugged.

"Either way, your face turned red when you saw the cock on the screen," Slim reminded everyone of the conversation we'd been having just moments before.

I grunted and waved him off. "No offense, but you three kind of suck," I said but I said it with a smile. "Just a wee bit."

Dex looked at Blake over his shoulder, one side of his mouth curled up. "She says no offense before she says we suck, can you believe that?"

I rolled my eyes at them. "I have manners."

Slim patted my hand like he had when I'd told them about my parents. "That you do."

The sound of a cell phone ringing faintly over the music in the pub had each of us fishing to look at our phones. It was Blake who pulled his up to his ear, frowning at the screen. It was close to two in the morning already and the bartender had already announced last call, so I couldn't blame him for looking confused when his phone rang unexpectedly. A second later he was pushing Blue out of the booth and stepping outside.

"I think it's his baby mama," Slim suggested in a hushed tone.

The mood shifted in those moments that Blake was gone. None of us said anything until he came back in, looking somber and flustered. He stopped at the end of the table, jaw tight. "I need to get going. Seth is in the emergency room. He's been running a high fever that his mom hasn't been able to keep down," he explained quickly, already taking a step back.

"Go, man."

Blake nodded, taking another step back before looking at Dex. "I'll call you in case something happens."

I forgot that they were supposed to be leaving the next day for Houston.

"Hope your son is okay!" I called out before Blake left. He shot me a grateful smile, tilted his head at the guys and took off.

Almost immediately, we all unanimously got up. Dex waved down the waitress and spoke to her briefly before handing a card over. Guilt washed through me as the waitress took off with his card. I reached into my wallet and pulled out a twenty dollar bill, folding it neatly while we waited around.

Before the waitress came back, I closed the distance between us, watching him focus in on one of the screens mounted over the bar that was showing a baseball game from earlier in the day.

"Here you go," I told him, handing him the bill as discreetly as possible.

Dex's gaze flickered from the screen to mine in a second, eyes widening as he looked down to see what I was trying to pass him.

"Here," I whispered.

He just kept looking at me, making me feel awkward for holding the money in my hand. Money he wasn't taking.

"Take it."

Dex did that slow blink again, the one that consumed planets entirely. "No," he said simply.

"I'm serious," I whispered, shoving the bill closer to him.

"No, babe. I said it was on me."

That was exactly what he'd said, but I felt bad. He'd drank anywhere from four to five beers. The other guys probably had as many, and there weren't friggin' happy hour specials going on. The bill had to be more than what I made in a day.

"Just take it," I insisted.

Dex plucked the bill away, holding it between his middle and ring finger, keeping those bright blue eyes on mine. "You serious?"

I nodded. "Yeah."

"Dex, can you sign here for me?" the waitress asked walking up to us with his receipt and card.

Relief flooded through me that he'd at least taken the money to cover something. Not like I thought he was hurting for it. He'd accidentally left the business' online checking account open a few days back, and I'd taken a peep before logging out. Needless to say, the figure in the checking account was impressive.

The moment I took a step away to head back where Slim and Blue stood, I felt a faint pressure on my butt and turned to look over my shoulder to find Dex's fingers creeping out of my back pocket.

Uh... what?

His fingers were in and out of my pant pocket so fast I almost wasn't sure whether it actually happened or not, and before I could complain about him giving me back my money—and sticking his hand where it didn't belong—he leaned his chest into me.

"Thanks for offerin', babe," he whispered, all hot breath on my skin.

It was unavoidable for me to shiver but at least I think I did it discreetly. Damn it, this laid-back Dex was something I didn't know how to handle. It was almost possible for me to forget the shit he said and did on a daily basis.

It was right there, I could feel it. I could sense that draw in him that made people put up with him and his insane mood swings and temper.

Looking up at him towering over me all relaxed, face loose, tension gone, I nodded. "Well, you're welcome at least. Thanks for inviting me."

And he smiled at me while we made our way out with Slim and silent Blue.

I had to mentally tell myself to stop looking at the strange man I didn't seem to understand, to focus on my slightly drunk coworkers. I had to physically shake myself awake to survive the next hour. Inspecting all three of them, I sighed with just a hint of exhaustion nipping at my shoulders and neck. "You suckers need a ride?"

CHAPTER ELEVEN

The last thing I expected to do the next day was to go to Costco.

With Dex.

In my car.

I mean, Costco, Dex, and my car shouldn't even belong in the same sentence, right? Dex and Costco?

But somehow that's where I found myself at five in the afternoon. Following Dex around the massive store, stocking up on toilet paper, paper towels, and random stuff like plastic utensils for Pins.

I'd shown up to work fifteen minutes early to find Dex outside—smoking. Gag. He'd given me that long, leisurely look that I didn't quite understand and tipped his head back, blowing a thick cloud of smoke from his lips in the opposite direction of where I stood. "We're openin' late," was exactly what he'd said before dropping the bomb on me.

Like I was going to complain. "Okay."

Dex had pushed off from the wall, dropping his cigarette to the ground and crushing it with the toe of his boot. "Is your trunk big enough for a Costco run?"

In my head, there were tires squealing in protest to his comment. He wanted me to go with him? "Umm...I think so."

He smirked right before leaning down to pick up the crumpled butt. "All right. Let's go."

Crap.

I kept repeating *crap* over and over to myself as we walked toward the lot. I'd worked out most of the tension I felt toward Dex over the course of the last few weeks, and especially after seeing how nice and understanding he could be... well, I didn't feel that same resentment. That didn't mean that I was mentally prepared to hang out with him.

Or you know, go buy stuff together.

Twenty minutes later, Dex was pushing around a massive cart and heading toward the food section.

It should be said that the couple of times I'd been to the megastore, I'd seen plenty of men. Usually, they were always husbands or boyfriends, ranging from twenties to sixties or seventies. Some were good-looking, others were not. Some had tattoos, most didn't.

But I had never seen a man like Dex pushing around a cart. With his full-sleeved tattoos, peeping red ink on his neck, and Levi's that had broken in perfectly around his thighs—and butt, too—he was a sight. Then again, maybe I hadn't pictured men like Dex at all. Ever. They were like abominable snowmen.

Yet there he was with his little scrap of paper that he called a list, hunched over the lip of the cart, tossing in enough paper towels to last three months, and massive packages of toilet paper.

The first and only thing he said in the time between us parking and winding through the aisles was, "Grab whatever you want."

"Thanks," had been the response I gave him.

Then, nothing.

"You pissed off again?" Dex finally asked after we'd arranged the paper products to make room for the other stuff he planned on buying later on.

We hadn't really spoken much on the drive—he took the keys from me while we were crossing the street to the lot—and I hadn't made much of an effort since we'd walked into the store.

I looked over at him, taking in the dark green t-shirt that made his eyes look nearly black, and shook my head. "No. Why?"

Those normally brilliant blue eyes made a lazy trail from my face down, reminding me for some reason of the fact that he'd tucked his fingers into my back pocket at Mayhem the night before. "You're bein' all quiet, babe. It's weird."

Uhh... What? "I don't really talk a lot."

His eyes narrowed just a little bit. "You talk to everybody else."

I don't think it was my imagination that his tone had dipped a little lower than it usually did.

Thinking about it for a second, I guess I did. At Pins, I was usually always talking to a client or Slim or Blake. It was more often than not that I'd be speaking to someone. Yet the one person that I didn't really ever talk to was Dex. Not that that was a surprise either. More than half the time I'd known him, I hadn't held him in the highest regard. The other half of the time, I'd mostly spent trying to stay out of his hair.

"Oh," I told him, giving him a droopy smile.

Dex blinked slowly, his gaze hard and unyielding.

Oh lord. It made my hands feel funny. I wheezed out an awkward laugh, reaching up to scratch at my head. "Thanks for putting me in bed that other night, by the way."

He didn't say anything, he just kept looking at me.

Well. I turned around to face the opposite shelves, feeling incredibly awkward that he didn't reply with at least a friggin' grunt. "You're welcome, Iris," I murmured under my breath, looking at the rows of granola bars on the shelves.

"What'd you say?"

Crap.

I tried to play it off by coughing. "Nothing."

The soft sound of his boots on the floor were my warning that he was approaching. "What'd you say?" he asked again, stopping just to my left. I could feel the heat of his chest on my arm.

"Nothing." God, I was a coward.

He took another step toward me, his abs brushing against my elbow. "Ritz, buck up. What'd you say?"

Oh boy. I swallowed hard and tilted my head up to look at him.

Dex was looking at me with that impenetrable gaze. "Didn't I already tell you to say whatever the fuck you want? I know you said somethin', so repeat it."

I really was a coward sometimes. Why wouldn't I just repeat what I'd said? Oh, right. I didn't want to get fired. "I said you're welcome."

"Why didn't you just say that then? You still think I'm gonna get pissed or somethin'?" he asked carefully, his voice low.

Buck up, he'd said. I eyed him carefully, taking in the dark stubble on his jaw. "I don't want to make you mad."

"Why?"

"Why?" I repeated.

"Yeah, why? I don't give a fuck about pissin' other people off."

Like I didn't already know that. I hummed in my throat for a second before reminding myself there was nothing about Dex Locke to be worried about. To be nervous around. He was just a man. A man with a temper. A man with a temper that asked for my honesty. "You're my boss. I don't want to get fired."

I felt the nudge on my ribs and looked down to see that he'd elbowed me gently. His eyes were narrowed. "Why would I fire you?"

The scoff in my throat just kind of came out. "Do you remember telling your friend on the phone that you didn't need a fucking idiot working for you? Or do you remember telling me that if I couldn't handle the job, I wasn't needed?" There was probably just a little too much edge to my voice.

"Ritz," he groaned. Groaned! Like he was embarrassed or something when the words had come directly out of his mouth.

I tightened up my shoulders and flattened my mouth to give him an incredulous look. It didn't really work because he just managed to look at my mouth curiously. "Well. It came out of your mouth, didn't it?"

The question had barely left my mouth before I physically flinched at the aggression in my voice. I'd told myself over and over again to stop, to move over, and I would. There were millions of things that were unforgivable and being a grumpy shit wasn't one of them. Even if I wanted to believe it was. I had to pry half the words out of my mouth to feed them to him.

"I'm sorry. I forgive you. I'll figure out how to drop it sooner than later."

Dex scrubbed a hand over his face and sighed, frowning just slightly down at me. "I wouldn't have said that shit if I hadn't been pissed off before," he huffed. "If you're hopin' to make me beg you to forget about it, you're gonna be holdin' your breath a while, baby."

Was it mean of me to snort? Yes. But I did it anyway without even thinking about it. Him? Beg? I'd be sending parkas to hell the day that happened.

I could forgive him but forget? Eh. Not so much, at least not so quickly.

When I looked over at him, the side of his mouth was tilted up in a half-smile. The tip of his elbow nudged my side again. "I'm not gonna fire you, all right?"

That didn't mean I wasn't planning on finding another job so that I wouldn't deal with his dick-ass but whatever. So I just tipped my chin down. "Okay."

"Yeah?" he asked slowly.

I nodded. "Yeah."

He didn't look completely convinced with my answer. "You're hangin' in there, babe." He paused. "Even when I gotta fix the shit you mess up sometimes. I'm not complainin' anymore."

Anymore. I snorted. Whether he was just being nice because my brother, Trip, or Luther had said something to him, I wasn't going to ask.

As long as he wasn't still being a dick, I'd take it.

"Have you heard from Blake today?" I asked him, trying to get away from all this talk about me getting fired.

Dex plucked a box of organic granola bars from the shelf and dropped it into the cart. "Yeah. Sean's got meningitis. He's still in the hospital."

A little kid in the hospital? My stomach churned. "God, that sucks."

He nodded, his eyes on another shelf. "Yeah. We need to stop by Sonny's and pick up your shit," he announced, glancing at my what-the-hell look out of the corner of his eye. "You're comin' with us."

CHAPTER TWELVE

"One of you please explain to me why we're leaving tonight and not tomorrow morning," I yawned, hoping my question made sense.

It was two-thirty in the morning and Houston was still two hours away. Dex was behind the wheel of a big, black GMC truck I'd never seen before—he always came to work on the back of his Dyna. Slim, on the other hand, was sitting shotgun and fiddling with the radio station. Again.

For the tenth time in less than twenty minutes to be exact. It'd be the last time if I had anything to say about it.

"We have to be there by eleven to set up the booth," Dex explained, looking at me through the rearview mirror. "I don't wanna risk not wakin' up on time tomorrow mornin'."

Ugh. I guess he had a point. I also guess I shouldn't be complaining since I wasn't the one actually driving. Regardless, I would have rather gotten a few hours of sleep in my bed—by that I meant Sonny's guest room that I'd made my own pad over the last few weeks.

"Go to sleep, Iris," Slim chimed in. "At least one of us can get a decent rest."

I thought about telling him he could go to sleep because there was no way I would be able to. Even as a kid, it'd always been hard for me to sleep in a car. I think I was just paranoid that something would happen along the drive and if I'd stayed up, I could have prevented it. It sounded crazy but it made perfect sense in my head.

"You can go to sleep. I can survive on a few hours," I told our resident redhead.

No joke, he looked at Dex for approval, nodded and promptly passed out with his forehead against the glass window within a three minute time frame.

"Well," I muttered, looking at him to make sure he was asleep. He was. I had a feeling this was going to be a fun trip.

Or not.

How I got wrangled into it, I still didn't understand, and I felt guilty. Really guilty.

Dex needed someone else to tag along to help set up the booth and have another person to sit there constantly. It was doable with three people but nearly impossible with only two. And Blue, damn her, rarely went. Something about her not being social enough. Considering I'd maybe only spoken about twenty words with her in a month, it kind of made sense.

Apparently, I won by default. Though I still wasn't sure whether this was something to consider a win or not.

An hour after we made it back from the store, Gladys from Smiling Faces Daycare Center had called to offer me a job nearly a week after my interview. Fudgesicle sticks. The "yes" that spewed out of my mouth was unintentional, at least so soon. I should have thought about it longer considering that the pay was considerably less than what Dex was paying me but...

Wasn't that what I'd wanted?

I had every intention of informing Dex that I was quitting but he kept interrupting me or saying we'd talk about things later. And later had turned into later and *later*, and the Houston trip had fallen into my lap like an unwanted pregnancy.

We'd dropped by Sonny's after Costco so that I could pack my bag, call my brother and tell him what was going on—he somehow already knew—and haul ass back to Pins for Dex's appointment.

That was exactly how I found myself riding along in the backseat with Slim and Dex in front, deciding that I should probably wait until we got back to Austin before I broke the news. Was I a coward? Completely. Was it noticeable that I was stressing? Definitely.

Dex was glancing at me out of the corner of his eye, one hand wrapped loosely around the steering wheel while the other rested on the door.

"You buckled?" he asked me in a lowered voice.

I looked down. No. "Yes."

Dex sighed, glancing at me again. "Buckle your goddamn seatbelt."

"Sheesh." I usually always had it on, especially if I was in the backseat but this time I'd been so distracted and worried about driving overnight that I didn't even think to do so until he mentioned it. With a huff, I pulled the belt across my lap and strapped in, mumbling, "Friggin' bossy," under my breath.

A moment later the truck swerved to the right quickly before aligning itself just as fast. In the meantime, despite the jarring motion, Slim stayed asleep while I freaked the hell out and leaned forward to pop my head between the two seats.

"Are you okay to drive?" I whispered.

He cut me another sidelong glance. "There was a dead raccoon in the road," he explained in an equally low voice. "And I'm fine to drive, quit stressin'."

Quit stressing. Like that would happen.

And it didn't. For the next thirty minutes, I rubbed my hands down the length of my thighs, thanking whatever divine entity that could be listening in, that the road was surprisingly empty. There had only been a handful of cars on the highway and if it weren't for that, I'd probably be freaking out even more.

"Would you calm down, Ritz?" Dex whisper-hissed at me.

"I'm calm," I argued. He turned to look at me over his shoulder for a moment, which made me squeal. "Keep your eyes on the road!"

"I can feel the little panic attack you're havin' back there," he mumbled. "Fuck, I'm surprised you haven't woken up Slim with how much stress you're puttin' out, babe."

I sighed, turning my attention outside the window to the right. So far, besides the swerving incident, he had been a good driver. Not that that meant anything because there wasn't any traffic but still. He was over the speed limit but not too much, and except for glancing at me a moment before, his attention had been glued to the road.

"What's freakin' you out?" Dex asked in that soft melodic voice he'd only used on me a couple of times before.

"I'm worried you're going to fall asleep driving or something."

Not even a heartbeat later, Dex responded. "I'm wide awake, babe. Swear. I took an energy drink before we started drivin'." There was no hesitation or annoyance in his tone.

I hummed in response.

A few more minutes passed by. Dex fiddled with the knobs on the radio. If I wouldn't have been paying so much attention I would have missed his quick glances to the backseat.

"Ritz."

"Yeah?"

Without an introduction or a ramp that apologized for being nosey, he asked, "What'd your ma die of?"

There was a knot in my throat I hadn't felt in a long time—a very long time. Such a long time that it was laced in rust and spider webs, foreign in my body. In the same way I'd avoided telling people about my parents being gone, I avoided telling them how Mom died, and mostly, people didn't ask. Mortality is a delicate subject. Most people don't like to get reminded of how fragile and unstable life is. Mom wasn't even near forty when she first got sick.

People asked about my family if they cared to get to know me. Most of the time I didn't get close enough to establish that type of relationship with anyone. I liked people in general but with life and work as unstable as they were, leaving people behind or getting forgotten hurt too much. I lived the last few years of my life being friendly and cordial.

But I was tired.

And Dex had cared enough to ask.

"Breast cancer." Something that constantly scared the crap out of me but I didn't admit that.

He let out a long, suffering sigh from his nose. His free hand went up to pull his cap off his head, tossing it onto the center console. "Fuck," he groaned. "How old were you?"

Just answering pierced me a little. Just a little. I'd accepted what happened a long time ago. "Sixteen. My brother was eleven."

Dex hissed long and low. Turning to glance at me out of the corner of his eye, his gaze was heavy and curious. "Fuckin' kids," he murmured in that low register.

One kid raising another kid with only the weary monitoring of *yia-yia*. Even before my mom had died, she'd been sick for a couple of years. By the time the aggressive disease had gotten to be too much, I'd already felt like a thirty-year-old in a teenager's body. Deep in my bones I knew that my life would have been completely different if my dad wouldn't have left.

I would have still gotten sick and maybe Mom would have still had useless mastectomies, and pesticides shot into her veins, and for all I know, she would have still passed away. But maybe the paragraphs that had been written in between Mom and *yia-yia's* deaths wouldn't have been so roughly drafted and eventually published. I may have still been in Florida, with a college degree, and married with the Golden Retriever I'd always wanted. And maybe Will would have done something else with his life that didn't involve running away to start over.

But like the few other times when the pity party started without my permission, I reined the thoughts in with a restrained mental lasso. I rarely went down that path of what-ifs. They were pointless and painful, and I'd come to accept that my life was the way it was because… it just was. It was the brew of a million decisions and possibly fate if you believed in it.

I didn't. Then again, I didn't believe in a lot of things anymore.

I had to swallow back the knot in my throat, push the focus of my family off while I still could. My brain leeched onto the first topic that came to mind. "Are you looking forward to the expo, Charlie?"

He made a choking sound. "Charlie?" Dex glanced at me through the rearview mirror, one eyebrow raised like he couldn't believe what I'd just called him.

Maybe I shouldn't have called him that out loud, but I'd already said it and I knew Dex wasn't going to let it go. Plus, I thought it was kind of cute. It softened up the impression I had of him. "Yeah. Charlie. Charles. Charles Dexter."

He grunted. "Dex, babe. Not...that."

"It's a good name," I told him. "No need to get extra grumpy about it. It's not like your first name is Leslie or Clancy."

Out of all the things he could have picked up on, like the fact that I thought his first name was a good one, he went for the obvious. "You think I'm grumpy?" he asked.

I didn't like lying and it wasn't like he'd kick my ass for telling the truth. I think. He'd probably leave me in Houston or fire me...

"Well you aren't going to win any congeniality awards when you're pushing customers out of the shop and always grinding your teeth away." I thought about bringing up his not-so-sweet actions but I'd told myself I didn't want to go there anymore.

And Dex snickered. "You tellin' me I'm an asshole?"

"Grumpy with a side of extra grumpy." Did that really just come out of my mouth?

He shook his head, biting his bottom lip in a way that looked pensive. "Huh," he paused like he was searching for words to explain his nature. "I have a temper." Like I didn't know that. "It's hard for me to shake things off."

"Like what kind of things?" I asked though it wasn't my place to. This was something I'd talked to *yia-yia* about multiple times. The inability of a person to let go of things that harmed or bothered them. Everyone was guilty of it. "I can keep a secret."

I swear I think he laughed nervously. "Well, when do you want me to start, babe? The day I said that shit to you? My ma had rung me up and said that Pa had called."

Okay, it was safe to assume he wasn't a fan of his dad. That I understood. Simply thinking of my dad had almost ruined my day in the past, too. Check. That was acceptable. "Okay."

"The day after that? I found out my property taxes were goin' up—"

"You get that pissed off about property taxes?" I asked him incredulously.

"They went up a fuckin' ton," he explained like that would make perfect sense.

"You were in a terrible mood, looking at me like I ruined one of your tattoos, all because your property taxes went up?"

Dex had the decency to grunt. Decency only because tracing the root of his anger to taxes was so absolutely ridiculous it didn't need to get cemented into a fact. I hoped it would have been something better, more worthwhile. Like...finding out his girlfriend had cheated on him or something. That I could understand.

"Then I'd found out that somebody was stealin' from the bar," he added in afterthought.

"Someone was stealing from the bar riles you up that much?"

Once again, he grunted.

Oh boy.

"The day after that, I got into an argument with Luther about him messin' around with girls who aren't old enough to rent a damn car on their own, " he prattled on until I blew a long breath out of my lips.

The idea that I could and probably should keep my mouth shut was right there, telling me to not bother saying anything. I couldn't do it though. It wasn't my place to give him advice or call him out on things he could fix. I had a whole list of things I should fix about myself but I'd never bothered picking it up to look it over.

"Dex? I completely understand that you get pissed off about stuff, but I don't think it's worth you getting so mad. You can fight your property taxes, right?" He didn't say anything. "You're smart, you can figure out a way to find out who's stealing. And Luther sleeping with girls that young…"

Was I going to say it? Yup.

"It's pretty friggin'… weird but they're old enough to know what they're doing. It's consensual, and you think it's going to stop him from doing it?" No answer again. "Probably not. So I don't think you should waste your time away brooding or calling innocent people bitches and friggin' idiots in retaliation. And the receipts missing? That sucks but don't let it ruin your day. You're going to give yourself a heart condition by stressing out so much about things that don't matter. Trust me. It isn't worth it."

Silence. More silence. Triple silence.

Dex fidgeted in his seat during all of this. Arranging then rearranging his butt position.

Failing to bring up how right I was, he sighed. "I did have a few ideas on how to figure out who's been takin' money from the register..."

An hour later, we were still talking over ideas.

The three of us dragging our way across the hotel lobby was more than likely one of the most pitiful sights any possible observers would ever see. I probably resembled some sort of hybrid zombie raccoon with my rundown eyeliner and sleepy groans. I know without a doubt that Slim had a line of dry drool from the corner of his mouth down the side of his neck that Dex and I had silently agreed we wouldn't tell him about. And Dex, carrying his backpack, my little duffel, and something that looked like a toolbox on absolutely no sleep, didn't look like such hot stuff anymore either.

Well, that was a lie. Dex, with his disarray of blue-black hair and dry, pink lips, still looked attractive. Just more like an attractive hobo with his wrinkled clothes rather than a stunning one.

Slim had explained to me through several yawns and eye flutters that Pins usually reserved one hotel room that three people shared to keep the guys focused—on tattooing, I assumed. Not landing between two thighs. Two people got beds and someone tackled the sleeper sofa. As nice as Slim was, he hadn't already said, "I'll sleep on the pull-out," so I wasn't going to assume he would either. Sleep and hunger always brought out the worst in people and I totally got it. If I went too long without eating, everything annoyed me. Plus, he was actually tattooing when we got up. My job was just to stand there and say hi to strangers.

"I'm gonna knock out," Dex finally yawned from a couple steps behind me.

I staggered, blinking back the fight of slumber. I'd already asked him about four times if he wanted me to help him carry stuff but each time he'd insist that he didn't. And shoot, I wasn't about to ask again.

Instead, I yawned as well. "Me too."

Dex's mouth was wide open, recovering from the nonstop trip that took us to the Hyatt closest to the convention center. The corners of his eyes wrinkled with another yawn, exhaling something that sounded like a groan. A two and a half hour drive in the middle of the night after a full work day would kill anyone.

After the confessional slash strategy session we had back in the truck—which he finally mentioned belonged to Luther—we'd exchanged maybe twenty more words. Each and every single time consisted of me asking if he was fine, and Dex responding with an assured "Yeah." One heart-to-heart was enough.

The second that the door was unlocked and the hotel room was open, I beelined toward the couch the instant I was inside. It was almost six in the morning and we had to be up by ten and parked in front of the convention area to unload around eleven before setting up the booth.

The idea of unpacking—even worse—the idea of even taking off my clothes to crawl onto the couch made me sleepier. I pulled the cushions off and threw them on the desk across the carpet before unbuckling my belt.

"Ritz."

My mind was completely focused on getting in that friggin' bed as quickly as I could, as I yanked the mattress out. "Yes?"

"What are you doin', babe?" Dex asked.

"Going to sleep," I said, shoving my pants down to my ankles. It was a blessing my shirt was so long it covered the most important piece of my anatomy.

"What the hell?" was Slim's lazily yawned question.

I barely turned my head to look over my shoulder. Barely. My eyes were somehow managing to stay open but they were about to lose the battle. So I hardly managed the effort to see Slim standing at the foot of the bed the closest to me, holding the hem of his shirt in hands. Dex meanwhile, stood at the sink across from the bed, a hand braced around the edge of the sink, eyes on me through the reflection.

I didn't even have the decency to blush.

"So sorry guys. I'm tired." It was the truth. I was embarrassed that I'd just been an exhibitionist and yanked down my pants in front of two men that I didn't think even knew my last name.

"Get the bed, honey," Dex said.

I waved him off. "You can have the bed. Just wake me up please," I muttered, smiling in the general direction of where they'd been standing a moment before. "Goodnight, suckers."

Two "goodnights" wafted through the room. I closed my eyes and tried to go to sleep. As tired as I'd been the entire drive and walk to the room, I couldn't shut off my brain. The sound of the sink running, sheets rustling, and low murmurs kept me up. No matter how hard I tried to fall asleep, I couldn't. The light from the guys' half of the room was right smack on my face either way I lay.

At some point, the whispers and the running water stopped. The sheets shuffled once more, and I heard one sigh after the other before silence ensued. I tried to steady my breathing, and I still couldn't fall asleep.

And then, I heard it.

It started as a whisper, a hiss, a *pssssssssst.*

And then it grew progressively louder before the smell hit me.

But by that point, my stomach was hurting. Pure, pleasurable pain stabbed me right in the gut. And I started giggling like crazy. *Crazy.* Tears pooled in my eyes and I gasped.

A deep growl of a laugh mixed with mine from the other side of the room. It was Dex. Dex!

"Oh my God," I wheezed, smothering my mouth with my hand. "Did you crap your pants?"

Another bout of grumbling laughter came over Dex that made me suck in a breath.

My stomach hurt even more as I heard his wind-breaking in my imagination. The badass Dex Locke that Trip and Sonny had told me about so carefully, the one who probably beat a man for talking smack to him, was passing gas like he was on the verge of pooping his pants. And he laughed about it.

"I thought you were sleepin'," he muttered before laughing even harder. The sound was even richer, more pure in the dark room.

I pinched my nose to keep from laughing louder. It was only a miracle that Slim was a heavy sleeper and didn't wake up. "Holy moly, I want my own room."

"Go to sleep," his gruff voice barked at the end of a laugh.

"Sleep?" I gagged so loud it was another miracle that Slim still hadn't woken up. "How am I supposed to go to sleep after that?"

Dex groaned. "Ritz."

My stomach hurt from how hard my muscles were cramping. "Your butt should be a weapon of mass destruction."

Dex chuckled low, rough and sugar sweet at the same time. "Get to bed."

I let out a long breath trying to control myself. It worked.

For about half a second.

And then I started laughing all over again, pulling the extra pillow over my face to muffle it. I really had no idea why I thought it was so funny. It wasn't like I hadn't been around Will the Farting Machine most of my life. His goal for the longest time had been to fart the alphabet. I mean, everyone passed gas. Everyone.

But this was Dex. My smoking biker boss that wore black on a regular basis.

I pulled the pillow away just long enough to hear him having another laughing fit as well.

So I said what came to mind. "You're funny."

Because he was, who would have known? My chest felt all loose and fun for the first time...in forever.

It might have been because the dark took away the intimacy of my admission but whatever. It just came out of my mouth. "I can't remember the last time I laughed so much."

"Me neither," his low voice carried across the room right before I felt something hit my stomach. It was a pillow. He'd thrown a pillow at me. "Night, baby."

I rolled over and tossed my leg over my new pillow with a snort. "Night, Charlie."

I fell asleep with my cheeks hurting that night.

"I don't fuck my employees, man."

Shane shook his head, and then tilted it forward just a little. "Not even that one?"

I was trying my best to pretend that I couldn't hear them. Like I was so wrapped up in watching Slim transfer the fresh stencil onto the customer in the chair, that I was able to zone out my boss and his friend. But I couldn't, and a huge part of me, the sadistic part, didn't want to.

For the last thirty minutes I'd been trying to ignore Dex and this Shane fella talk about who'd they'd seen up until that point at the convention. Up until Shane had shown up, I'd been having a good time with both of my coworkers. Dex had teased me about how I thought everything was cool while we'd walked around bringing the shop's things in.

That's right. Dex was teasing me. Apparently our middle of the night hysterical laughing session had been a transition in the Iris/Dex battle. Who would have known? I still felt a little uneasy and unsure but it wasn't anything like before. I'd take it. I had told myself before I wasn't going to be pissed off at him anymore, and I was going to stick to my guns and go with this new attitude for however long it lasted.

Because it wouldn't last but I'd worry about that when the time came.

We spent the morning making our way around like zombies trying to set up the booth before opening. The people, the colors, the designs, everything in our surroundings sucked me in with the back and forth trekking from the truck.

The people and the piercings were beyond interesting. I'd seen one girl who had rows of piercings that lined up her back with streams of ribbon laced through that made it look like she was wearing a corset. Another man I'd seen setting up a table down the row from ours had tattoos all over his face. There was literally no inch of clear skin on his entire head except around his eyes. That was just the start, Slim had warned me.

It was fun. Taking in all the unconventional people, imagining what kind of stories the tattoos on their bodies told. There was no doubt in my mind both Slim and Dex could sense my curiosity and excitement.

We were having a really good time.

Until Shane came in with his big, ringing words, retelling stories about how many girls he and Dex bagged every time he visited Shane's shop in Dallas. From the amount of time he'd spent with us, I figured his booth wasn't exactly busy. I'd stood up to grab Slim a new water bottle for rinsing, and that was when Shane noticed me. Leading to the question that made me wary. The same question that had me clocking in our wagon of friendly as a twelve hour truce.

Well, it'd been fun while it lasted.

I saw Dex cut me a glance out of my peripheral vision, though I'm not sure whether that was a good thing or a bad thing, before sighing out, "No."

Sheesh.

"Especially not that one," he added.

Dick!

The stab to my pride flared up my chest painfully.

Screw him for not wanting to sleep with *especially me*. Dick face. It's not like I wanted someone like him to add to the nonexistent list of people I'd slept with in my life.

I flicked my gaze over in their direction, catching Shane's eyes on me, and forced a hard smile to my face. I wasn't a vain person. I was happy with myself and regardless of whether Dex thought my B cups were too small or whether my facial features weren't up to par. I had some pride. So I gritted my teeth, locked my gaze on Dex's throat and grabbed the bottled water I'd filled up hours before.

Dick. Dick. Dick. Dick. Dick.

"What's wrong with her?" the snooty little jerk asked.

Was there something wrong with me? Besides my arm, which no one friggin' knew about, I didn't think there was anything *wrong* with me. I wasn't going to be on the cover of a magazine anytime soon—or ever—but I didn't look like I'd gone head to head with a surgeon's scalpel and lost.

"Nothin' besides the fact Sonny would rip your asshole outta your mouth if he saw you lookin' at her ass," Dex replied in a low laugh.

There was a low groan. "That's Son's sis?"

"The only one we know of."

God, the thought that there could be another Curt Taylor offspring in the world made me want to vomit even more than the realization that Dex didn't find me at least attractive enough to stand up for me.

Dickface.

Shane made a humming noise. "So I can't try—"

"Shut the fuck up, man," Dex groaned.

"Dude. You can't tell me you haven't thought about hittin' that."

Oh God. Was I mad or annoyed? I should feel insulted or pissed that I was being objectified, but strangely, I think I was more annoyed than anything else.

Dex's answer only fueled the part of me that was pissed off. Completely overshadowing my annoyance. "Why would I?"

And here I thought we were sort-of friends. Jerk. Slimy, moody, tiny balls. Weren't recluse spiders common in Texas? Maybe I could—

"I think we're talking too loud," Shane stated.

There was a short pause before Dex stated evenly in the same volume, "Ritz."

I ignored him, focusing at the thought of finding a spider to bite his precious arm.

Here was this man I thought was beautiful, nearly perfect on the outside, hotter than a light bulb that had been left on all day—a bit of a dick but whatever. And he didn't even find me attractive enough to be polite when referring to my looks. Not even a little and it made my sternum burn.

"Ritz."

Dick.

"Iris," he said that time.

I looked over my shoulder at his chin, clenching my jaw. Dick. "Yes?"

Dex waved me forward with a flick of his tattooed fingers. "Babe, come here."

I didn't.

"Iris, come here."

"I'm fine over here, Char-lee," I told him. Was I trying to piss him off by calling him that? Probably.

I could see Dex shake his head in Shane's direction before splitting the distance between us. His gaze dropped to my eye level as he rolled my chair away from Slim's vicinity for me to face him. Dex's hand reached out to tip my face. I looked up at the rafters.

"No." He pressed his fingers deep into the skin under my chin.

Touchy-feely Dex? *Okay.*

"No what?" I blurted out the question like a moron.

He made some sort of disapproving noise in the back of his throat. "I hate it when you look away," Dex murmured. "Quit it."

I widened my eyes but still didn't listen to him.

"Look at me," he insisted. "You pissed again?" he asked in a low voice meant only for me.

There was absolutely no hesitation in my answer. "Yes."

He groaned. "Babe, fuckin' look at me. I like your wounded deer eyes."

Dick. I shrugged.

Dex slid his thumb down to replace the two fingers beneath my chin, and then swept it across the line of my jaw to nearly my ear. "Please."

God. He got on my nerves. Tired of playing the petulant child and kind of pleased that he'd said the magic word, I finally looked at him. The expression on my face was the best blank one I could muster.

Those cobalt colored eyes shifted from one of mine to the other. Because I'd gotten to know him in my own secret way, I could see the strain on his lips. The strain that told me he was trying really hard not to be amused. "You heard what I said?"

I gritted my teeth. "I'm not deaf."

Oh yeah, he was trying not to smile.

But he forced a slow blink. "And?"

"It's fine that I'm not your cup of tea, Dex, but you don't have to be such an ass about it and tell the entire world." I swallowed. "I don't have friggin' herpes or the Black Plague."

A frown twitched his pink lips, a crease forming between his eyebrows as he looked from one eye to the other again. "Honey." His finger slipped just behind my ear.

"Please go away."

"No."

Of course not. I had to try a different tactic. "You're embarrassing me."

What did the asswipe do? He grinned goofy. His good mood apparent over every pore of his face. "I think you're embarrassin' me."

"Oh please," I snorted, tipping my head back out of his reach. "You're just being honest. It's fine. I'm serious. I don't like chocolate, it's kind of the same thing, right?"

His eyes widened for a moment, sweeping leisurely over my face and down to my mouth. "No. It's not, babe." His grinned flattened in a way that spelled trouble. "You don't need to be fishin' for compliments."

"I'm not fishing for compliments!" Was I?

His tongue peeked out to tap his bottom lip. "Seems like it."

What? A shiver wormed its way down my spine. A shiver that I was barely able to control until I felt something soft, hot, and feathery in my throat. "It seems you're out of your mind."

He raised a heavy eyebrow. "Why?"

I swallowed hard and leaned further away from him. "Where do you want me to start?"

He looked at me for a little longer than I expected before he laughed that same guttural version I secretly liked. Dex smiled, never losing eye contact even after calming down.

Something changed in his expression. Maybe not even in the contours of his face but in his eyes, something definitely changed just a little. Whatever it was, I liked it.

Plus, I wouldn't get to see much of him pretty soon. The reality that I needed to tell him what was going on made me feel guilty.

I still kind of hated him for being so damn hot.

Especially since he'd decided to let himself all hang out while at the Expo. Unlike his daily attire back in Austin that mainly consisted of t-shirts, jeans, and the occasional gingham print shirt, Dex had shed his normal attire for a black undershirt. A sleeveless black tank that let me see every inch of those cut arms beneath layers of thick ink, and a better view of the red tattoo that went from his back over his shoulder and neck to his chest.

Damn him.

Damn him to hell.

Dex looked at me for a second longer before straightening up and saying, "I'm gonna get goin' for a while. If someone comes lookin' for me, call."

I nodded, knowing that I didn't have his number but assuming that Slim did.

He paused for a minute, straightening up to his full height before leaning back down and over me. The hot heat of his skin radiated onto mine so intently the warmth of his skin seeped into my muscles. "Son would skin my balls if I let somebody take advantage of his pretty baby sister."

Oh my mother heifer.

As if that wasn't enough, I swear to Mary and Joseph I felt his bottom lip press to the skin over my right temple. "I like it when you're all cute and playful," he added.

And, it was a miracle I didn't croak when he stepped away. What in the *hell* was that?

When I glanced over in Shane's direction, he was watching me curiously before taking off with Dex.

Well. That was awkward. And, and, and... holy crap. What was that about cute and playful? It made it sound like he thought of me as a puppy or something. I had to shut down my brain and push what he said out of my head.

Dex is a dick. Dex is a dick. Dex is a dick.

Gah!

I shut the thought in the back of my mind indefinitely.

Debating whether to keep watch at the table or keep my eye on Slim's masterpiece—for the record, it seemed that everything Slim did was a masterpiece of fine lines, delicacy, and color. All the guys at Pins were really good, some better at certain things than others, but I'd always thought that Slim was the most talented. Maybe tied with Dex when he actually worked but usually he won.

After deliberating my options for a split second, I rolled my chair over to watch him tattoo the guy he had hunched over, working on an old pirate ship right smack on the middle of the man's brawny shoulder.

I didn't say a word as I watched him, not wanting to distract him from the man who had been all too excited to request Slim's work an hour before.

But my friend Slim had other thoughts. His green eyes flashed up at me. "What was that about?"

"Huh?" I played stupid.

Slim pulled the gun off the customer's skin, dabbing at the beaded blood before continuing with a shake of his head. "Since when are you guys BFFs?"

I'd learned over the last month how chatty all the guys were, well, specifically Slim and Blake. If I answered his question just remotely weird, I'd bet my first born Slim would jump to some kind of crazy conclusion that I wanted no part of. So I went with the truth. "I heard him fart last night. It kind of broke the ice."

The little whistle he let out told me that was good enough. He snorted and raised an eyebrow before getting back to work. "That'll do it."

CHAPTER THIRTEEN

I was swooning. Unfortunately it wasn't because someone had said something sweet—no one had—but because I was bone tired. After the four hours of sleep we'd gotten after the drive, then all of the running around to set up the booth, and finally the nine hours we had to work the Expo, I was crabby and swooning.

And these guys had dragged me to a bar with Dex's friends.

Apparently no one cared that I was really tired and that I didn't drink. They especially didn't care that all I wanted to do was veg out on the bed in the hotel room with a meal that was more than the nachos and stale fries I had to down at the Expo. If I never saw another plate of nachos or another paper plate with over salted fries on it again, it'd be a day too soon.

"We'll only stay for a little bit," Slim had sworn.

That had been two hours ago. Two hours was not what I considered a little bit. Two hours was the length of a movie. A movie I could gladly be watching in our hotel room beneath the covers of the pull-out. But more than likely I'd probably be asleep the second my head hit the pillows.

"Are you okay?" Shane asked from his spot on the stool next to mine.

I shook my head, giving him a drowsy shrug afterward. "I'm exhausted."

"I was planning on leaving in a minute. Want to catch a cab back to the hotel?" he asked.

Hmm.

I was really tired…

Not tired enough to be stupid and irresponsible though. "I'll just wait for Slim or Dex." Or leave by myself. That was an option I'd willingly pay extra money for to be safe and not take a chance with a stranger.

Dex had disappeared a few minutes ago, leaving the table we'd taken up in a corner. Slim was over at the other side of the bar speaking to people that he knew. It was only my antisocial ass that was still sitting in the same spot we'd been in for two hours while my two coworkers were social butterflies. The bar wasn't exactly some upscale downtown hot spot. Saying it was seedy would be an exaggeration but it wasn't somewhere I'd go by myself. So I used that as an excuse to stay where I was.

Shane shrugged, and it was at that very moment that Dex reappeared, taking his seat on the other side.

As if he could read my mind, he leaned over and sighed. "I'm too old for this shit. You ready to go?"

Hallelujah!

I nodded so quickly and grinned so widely, I knew it was the reason why Dex smiled then. "Be right back."

He got up again and made his way over to Slim who stayed where he was. Dex said something to him before bulldozing his way back where Shane and I were. Only he'd barely covered half the distance when a man standing in his way turned around too quickly and bumped into his chest.

Spilling a small glass of alcohol all over Dex's signature black v-neck.

Obviously I couldn't hear what Dex said to the guy but from the angry lines across his forehead, it wasn't nice. The man who had spilled the drink, only a couple inches shorter than my boss but easily twenty or thirty pounds heavier in the gut, lifted up a finger and pressed the tip of it into Dex's chest.

Even I knew that was the absolute stupidest thing he could have done.

"Shit," I heard Shane mutter as his friend—my boss—lifted both hands up to shove the drunk guy back into a table. "C'mon, let's go get him. He can't get arrested again."

Oh crap.

Shane passed right by me, ticking his head over in the direction Dex was. Climbing over the chair, I followed after him, trying to peep around his figure to see what the hell Dex was doing by that point. From the stable conversations and tones around me, no one had gotten punched. Yet.

"Dex!" Shane yelled futilely. The bar was too loud to hear anything more than a foot in distance away.

I twisted around his frame to see that Dex was fisting the drunk guy's shirt, shaking him pretty violently. All over a spilled drink? Jee-zus.

Shane cut the distance between them. "Dex! Let's go!"

I happened to turn and look over my shoulder at that moment to see the big bouncers at the door fighting their way toward the small—and stupid—spectacle.

"Dex!" Shane yelled again.

This idiot was going to get arrested, and then how would Slim and I get home? Annoyed, I made my way around Shane to reach out and grab Dex's thick forearm. "The bouncers are coming." I shook his arm.

Not paying any attention to me, Dex pulled the drunk guy closer to his face.

I looked over to see that the bouncers were even closer. So I did what *yia-yia* used to do when Will was being a little shit. I pinched his side as hard as I could.

That got his attention.

He swung those bright blue eyes over to me, jaw clenched, mouth grim.

I pinched him again. "Don't get arrested, you friggin' behemoth. C'mon."

Dex blinked twice. He glared at me for a moment before whatever anger or frustration he was feeling melted away in the blink of an eye. He nodded stiffly once, dropping both hands to his sides. With a glance behind my head, he cocked his head in the direction of the exit. Dex gestured me over to him, eyeing the door as his sign that we should get going. Shane followed behind me until we got to Dex, who maneuvered me in front of him as we made our way outside. By some miracle, we caught a taxi in complete silence almost immediately.

Shane slid in first, and as I started to duck to sit in the middle because that was the way we had ridden over with Slim, Dex's hand on my arm stopped me. "Me first."

Okay.

I slid in after him, listening to Shane give the driver the name of our hotel.

Heat hit the side of my face almost immediately.

"Did you call me a behemoth?"

I tilted my head just a little to see that Dex's muscular body was angled toward me, his legs spread wider than necessary, his thigh pressing into mine as his mouth lingered way too close. "What?" I breathed out.

His lips twitched. "You called me a behemoth." I swear the corner of his mouth tilted up.

"Oh." I grinned because yeah, I had. "I did."

Shane's head peeked over Dex's shoulder. "Did you pinch him or was I imagining that?"

At the reminder, Dex started pulling up the side of his shirt where I'd gotten him. All I could see in the dark cab was the sleek outline of his lateral muscles rippling.

I think my mouth watered a little before I caught myself and snapped my eyes over to Shane. "He wasn't listening."

"Don't think anybody's ever pinched me in my life," Dex claimed with a frown.

"You weren't listening!" I insisted.

"I'm gonna have a goddamn bruise. From you," he pointed out the obvious.

"Bro," Shane hummed. "You know your ass can't be getting into trouble again."

I wanted to ask him if he was still under probation. I mean, he'd lost his mind over some guy accidentally spilling a drink on him. What *wouldn't* make him lose his mind?

Almost as if he was reading my mind, Dex made an irritated noise in his throat. "He spilled shit on me."

I snickered and mumbled under my breath, "Wearing a black shirt." Like that was noticeable.

I must have spoken too loudly because Dex's head snapped around to look me in the face.

With a one-shoulder shrug, I twisted my body to look out the window. "Just saying. Spray a little Resolve on it and it's fine. You didn't need to get your panties in a wad."

Shane snorted.

Dex grunted but I ignored him and settled my forehead against the window of the cab, listening to Shane strike up a conversation about having watched The Avengers recently. I'd overheard from Slim that Dex's first tattoo had been a Captain America shield somewhere on him. Where exactly it was located, I had no clue.

To be honest, I thought that was sort of cute.

Big, bad Dex with his inked up arms, black bike, the f-bomb dropping dick in a motorcycle club… liked superheroes? Unreal.

So all right, it was pretty friggin' cute.

I pulled out a twenty dollar bill from my purse to pay for the trip when Dex pushed my hand away and nudged me out of the cab. I felt like a drunken prostitute on the way through the hotel lobby and up the elevator with the two friends. Shane said bye on his floor while we went up silently to the twelfth floor.

We were about halfway down the hall when I remembered something Dex had said at the bar about being too old. "How old are you?"

"Thirty-three," he answered.

I stopped walking and stared at him. Thirty-three? I guess it made sense. He had his own business. A business that had been open for six years, so it wasn't like he could have been too much younger despite the fact that his looks landed him somewhere in his mid twenties instead of early thirties.

"Huh," I huffed, taking in the lean frame in a fitted shirt. "You don't look like you're thirty."

Dex shot me a sidelong look that could have passed as a smile. "I feel like it most of the time."

Neither one of us said anything else as we made it into the room. I grabbed my pajamas and ducked into the bathroom to shower the smell of sweat from the bar off and get ready for bed. By the time I made it back out, Dex was sitting on the edge of the mattress in basketball shorts and a t-shirt with a bottle of lotion between his legs, one hand massaging his opposite arm.

"Are you putting lotion on?" I asked.

Those true blue eyes flickered up to mine. "Yeah. It preserves the colors. See?" He slid the sleeve of his t-shirt up to his shoulder, pointing at the solid shiny black ink of his right arm. "Gotta be careful with all this black. I don't want it lookin' gray in a few years."

"Oh," was my brilliant response. I blinked. "How many do you have?"

Dex smiled, that slow creeping smile that I recognized as a sign that he was amused. "Only five." He watched me standing there for a minute longer. "Wanna see 'em?"

No.

Who was I kidding? I nodded anyway.

He slid forward on the edge of the bed, his hands dropping to his knees before he started yanking up the material on one side of his shorts. Heavy muscle filled in his thigh covered in black ink. A tattoo that looked like the outline of a sugar skull—the ones I'd studied in my Mexican Folk Art class in high school—stamped his leg. The letters 'WMC' and 1974 were tattooed in individual banners directly below the figure with loose, almost loopy lettering.

"This is my club piece," he explained.

My eyes were glued to the huge skull that wrapped around the side of his thick thigh. "Why'd you do your thigh?" My Dad and Sonny had theirs on their arms. I'd caught the bottom of Trip's on his back.

Dex shrugged. "I had other plans."

I coughed. "So... where are the rest of your tattoos?"

Oh boy.

His mouth slowly melted into a smile, that unblinking gaze absorbing everything in its path—me. After a minute, he sat up and held his arms out in front of him. "You've seen these."

I had but not in great detail and not without checking them out on the sly.

"What are they though?" I asked him, genuinely curious.

Dex looked down at them. "Different ideas I came up with." Flexing his right wrist, and his left, he looked up again and shrugged. "Sometimes I'll get ideas from random shit I see. Like this one," he held out the arm with the configuration of fading triangles. "Went to the planetarium with my niece and I just couldn't get it out of my head."

He then held up his other arm, the one with the wing wrapped around it. "Other times I'll dream of stuff."

But it was more than that. He dreamed of things that looked angelic? I had dreams of zombies chasing me and breaking into houses, not things like his. Not landscapes of abstract colors. Then again, maybe an artist had thoughts like those and I definitely wasn't an artist.

He started tugging his shirt up and over his head, and I had to physically tell myself not to say anything stupid because I'd gone brain dead. All I could think of while watching Dex sitting there with his bright, beautiful tattoos and his equally beautiful but tired face, was that the world was unfair.

"This was my first one," he said, pointing to the infamous Captain America shield on his left pectoral while I ogled his six-pack instead. Or was it an eight-pack?

"And this is Uriel," he explained, pointing at a huge red octopus that wrapped over from his back to the right side of his chest. The same one I'd seen framed in his office. Shirtless, I could tell that the red I'd seen on his neck was a tentacle so detailed it almost looked alive.

Uriel was forgotten the moment I saw his flat, dark nipples. I didn't think anyone could blame me for caring less about his tattoos when I could use my eyes to visually molest the definition of his bare chest and the two friggin' rings he had through his nipples.

"You don't like 'em?" he asked.

I couldn't remember how to speak.

"Uh…" I blinked, searching for those things called words and sentences that people had been using for millennia to communicate. "Wah… why Uriel?" I somehow managed to ask.

But really, I was still looking at his upper body and not at Uriel, his red octopus, specifically.

And as hot as Dex was, when he smiled broadly it was enough for me to tear my eyes away from the dream he was half-naked. Because Dex's smile was the nicest I'd ever seen. It was wide and genuine and playful and so rare. And it made my insides flare.

"It's my favorite animal," he answered casually.

"An octopus?" I'd figured he'd go for something different. Way different. Maybe a tiger? A dragon?

Dex nodded, not disturbed at all about my confusion. "They're smarter than people think," he explained. "They know how to problem solve. They're curious little fuckers—"

"And they squirt ink," I told him with an understanding laugh, though I had no doubt he knew that already.

Another glorious smile lit his face. "Exactly."

"Huh." Feeling just a little like a jackass, I smiled back. "That's pretty perfect."

He shrugged, just a hint of color on his tan cheeks. "It's all right."

"It's really cool."

Dex grinned even wider. "Ritz—"

"Why do you call me that?" I finally asked him after more than a month of silently letting him get away with it.

Another slow smile welcomed me. "That day you got hired? Sonny called to rip me a new one, I couldn't hear him well when he called you Ris. I thought he called you Ritz. By the time I figured it out," he shrugged, "I'd already gotten it stuck in my head."

Another brilliant response. "Oh."

When neither one of us said anything, and suddenly uncomfortable, I walked over to the pullout bed I'd left a mess and fell onto it. Yanking the covers up and over my body with a yawn. I could hear Dex settling onto his bed, the springs on the mattress creaking under his weight, the sheets shuffling every which way.

"Dex?"

"Yeah?" he answered.

I yawned again, rolling to my side. "If you feel another Northern wind coming on tonight, aim it the other way, will you?"

The laugh that blasted out of him put a smile on my face as I fell asleep.

CHAPTER FOURTEEN

By the end of the second day at the expo, I would have bartered my first born for some sort of cloaking spell that made me invisible to douche bags.

My brief conversations with the drunkards that stumbled to the booth with one hand wrapped around a beer bottle and another shoved down the front of their pants usually all went along the lines of:

"So if I get this expensive ass tattoo, do I get you for free?"

"No."

"How about a kiss?"

"No."

"Just a little one."

"No."

"A hand—"

The time Dex was around when a guy started going down that route had ended with Dex grumbling out, "Fuck off."

Oh Jesus.

He didn't even spare a glance behind him to see the man who was bothering me, but apparently, the drunk idiot didn't even need to see his face to get the message.

"Dex!" I hissed at him for being so rude when the guy only partially deserved it.

"Babe," he responded, completely unapologetic and not giving half a shit. Then again, when did he? If I thought he'd pay attention, I'd try to give him a lesson in being polite.

Pointless, right?

Then there was Shane. Shane who came over every chance he got and what felt like every chance he didn't have. If I wouldn't have heard so much about him sleeping around with random women the day before, I would have sworn he had a man crush on Dex.

Maybe he did.

He must have warmed up to me after the night before because he'd make his way to the counter and look me right in the face or down at my chest. Blatantly.

Like there was anything there to look at.

It had first started off with him, smiling, and leaning in. "Can I see your ink?"

Before we left Austin, I'd been mentally prepared for how hot and humid the city would be when I'd stuffed elbow-length sweaters and cardigans into my duffel bag. Neither one of the guys had said anything but I didn't want it to be completely obvious to a crowd of body art lovers, that my skin was naked.

"I don't have any," I told him in a low voice.

He totally didn't believe me at all because he frowned but mysteriously let the question go. "Got a boyfriend?"

I'd been busy organizing invoices from the day before, so I only bothered to glance up at him before shaking my head. "Nope."

"You really aren't fooling around with Dexter?"

"Nope."

"I don't believe it."

He left and came back a couple hours later, this time Dex had run to the bathroom between appointments. Slim was busy with a client and I'd been sitting there, people-watching.

The first thing Shane did was tilt his chin up. "You sure you aren't...?"

Wanting to hide my irritation because *Jesus*! How many more times did he have to kill my self-esteem by reminding me that a man that looked like black sin on tan skin didn't like me in that way? There was only so much my pride could handle.

"Nope." I popped the last consonant to emphasize the fact that I wasn't and would never ever sleep with my boss.

"I don't get it," he murmured like he was trying to disprove a mathematical theorem.

A groaned sigh managed to escape from my mouth. "I'm not his type." Okay, wrong thing to say. I amended my words as quickly as I could. "He's not my type."

The noise he made in response sounded like a mixture of a hiccup and a snicker. "You need glasses?" His eyes drifted to my cleavage again. "He threatened to break my fingers if I made a move on you. We've never had a problem sharing before..."

There went my appetite.

Before he had the chance to make my stomach roll, I spotted Dex coming down the aisle, wiping his hands on his jeans as his eyes locked in on Shane's form. The minute he was within speaking distance, he darted his gaze over to me. His gaze dipped down to my collarbones in annoyance.

"Babe, button up your fuckin' sweater. Everybody can see your tits like that."

Holy crap.

I glanced down to make sure that my boobs weren't hanging out for everyone to see, and they weren't. My shirt was racerback tank, the scooped front hit clearly above my bra-line for the friggin' record. I opened my mouth to argue with him, and then closed it. The last thing I wanted was to argue with him back and forth, then have Shane assume that that was... foreplay or something ridiculous.

I buttoned up the length of tiny buttons, looking everywhere but in front of me. Dex was talking to Shane in a low voice. His lips were moving but I couldn't hear what was being said between the two of them.

After a minute, Shane inclined his head and took off in the direction of his booth. I'd walked past it a couple of times already and I knew exactly where it was.

When he turned around, Dex glared at me. It was immature but I was irritated by what he'd said though I really would prefer not getting hit on by drunk strangers. The look I gave him in return was scathing. Well, as scathing as I was capable of.

There were a great many things that I learned in the three days we spent in Houston. Some things were more informative than others. Some things I would have rather not learned. And, a fraction were inevitable in this path called life.

I learned more about tattooing techniques than I could ever have imagined. With Slim and even Dex leading me around to different booths on Saturday and Sunday, they showed me the best and unfortunately, the worst too. The best: creativity. The worst: inexperience. The inexperience was spelled out with sloppy letters and terrible outlines. Another big thing I learned that seemed essential: Pins was well-known. There was a constant stream of people looking at the binders we'd brought and asking to see who was available. I was surprised by the pride nipping at my chest when I saw how respected they were.

I also learned that there were a lot of exhibitionists into body art. A lot. I hadn't seen that many half-naked women in my life and that included the time I spent trolling porn websites when I was itching to relieve some tension. I also learned that there was no inch of flesh on a body that couldn't be tattooed. For example, an armpit. A penis. Balls. Palate. Tongue. The inside of a lip. Downtown lips! Face! I mentally made a decision that if I ever did get a tattoo, it wouldn't be in any of those places. I'd leave that to the souls that were way more brave than I could ever be.

Lastly, the thing that was slapped in my face over and over again was that Dex was a vagina magnet. I already knew that from the conversation I'd overheard with Shane, but I swallowed it and shoved away. He didn't stop to speak to any of the women who dropped by our booth, and I wasn't sure how to take that, so I didn't. Back in Austin he'd kept that part of his life private at least since I'd run into him at the body shop. I refused to waste a minute wondering what his numbers were like.

It wasn't any of my business but lord knows I would have paid for his ass if he wasn't my boss and I wasn't confused with the way I felt about him.

After an exhausting Saturday, where we spent more than thirteen hours at the Expo, we ate dinner at some Chinese restaurant nearby and then promptly passed out watching Rush Hour in the hotel room with Slim narrating the entire movie perfectly.

Sunday was just as hectic. It seemed like every other person who had bought a ticket to the convention wanted Dex or Slim to tattoo them, so I had to balance out the requests as well as I could while also taking advantage of watching them work. It'd always seemed weird to me when we were at Pins to look at them but in Houston our proximity was so close and it was different circumstances, that it felt fine. If you were shy then you wouldn't exactly get tattooed in the middle of an expo, right?

Just before we started taking our stuff down, Slim let me tattoo the tiniest heart in existence onto his wrist bone in celebration of our successful visit to Houston.

"But what if I mess up?" I'd asked him in a panic, holding the gun somehow without shaking.

Dex was sitting next to him, wrapping a client's new inner bicep tattoo.

Slim grinned. "Iris, it's a little thing. I'll fix it if you mess up or Dex will. It's not a big deal."

My mouth curled down into a grimace. "I'm scared."

"Just try it," he insisted.

I shot a glance over at Dex who was looking at me in amusement. "Can you fix it if I mess up?" I asked him in a whisper.

He gave me the most indulgent smile in the world. "Course I will, babe."

"You're sure?" I asked Slim, who waved me forward. I blew out a deep breath and nodded. "All right." A few minutes later, I'd somehow managed to hold down the right amount of pressure, follow the outline better than I expected, and then I thrust the gun at Slim. "You finish it, I can't do it."

He blew out a raspberry, shaking his head. "You can finish it another day. Deal?"

"Maybe," I offered him.

He winked. "Deal."

Dex leaned over to inspect my job as he plucked the gloves off his hands. "Nice work."

These guys did the most intricate, multicolored pieces I'd ever seen and they were complimenting me on a simple heart shape? Guh. I think I was kind of growing fond of them and that only made me feel worse about putting in my notice when we got back home.

We packed up our crap, hauling it back and forth from the convention hall to the truck in what seemed like a million trips. After the last one, Dex waved me into the front seat while he got into the driver side. "Ritz, you can sit in the front since you aren't gonna sleep."

I shrugged, thinking that made total sense. Slim didn't argue or bat an eyelash as he got into the backseat. They talked about the things they'd liked the most, the people they had seen, and chatted about how popular fluorescent tattoos had gotten and how they might have to look into the ink needed for them.

"Rainbow-Ris, did you have a good time?" Slim asked, adding in the nickname he'd picked up from a client on Saturday.

Shifting in the seat to look at him from around the headrest, I nodded, smiling because he'd been the one that went out of his way to make sure I did. "A lot of fun even though you snore." I tilted my head in Dex's direction, waggling my eyebrows at Slim, "and this guy's gas could fuel my car."

"I don't snore," Slim argued, but I was too busy looking at Dex over my shoulder while trying to hold back a laugh. Dex smirked, keeping his attention straight forward.

"Thanks for bringing me, guys." I told them shyly after a few minutes of traveling. Settling back into the front passenger seat, I glanced at Dex, who had his eyes on the road.

Dark eyes slicked over to mine for a split second before he resumed his focus on the highway in front. Slim rattled on about random things for a while before falling asleep, leaving only old Pantera playing faintly in the background.

"I swear I won't fall asleep," Dex muttered some time later.

"I believe you," I told him, taking in his silhouette. "But I'm too paranoid to sleep. Sorry."

His fingers drummed on the steering wheel. "You're not flippin' out as much," he noted.

That was true. I wasn't. "You don't drive like an idiot so it doesn't make me as nervous, I guess." Was that rude? "No offense," I added.

Dex chuckled, smiling just barely. Those eyes darted in my direction again. "You're a vegetarian?" he asked out of the blue.

I did that whole creepy side-glance thing at his comment. How the heck did he know? "Yeah." I paused. "How'd you know?"

He made a little noise with his tongue. "Never seen you eat meat, and then I saw the way you looked when we brought you that hot dog. I thought you were gonna puke."

He did notice. How about that. "I threw up in my mouth a little bit."

"That's pretty fuckin' disgustin', babe." What was funny was that he laughed instead of making a face.

I snorted. "Sorry." But I wasn't sorry. It was true. That hot dog had looked like an old turd.

"Don't be sorry," he grunted, cutting me another glance. "You don't eat meat, you don't eat meat. Next time just tell us so I don't have to see you lookin' like shit."

Looking like shit? I turned to look at him and made an ugly scoffing noise in my throat. "Jesus, that's rude."

"You know what I mean."

Yeah, I did know what he meant. He thought I looked even worse than usual. Dick face. "Yeah, yeah. Whatever you say."

He didn't say anything else but he did shake his head in response. "I got two good eyes, Ritz. You're fine. You should already know I don't mean half the shit that comes outta my mouth."

He had. At least half a dozen times, so I should know better than to take too much of his verbal crap to heart. Plus, why should I care? It wasn't like I was planning on being best friends with him. Right?

"I know," I sighed, turning my attention to look out the window.

Neither one of us said anything else for the longest. I sat there and thought about telling Dex that I was quitting and the guilt swamped me. God, I felt like a jackass when I had no reason to. It wasn't like I was a special employee. The work was pretty easy, he could find a hundred other people to fill the position.

Still, it sucked.

I felt like my father. A coward.

A coward that had come into town and asked his long-lost son for money.

And a coward that had disappeared as quickly as he'd popped up. Which speaking of, I hadn't brought up to Sonny again after he'd been so pissed off over the situation. Dex might know more and he'd be a more reasonable person to talk to since he wasn't emotionally attached to the situation.

"Hey, Dex?"

The smartass that had somehow popped up over the course of the last three days replied, "Hey, Ritz."

Oh lord.

"By any chance, did you see Sonny's dad when he was here?" I asked him as casually as possible.

Keeping his eyes straight ahead, his mouth twitched. "Nope."

Nope? That was all I was going to get out of him?

"But I did hear about it," he thankfully kept going. His eyes flickered over in my direction. "Why?"

"I'm just curious." Extremely curious but he didn't need to know that.

"I know he asked for a loan," he offered in a gentle voice that made me wary. "And I know Luther didn't give it to him."

"Oh." I paused, redirecting my eyes to the window. "Huh."

I wanted to know what the money was for. And even though I didn't want to, I wanted to know what he'd been doing the last eight years. Why he hadn't bothered coming to see Will—to see me.

The questions sank to the pit of my stomach like lead, dragging my mood down with it. Until I thought about what it was like to go through a million and a half things without my father.

I didn't need him.

I didn't. Not today. Not tomorrow. Never.

"Trip told me the shit he pulled on you and your ma," Dex spoke suddenly.

My muscles tensed up.

"I remember hearin' about him movin' away when I was a kid," he explained. "I didn't know he left y'all though."

The urge to blabber out that he'd left a year before I got sick was right on my tongue but I fought it back.

"He never came back after your ma died?" Dex asked in a low, gentle voice.

I had to swallow back the bitter sting in my throat. "Nope. I mean, he came right at the end. Right before she died. Then he left again the day afterward." My voice cracked just a little but it was enough to shame me for being so emotional about something that had happened forever ago.

And it was enough for Dex to notice.

He reached over and tapped the side of my leg with the back of his tattooed index finger. "That shit's not worth your tears, babe."

It wasn't exactly comfort in *yia-yia's* arms but his light nudge was enough to center me. To make me remember that man wasn't worth my tears or even my thoughts. My mind was all for it but my body felt otherwise.

I sniffed.

"I'm serious, don't go cryin'," Dex added in that same even tone he'd used a moment before.

I nodded. Whether it was to his words or myself, I'm not sure, but I sucked in a deep breath and thought of my mom. My sweet mom who had loved a man, lost him, and never fully recovered. I never wanted to be like that. I never wanted to end up in the same shoes. I'd lost enough in my life to risk losing even more.

"I remember when your dad came back once a long time ago. He came by to see Sonny but Son didn't a give a shit by then, ya know. Told him to fuck off because Son was pissed at something."

Something.

The memory of Sonny's call a few weeks after my mom had passed away was an easy memory. One of us always called the other at least every month back then, my half-brother had always been super easygoing. But that call, when I'd told him that our dad had left again, Sonny had lost it.

Absolutely lost it.

It might have been because the older Taylor had only stuck around a few years in his life, and even when he was in Austin while Sonny was a kid, he was a distant figure. Our dad had never committed himself in any way to Sonny's mom, though I'd learn years later that the word commitment meant nothing when he broke three hearts in Florida.

Regardless, it didn't hit me until I was a teenager and Sonny had gone out of his way to have a relationship with Will and me. At least we'd gotten Curt Taylor longer than he had.

So when Sonny found out that our birth father had left—again—right after Mom died... he'd been furious.

And I think that Sonny swallowed up all the anger that Will and I had, for us.

"Your old man is a fuckin' prick."

That wasn't the first time I'd heard those words. I shrugged. "You should have heard the Greek names my grandma had for him. I wouldn't have been surprised if she had a voodoo doll in his image under her bed."

He pursed his lips together. "She's gone?"

Almost immediately after I went into remission but I wasn't that specific with him. "She had a heart attack in her sleep a couple years ago." What I also didn't explain to him was that she'd sold her house a few months before she passed away to pay my medical bills.

"Goddamn." Dex's long, masculine fingers tapped against the steering wheel. Lifting a hand, he pressed the back of it to his face. "That...that fuckin' sucks, honey."

I blew out a breath and laughed just a little, more nervous and resigned than anything. "It could have been worse. He could have been abusive, or...I'm not sure. I just know that it could have been a lot worse, I guess."

Dex glanced at me out of the corner of his eye, jaw shifting in the brief silence that followed what I said before he spoke again. "My pa was a piece of shit, too. Always yellin' at my sisters, talkin' smack to my ma, tryin' to beat my ass when he could. Constantly drunk, stealin' money from Ma or whoever was stupid enough to hang around him so he could hit up the bar and get so shit-faced he'd fall asleep on the floor most days. Worthless waste of life especially after they kicked him outta the Widows when they got tired of his shit."

By about halfway through him speaking, I'd been so stunned that I'd shifted in my seat to look at him. Where the heck his honesty had come from, I had no clue but I was sucked in completely.

When there was an awkward break in the conversation, I blurted out a question. "What happened to him?"

He sighed so painfully, I wouldn't have imagined a man like Dex could harbor so much resentment in him. He'd never seemed like the type to be disappointed in others. He usually went from normal to straight up pissed off.

"He got arrested for distributin' when I was eighteen. Haven't seen his face or spoken to him since."

"Not once?" I asked him in a low voice.

Dex shook his head roughly. Anger and frustration seeped from his pores, stinging my chest with his unease over the past. "Not since he blamed me and Ma for his mess. Told us it was our fault for lettin' him get away with his shit for so long. Said we should've gotten him help. Can you believe that shit? I spent years tryin' to get him to spend time with me and my sisters instead of with his vodka and he blames us for bein' a drunk motherfucker?

The last time I talked to him he said I should get used to bein' a disappointment 'cuz that's all I'd ever be." He snickered bitterly. "Just like him."

Anger flooded my veins. "What a piece of shit."

Holy crap. Did I really just say that?

I looked over at Dex to see him glancing over at me. Whether he was shocked or amused, I had no clue. All I got was a bob of his head. "You have no idea, babe."

I didn't know Dex well, but I felt confident with what I told him next. I wasn't trying to suck-up to him—why would I?—or make him feel better, but I thought he should know I didn't believe his dad's prophecy. "You're nothing like that—like him—you know that, right?"

"I hope to God I'm not."

"You're not," I confirmed. "You're a good man, Dex."

He shrugged, but I could tell he was thinking, processing. "I don't ever wanna be half like him. Back then, I was out on bail for some dumbass charges—," I wouldn't call assault a dumbass charge but I'd keep that thought to myself. "Hearin' those words outta his voice. Doomin' me to repeat his miserable, drunk life? I swore right then I was never gonna be like him. I have his temper. I say stupid shit I don't mean sometimes but that's it."

I said the next few words without even thinking. "You're not." I looked at him. "At all."

The silence after that was so crushing, it made me feel awkward. Heavy. Pressurized. I knew this chance was rare, so for some reason, I kept going. "What happened after that?"

"After I got out of county, I left Austin, went up to Dallas for a couple of years and sorted my shit out. When I was ready, I came back home."

His version of the story was so short and perfectly cut out, I couldn't wrap my mind around it. He'd paid his penance, and then gotten out and tried to steer his life in a different direction. That was admirable.

Dex turned to look at me over his shoulder. He looked at me so long I should have worried about him keeping his eyes on the road but there was no one there. "You think I'm an asshole, babe? Like really an asshole? Not just a grump or whatever the hell you call it?"

He was being serious. So serious, so innately vulnerable right then that I felt something warm and heavy paint over my insides, warning me that this moment was something for Dex.

Something that I had a feeling, an instinctual confirmation, he didn't share with anyone.

"I think you do some asshole things," I answered him honestly. "But I don't think you're really an asshole, Dex."

Truth. Truth. Truth. This was the man who sat me on the counter after I'd been yelled at, bought me a coke and fed me bread. This was the same man who bitched at me for walking to my car alone. The same man who carried me to my bed. Dexter Locke was the man who didn't give me a hard time about not drinking and kindly praised my attempt at a tattoo.

He had more points going in the opposite direction of the asshole-meter than he did going toward it.

"You're actually probably one of the kindest people I've ever met when you aren't—"

"Bein' a dick?" he suggested in a low voice.

It was impossible not to smile. "I was going to say grumpy but that works too. The point is, you two are polar opposites. I'm pretty confident you wouldn't treat your loved ones the way he did."

He cocked his neck from one side to the other as if trying to stretch the muscles. A long huff escaped from his mouth. "I've always told myself that when I have kids, I'm gonna to spoil the shit out of 'em."

I couldn't help but smile, though I kept my gaze forward. Dex as a dad? A bad-mouthed dad?

Dex smiled right then, morphing something inside of me that I couldn't completely recognize. The moment and intent was too heavy for me to bear. I didn't want to think of what all this honesty was doing to my insides. "You know what?"

He grunted.

"Your kids will probably come out of the womb saying the f-bomb."

"Fuck," he laughed loudly, confirming my guess. "You're probably right, babe."

I tilted my face to look at him, meeting those blue eyes that I knew even without the light, were the brightest blue I'd ever seen. "Little f-bomb dropping hell raisers. I can totally see it."

CHAPTER FIFTEEN

Don't vomit.

Don't vomit.

Don't vomit.

Oh God, I was totally going to vomit.

You will not throw up, balk, or gag, I told myself.

Over and over again.

The letter I'd typed up the night before shook in my hand. The paper that stated to my employer I was giving my two week's notice to find a replacement. Ef me.

I'd felt so guilty the days before as I hooked up my laptop to Sonny's printer. I kept thinking about Slim and his friendliness, Blake and his patience, and Blue and her quiet nature.

But I'd be lying if I said the person I thought of the most wasn't Dex.

All I could think of was the version of Dex I'd encountered in the truck on the trip back and forth to Houston. The one who talked to me about installing cameras and putting in extra bills into the cash registers at Mayhem to find their thief. The man who had opened up to me about his own crap-ass dad.

That was the person I'd thought of as I waited for the printer to give me my notice.

And it was that man that had me shaking in my boots at just the idea that I had to tell him I was leaving.

To my surprise, only Blake and Blue were at the shop when I'd driven by on my first attempt to drop off my notice on

Monday. When I'd shown up for work on Tuesday, it was Slim who opened with me.

Each moment longer I had to wait, the more nervous and guilty I felt.

So when Dex showed up about halfway through the evening at Pins on Tuesday, I had to double check to make sure my big girl panties were on and finally go break the news.

And still, I wanted to vomit out my nerves.

Only the problem was that he'd shown up in a mood. He'd tilted his head up at me and Slim as he walked passed us and disappeared into his office. And that was my sign that something was adrift in the world of Dex.

Shit.

By the time I made my way into his office, he was sitting behind his desk looking too intently at the computer screen on front of him. The rim of his cap was tugged low on his head. A cigarette peeped out from between his ear and hat.

"Dex?" I asked him in a small voice from the doorframe.

He didn't even bother looking up. "Sup, Ritz?"

"You have a minute?"

"Now's not the best time," he warned. "I'm tryin' to sort this shit out."

What shit he was trying to sort out...I had no clue. But time was a ticking.

"I really need to talk to you though," I insisted.

Dex blew out a raspberry from between his pink lips. "One minute, babe."

Sheesh.

"What'cha need?"

I couldn't summon the courage I needed to tell him verbally, so I shoved the paper across the desk.

Wordlessly, Dex picked up the paper, his smooth forehead was already lined with rows of frustration at whatever was bugging him. Those bright blue eyes moved in a line across the paper twice.

And then he balled it up and tossed it into the trash can, his expression unchanged.

Dex said one word and one word only. "No."

Umm...

"What?" I asked him in a squeaky voice.

His attention was already back on the computer screen he'd been glued to when I walked in. He simply lifted a single shoulder in a shrug and repeated himself. "No."

"No, what?" What the hell?

Dex repeated the two letter word again.

"No...you don't want me to finish out my last two weeks? Or—"

He huffed, his eyes still locked on the monitor. "No, you ain't quittin' on us."

That was absolutely the last thing I expected him to say. I scratched my nose. "I mean, I can probably swing both jobs if it takes a little longer than two weeks to find someone else."

"Ritz, I don't have time for this shit right now," he huffed. "You ain't leavin' and that's that. You want more money or what?"

"No! Jesus, Dex. I'm not trying to play a mind game with you or something. You have no idea how much I appreciate everything you've done for me, but I figured you could find someone who fits in better than I do," I explained to him honestly. Well, as honest as I could get without admitting that I'd started looking for another job almost immediately after he hired me.

"You fit in fine."

"I don't have any tattoos. Half the time I think you don't really care for me either. You can find someone else that you like more."

The way he looked over at me was so slow it threw me off. Like he was thinking, or absorbing what I'd said. Dex tugged his signature black cap off his head and tossed it onto the edge of his desk, sighing loudly. "Babe, seriously, I don't have time for this. You aren't leavin'. I don't give a fuck anymore if you have ink on you or not, and if anybody else gives a shit, they can shut the fuck up. You're fine here. You're stayin' here."

His words felt like a punch to the gut. You know, if a punch to the gut could be a pleasant thing.

Because, I mean, The Dick wouldn't just instruct me that I wasn't leaving if he genuinely didn't feel that way. I knew it. I knew that. I should be outraged that he was telling I wasn't allowed to quit. Then again, I'd been having issues accepting the idea that I'd be leaving Pins behind to work at a daycare for nearly half the hourly pay.

If I really wanted to go, I could just walk out right then and never come back.

"Don't even think about it, Ritz," Dex grumbled from his spot. He wasn't paying attention to the screen anymore, he had his gaze locked on me, his eyes intense. "You walk out, and I'll go get you."

It was completely inappropriate that his words brought a shiver up my spine.

"Call your other job back, tell 'em you aren't comin' in, and then I have an order I need you to place."

"I already told them I was taking the job."

He raised an eyebrow. "And I'm tellin' you you aren't takin' it. I've already trained you. You want more money, I can swing a little more your way until it's been a year. I already told you I'd add you to the insurance plan in September. And I don't wanna talk about this anymore, babe."

What in the world had told me that this would be easy? That I should be worried about telling him that I was quitting?

Arguing with him was futile, I knew that but I tried again anyway. "But—"

Dex scrubbed his hands over his face, his eyes wide with intent. "Babe, I've handpicked everythin' and everyone in here. I know what I want and I get what I want," he breathed. "And I keep what's mine."

After cleaning up and making sure none of the guys needed anything before I left, I was running home a bit later than usual. There were a few things I wanted to get from the drugstore that I forgot to pick up before work. I pulled into the first Walgreens that didn't look totally sketchy, bought new razors and lip balm, and headed the rest of the way to Sonny's.

My mind was usually in a million different places, but all I was focused on at the moment was getting in, eating and vegging out on the couch to relax. With only Monday off because of the Expo and the stress I'd put myself under at the thought of quitting Pins, my body was suffering from the long days we had. Not to mention the fact that my brain hadn't stopped running different scenarios and ideas on what I could do to change my life's current situation forever for the better.

I'd been given a second chance, it only seemed fair that I take advantage of it. What was the purpose of wasting years, months, weeks, days, minutes, even friggin' moments of life, after everything I'd been through? My mom and *yia-yia* had done so much for me. I had to figure out something.

Sonny hadn't come from beginnings that much more different than mine. He had a good job, a house and—except for this crap with our sperm donor—security. There was a reliable future ahead of him.

If Dex could come out of his father's shadow, somehow manage to stay in the supposedly reformed version of the same motorcycle club who had lost half its members over the years, moved passed the years he spent in jail, and built a successful business... there was newfound hope in the world.

If they could do it, so could I. It was just a matter of time.

I'd barely pulled the car into the open spot right in front of the house when I happened to look down the street in the opposite direction I'd come in from. And what I saw made the hairs on the back of my neck prickle up. I forgot all about eating and watching the History Channel.

There were three men straddling old school bikes two houses down. Three men I could barely see in the dark under the luminescence of the street lamp. It was the same friggin' guys from the party and two of the same guys who had driven down the street. The one with the shaved head was in the middle as before, his big body looked incredibly imposing from where he was rooted.

Shit!

Double shit.

Something in me told me that wasn't right. These guys weren't like Trip or Luther, or the other people I'd watched while at Mayhem. These guys weren't a part of Sonny's club.

So I did what any somewhat intelligent woman that's watched too many movies did—I hauled my ass out of the car, kept my focus on the door, slid my three keys between my knuckles for protection Wolverine style, and slammed the door shut the first nanosecond I was in.

And then I shrieked, "Sonny!"

"You're sure?"

I glared at the dark haired man across the table and nodded slowly. We were sitting at the dining room table while I scarfed down toast and a warm glass of milk before bed. This was normal behavior.

If only there weren't creepy ass bikers down the street.

And if only Sonny didn't currently look like he was fighting every cell in his body to unleash something ugly that was residing beneath his light brown eyes.

"They're the same guys." I bit into my toast. "I recognize them from when I left the bar that night, and I swear they drove down the street a couple weeks ago looking over here in a weird way. They have jackets instead of vests, and there's a big bald guy that looks familiar."

His attention was focused on the wall while his hands propped up his chin. "Fuck," he muttered. "Fuck, fuck, fuck."

My question was calm. "What is it?"

His eyes stayed on the wall.

All right, he wasn't going to tell me that either, so I was going to plan B.

I reached out to touch his hand, trying so hard not to let the tiny nip of fear in my gut swallow me whole. "Sonny, did you do something?"

He slammed his eyes shut and grunted. His hands fisted into tight balls on the table as he blew out a long breath.

"If something happened, I'll help you," I promised him. Because I would. There wasn't much I wouldn't do for him, and that included letting him use me as an alibi if he'd done something awful.

Sonny's fingers uncurled just enough to wrap around my elbow, squeezing just lightly. "I didn't do anything, Rissy."

Jesus F. Christ. He called me Rissy. He only called me Rissy when he had bad news to tell me.

"What is it?"

He groaned, earning him a poke in the rib.

"Are they like your… arch enemies or something?" I asked him quietly, setting the bread back onto the plate. I probably sounded like an idiot with that terminology, but I didn't know his biker lingo, and I thought that description worked well enough when his cheek quirked up for a split second before his lips hardened.

He leaned back in his chair, clenching his eyes closed. "Kind of but it's not like that." He paused. "They're part of a group of wannabes in San Antonio that aren't exactly fans of the MC's territory here."

Oh my God, I was living in a real-life television series.

I blinked at him, confused as hell. "I thought you said you guys weren't doing stuff anymore." I pushed the plate away, leaning toward him.

He was going to tell me the truth, damn it. My mom had told me that back when my dad had left the MC, they'd been associating with drug distributors, whatever the hell that meant. I could clearly remember Sonny telling me that president, Luther's old nutted self that'd been making out with a much younger woman at the bar, had split the club up, cleaning it out after his wife had gotten murdered in retaliation.

He dropped his gaze down to press his forehead to one of his upturned palms, closing his eyes in the process. "It's nothing like that, Ris," he promised. "It's not me or the Club they have business with."

That little bit of information was better than nothing, but it didn't mean I wasn't going to fish for more. "Okay, so why are they here?"

"I'm sorry, kid, but I can't drag you into this, okay?" he murmured, still looking down. "Don't worry about them, all right?"

Telling me not to worry would be the equivalent of telling me not to have my period.

But I wasn't about to stress him out more than he already was, so I mustered my most bullshit face. "You're sure?"

He nodded slowly, darn it.

"Okay," I agreed hesitantly.

Sonny's features softened at my weak ass smile. "Iris." In a second he had dropped down to his knees, placing his palms on each of mine. "It'll be fine," he assured me.

Listening to him was one of my life's dumbest decisions.

CHAPTER SIXTEEN

There were a lot of things that immediately let me know as soon as I woke up that something was wrong.

Seriously wrong.

The top drawer of the dresser was open, and I never left any drawers open. Keeping them closed was a neurotic tendency of mine.

My cell phone was on the bed instead of the nightstand where I'd left it charging before I fell asleep.

And the third was that the door to the bedroom was also closed. I never closed the door because I was paranoid about screaming and not having someone hear me.

My first thought after my brain decoded the clues was that Sonny had come in at some point during the night. Everything besides the drawer and my phone was in place, so I tried to think of what I should do. Luckily, my first instinct had been to check my messages and when I unlocked the screen, I saw that it'd been the right step.

If I don't leave you a note on the kitchen counter,

call Dex ASAP. My phone and other stuff is in your drawer.

Tell him what you saw.

The three messages were from Sonny at two o'clock in the morning. Thirty minutes after I'd gone to bed and left him sitting in the kitchen shooting off several text messages one right after the other.

I'd known something was wrong and that realization choked my insides, making me throw back the sheets and run out of the bedroom as quickly as I could. But what I saw wasn't what I wanted to find. There was no note on the counter.

Fuck!

Never in my life had I ever moved so fast besides the time I tried to dodge Will when I took off with his secret stash of Playboy magazines to parade around the house. And this was Sonny. I'd just gotten him back in my life.

His wallet and another set of keys that looked to be too small for any door or car, were sitting right on top of my pile of socks. My fingers trembled as I flipped open his old, basic flip phone and tried to get through the menu with a panicking, freaked out mindset, searching for Dex's phone number. When I found "Dexter" under the contacts, my thumb was hitting the call button before I even thought to do it.

"Please, please, please, please, please," I begged to myself, listening to the ringing on the speaker. My heart was hammering its impatience. "Dex, c'mon—"

"What the fuck?" a sleepy, throaty voice answered with a yawn. "It's nine, asshole."

I sucked in a breath. "Dex?"

There was a clearing of a throat and another sleepy sigh. "Uh… Ritz?"

"It's me," I confirmed quickly. "Sonny's gone."

In the span of a millisecond, Dex's sleep laced voice froze over. "What do you mean Sonny's gone?"

I didn't notice until I heard the trembling in my voice that there were tears in my eyes. "I think these guys took him."

I was kind of a mess following my brief conversation with my new ally, The Dick. After having him basically demand that I calm down, I managed to tell him in ten seconds about the guys I'd seen parked down the street, and what Sonny had texted me. Needless to say, I was really friggin' glad that I wasn't having this conversation with him in person.

Using the word "pissed" to describe his reaction would be like saying that the Pacific Ocean was a body of water. The term didn't give any justice to what was said over the phone. I didn't even get a chance to say "bye" before he'd hung up, giving me a thirty minute notice on his arrival.

Twenty-nine minutes later, I'd taken the fastest shower of my life, cried over my missing brother, and freaked the hell out all over again. Even though I knew it was coming, the knock on the front door made my hands shake and heart rate speed up. Keeping in mind what the hell had just possibly happened to Sonny, I checked the peephole to make sure it was Dex—it was—along with Trip and another guy I'd never seen before.

"Open up, Ritz," Dex barked from the other side of the door.

"'Kay," I mumbled, unlocked the bolt and took a step back to let them inside.

Dex's eyes were on me as he strode in, his walk full of that same swagger that made me think he either practiced it or he just got really lucky. That gift kind of seemed unfair but whatever, this wasn't the time to think that.

"You okay?" Trip asked me, following in after Dex, who also watching me closely but without a crease between his brows.

I should have been tough and said that I was, but realistically, I wasn't. "Kind of."

The new guy walked in with a nod and a, "Sup," which I answered with a weak "Hi."

"Where's his stuff at?" Dex asked me as he made his way into the living room like a mother goose leading its babies to water.

"On the coffee table."

He nodded to himself, bending over the table with his faded but fitting jeans winking at me. "Trip, go check his room. See if anything's missing. Buck, check out the garage," he ordered them as he flipped through the slots in Sonny's wallet.

The two guys didn't say anything in response but split up, going in opposite directions in the house to do as he'd asked. I just hovered in the corner at a loss as to what I could do without getting in the way of whatever their plan was.

"Can I do anything?" I asked hesitantly.

Dex's eyes drifted up to mine, slowly. He was still pissed, I could tell, but he was trying to rein it in. "No, babe. We got this."

"You sure? I don't have very much money, but if that's what they want, I'll give you what I have to get him back," I told him, feeling my chest constrict. This shit was straight out of an action movie, only this time I couldn't be certain it would have a happy ending because life wasn't always like that, unfortunately.

Dex looked at me for the longest before shaking his head and lowering his voice. "No, no. Don't worry about that. It's not your money they want."

I almost asked what the hell else they would want. I almost also asked who "they" were. But my survival instincts said this wasn't the right time to ask so I bit back the questions and nodded at him.

"Babe, this place is about to get packed. Got any errands or something you can run before you go to the shop?" he asked me in that same soft tone he'd just used.

I didn't but obviously he didn't want me to be at the house when the other guys from the WMC showed up. But if it helped Sonny, then I'd move back to Fort Lauderdale or drive down to Venezuela if that's what he wanted.

"Yeah, I can go do a few things." I just didn't know what.

His head tilted down so that he could look at me through his long, dark eyelashes. "All right. Already talked to Blake and he's openin' with you instead of me but put my phone number in your cell so you can get in touch with me if you need to." He pinned me with this concrete-like look, his tone attempting to be reassuring. "Don't worry about Sonny. We'll find him."

I wanted to believe him, but those were pretty much the same words Sonny had told me right before he'd let some assholes do who knows what to him.

"Babe."

Make it stop.

"Babe."

Oh God. Please. Stop.

I'd barely fallen asleep following an hour long staring contest versus the ceiling. The tension in my body after my shitty day had finally seeped out of my bones enough to let me relax. I hadn't been able to stop thinking about Sonny. Kidnapped Sonny. Missing Sonny. Possibly injured Sonny. I wouldn't let myself even think that something else could happen to him, but wasn't that what people did in movies and in real life? Torture and… do other things?

I buried my face deeper into the pillow.

All day, I'd been worried sick. After Dex had pleasantly kicked me out of the house, I'd gone to the mall. I watched a matinee by myself at the theater to kill time until work while also distracting me just a little from the uneasy goldfish swimming around in my stomach. I couldn't remember anything clearly, not the movie or the things I'd seen in the stores, or even the customer's faces I'd helped throughout the day at Pins.

Blake and Blue must have known something was up because they'd been even nicer to me than usual. They gave me space by not asking a million questions I couldn't answer but came by to sit with me silently each opportunity they had. I'd tried calling Dex a few times but he'd only answered the first time, sounding annoyed beyond belief but promising to call me if he found out anything. I never got such a call, so I called him again and got no answer.

Fucking Sonny.

The more I thought about what happened, the more pissed off I got. He'd known they were out there. The men hadn't broken into the house and taken him. Sonny had to have walked out of the friggin' house and gone to them. What the hell had he been thinking? Obviously, I wasn't the only one who was an idiot.

So I stewed all day. Thinking about friggin' Sonny and how much of a dumbass he was. Thinking about what reasons those men could want him for.

Sonny didn't tell me enough about what he did when I wasn't around or when he magically disappeared at night, so I had no idea the kind of crap he got into. Mainly, it was blind trust between us. Neither one of us was used to having someone to answer to.

As soon as we closed down the shop that night, Blue had asked me if I needed anything—which was extra sweet because she rarely spoke to anyone, much less me—and then we'd all gone our separate ways. The thought of not going to Sonny's hadn't even entered my mind, so I drove straight there, showered again, forced myself to eat two-day-old leftovers, double-checked to make sure all the locks were secure, and went to bed. The bed where I tossed and turned for more than an hour before I somehow managed to fall asleep, pushing away that little voice that warned me here was someone else that I cared about that I could lose.

And now, I was quickly losing that sweet reprieve from reality.

"Honey, wake up," someone whispered in the dark.

Someone?

Shit!

I knifed up in bed, my heart jack-hammering against its house of bones. I blinked away sleep, expecting to see one of the bikers, or I don't know, a serial killer sitting on the bed next to me with his hands on my arm, thumbs making lazy circles on my skin.

"What the—!" I panted, blinking in the dark to see that strikingly familiar facial structure inches away.

"Chill, Ritz," Dex murmured gently, thumbs still circling.

My hand flew up to press against the skin over my heart, willing it to slow down. "Jesus, you scared me," I panted.

In true, normal Dex fashion he didn't smile in amusement or apologize. "What are you doin' here?"

"Sleeping?"

He sighed. "Blake didn't get my text?"

What was he talking about? I shook my head.

"Get up," he ordered. "You need to go talk to your bro before we get outta here."

I blinked again slowly as his words settled in. Talk to my bro? "Sonny's here?" My voice hitched up.

Dex nodded. "He's packin' some shit up. Pack a bag so you don't have to come back here for a while, then go talk to him."

Confusion swamped me in a million different ways. Where was Sonny going? Where the hell was I going? But mainly, I was wondering what was going on, period. There was too much secrecy to make me feel good.

Like a good girl, I tried to focus on what to pack so I could figure things out as soon as possible. Luckily, I had enough good sense before falling asleep to keep a pair of sleep shorts on because I usually slept in just my underwear and a bra. Dex flicked the lamp on while I grabbed a bunch of random clothes from the dresser.

"Where was he?" I asked him while stuffing my duffel with what I'd absently picked. I couldn't even look at Dex as I asked him the question, it made me too nervous. I'd ask if Sonny was fine but he wouldn't be home packing if he wasn't.

"County hospital."

My spine snapped up to standing, the muscles along my back tensing. "What?" I'm pretty positive I screeched out the words.

"The county hospital, babe. Some lady found him by the park unconscious this mornin' and called in an ambulance for him," he explained.

Without even thinking about it, my legs became unglued and started leading me around the bed to skip the whole packing thing and find Sonny instead. But Dex held up his arm, blocking me from going around him. "Calm down, Ritz. He just had a little concussion, a few bruises. He's all right," he said softly. "Finish packin'."

What the ef constituted a little concussion?

I was going to be sick. Breathing in and out of my nose a few times, I looked up at Dex's eyes to see if I could catch a hint as to whether he was being honest with me or not. Those fathomless dark blue eyes were intent and clear in a challenge of the wills, like he could tell I was trying to catch him in a lie.

"He's okay," Dex insisted, nudging me back with the muscles of his forearm. "Finish up, babe."

Holy crap. He probably wasn't lying. For about the hundredth time in five minutes, I nodded, pushing back that sickening sensation in my chest again. "Okay." Zipping the bag halfway, I yanked it off the bed and looked at him. "I think I have everything, I'm going to go hunt this moron down."

I didn't bother waiting for a response before I took off down the hallway to the opened door of Sonny's bedroom. The fan light was on, illuminating the room and the figure sitting on the edge of the bed with a duffel bag next to him. Even from behind, his features looked loose. Tired. Worn-out.

But it wasn't until I rounded the bed and saw the side of his face that made me gasp. "What the hell, Son?"

His cheek was swollen to twice the size it should have been. The skin was broken and purple, only slightly worse than the awful split on the corner of his mouth. Yet, he managed to give me a little grin out of somewhere.

"Ris," he greeted me in a lower voice than usual. He patted the bed. "I'm fine, kid. Come sit down."

"My ass you're fine," I told him, taking a step to stand in front of him.

Sonny tilted his head back to give me a better view of the ass-beating those sons of biscuit-eating whores gave him. The entire right side of his face looked deformed from the swelling. I was kind of worried that maybe he'd lost some teeth but I couldn't be sure.

"I've had worse, believe me," he argued softly. "Come here and quit worrying."

I gave him a look that said it'd be a cold day in hell before I stopped worrying about him.

"C'mon, I don't have a lot of time before Trip gets here," he said, patting the bed again.

I wanted to argue with him but logic told me not to. My poor, poor brother looked like complete crap. It made my stomach tense horribly, like I was having contractions or something. My hand was out and clinging to Sonny's instinctively.

"You remember I told you the sperm donor came down and asked me for money?"

Like I'd forget. "He asked Luther for money too, right?"

Sonny nodded slowly. "Yup, and he didn't give it to him either," he explained. "He didn't want to tell anybody what the money was for, except he just needed it real bad."

"How much was it?"

It looked like he tried to make a face but immediately stopped the effort once he remembered he looked like the Elephant Man's cousin. "Ten grand."

An ugly guffawing noise sprang out of my throat. "What?"

Sonny nodded again. "Exactly. No one in their right fucking mind is gonna let him borrow that much money for no damn reason. So nobody in the Club did." And I suddenly had a really bad feeling about the word choices my brother had chosen. No one in their right fucking mind...

"So what does that have to do with you exactly?" I asked him hesitantly.

"It turns out this wasn't the first time dear old daddy asked for money. A few months ago, he'd come down and borrowed a healthy chunk from the Reapers."

Oh crap. Oh boy-crap.

I'd never heard of the Reapers before but the puzzle pieces were making too much sense. "Those men?"

He sighed. "Yeah, Ris. Daddy didn't stick to the payment plan, and from what Trip figured out today, they aren't exactly happy that he came into town, and then bailed. They want their money."

This had to be a bad dream. An awful dream.

"But you don't even—" What was I going to say? That he didn't matter to our father? It was the harsh truth.

He must have known what I was trying to explain because he lifted a shoulder in lame agreement. "I know, Ris. I know. But I'm not paying for his shit, and I'm not lettin' them come after you next now that they know you live here. I'm sure they know you're his too."

I gagged, earning a slap to the back from my brother.

"Quit it, kid. It's fine. I'm gonna go find this motherfucker and make sure he pays his shit now. I'm not sitting around, waiting for God knows what to happen. The last thing he deserves is to get rescued by one of us. I'm not paying for his mistakes any longer and neither are you," he stated evenly.

Every minute just seemed to make this entire scenario seem so much more like a dream. A very hard dream that I couldn't swallow. "So we're going to go find him?"

Sonny didn't agree. The hand he'd left on my back after slapping it, slid up to rest on the shoulder furthest away from him. "No, Ris. I'm gonna go find him. Trip's coming with me. We don't know what other kind of pile he's dug himself into and you're better off staying here with Dex until all this shit gets sorted out."

The sound that came out of my mouth sounded like a squawk. "What?"

"You're staying with Dex. The house isn't safe and I don't trust you to stay with anybody else in the Club," he explained, squeezing my shoulder. "Hopefully I can find him in a few days."

But what would he do once he found him? The old man had obviously taken off because he didn't have the money to pay back the Reaper assholes. I almost, almost asked Sonny but by the look on the half of his face that didn't look like it'd gotten friendly with a baseball bat, Sonny had no limits on what he was capable of.

So making Curt Taylor find ten grand was going to happen one way or another. Of that I suddenly didn't have a doubt.

"Shit, Sonny," I whispered. How the hell had this mess fallen on us? On him? The one Taylor offspring who had less to do with his father than the other two. Christ.

The hand on my shoulder tightened. "Ris," he whispered, pulling me closer to him. The side of his forehead rested against the top of my head. "I'm coming back, all right? I swear to God I'm not leaving you here. I'm just gonna go find this asshole so we can get back to Tofu Tuesdays and shit," he assured me. "I'm coming back."

The intent behind his words weighed my sternum down. He was leaving. Leaving me in a new city all alone with his friend. I wasn't going to have a panic attack. I had a panic attack once when Will had first left, and then I'd dealt with it. But Sonny was coming back.

"It's only for a little while," he promised.

Leaning into his side, I nodded against him. I couldn't remember the last time anyone had hugged me like this. With so much reassurance and promises that I didn't doubt even a fraction that he wouldn't come back. It wasn't at all like when Will left. My own full-blooded little brother who gave me the quickest hug in history and pinched my arm before leaving.

"Are you sure you're okay?" I asked him, pushing away the fact I hadn't heard from Will in months.

Sonny laughed just a little, low and pained. "I've been better. I'll be all right once this all gets straightened out."

I slid my arm around his back. "I'm sorry you got dragged into this mess."

"Me too, kid, but I'd rather it be me than you who gets caught up in the shit-hole he's dug himself into." Sonny sighed and it pained my heart. "I need to get going though. Stay with Dex until I get back, okay?"

I wanted to argue with him but what was the point? We all had to do things we didn't want to at some point, and if the Reapers would beat the shit out Sonny for the mistakes of our estranged father, what else were they capable of?

"Maybe I should go to Lanie's," I suggested. "If they did that to you, won't they try and—"

"No, Ris. I'm a sign for the sperm donor, and Dex knows better than to be a dumbass. You'll be fine."

Oh man. This was a mess. A huge, surreal mess all caused by a man that had no connections to our lives anymore.

"You won't get in trouble at your job?"

Sonny laughed before loosening his hold on me and climbing to his feet slowly. "Don't worry about it. It's all good."

I blew out a breath and nodded, getting off the bed. His face looked bad, so bad, but Sonny was his own man. I couldn't and wouldn't beg him to stay.

"You got all your stuff?"

I nodded.

"Your bathroom stuff, too?" he asked.

In that moment, I suddenly wished that I'd had Sonny in my life from the very beginning. I mean, who else would remember bathroom stuff of all things? "No, I forgot."

He ruffled my hair lightly. "Go get it and I'll meet you outside."

I followed after him but split off to grab my toiletries from the bathroom. There wasn't much so it only took a second to put my things into my duffel. Just as I was about to walk out of the house, I heard Sonny and Dex speaking on the other side of the door.

"—been through too much, man. She doesn't need to go through anything else," Sonny spoke.

"I said I'd watch over her." That was Dex who replied.

"Fuck, I'll stay and this one can go with you." Another voice suggested. Trip, probably.

Dex made a noise I couldn't recognize through the door. "I'm stayin'."

There was a pause. "Keep your dick in your goddamn pants, Dex. I swear to God…"

Sonny murmured something else I couldn't hear because he must have been further away from the door than Dex. Feeling creepy enough for eavesdropping, I pulled open the front door to all three of them on the deck. Sonny standing just off the stairs, Trip and Dex right in front of me—well, the door.

A tired smile crept over my brother's face. "You ready?"

"Yeah." I looked over at the blonde standing next to Dex. "Hey, Trip."

"Hey gorgeous," he murmured. The color under his eyes made him look like he hadn't slept in a while.

Dex's hand landed on my lower back, urging me forward. "Let's get going, Ritz. I'm tired."

"All right." I walked over to Sonny and wrapped my arms around his chest. "Be safe, all right?"

He pulled me in for a hug. "I'll be back as soon as I can."

I pulled back just a little and kissed his beard covered cheek. "Okay. Let Trip drive though."

Sonny snorted and put both hands on top of my head, pushing my face down so that he could plant one on my forehead. "Whatever you want, kid."

Oh, the irony. If anyone knew you didn't always get what you want, it was Sonny.

"See ya, Son." I waved at him. "Bye, Trip. Be safe."

Sonny inclined his head forward, smiling just barely. "See ya, kid."

Trip added a sigh with his goodbye but I already had my attention forward, just past Sonny's frame.

Dex and my brother shared a strange look between them as the dark-haired one made his way down the stairs. I started to round the front bumper of my car to get in when he reached out to wrap his fingers around my elbow.

"Where ya goin'?"

Uh... "I'm following after you."

He made a tisking sound under his tongue. "No. You drive too slow. Hop on my bike and we'll get your car tomorrow."

I hesitated, looking back at my car.

"Iris." I really liked it a little too much when he used my name. "Babe, get on. We'll get your car later."

I must have waited too long because the next thing I knew, he had an arm hooked around my waist and was half carrying me-half dragging me the distance to his Dyna. Dex took my duffel, handed me a helmet that had been left on the seat and replaced the empty spot with my bag, strapping it down.

He turned back toward me, took the helmet from my hands, and then lowered it onto my head silently. Once it was buckled on, he straddled his bike and tilted his head in my direction. "Hop on."

Well then. Bossy ass.

There was all of about eight inches between Dex's back and my bag, but what could I do about it? I had a feeling that if I argued with him more about whether I was riding with him or not, I'd lose anyway and to be honest, I was really tired. Having been on bikes with Sonny in the past, it was easy getting on but awkward when I had to shift forward on the seat so much that my crotch and thighs left no room for a sheet of paper between them and Dex's outer thighs and beefy butt. Grudgingly, my arms slipped around his ribs as he started the bike up and backed onto the street.

Sonny's house was already on the outskirts of Austin, so when Dex got on the freeway leading us further out of the city, I wondered where the hell he lived but didn't ask. My cheek was technically to his back, arms tight around his chest. I didn't realize until then that he had a leather jacket on that did nothing to hide how solid his build was.

Damn it.

It was too dark to see anything well, but I could tell that we were pretty much in the middle of nowhere. The trees were huge as we zoomed off the freeway ramp with only the loud roar of his bike breaking the monotony of the ride.

After about five minutes, he turned onto a farm road that had no name or real sign. An outline of a house was visible in the near distance over a hill. The closer we got, the more I was able to see under the moonlight. The house was a long one-story ranch style home. A huge front yard dotted with tall trees gave way to the light colored paneling of the home. It wasn't at all the kind of place I expected Dex to live in. He seemed like the typical bachelor with a dirty apartment.

But maybe I was just assuming that of every member of the MC. To be fair, Trip lived up to the stereotype I'd built up. There had even been socks crammed into the corners of his couch.

When he parked the bike right in front of the paved driveway, he dismounted first before holding out a hand and helping me afterward. I yanked the helmet off while he unstrapped my bag, tilting his head in the direction of the door as his wordless come on.

I followed in after him, taking in the minimal furniture in his living room: a brown microfiber sectional sofa, a large flat screen television mounted to the wall, an entertainment center underneath, and… that was it. Dex had dropped my bag onto the couch before turning to look at me.

"You can take the bed, babe. I got two other rooms but not another bed to sleep in," he explained.

I was still looking around, past the living room to spy a kitchen that opened up directly to it but at his words, I shook my head. "No, I'll stay on the couch. I can sleep just about anywhere."

While it was the truth, I wasn't about to point out that our sixty or seventy pound weight difference on top of half a foot in height difference would definitely make me a better candidate for his long but still somewhat narrow couch.

He opened his mouth to argue with me before I cut him off.

"Seriously, Dex. I'll stay on the couch, don't worry about it. If you can just get me a pillow and a blanket…?"

The flat, completely ill amused look on his face made think he wanted to discuss the sleeping arrangements more, but I think he understood my secret reasoning and was probably too tired to fight it. With a nod, he disappeared into a hallway to the right of the living room and couch for a couple of minutes, coming back with a pillow covered in a dark blue pillowcase and a white blanket under his arm.

Dex handed them to me silently, watching as I laid out the blanket with a yawn and dropped the pillow onto the end of the couch closest to the front door.

"The bathroom is down the hall, first door on your right, and my bedroom is that way," he pointed toward another hallway on the left side of the living room. "Last door."

"Thanks," I mumbled with another yawn, dropping my butt onto the cushion.

He took a step back, locking those Crayola blue eyes on me. "Make yourself at home, and wake me up if you need anythin'."

I nodded my answer, smiling at him sleepily. "All right. Night, Dex." I paused. "Thanks for everything."

His nod was slow. "Night, babe."

I didn't waste any more time trying to watch him disappear into the hallway. The moment I slipped beneath the blanket and my head hit the pillow, I realized how wide awake I was.

Ef me.

Small sounds creaked throughout the house. The rush of water through pipes pulled at my attention while I lay there, chin to chest, staring at the darkness. I closed my eyes and tried to will my body to wind down.

And then I tried some more.

CHAPTER SEVENTEEN

I woke up the next morning both way too early and in almost the same way I'd gotten scared awake just hours before at Sonny's. Dex's ass was on the couch crammed into the area where my hips were, one hand on my shoulder shaking me.

"Time to get up."

I opened one eye, immediately focusing on the digital clock of his DVD player. I groaned, shutting it right back again. "It's barely seven." I'm not sure if what I said even sounded like what I'd intended it to, but it must have been enough for Dex to understand.

"Yeah, babe, but we got a busy day. Gotta run some errands."

What I meant to say was, "I don't know what errands you want to run at seven in the morning," but it probably sounded more like "I…errands…seven…"

Fingers swept back the black hair plastered to my face in a gesture I was too tired to appreciate. "I need to go sort Sonny's shit out."

Sonny. Right.

With a grunt, I rolled onto my back and blinked at the white popcorn ceiling. I sat up half-delusional, sounding more like a man than a woman. "Okay, okay. I'm up."

After giving me instructions on where the towels were and how to use the tricky hot water, Dex dumped my bag in the standard guest bathroom with a tub blocked off by a neat blue and green striped curtain. I took a quick shower and pulled a brush through my hair before throwing it up into a ponytail. I bumbled out, still half-asleep to find Dex sitting on the couch watching television with my neatly folded blanket and pillow to his side.

"Ready," I yawned.

He glanced up, looked back at the TV screen for half a second before darting his attention back at me. Well, specifically my legs. In my haste hours before, I'd thrown random clothes together. Apparently, I'd dug into my NSFW—not safe for work—clothing. All I'd found in the bag were shorts, yoga pants, and the three denim mini-skirts I owned. The mini-skirts were a memory of the heat and humidity in south Florida. Heat and humidity that I swear Austin compared to.

And there was no money in the world that would get me to wear one of my skirts when I was stuck riding on the back of Dex's bike.

So my short shorts it was.

By the length of time it took Dex to stop looking at my—thankfully—shaved legs, I'd gone from being flattered to uncomfortable. The only time people stared at me that intently were when they were looking at my arm. An arm that I'd thankfully managed to subconsciously pack smartly enough for by grabbing a handful of elbow-length cardigans. "I'm ready," I repeated.

"Right." He stood up, huffing under his breath while turning off the television, and then striding toward the door. He gave me another sidelong glance. "You might wanna take that sweater off. It'll be pretty hot outside in no time on my bike."

Shoot. I hadn't even thought of that. I only had a tank top beneath the cardigan and... *yeah*. I'd rather have pit stains than pitiful looks. "I'll be fine."

Dex looked like he wanted to argue with me but luckily he dropped the issue.

The ride back into town was silent, and I got to appreciate the scenery of what was outside the Austin city limits. Except for traffic and pollution, and the feel of Dex's bare bicep and forearm touching my knee every few minutes, the ride back was fine.

"Where are we going?" I asked him at a stoplight once we were back in the city.

He tilted his head to the side, talking loudly over the roar of the bike. "Luther's place," he answered. "You remember him?"

I nodded, reminded of the time I'd taken the package over to him and the night I'd caught him fondling up a twenty-something. Yet again, still friggin' gross.

We pulled into a large two story red brick home in an upper middle class neighborhood. The same truck we'd taken to Austin was parked in the driveway alongside a Harley that looked differently than Sonny and Dex's. As soon as he'd gotten off the bike and helped me off too, knocking on it so loud I'm sure the neighbors heard.

The door opened up much quicker than I would have expected with a disheveled looking Luther standing there bare-chested and bleary-eyed.

"Jesus, Dex, you know it's my day off, it's too early for this shit."

Dex's broad shoulders shifted tightly beneath the plain white tee he had on. Someone was on the verge of being a grumpy butt. "Sonny took off last night."

Luther let out a long and drawn out sigh from between his lips before waving Dex—and me by default—inside. "What do you mean he took off?"

"He's goin' to look for Curt, Lu. Took Trip with him."

The older man's features tightened, his jaw locking right before he rubbed a big palm over it roughly. "Fuck."

"What do you expect? You saw him at Seton. You know what those pieces of shit will do if they don't get paid."

It didn't escape me that they both glanced at me as Dex spoke the last sentence.

I might have flinched just a little inside.

Luther groaned again, scrubbing both hands over his face. When he dropped his palms, he slowly turned to look at me. It hit me right then that the older man had the same sky blue eyes Trip did. Huh.

"Honey, don't go anywhere without one of the club members with you."

The second time in my life that the "Prez" had spoken to me and he was warning me. The urge to go visit Lanie was right smack on my forehead, but I knew I shouldn't.

Dex let out a long sigh. "I got this. Don't worry about it," he assured the older man.

I, on the other hand, had a really bad feeling about this.

"Who are those guys?" I asked Dex over breakfast.

After we left Luther's house, we'd loaded back on the bike and made our way over to a diner nearby. We squeezed into a booth across from each other and ordered breakfast in a murmur of low requests.

Dex looked up at me as he shoveled half of a breakfast sausage into his mouth. "What guys?" He even had the nerve to look around the diner like I'd be asking about any other guys besides the ones who had taken Sonny.

"The guys at the bar. The ones my dad owes money to," I explained, eyeing the dark circles under his radiant blue eyes. Dex had some seriously thick eyelashes.

He chewed on only one side of his mouth, eyeing me wearily. "They're another club in SA."

That was something I already knew.

"They don't like us," he added vaguely.

You have got to be kidding me. "They don't like you guys?"

"Yeah."

"They don't like you guys so they beat up Sonny instead of looking for our dad?" I could smell his bullshit a mile away.

He knew I had him, so he nodded his answer. "It's more complicated than that, Ritz. They're all Widows' rejects. They'll try to start shit with us for whatever reason they can come up."

"Explain that."

He lifted a brow. "Explain what?"

"What do you mean by them being rejects?"

Dex sighed, his mouth twisting. "Your pa never told you this?"

I gave him a flat look.

"You know the Original 12?" he asked.

I shook my head, earning another sigh. "They were the first Widowmakers. Twelve pissed off vets. Tough as shit, hated every single thing about the government. My granddaddy on my ma's side was one."

That made a heck of a lot of sense. One badass passing on the gene to another badass.

Dex kept going with his story. "They got into shady shit. Drug runnin', enforcin', shit that gets everybody into trouble." He shook his head. "Gets people killed, babe, but what the hell did they care? I remember my granddaddy was cool as fuck but he wasn't right. None of 'em were."

I suddenly had the urge to find out what Dex considered as "not right." Then again, I probably didn't want to.

"As the club grew with more and more assholes wantin' in on the money and the respect and the ass, they got into more shit. Girls—"

Prostitution?

"—bad shit, Ritz. Years, that was the way things were run. Once the 12 were all too old to give a fuck, Luther took over the club. He knew we were in deep with the Mexicans when he took over. Some of the brothers were gettin' restless, sloppy. They wanted more money, more drama. More, more, more, more. Then, a run got fucked up. The Mexicans got pissed, and took care of Luther's wife in retaliation."

I made a face that earned me a slow nod of understanding from Dex. Even hearing it again after so many years, it sounded just as terrible.

"Yeah, babe. It was bad. I was a little pimple-faced shit back then but I remember. Lu lost his fuckin' mind. I mean, lost it. He made it his mission to clean us up after that. The club was all cash capital back then. He wanted to open up businesses and make the money legit. It was a good plan. Better for everybody even if the money wasn't goin' to be as good first, it would've worked. The problem was, not everybody wanted to get clean."

That I could understand. Men living in their own little world with no regard for society, making money, scaring the shit out of people? It made sense though it didn't seem like a life I'd want to live.

"There were more brothers who wanted to get clean after Darcy's death than not. It scared the fuck out of everybody with families, babe. They saw that Lu had his shop. It'd never been tied up with club finances. Lotta members left when the club voted to try the clean way. They left but they were pissed. Felt like they'd gotten fucked over, and men like that don't get over shit. Ever. They all hooked up, started up the Reapers."

And then I winced. I could understand why the men would have held a grudge. I did. They'd join the WMC for one reason and then that reason had morphed into something completely different. After everything they'd lost—friends and family—they'd gotten kicked out.

"It took a couple years but the MC bought the bar. Lu wasn't starvin' for money and he financed us buyin' an auto parts store." He lifted a shoulder like the conclusion was inevitable. "That didn't help the situation out."

"I bet."

"Just the way shit is."

I tried to process everything he'd explained. Why the Reapers hated the Widowmakers. Why they'd be such jackasses. But there was one thing about his explanation that didn't make any sense.

"Why did they let my dad borrow money if he was a Widow?" Right?

Dex slid a piece of pancake between his lips, his dark blue eyes hooded. "No clue, babe. Maybe they were expectin' him not to pay up. Who knows."

Well, shoot. That didn't add up but it wasn't like I could hound Dex for an answer he didn't have.

"I just don't get it, I guess. Neither one of us is close to him," I didn't need to be specific about who him was. "He won't give a crap about either one of us paying for his mistake."

As soon as the words were out of my mouth, disappointment and sadness pierced my belly.

It was the truth. The awful truth. Curt Taylor wouldn't give a shit about his son getting beaten up. Getting a freaking concussion and left behind at a freaking park. Alone. Unconscious.

Just as quickly as the sadness had poked at me, it disappeared, replaced by pure anger. It was red and hot and just... dark. And I hated it. Hated that I could feel so much disdain toward a man that I should have loved.

A man that should have loved me.

Should have loved his sons.

"Babe," Dex murmured, reached out to place a hand on my forearm. "Baby, quit it."

"Quit what?" I asked him in a gloomy voice.

He squeezed my forearm. "Quit thinkin' about him. I already told you that prick's not worth you gettin' upset."

How the hell did this man know what I'd started thinking about?

I had to swallow back that weird feeling and try to plaster a smile onto my face. "I wasn't—"

"You were."

Crap. I sighed. "I know he's not worth it but it still just... gets me." My fingers flexed around the silverware I was holding. "I want to punch him in the nuts so bad."

Dex choked. "What?"

"I said it." My tone was husky, almost a growl in frustration. I shouldn't be calling him an asshole. I told myself that I wouldn't but he'd gotten Sonny hurt. I could forgive the old man for a lot of things, ignore a lot of things but this had crossed the line. "He's so stupid."

Stupid for messing around with a group he had to know would only bring trouble. And so friggin' stupid for the dozens of other mistakes he'd committed along the way. I don't know how long I sat there, breathing in through my nose and out through my mouth to calm down but when I managed to, I caught Dex looking at me with an amused tilt to his mouth.

"I don't like feeling this angry," I admitted to him, feeling incredibly vulnerable.

Like all things Dex, his response was so simple I wanted to laugh. "Then don't."

We pulled into the parking lot opposite from Mayhem about twenty minutes later, parking the solid black motorcycle into the closest open spot next to another Harley. Hoofing it across the street, I spotted the same guy that had come into Pins a few weeks ago standing by the door. The one who had gotten into an argument with Dex my first night in Austin, I finally realized.

"Dex." The man tipped his chin up before looking over in my direction, a smug grin crawling over his lips. "Sweetie."

I smiled at him weakly. "Hi."

"How you doin'?" His thick eyebrows went up.

"I've been better, and you?" Crap, what was his name again? I couldn't remember.

That smug grin grew wider. "My day just got a whole lot better, sweetie."

Dex's presence, broader and slightly taller than the other man, maneuvered its way between us like a barrier. His eyes burned a hole in his direction. "Don't you have shit to do?" he asked brusquely.

The man shrugged, that pleased smile still plastered on his dark pink mouth. "Yeah."

"You don't get paid to stand around scratchin' your balls," The Dick, who had apparently come out to play, bit off before pulling the bar's door open and pushing me through a little more roughly than he needed to.

I looked at him over my shoulder, frowning. "Watch it, would you?"

He looked at me out of the corner of his eye and waved me forward. "My bad, babe."

With a flick of fingers, Dex led the way through Mayhem. The place was empty and dark as we crossed the hardwood floor to the stairs that were on the far end of the floor. On the second floor, he turned and pushed open the door that closed off the stairwell from the rest of the building, holding it for me. I got a chance to look and see that the stairs went up another floor.

I'm not sure what exactly I was expecting to see inside, but it wasn't the short bar directly off to the right with neon signs mounted on the wall around it. A pool table and a separate foosball table took up an open space to the left with beer brand lamps mounted on it. It looked like a replica of downstairs except on a smaller scale.

"Babe, take a seat and hang out for a bit, yeah?" Dex asked me.

I nodded.

"Grab a pop or whatever you want from the fridge behind the counter," he offered. A second later he'd disappeared down a halfway off the end of the bar. Like a siren's song, a couch pressed against the far side of the wall called me to it.

I really didn't mean to fall asleep but with the four hours I'd gotten the night before, it was inevitable. Except all I did was dream of my mom.

"We'll get your car tomorrow," Dex said as we got off his bike that night after closing up Pins.

I'd been surprised that he even came back to the parlor after he'd dropped me off with Blue that afternoon. He'd left me sleeping at the bar for four hours. Four hours of sleeping on the couch with my neck twisted, my drool a little river from the corner of my mouth down my chin.

The only reason why I'd gotten up was because I felt something dabbing at my face. That "something" was a napkin Dex was holding while looking like he was trying his best not to smile.

Not cool, and when I told him just that, he threw his head back and laughed.

His laugh still unsettled me.

Work had been steady like usual until Dex showed up around nine, cool as a cucumber to tattoo his nighttime appointments. The only sign he'd given me that this day was different from every other one before spending the night at his house and spilling his guts about his family back in Austin, was when he stood behind me after tattooing a client and wrapped his fingers around the back of my neck while I typed in a follow-up appointment for him.

I tried my best not to react to his touch but this was Dex. Hot Dex. Hot Dex that screamed at scary, mean men for me. Hot Dex with a piercing in his thing. Supposedly.

God, guessing where that piercing was located was a game I had no business playing.

"What do you wanna eat for dinner?" he asked as he held a hand out to help me off his bike.

"Anything really."

"You know how to cook?" He watched as I pulled off his helmet.

"Yeah. Do you have groceries?"

He nodded. "I have shit in the freezer."

"I have shit in the freezer," I repeated his words back to him, walking into the house. So eloquent. "Well, I can probably figure out something. No promises it'll be good though."

He shrugged, still facing forward before detouring to head in the direction of his bedroom. "Gonna shower. Make whatever you want, babe. I'm not picky."

The stuff in his freezer wasn't exactly shit, but compared to Sonny's house, it was like this guy visited the grocery store once a month instead of weekly. I found cans of diced tomatoes, pasta, and dried herbs in the pantry that I set out, while a big pot of water boiled—after spending ten minutes trying to find pots that were scattered in random cabinets throughout the kitchen. For as organized as Dex made sure we kept Pins, he didn't have the same standards at home.

"What are you makin'?" Dex asked from just a few feet behind me.

I turned to look at him over my shoulder. "Spaghetti." I gave him a little smile, taking in the worn white undershirt he'd put on. "If you want to take out some of that chicken you have in the freezer, I'll cook it."

He hummed. "Sounds good. I'll pop the chicken in the microwave, babe. No big deal."

I smiled at him from over my shoulder. "Well, it probably won't be that good since there wasn't much to choose from in the pantry but...hopefully it won't taste like crap."

Dumping the box of noodles that were in his cupboard into the big pot of water, I saw him pull out the freezer bag with precooked grilled chicken and set two breasts onto a plate. "I'm sure it'll be better than anythin' I can cook," he chuckled, putting the plate into the microwave and setting the timer.

"You better hope so." I made a face, stirring the pot.

He snickered.

The silence felt pretty awkward while I dealt with the food cooking. Trying to kill the tense silence, I tried to think about something to talk about. "So you've known Sonny for a long time?"

Dex was sitting there next to the bar with both elbows resting on the counter, hunched over it. "Ever since your pa used to drop him off with my ma durin' club meetings."

"You didn't go to school together?"

He shook his head. "Nah. We lived in different hoods. Him and Trip went to school together." For a brief moment, he got this far off look in his eye that made me wonder what kind of crap he was remembering. Probably nothing good.

"Oh. I don't know why I got the impression you two were pretty close."

Dex pushed away whatever had caught his attention on memory lane. "Close enough. I didn't even know he still kept in contact with you 'til a few years ago. He used to take off and not say shit to anyone about where he was goin'."

Yeah...that sounded like Sonny. I lifted up a shoulder at him.

"Thought you were too good to come see him."

And that had me narrowing my eyes over in his direction. It was a fact. A statement, and if I took the time to absorb what he was saying, I'd understand his point. So I saved my smart ass comment and went for a scowl. "I didn't have money or time."

He gave me a long look before nodding. "Yeah, I get that now."

When he didn't say anything else, I tried to think of what else to talk to him about. The distance between us wasn't so painful at Pins, but at his house? It was. Oh lord, it was. I was grateful to him for letting me stay and sitting there quietly, well, awkwardly quietly, seemed wrong.

"I like your house," I blurted out the first thought that came to mind.

He glanced up and looked around his kitchen, tipping his chin down. Dex's mouth formed a serious straight line. "Me too."

"Have you lived here long?"

"Almost a year in November," he answered.

Why was he making this so difficult? I glanced at the bare walls and clean counters, listened to the cicadas outsides, thinking of the fact he lived out of the city limits. "I'm a little surprised you have a house out here and not an apartment like Trip's." A little shudder curled through my spine when I thought of the state his toilet seat had been in.

In typical Dex fashion he picked up on the last thing I would expect. "You been to Trip's place?"

Did his tone sound off or was I imagining it? One look at the straight line of his jaw had me deciding I'd imagined it. "Once."

"Huh," he huffed. Those dark blue orbs narrowed for a split second. His fingers tapped against the counter before he started talking again. "I used to live in the same complex before I bought this place. Fuckin' hated it there."

"Really?"

Dex lifted up a shoulder. "Made me feel like I was livin' in a beehive. Kinda reminded me too much of bein' all cramped up in a double-wide as a kid, too." When he went to start scratching at his throat, I understood how awkward and uncomfortable the memories of living in a trailer made him feel.

Then I remembered everything he'd said about growing up with his drunk of a dad. That kind of man in such a small place? Oh hell. With two sisters? Where the hell would he have even slept?

Acid built up in my chest and throat so quickly it caught me off guard. I was suddenly the one that felt uncomfortable. "I had to share a room with my little brother—bunk beds—until I was nineteen." *Yia-yia*'s house had been so small, but it'd been home. I swallowed hard at the memory of sleeping on the couch at the apartment we'd moved into after selling the second home I'd ever known. "So I get it."

And then, nothing. Silence.

O-kay. I could let that topic go.

I fumbled my way through making sauce for the pasta, hoping it wouldn't taste completely bland since I didn't have the right ingredients. In the mean time, Dex watched quietly, only getting up to grab a beer from the fridge and asking if I wanted a drink.

We sat on opposite sides of the kitchen bar, Dex drinking a beer and me with a bottle of water he'd pulled out from somewhere in the fridge I hadn't seen. Considering the absence of necessary condiments and herbs, I thought the food came out pretty good. Dex's murmurs of enjoyment told me he was either a great liar or it wasn't too bad.

"Good food, babe," he finally muttered after twirling ribbons of pasta around his fork, gaze leveled on me.

I smiled at him, taking a few more mouthfuls of food. I glanced up again only to see him still looking at me.

O-kay.

"Is there spaghetti sauce on my face?" I asked.

He shook his head, stringing more noodles along the tines of his fork.

I let it go until I caught his eyes one more time. "I'm not kidding, what's on my face?"

"Nothin'."

I narrowed my eyes in his direction but kept watching him. Until he did it again.

Oh dear God.

I put my hand over the middle of my face. "There's a booger in my nose, isn't there?"

He looked at me for a long moment, a moment that stretched light years and galaxies. Time-wrinkled centuries and possibly eons. Generations—

And then Dex was laughing. Laughing and laughing and laughing. Muttering something that sounded suspiciously like, "You're the goofiest fuckin' girl," between bellows of barrel-shaped laughs.

And I might have had a booger in my nose, though I'd probably never know for sure, but that laugh coming from that man.

So worth it.

CHAPTER EIGHTEEN

"That's fucking outrageous!"

Dear God, what in the hell had I been thinking working at a tattoo parlor? A tattoo parlor that was right around the corner from a body shop. A body shop that was owned by the president of a biker club. A biker club that owned a bar, which seconded as headquarters for said club, who were enemies with stupid asses that beat up innocent—err, pretty innocent—people.

Where had my quiet life disappeared to?

And why hadn't I insisted on going with Sonny?

With the exception of Rick, the drunk guy who had yelled at me and called me a bitch, every other client had been incredibly nice. Even when they had to pay the steep rates that the shop charged—with good reasoning. The reasons were framed all over the shop in printed acclaims.

The first time I heard how much Blake charged his client, I had to stop myself from choking. The prices could be down payments on used cars. I'm not exaggerating. But it was standard practice to agree on a fee before any piece got started so the customer didn't have a fit at the end.

Obviously, not everyone functioned on the same wavelength.

This customer had been in once last week to talk to Blue about having some detailed script done on his ribs. Blue had drawn out the idea, spoken to the guy about the pricing and the man had scheduled an appointment to come in and get it done.

So why the would-be client was now standing in front of me while I was trying to take payment and having a fit to end all shit-fits—and this included the year I worked at a daycare—was beyond me. "Blue had already spoken to you about the pricing last week," I reminded him.

Blue stood directly behind me, silent.

"You never said it was going to be that expensive!" the guy shouted at Blue, completely ignoring me.

Yes. Yes, she had.

"Sir, before we schedule anything in advance for custom artwork, the rate is agreed on," I told him.

Pissed Off guy just shook his head. "Fuck that. I'm not paying that much for a goddamn tattoo."

Blue and I looked at each other and shrugged. "Okay."

There were payment options that Blake had told me about, but that consisted of the customer paying in advance for artwork or doing bits and pieces at a time as they could afford it. But if Blue wasn't going to say anything about it, then I wasn't either. I think we both could be perfectly happy having one less belligerent customer coming in over a period of time.

"Fuck that and fuck you guys!"

Blue and I glanced at each other again and shrugged.

"Fuck this place! You fucking thieves. Your shit ain't that good."

We just stared at him.

"You short little shit." He pointed at Blue.

Blue blinked like she didn't give half a crap what he thought, but I did.

"Hey, that's unnecessary," I snapped back. Why did people have to be so rude?

And then the pissed off man moved his finger in my direction, ignoring my outburst. "And you, you—"

"Get the fuck out, man."

Blue and I both whipped our heads over our shoulders to see Dex come prowling down the hallway from his office.

Oh snap!

With the mood he'd been in all day, I'd been relieved when he'd locked himself in his office as soon as we'd gotten to the shop. That morning he'd come out of his bedroom with his lips pursed, jaw locked, angry at the friggin' world. He'd snapped at me for just asking if he'd heard from Sonny. Sheesh. I wasn't sure what had gotten him so ripe but even I knew better than to ask.

So when the man yelling looked relieved, I didn't understand why. Obviously, he'd never spoken to Dex before because if he had, he would have known the look on his face was the opposite of anything that could resemble salvation or relief of any kind.

"Bro, your two drones here are trying to charge me an arm and fucking leg for my piece!" Pissed Off Guy said with that same relieved smirk on his face. "Can't I get a hook-up for being a new customer?"

Dex had closed the distance between his office and my desk by the time the guy finished talking. At that point, he was standing right next to me, seven inches of space between us. If I moved my arm, it would touch the muscular tattooed thigh he'd shown me days before. The muscular thigh then made me wonder, for all of a microsecond what kind of piercing Dex had on his penis before I snapped myself out of it. Somehow I'd gone from a relatively content virgin to a woman who was constantly thinking about pierced genitals and nipples.

"No, bro, I won't, and if I did, I wouldn't give it to someone who comes into my fuckin' shop, hollerin' and callin' my employees little shits and whatever the fuck you were gonna call Ritz," he ground out with a slight grumble to his voice.

Pissed Off Guy sagged, shaking his head in a way that told me he didn't think this conversation with Dex was over. "Aww, c'mon, bro."

"Get the fuck out before I throw your ass outta here, *bro*," The Dick warned.

Ooh, wheee. I somehow caught Blue's gaze and we each made our eyes wide.

Dex inhaled a long, deep breath through his nose. "You got five seconds to get the hell out."

There was no room for interpretation. I would have left and taken my carbon footprints with me. Dex was pretty scary when he was pissed off—though Dex on a daily basis was pretty scary. I used to think it was all that ink on his arms but it totally wasn't. Since he usually wore t-shirts, his tats were always visible. All that black and gray on tanned skin was the first thing your eyes went to when speaking to Dex. Now, the more I got to know him, the more I realized that it wasn't just the tattoos that made him intimidating.

Dex was a scary asshole period. He just radiated this pure "I-don't-give-a-fuck" attitude, and that was scary. You couldn't control or anticipate a person who didn't care. They were wildcards. Add that in with his Dyna and his tattoos, and yeah—intimidating on the outside.

When the Pissed Off Guy held his arms out in a what-the-hell gesture, Dex shook his head.

"Five," he started counting. "Four, three—"

"God. Fuck you guys and fuck this fuckin' overpriced bullshit!" Pissed Off Guy's voice had taken a slightly shrieking edge to it.

"Two—"

With all the class in the world, the guy shot us a one-finger salute and got the hell out.

Well.

Long, warm fingers wrapped around the back of my neck as Dex dropped down to his haunches, eye level with me. "You all right, Ritz?" His bright blue eyes were on mine, all traces of annoyance gone from his features.

"Yeah," I told him. "He was just pretty dumb and rude."

The smile he gave me in return was so soft it was hard to understand how his mood went from one side of the linear line to the other in seconds. It also reminded me of exactly what I'd told him on the ride back from Houston. The kindest, grumpy ass man in all of Texas.

"Yeah, he was," he agreed. Dex's fingers gave my neck a squeeze. The action made my throat close up momentarily. "C'mon, I'll buy you a Coke."

Like I was going to tell him no.

"You want a pop?" he asked Blue as he turned around.

She scrunched up her nose and shook her head. "I'm good."

I followed after him, waiting patiently while he put in the dollar bills to get our drinks. He popped the lid for me, handing over the drink with a frustrated smile.

"I can't stand assholes like that," he grunted. "What I wanna do is go beat his fuckin' ass."

Both my eyebrows went up. "Calm your horses. It's not worth you getting into trouble," I reminded him of what Shane had hinted at back in Houston. "Or messing up your hands, dumb-bum."

"Dumb-bum?" He blinked.

I shrugged. "Yeah. What would you do if you broke a couple fingers?"

"Babe, you only break fingers if you don't know what you're doing."

Blinking slowly, I opened my mouth and closed it. "I know you're not kidding and yet…"

The corner of Dex's mouth tilted up, but it wasn't a smile of amusement exactly, it was more of a knowing smirk. "Babe."

"I'm being serious. You have to take care of yourself. Keep that rage under control."

"I'm good."

The look I gave him was half disbelieving, half resigned. Then the opportunity hit me, and I stopped caring. "You weren't good this morning."

He scowled. I hit the battleship!

"What happened?"

"Nothin' important. Don't worry about it."

What was it about that saying that grated on my nerves? I should shut up. I should mind my own business. The only thing was, I didn't want to. "Did a bird poop on your bedroom window?"

Dex's cheek ticked up in agitation. "Smart ass." He blew out a long breath from between his lips. "My pa called my sis askin' for money to buy new shoes."

"Okay…"

Then he burst out unexpectedly, "And the dumbass gave it to him!" He squeezed his eyes shut, thumb and index finger pinching the bridge of his nose. "I don't get what the hell is wrong with 'em. I can sleep at night knowin' he's runnin' around with holes in his shoes."

Well, what could I say? *Don't be mad?* Please. No way. If he disliked his dad half as much as I disliked mine, then...yeah. That didn't mean I had to let him wallow in his frustrations even if it seemed to have passed. "There's nothing you can do about it now though, is there?"

When his cheek ticked up again, I lifted both of my shoulders and wiggled my fingers. "Just let it go, your highness. Just let it all go."

The look he gave me could have seared the flesh off of my muscles and made me break into hives if I hadn't recognized that little gleam in his eye that assured me he would never physically hurt me. Yell at me? Sure. Call me names I'd use on my future dog? Yeah. But hurt me? Nah.

"Babe?"

"Yeah?"

"Get your ass back up front."

Oh.

"I like having you around," Slim told me while we were seated on the couch, waiting for Blue and Dex to finish up whatever they were doing for closing.

"Why?" I asked him carefully, smiling a little.

"Because Dex is hilarious when he's pissed off."

I gave him my best bug eyes. "You like seeing him mad like that?"

He nodded like it was the most obvious thing in the world. "Trust me, you know Dex a few years like we do, him getting pissed is like an early Christmas present. He never gets riled up enough to lose it at Pins. Mayhem is another story but here? Never."

I'd thought about that after I'd finished off my soda with him in the back. His mood had switched to laid-back Dex in the blink of an eye. He'd asked me about what my life had been like back in Florida, and if I'd ever dealt with so many insolent people before at any of my other jobs. The answer to that last question had been a blatant "no" that made us both laugh.

Despite the fact that I had no doubts Dex would have kicked that guy's ass if he hadn't left and that it was kind of scary that someone could get so angry, I had to say, it was kind of hot.

Pretty hot.

All right, it was plain hot.

But I didn't know what to do with it and knew I shouldn't do anything with that thought.

Dex was my boss. My boss who'd been a dick to me in the past, but still was a dick to other people. On the other hand, this was still the same man who had opened up to me about things that were undoubtedly difficult for him. And the same one who knew things I hadn't told anyone. The caring grump.

"How's your piercing?" Slim asked.

Not wanting to pull up my shirt while I was sitting—my pants were really tight and that was the excuse I'd use for the little roll hanging over the waist band— I stood as I told him. "Good, I think."

I pulled up my shirt, just over the belly button. "It's only sore if I touch it, but that's normal, right?"

Slim nodded, leaning forward to rest his elbows on his knees to look at the green gem in the middle. "Yeah, that's normal. It looks good."

I pushed the ring up and down like he'd told me to, to keep the skin from healing around the metal. "I like it."

The alarm beeped from the hallway, followed by the sound of motorcycle boots on the tile floor as Slim reached up to poke at my rib cage with his index finger. "One day, you have to let me do something here. I think it'd look pretty wicked, Ris."

I snorted at the same time that familiar figure came into my peripheral vision. "Let me think about it."

Dex stopped and eyed our placement critically through narrowed eyes before I yanked my shirt back down and shot him an innocent smile.

"Ready?" I asked.

He nodded his reply.

I called out a goodbye to Blue and Slim when we were out of the shop. All of us except Dex were used to walking toward the lot together each night. Dex always parked in front of the shop. Every single time. It was like the universe and all of its inhabitants knew that spot in front of Pins was his and only his.

Dex had barely gotten on his bike, having passed me the helmet when he said, "I got somewhere to go tonight. I'm taking you to your car, and you can drive back to my place from there."

I pretty much knew how to get to his house, and while I wasn't crazy about the idea of staying there alone when he lived in the middle of nowhere, I couldn't really argue or be a baby about it. "Okay," came out of my mouth but it was reluctant.

He parked in front of the driveway again when we stopped at Sonny's place. It was eerie how quiet the house seemed. Usually by the time I came home from work, Sonny had already turned on the porch light, and another light inside of the house would be on as a welcoming beacon for me. But there were no lights anymore, his SUV was gone, and his bike, along with Trip's, were under the carport. It hit me how mad the sight of it made me.

All because of our dad.

I'd barely taken the helmet off when I frowned at Dex. I asked him the same question he'd snapped at me for earlier. "Still nothing from Sonny?"

His head shake was grim. "Not yet, but it ain't a big deal. Knowin' them, they're drivin' nonstop, babe."

I let out a deep breath and nodded. There was no way I could realistically expect Sonny to keep tabs with me, and especially not with Dex. I couldn't imagine a man in his thirties calling his little half-sister to tell her every single time they stopped for gas. "Okay. Well, I guess I'll get going."

He extended his hand out to wrap around my wrist. "Text me when you get there." His heavy eyes stayed on me the entire time. "There's a spare key under the garden gnome in the front yard."

Ahh, that would explain the garden gnome's existence. He'd seemed so out of place in the plants that hadn't been tended to in way too long.

"Will do." Taking a few steps back toward my car, I wiggled my fingers at him. "Be safe."

I tried to tell myself that there was nothing to be mad at.

I did.

I shouldn't have been worried that Dex hadn't come home that night, that he never texted me after I messaged him that I made it to his house. He was a big boy. He could do whatever he wanted.

I swear, I really tried not to be mad, but I was.

Falling asleep on the couch was nothing new. Being paranoid that someone would break into the house that was in the middle of nowhere—without a friggin' alarm!— was too much. I kept envisioning those men who had taken Sonny showing up. When that disaster ended, I'd start thinking of serial killers with masks on breaking a window and killing me, and then flaying my skin off to mount on their wall. Dramatic? Maybe a little.

So maybe my lack of sleep was part of the reason why I was so annoyed—not mad—that Dex hadn't made it back. Or texted me.

I'd sent him another message that he didn't respond to.

Feeling weird being at his house by myself and not wanting to deal with it any longer, I left a note on top of his dining room table telling him that I was going to run some errands. First, I stopped at the YMCA and swam as many laps as I could push through. Then I ended up going to the mall and bought new pants and a couple of shirts so that I wouldn't be walking around worrying about clean cardigans that covered what my tank tops didn't. After that, I watched another movie and went to work.

Almost immediately, I regretted making it in.

I'd been in the middle of trying to look up videos on how to fix the thermo fax when a little hussy—I say little but she easily had three or four inches on me while I probably had about five pounds on her—appeared. She came in wearing a mini-skirt that looked like something made for someone my height—or a ten year old's—and thick red hair that made me a little jealous. And she was carrying a vest that looked familiar.

Her thin, pretty face pinched into a scowl when she stopped in front of my desk, looking at me through the dark tint of her huge sunglasses. "I need to drop this off for Dex."

"All right," I told her, already extending my arms out to take it as my annoyance factor went up about twenty degrees.

"He left this at my house last night," she added. Why she mentioned that I had no idea.

Why I felt a twitch at my eye, I had no idea either.

I just blinked at her, taking the vest from her hands before I stood up, my stomach fluttering. "All right."

"All right," she repeated in a low voice. "Later."

And just like that she was gone.

Then, just like that I got even more annoyed.

I'd sat there worrying about goddamn Dex doing something stupid to help us out with the Reapers, while in the meantime he was off at some woman's house? I swear even my butthole tensed up in frustration as I carried Dex's jacket to the back and hung it up on a chair in the break room.

I knew it wasn't worth the effort worrying about a grown ass man like Dex. I knew it, but still, I'd lost sleep over it. Asshole.

"Skyler bothers the fuck out of me, too."

I turned around to see Blake standing at the doorway to the room, hands shoved into his pockets. "You know when you meet someone and you're immediately annoyed?"

He laughed. "It's her face, and maybe those windshield sized sunglasses she's always wearing."

They really did look like tinted windshields, the visual made me grin at Blake as I ignored the fact he'd hinted that she'd been in before. "Yeah, you're right. That's probably it."

Blake's easygoing expression melted into a worried one as he crossed the room toward the vending machine. "I heard about Sonny."

Ugh. I frowned at the reminder.

"You heard anything from him?"

I wished.

"No, but then no one tells me anything either." I paused for a second to look at my fingernails. "I'm sure he's fine."

Oh boy. How many times had I used and heard someone use the word "fine" to describe how they were doing? I could happily go the rest of my life without hearing that vague term ever again.

Blake sighed. "Sounds like a mess. That crew's nothing to fool around with though." He raised both his black eyebrows. "You need to be careful until it all gets sorted out."

The urge to laugh was right on my tongue. Sleeping at Dex's alone was definitely being careful. Right.

I flinched a little at the thought. Where the heck had I gotten so negative? It was weird.

He shrugged. "Well, let me know if you hear anything about him. I need to go set up for my next client."

The bald man I'd seen twice flickered through my brain. Then the memory of being terrified at Dex's house pushed that one aside.

The need to work out the issue going on with my dad seemed too important all of a sudden to leave Sonny to deal with it alone. It wasn't friggin' fair for either one of us. Plus, would they really do something to me? Oh boy, I hoped not. "Wait! Blake!"

He paused at the door, looking over his shoulder. "Yeah?"

I snapped my fingers together to play off the question poised on my tongue. "What's the name of the president of that Reapers club? The bald guy?" I was so full of shit but I knew Blake wouldn't tell me if I made it seem that Dex had hidden something like that from me.

Blake's face scrunched up. "Liam?"

I snapped my fingers like a little liar. "Yeah, I couldn't remember." I smiled at him as he shrugged and made his way toward the front, leaving me in the back to try and figure out a way to get the guy's last name without being conspicuous.

And that would be by asking Slim when Blake was busy. Sometimes a girl's gotta do, what a girl's gotta do. In my case, it was finding a way back to Sonny's.

CHAPTER NINETEEN

Standing outside of the strip club, I knew what I was about to do was monumentally stupid. Astronomically dumb. And if—okay, *when*—my brother found out, he'd more than likely try to strangle me.

But screw it. Desperate times called for desperate measures, and I was used to dealing with things on my own. If the tables had been turned and I'd been the one who had gotten the shit kicked out of me, every nerve cell in my brain was confident that Sonny would have done something equally as stupid to get me back.

I wasn't about to let him down when he needed me for the first time.

That's exactly what I kept telling myself as I flashed my license at the bouncer standing at the entrance. He looked at me, then my ID, and then back at me before waving me in.

I really was a moron.

After asking Slim in passing what the last name of "that Liam guy" was, I'd then asked him "where do the Reapers hang out again? Dex told me not to drive by there but I can't remember the name." My poor, sweet Slim had answered so nonchalantly, he never could have expected that I was planning on visiting the rival motorcycle club.

Or...maybe he just didn't assume I'd be that dumb. You know, being the daughter of a former member of the Widowmakers, and that specific member happened to owe them a crap-ton of money. And the half-sister of a current member that they'd beat the crap out of. Triple the shit factor, and also the employee of a short-tempered Widow.

Well, I'd had a good run while I had the chance.

Using the excuse that I had a "girl emergency", I'd stormed out of Pins a little after seven. It'd taken me nearly an hour to drive to the strip club the Reapers hung out at in the outskirts of San Antonio. Judging by the five motorcycles I'd seen parked in the lot, I figured at least a few of the members were there.

Hopefully the bald guy was there. He had to be one of the main guys in the MC.

No sooner had I walked into the smoke-machine infested club with two dozen strobe lights and black lights dazzling the room, did I spot the corner where five very gruff looking men sat like kings.

The bald guy was hanging off the edge of his seat, looking more bored than entranced by the monstrous E-cup breasts onstage. My hands had started shaking at some point, so I clenched them into fists and took a deep breath.

Sonny would do worse than this for me.

Plus, they wouldn't kill me or do something crazy like that in public? Right? I friggin' hoped so.

Those twenty steps around the club to the corner of doom were the longest of my life. At about fifteen out of the twenty, the bald guy—who didn't look like he was actually bald the closer I got—spotted me. He didn't tense up or look alarmed as I sucked in a breath and steeled myself to beg for something. Was that what I was doing? Begging? For my dad?

Apparently, I was, but I liked to think that I was doing it more for Sonny than for our deadbeat father.

The other men had turned to look too, all at least ten years older than me if not twenty. They looked more interested than I'd like. It might have been because I was the only female in the building wearing more than tiny shorts and a top that ended half a dozen inches above my waist.

I was two feet away from the bald guy—not bald, his hair looked like it grew in everywhere but must have been shaved often— when he tilted his chin up at me and my nerves kicked in. When that happened, I turned into an idiot—a blabbering idiot with no social skills.

"Hi," I squeaked out. And then I waved.

Jesus Christ, what was wrong with me?

The bald man, Liam McDonaugh from the intel I'd gathered from my unsuspecting coworkers, raised a single dark eyebrow. "Hey," he replied hesitantly, more than likely believing I was nuts.

If they didn't kill me, I'd kill myself for this stupidity.

One or two of the other men grunted in response, making my nerves worse.

What in the friggin' hell had I been thinking? Seriously? What? That these men would compromise with me? Give my dad an extension for his debt? God, why the hell hadn't I at least told Slim or Blake where I was going?

"Not that I don't mind a pretty face standing in front of me, but you look like you're gonna puke, doll. I don't wanna get thrown up on," the Liam man drawled.

Screw me. Screw me now.

"I won't throw up on you. I swear." I smiled nervously, trying so hard not to think about bursting into frustrated tears.

Liam just looked at me in that same intense way Dex did, stripping me of my dignity and strength slowly.

Shit!

"My dad—," crap! That wasn't the picture I should paint. "Curt Taylor owes your club money and you went after my brother for it—," I had to suck in a breath to try and steady my speech. It sounded like I was trembling. "Is there any way you can give him an extension? He doesn't even like us," I blurted out.

The bald man, Liam, smiled crookedly. His eyebrows tented up. "That so?"

"I haven't seen him in almost ten years," I told him honestly. "I swear he won't give a crap what happens to either one of us."

That smug, crooked smile stayed in place. "I find that hard to believe, doll."

Holy moly. My hands shook though they were still in fists at my sides. "Look, I don't know why he hasn't paid you back but I'm sorry. I'm really sorry." I could feel the tears singing in the corners of my eyes as panic swelled like a tidal wave in my chest. "If I had the money, I'd pay it back so that you wouldn't go after my brother again."

I had to purse my lips together so that I wouldn't start sniffling.

Liam's eyes widened. In the dark building, I couldn't exactly see what color they were but I'm sure they were dark on his pale face. In fact, it was a pale, handsome face if you liked that rugged, late-thirties bad-man type.

He leaned forward, elbows on his knees, hands dangling between his outstretched legs. Those murky eyes roamed over me quickly, once, twice, three times. "You new here?"

I'm sure he already knew the answer but I nodded anyway.

"It's safe to say that you don't know how shit is run then, doll. You didn't know that bitches—excuse me, *ladies* don't come around dipping into their men's business. The last thing your cute ass needs to be doing is coming to my place and asking me for something I have no obligation to give you," Liam said carefully.

This wasn't exactly going the way I wanted it to.

I must have made a face because he held up a finger to interrupt me. "But, you're here and I can tell you're scared out of your mind." This was true. Totally true. Now standing, Liam didn't exactly tower over me like Dex, but he was still at least six feet. His build was broad, more bodybuilder type than lean and hard-packed. And his personality? Guh. Made him seem even bigger. It might have been the intelligent, crazy look in his eye that seemed oddly familiar. Hmm.

"I can appreciate the guts it took you to come over here, asking for your bro's sake," he said, coming to stand directly in front of me while I stayed rooted in place mainly from fear. His gaze, which I could now confirm as being brown, bore into mine. "And you're smoking hot. That helps out my temper, too."

There was a frog in my throat. Maybe several because I croaked as he leaned into me. A violent urge to push against his chest was at the forefront of my brain but realistically, there was no way I could make it out of the club in one piece.

"Give me some sugar and I'll let you get out of here without a problem. I might even think about only charging your damn daddy for nine instead of ten more in interest," he breathed.

Oh friggin' hell. Nine thousand? In interest? On top of ten? Crap.

"What do you say?" Liam tucked his chin in, staring down at me.

I froze. "You want sugar?" I had a feeling he wasn't asking for the thing I liked to put in my coffee.

He nodded slowly.

My mouth had to be gaping wide. It had to. "I don't think so," I whispered, still not moving.

Play opossum, Ris! Play opossum!

Liam smiled grand. Okay, it was too late to play dead. The movement made him appear even more good-looking than before. "You do," he chuckled, coming even closer to my face. "Nine instead of ten, doll face."

I don't know why I inhaled, but I did and he smelled like a musky cologne. It was pretty nice but all it succeeded in doing was making me feel a bit dizzy. My emotions and fears were all over the place.

"He doesn't give a shit about us." I swallowed, keeping an eye on his ever descending lips.

Holy cow, his mouth was literally a few millimeters from mine. *Don't do something stupid, Iris! Don't do it!*

Liam chuckled again, sounding deeper. "Whatever you say," he whispered... right before he kissed me.

I wanted to kick my own ass.

Getting behind the wheel of my Focus with my lips still tingling from their visit with Liam's mouth, and what seemed like a ten pound weight settled nicely in my belly, I felt sick. Like I'd done something horribly wrong. Terribly, terribly wrong.

It also didn't help that I knew I'd been a complete idiot walking into that strip club. Such an idiot—

The wailing ring of my cell phone snapped me out of the mental ass-kicking I was giving myself. Pure, sickening dread lined my belly. Because I knew, I knew *somehow* that I wasn't going to want to answer the call. Don't tell me how I knew, I just did.

And when I picked my phone out of my purse—the one I'd left in the backseat of my car when I'd gone inside—the screen flashed the name of possibly the only man I dreaded speaking to occasionally.

Dex.

Shoot me now.

I sucked in a breath and let out the exhale as soon as I hit the button to answer. "Hello?" My voice might have been a little more squeaky than I would have liked.

"Where the fuck are you?"

Oh boy.

"Ahh..."

Dex didn't even wait a second to bark out, "Where the hell you at, Ritz?"

"I'm driving back to Pins," I croaked, hitting the mute button while I turned the ignition and put the car into reverse so he wouldn't hear anything that would give me away.

"By yourself?" he asked in a slow, careful voice that did nothing to ease my anxiety.

"Yeah." I wasn't going to lie to him about that.

The pause it took for him to respond made me steel my spine for whatever was going to spill out of his mouth. "Iris," he said in a low, low voice. "Meet me at Mayhem." His tone was way too controlled. Crap!

"I should get back to Pins, I've been gone awhile."

I could hear him breathing over the phone. "No. See me at Mayhem."

Before I got a chance to argue with him anymore, he hung up. Hung up on me. That dick. Shit! No!

The realization that they had no idea I'd driven all the way to San Antonio was right on the front of my thoughts. I was going to need to do some serious speeding to remotely save my ass because there was no way in hell I was going to tell him where I'd gone if he'd gotten that pissed off over me leaving to begin with.

Unfortunately, I sped. The speeding caused me to get to Mayhem a lot quicker than I liked, even though I knew that I still hadn't gotten back fast enough to really play off being nearby.

The lot for the bar was packed for it being a weeknight, then again, I probably shouldn't be surprised. I highly doubted most of the people inside cared whether they drank during the work week or not. I'd barely stepped into Mayhem after flashing my license at the bouncer, when I caught sight of the blonde I'd seen Dex with back at the body shop so long ago. She was sitting at the bar, right next to a Widow by the patches on his heavily weathered vest.

Well, I guess Son wasn't kidding about the girl getting around.

I didn't see Dex anywhere but that didn't exactly ease my nerves. I mean, he couldn't kill me with so many witnesses around.

"Have you seen Dex?" I asked the first bartender that walked by me.

The lady tipped her head up. "Upstairs, sugar."

Sheeeit.

It felt like I'd just been doomed to participate in a Death March. God. Sucking in another breath, I reminded myself that Dex wouldn't do anything to me. He wouldn't. Except maybe rip me a new butthole with his mouth. Well, with his words.

The same WMC member that had come into Pins when I'd first gotten the job—the one with the beer belly—stood at the bottom of the stairway that I'm sure was about to lead to hell. He cocked an eyebrow at me . "Sonny's sis?"

I nodded.

A smirk inched across his face. "All the way up," was the only thing he said.

I will not gag. I will not gag. I will not gag.

"Thanks," I muttered, making my way up the first, and then the second flight of stairs. Despite the loud music blaring from the main floor, I could hear the deep rumble of voices coming from the third floor.

The doorway led to a large room with two loveseats and a futon closest to the door facing no particular direction. Just behind the seating on the far side of the wall, three desks took up the remaining space.

And seated at the desk in the corner, surrounded by Luther and two other Widows, was Dex.

Dex who was staring at me like he was plotting my murder.

I did the only thing a logical person who feared for her safety—kind of—would do. I pretended like nothing happened by flashing the most fake grin in the natural world.

He stared at me, the tick in his jaw was noticeable even so far away.

Dex's gaze didn't waver for a second. "Get your ass over here, Ritz," he demanded in a cool voice.

Nothing was going to happen. Nothing.

My feet moved on their own with no regard to the fate they were leading us to. "Hi."

Did I get a "hi" back? Nope. Four faces stared back at me, completely unemotional.

I stopped just next to the member I recognized from the day Dex had shown up with Trip after Sonny's disappearance. He happened to be the only one who didn't look like I'd stomped all over his sand castle.

"Baby." Dex sat back in his chair, crossing those long, heavily tattooed arms over his chest.

I swallowed.

"Where you been?" He enunciated his words a little too carefully.

Well, there was no way in friggin' hell they were going to get the truth out of me, and in retrospect, what I blurted out my mouth really wasn't any better. At all. "I went to go buy some tampons." That wasn't so bad, but the rest...? "And then I had to run over to Sonny's house to change my pants since I bled all over them."

Kill me. Kill. Me.

Tampons. Bleeding on myself. Sonny's place.

Dex leaned forward over the desk, his elbows coming down hard on the surface. I could see the movement of his tongue sweeping over his teeth beneath his closed mouth. And then his jaw locked. "You went to Son's?" His lips peeled back to reveal a line of straight white teeth. "By yourself?"

I'd crapped all over that explanation, hadn't I? It wasn't like I could backtrack, dang it. "Yes," I tried to tell him as securely as I could.

He blinked, shifting his eyes to Luther's looming frame just to his side before returning to me. He blinked again, reaching up with one hand to run his thumb and index finger down the sides of his mouth. The pause was pregnant and heavy.

Out of the corner of my eye, I saw the member I didn't recognize shaking his head.

"You dumb little shit."

Uhh, what?

The muscles in Dex's biceps popped as he gritted his teeth, talking to me. Me! A dumb little shit?

"You know your pa owes the Reapers twenty?"

Why, yes, yes, I did but I couldn't tell him that and regardless, it didn't seem like he wanted an answer because he kept talking.

"What the fuck do you think they'll do to you, Ritz?" I think he may have gnashed his teeth. "They beat the shit out of Son back before they decided to up the debt. What the fuck do you think they'll do if they get you?" he asked in a louder voice than I'd ever heard him use. His features were too tight, too pissed off. "Huh? You can't be that fuckin' stupid, can you?"

Holy crap.

Something nasty knotted in my chest and all of a sudden, I couldn't bear to look at him.

"Iris!" he yelled at me. Yelled! "This isn't a fuckin' joke. You can't run around town doin' whatever the hell you want. Nobody has time to babysit you all day, do you understand me?"

Don't cry. Don't cry. Don't cry.

It took me a second to realize that I was blinking a lot. Blinking while I looked up at the ceiling instead of my boss' face.

"Iris," he grunted, his tone still holding the slightly hysterical note that relayed the extent of his anger. "Do. You. Understand?"

I didn't have it in me to answer him with words, so I had to settle for a nod. A nod I directed at the ceiling, while I had to tell myself that I wouldn't cry in front of him—them.

I mean, I get that he had a point. And I completely understood that he was watching out for me. But seriously? Was this the way he was going to go about it?

Just like my mess of an explanation came out of my mouth, so did the small amount of pride I still managed to have after getting yelled at.

It also might have also been just a little childish but I was too hurt and humiliated to care. "I didn't think it mattered after I got left alone all night and day, Charlie." By Charlie I really meant Dick.

He opened his mouth just a fraction before closing it. His dark blue eyes narrowed. "Get back to the damn shop," he snapped.

This jerk was going to get punched in the nuts. If I wasn't stuck staying with him, he'd get punched in the nuts and I'd put dish detergent into his food. Dex had a point. Of that there wasn't a doubt, but making a point didn't mean you have to be a complete asswipe.

Plus, hadn't Sonny told me that Dex needed someone to tell him when he was being a dick? Sure, I'd done worse but that wasn't the point. He didn't know that, and he never would if this was any indication of how he handled stuff.

So fuck him. I sucked in a deep breath to ward off the tears that were right there and forced a smile on my face. It was ugly and unnatural but at that point, I didn't care. The guy was a man of his word. He'd put up with me until Sonny got back.

I think.

Smiling that creepy smile, I curtsied, staring straight into those dark eyes. "Whatever you want, your majesty."

Luther snickered just barely.

But Dex? Dex just stared right back.

"You gonna let her talk to you like that, man?" the Widow I didn't recognize asked.

Those blue eyes swung directly from me to the man. Dex looked at the man even more aggressively than he had me. "I don't remember askin' for your opinion, shit for brains, so shut the fuck up."

If I wasn't so mad and hurt, I'd probably get a kick out of his words, but I was.

The man made a noise in his throat. "D—"

I coughed and took a step back. "I'm going back to the shop," I told them in a quiet voice, watching Dex as he kept his gaze steady on his MC brother.

"Text me when you're headin' home later," he grunted, still not tearing his attention away from the man.

I looked over at Luther to see him watching the two younger men.

Whatever.

I didn't bother saying anything else before turning around and heading toward the door. I jogged down the stairs as fast as I could because all of a sudden, I felt like crying all over again.

CHAPTER TWENTY

The look on Slim's face when I pushed through the door of Pins said way too much.

If he were prone to biting his fingernails, I think he would have been in the process of doing it. Instead, he smiled apologetically, lines creasing his forehead. "You okay?"

I tilted my head down and looked at him with wide eyes, rounding the reception desk to drop my purse on the floor. By some miracle, I'd managed not to cry.

No sooner had I gotten into the car had I realized that I couldn't exactly burst into tears at how upset and embarrassed I was. It made sense that Dex would be mad. I understood that. I really did. The problem was that he'd ripped me a new one, and the fact that it'd been done in public just made it worse—a heck of a lot worse. It was clear I was an inconvenience, but was it necessary to put things like I was a stupid child?

My chest hurt and I'd started hiccupping like crazy while I drove the two blocks down to Pins.

But screw it, I wasn't going to do it. I wasn't going to cry for no reason.

All right, there was a reason but that was beside the point. Deep down, I knew what I'd done was beyond foolish. If anyone had found out, I could only imagine what kind of shit storm The Dick would have raised. Hell, Sonny would have probably found out and I truly doubted he had any issues with actually knocking some sense into me.

So I'd be taking that little tidbit to the grave with me from the looks of it.

"I'm fine," I told him but the reality was that my voice seemed higher than normal. Obviously, I wasn't completely fine.

The last thing I wanted was to see any of the Widows anytime soon, especially Dex. Which didn't exactly work since I was staying with the guy. Damn it.

Slim gave me a disbelieving look that just barely overshadowed his apologetic one. "Was he pissed?"

I snorted, making my redheaded friend wince.

"Yeah. Sorry, Iris. You know we don't care if you leave for a while but Dex called right after you left. Then he called again every ten minutes after that, checking to see if you'd made it back." He bared his teeth. "Sorry."

Like I could get mad at Slim for being honest. I shrugged and fished through my purse for a stick of gum, tossing a piece at him. "It's okay. I shouldn't have been gone that long." That was kind of the truth.

"We were all a little worried." He flashed me a bright smile. "It just means we like you."

If calling someone a dumb shit was a way of showing them affection, then I definitely didn't want to have any friends.

For the next few hours, I tried my absolute best to not think about what had gone down on the top floor of Mayhem. I was a little sad, a little mad, and a lot frustrated. Frustrated because I wished this crap with the sperm donor wouldn't have happened because then Sonny would be in Austin, and I'd be at his house, and things would just be fine.

It made me feel selfish but oh well.

We closed up the shop a little after midnight, and I sent Dex a text as soon as I'd gotten into the car. With any luck, I'd get back to his place before him and could feign being asleep to avoid any other crap. Now, if he was home already, I was screwed and wanted a minute to mentally prepare myself for him.

So I thought it'd be a good idea to drive by Mayhem and make sure he was still there, otherwise...

Yeah.

I slowed down to drive by the parking lot, but I recognized him even before I was close. After seeing him outside of Pins so many times, leaning against the wall with his cigarette between his lips and fingers, his stance was identifiable. It was all Dex. Relaxed and strong, reeking of all the shits he didn't give.

And right next to him was the same redhead that had come into the shop earlier.

They were talking but his attention was focused on the biker I recognized from Sonny's place, the one I'd stood next to just a few hours before.

Jealousy and I don't know what else it was—it was bitter and stung my throat—rose up into my mouth. Because...

What did I expect? That Dex was some kind of celibate saint? He was attractive. Incredibly attractive. And he was really nice when he wanted to be. He was even nice in his own way when he didn't want to be. And he'd told me things about himself that I was confident he didn't share often. And he took care of me in his rough, Dick way. I liked Dex.

Holy shit.

I liked Dex.

I don't know why it hadn't hit me before. Maybe because he was my boss and he still got on my nerves pretty often.

But mainly because I realized deep down inside of me that there was no point in accepting or recognizing any feelings I could have for a man like him. A man who did his duty to his friend's sister.

God, I was such an idiot.

Such a friggin' idiot.

I hit the gas to accelerate at the same time I reached out to grab my phone, hitting the second person under my favorites to call.

It rang for a while, almost too long but right at the last moment, he answered.

"Ris?" Sonny answered in a raspy voice.

A shuddering breath made its way out of my lungs. "Hey, Sonny."

There was a bunch of noise in the background. The sound of a door opening and closing. "Hey kid, I was just thinking about you," he said. "You doing okay?"

Ugh. The one day out of so many when I wasn't fine, and he'd ask. "Eh," I answered him honestly. I mean, I'd already lied enough today. No need to tarnish my record anymore, especially not with my brother. "You?"

He sighed. Long and deep. "I've been better, too."

Something about his tone nipped at me. "What's wrong?" I asked him carefully.

"Ahh, kid," he hedged.

Like that would stop me. "Where are you?"

"Almost to Denver. I don't know what the name of this shitty little town is but we're in Colorado."

Colorado? "Is that where you think the sperm donor is?"

The three second long hesitation should have been my warning sign. "Maybe. My friends in Arizona said they know he'd passed through a couple weeks ago, so I'm hoping he went up north since he used to live there."

"Oh." It frustrated me how little I knew about my dad, though it shouldn't. "Did he live there recently?"

Another pause. More hesitation. "Uh, not really. I just don't think he'd be dumb enough to go back to Cali if he knows there's people looking for him."

So, Curt Taylor had lived in Denver for a while before ending up in California somewhere? What was it about this guy that made him unable to settle down?

And then it hit me, caustically, like a massive stone stuck in my kidneys, tearing a fresh line of pain through my insides.

What was the one thing this man always ran from, Iris? My brain screamed.

"Son," was all I could manage to get out of my mouth while I maneuvered across the freeway.

"Ris." He was being too different. Too guarded.

Neither one of us said anything for too long. Only the steady in and out of our breaths crossed the cellular connection. I was scared to ask, scared to desire the confirmation of the fear that had rooted itself into my stomach, and Sonny? Sonny was probably nervous about answering any more questions I had.

He knew. He knew that I had an idea.

As much as I genuinely didn't want to know, the question just kind of came out in a gasp. "Is there—?"

My brother, my beloved half-brother, sighed. "I'm sorry, Ris. I didn't know how to tell you."

Of course he wouldn't. Fuck. Fuck. Fuck!

"Lu told me about it fucking forever ago. Your mom had been really sick back then, and you were just a kid—"

It felt like the blood instantly drained from my body. Back when my mom had been sick?

I must have made some sort of sound because Sonny let out a long line of colorful curse words that I would have appreciated if I hadn't just found out that my father had more kids while he was still married to my dying mother.

That time I did hear the ugly choking sound that exploded out of my mouth.

"I'm sorry, Ris. I know I should've told you but I couldn't," he murmured, his voice straining. "I love you, kid. I love you so fucking much and you've been through enough shit already, I just couldn't do that to you."

For being the kind of person that cried whenever I felt anything slightly more than normal, later on, I could wonder why I didn't burst into tears at Sonny's words. At his explanation. His truth and lies. At my father's indiscretions and mistakes.

But in that moment, all I could focus on was the burning that scorched my guts and throat. It was betrayal and jealousy and anger in its purest form.

"Talk to me," Sonny pleaded over the line, pulling me back from the insane thoughts going through my head.

I shouldn't be mad. I shouldn't feel anything.

But the problem was, that I did.

"Iris," he called out.

"Shit," I muttered into the phone, somehow managing to keep on the barely familiar drive toward Dex's place. "I just—I just can't wrap my head around it. How old...?"

He groaned, telling me that this definitely wasn't a conversation that was easy on him either. "I don't know for sure. I'm guessing like ten, eleven."

That son of a friggin' whore.

Lava-like anger flared through my chest again. When I was fourteen, I'd been in the middle of radiation. My Mom had been getting weekly chemotherapy treatments that ravaged her. And what had that asshole been doing? Making babies? Babies that he apparently didn't take care of.

Another ugly choking noise sprang out of my throat no matter how hard I tried to repress it.

I mean, how the fuck could he have done that? Sure my parents were separated, but seriously?

"What's wrong with him?" I gasped into the receiver.

"I don't know," Sonny replied, sounding way too glum. "He's fucked up in the head, kid."

He was fucked up in the head and he was a huge asshole. A monstrous asshole.

"I can't believe it." Because I could remember his face when he'd come down right before my mom died two years later. His face when he came into the hospital room to see her, was etched into my memory. There was no way he could have faked his devastation, but maybe that had been my problem.

I hadn't really thought about it. He'd been devastated for my mom. But I'd been in remission at the time of his visit and not once had he ever even made a peep about my arm. About my own situation. I'd caught him looking at the scarring from time to time, this man I wasn't sure what to think of, but he never said a word.

That reminder just refueled my resentment.

"Are you with Dex?"

I sucked in a deep, ragged breath. "No."

"Where are you?" he asked in a gentle voice.

"Driving to his house."

There was another infamous pause. "By yourself?"

Damn it. I could have lied to him or at least not mentioned the earlier incident but I didn't have it in me. If he'd finally confessed to the existence of our other half-sibling then I could at least tell him something. "He's pissed off at me." My voice was still too ragged. "I left Pins and stopped by your house without him. He got really mad."

The only response I got was a long, low groan. He was trying not to blow his lid. Sonny knew I didn't need or want to hear him bitching at me. "Goddamnit, Ris," he sighed. "Don't do that again."

"I won't." God, I sounded so meek.

Another long pause filled the line. A million thoughts being processed by two different brains, I could only imagine. "Look, I'll let you know how everything goes. I want to find him as soon as possible, and Trip's helping. Once I get back, we'll figure shit out."

I didn't know what shit there was to figure out but a small voice told me that he was probably referring to the child in Colorado that, at least at the moment, neither one of us were fans of. I'm sure that once I wasn't so mad anymore, I'd come to my senses. From what Sonny had said, our dad hadn't stuck around there for long either. That man was a creature of habit.

Damn it. I could feel myself getting pissed off all over again. Even more so than before.

"Okay, Sonny." I wanted to bang my head against the steering wheel, but there was still another five minutes of driving left ahead of me.

"Are we gonna be okay?" he had the nerve to ask.

My heart swelled, only momentarily eclipsing the fury I felt toward our asshole sperm donor. My vow to not call him an asshole had apparently disappeared at some point.

Will might not answer my emails or bother to pick up a phone and call me, but Sonny had always looked out for me. It had always been an even give and take between us. We weren't forced together by obligation, but instead he'd gone out of his way to be in my life and I'd gladly accepted it.

And I hoped—I knew—I always would.

"I love you, dude. We'll always be fine."

The long sigh he answered with was relief for both of us. He promised to call me again soon and let me know what he found out, and I promised not to do anything stupid again. If he only knew.

I pushed all thoughts of my dad out of my head over the last minute of my trip to Dex's. I didn't think of him as I parked the car and made it in. I didn't think of anything as I grabbed clothes out of my duffel and headed into the shower.

But about a minute after I'd stepped into the stall, I thought of him.

And I screamed.

Not like a horror-movie scream, but the same kind of scream I'd expelled when I knew without a doubt that there was no hope for my mom. It physically hurt me.

The tears that followed afterward were just as painful.

Sonny had told me once that I'd felt everything more with our dad because I was the one who'd had him the longest. More than Sonny by far. Will was only five when he'd left us, and I doubted he remembered much about the bearded man that used to tuck him into bed. The man he'd cried over for months. I'd been the one with the most memories. The kid who had cried over him for longer than a few months.

Those memories, right then, I damned. Because I was too old to feel so territorial, so betrayed. I had no right. I had no reason.

I couldn't help it though.

The fact that he'd had another kid while we'd gone through so much made me feel insignificant. Whatever issues I think I'd secretly harbored with abandonment flared up.

I thought of Will. Of my poor mom, and I wondered if she'd known about Colorado. The idea that she might have found out killed me a little inside.

Before I knew it, the tears had turned into sobs, then the sobs had turned into whimpers, and the anger and sadness was replaced with cold indifference.

By some miracle I managed to turn off the water—I hadn't bothered with soap or shampoo—and I tugged my clothes on, fighting back those pathetic tears that were ready to commit suicide again. The reflection in the mirror showed me that I was a mess. I didn't have an appetite and all I wanted was oblivion for the night.

The problem was that the home I was in wasn't mine.

And the man who owned the home happened to be standing in the hall outside of the bathroom, waiting for me when I opened the door.

Dex's eyes were hooded, his normally sensual mouth parted, and his gaze bore a hole straight into me.

I dropped my own eyes down to the floor, the memory of what exactly had happened at Mayhem only stacking onto my misery. "Not right now, Dex," I told him in a voice that sounded more of a croak than anything. I walked right past him, heading into the living room where I flopped onto the couch, taking over the main length of it, face-down like a fussy kid. My face buried into the soft material of the pillow I set on the end of the sofa that morning.

The floor creaked with his weight. I could sense him standing just off the side of the couch. If I turned my head, I'm sure his feet would have been in my vision but I didn't do it. He just stood there for what seemed like forever.

"I'm not kidding, Dex."

He huffed. "Why?"

Why? Ohmigod. I wanted to scream again. "I'm feeling pretty worthless right now, all right?" I whispered into the cushion, just loud enough for him to hear. "The last thing I want is for you to make me feel like a pathetic moron again."

Did he say anything? No.

Instead, I felt the heat of his body get even closer right before the pillow below me was lifted, raising my head right along with it. A heartbeat later, he plopped into the empty spot, dropping the pillow on top of his lap so that my upper body rested on his thighs. The weight of his hand settled between my shoulder blades.

I tried sitting up onto my knees but his hand kept me down on top of him—well, the pillow. My boobs were smashed against his thigh but I didn't care. The last thing I wanted was for him to see me cry.

"Dex," I kind of whined.

He palmed the back of my neck, shifting down the couch just a bit. "Ritz."

"I don't want to hear it right now."

Dex made a humming noise. "I'm not gonna talk shit to you right now," he said in a silky, low voice. "I wanna know what the fuck had you screamin' in the shower, babe."

I hated him. Just a little.

"First I thought it was me that was makin' you cry but after a while, I figured I couldn't have made you that mad."

"Don't flatter yourself," I groaned. "You made me mad," I turned my mouth just to the side so I wouldn't drool all over the pillow. "But no, I'm not going to cry over you calling me ugly names and being a total dick."

He groaned, the hand on the nape of my neck tightened. His fingers massaging the sides. "I was pretty fuckin' pissed."

"Anytime you're pissed, you're always really friggin' pissed," I explained to him, earning a snicker from the big man beneath me. "You were a jerk."

Another groan. His hand slid over to my right shoulder blade. "You were bein' an idiot, Ritz."

"So you had to call me a dumb little shit in front of your friends?"

He didn't answer. Dex's large palm swept over to my other shoulder, cupping that one, too. "Lu told me I was too harsh with you," he admitted in what I could only assume was a contrite voice. "I was worried, all right?"

Hmm.

"I was plannin' on gettin' home and tannin' your ass like Ma used to do to me." His fingers went right back to my neck, the palm kissing my spine. "I don't really think you're a dumb little shit," he said.

I turned my head the other way to face his stomach. "Oh?"

"You're just a little shit, babe," Dex murmured. "You wanna tell me what all that mess in the shower was about?"

No, I didn't. Yet, there I was opening my mouth. "My dad's an asshole and an idiot."

"Whoa there, tiger. Watch the potty mouth," said the man that dropped the f-bomb at least one hundred times a day. Dex's long fingers swept down my spine all the way to where the elastic on my shorts were. A small part of me recognized that this was too intimate but the warm reassurance was exactly what I needed and wanted. "What happened?"

"He has another kid." I totally wheezed out the words. "My mom was friggin' dying, losing all of her hair, throwing up every day, and this asshole was off having babies with some lady, Dex." I gasped. "Does he not know what the hell a condom is used for? What kind of a selfish jackass does that?"

Of course, he didn't respond but I didn't care because the words just kept pouring out of my mouth.

"He loved my mom, was married to her, had kids with her and he left us. Just like that. Like we were nothing to him. One day he was there and the next he was telling my mom he couldn't stay any longer. *He was restless,* he said. I always hoped that maybe he'd come back. Maybe he'd miss us enough," I rambled. "But no. Nooooo. That fucking asshole doesn't give a shit about anyone. Not really."

Dex's hand slid up my back again, circling one side of my shoulders before moving to the other.

"And he has another kid, and he left that one too." God, I was pretty sure I was wheezing. "I hate him, Dex. I hate him for breaking my mom's heart, and leaving us, and for not caring. God dammit. I needed him—," Screw me. I'd started tearing up again, my voice cracking. "And he didn't give a fuck."

A watery cough escaped my body. "I just want life to quit taking a shit on me."

That large hand kept up its circling swipes, down one side of my back before moving over to the other while I sat there, trying to compose myself. Trying to bottle up the momentary anger that had made its way out of me. For a long time, we just sat there. Me still laying partially over Dex's lap, Dex with his hand moving around my back over my t-shirt. The silence was okay because I'd said what I needed to. I'd released the crap I'd held in for so long.

Because apparently, whether or not I'd stopped thinking about my dad years ago, the effect he'd left on me had been stored into the recesses of my conscience.

After a while, I tried to sit up but the heavy hand on the middle of my back kept me down.

"You feel better now?" Dex whispered.

I sniffled. "I guess."

"You better, babe." His fingers inched down like he was acting out the Itsy-Bitsy Spider on me. "I know you're hurtin' but that's enough."

Who the hell was this guy to tell me I'd cried enough or not? I tried to push back again but he wasn't having it. Dex made a tisking sound.

"No, no, no. You're gonna listen to me, Ritz. And you listen good."

Holy crap, this was going to be just like *yia-yia*'s lectures.

"That fuck is not worth your tears. He is not worth the love you've given him. He doesn't deserve it and he never will. I'm sure you needed your dad as a kiddo, honey, but you got a shitty one. And that shitty one is not gonna define you. He is not gonna be the reason you cry or don't trust people ever again.

"You're beautiful, and you're so fuckin' sweet, and you're smart, Ritz. You have to get that from your ma because you definitely don't get that shit from your pa. Knowin' Son and how much he feels for you, I know your ma wouldn't want you to suffer like you are."

His fingers tightened on my nape. "You are never gonna cry over that asshole again. I don't even want you to get mad when you think of him. He doesn't exist anymore. His shit will never hurt you again. Do you hear me?"

I hiccupped into the pillow, nodding just barely. I felt so overwhelmed, so raw, it was draining. I'd think about him again, there was no way I couldn't but at the moment, it was nice to believe that I could wash myself of Curt Taylor.

Dex's fingers extended to where the palm covered all of the back of my neck and his fingers wrapped around most of my throat. "My ma used to tell me you have to fight through some shitty ass days to get to the best days of your life. So I'm tellin' you now, that you gotta hang in there. I swear to you, after this shit is over, you're not gonna have to worry about him ever again." His thumb dug deep into my flesh.

I made a noise that sounded like I was dying. "Oh Dex."

"Babe, you're the sweetest little girl I've ever met. You deserve better than this broken heart bullshit." His fingers kneaded the muscles on my neck. "If I ever see that beautiful face cryin' again over somethin' that worthless sack of shit did, I'm gonna make your daddy regret ever meetin' your ma, you got it?"

A different kind of emotion overwhelmed me, temporarily blinding all the anger and resentment that had pierced my body. It made my insides clench and want to cry all over again. Because here was this man who had just called me a dumb little shit earlier, rubbing my back and promising things that were like some kind of super salve.

The words meant more because they came from Dex. Dex who wouldn't spout crap for the sake of being nice.

So when I sat up abruptly a minute later, letting his hand drop back to his lap, I inhaled this suffering, shuddering breath. I curled my lips behind my teeth and took in the dark scruff lining his jaw, the hard clench of his mouth, and I gulped.

"Would you mind giving me a hug?"

His mouth opened for a split second and his eyes flashed to mine, a trace of something in them. He was silent though, unmoving. I noticed a nerve under his eye twitching.

Dex's pause had me feeling like a jackass for a minute. If I really thought about it, he didn't strike me as the hugging type. Plus, I mean, who asks for a hug? Who—

"C'mere," he urged in his low voice.

I looked at him for a heartbeat, still feeling a little pathetic, but when he shifted onto his hip and lowered his chin to give me this look...I stopped caring. I shuffled forward and just went for it. Arms around his ribs, my forehead to his cheek.

It took a second but his arms wound their way around me. One band over my shoulders, the other around the middle of my back. And he squeezed. Dex held me to him, the faint smell of laundry detergent and Dex filling my nostrils. Warm skin, warm body, warm, warm, warm. So much warmth, this wild choke lodged in my throat.

I took a deep breath and shut my eyes.

He didn't say anything either, but I felt the deep breath that inflated his chest before he let it out over my ear.

CHAPTER TWENTY-ONE

"Would you quit looking at me like that?"

For the last five minutes, Dex had been sitting across the counter from me, staring. With his coffee cup raised just over his mouth, those dark blue eyes had been locked in my direction. At first I'd thought that there may have been maple syrup smothered somewhere on me but I'd touched all over and there was nothing there.

Those sleepy eyes were curious and way too intent. And it was probably because I hadn't slept so well after the long crying jag I'd thrown myself into, that it took me what felt like forever to figure out why he was looking at me with so much attention.

"I'm not going to spontaneously burst into tears, Dex," I finally advised him, rolling my eyes before shoveling another spoonful of oatmeal into my mouth.

From the sides of the coffee mug, I could see his lips tilt up just the slightest. What was up with that look in his eye? So. Weird. "Oh, I know you're not," the smug jerk said.

Both my eyebrows went straight up. It was impossible to understand what it was about his little challenges that had started baiting me every single time. "How do you know that?"

Those pink corners of his mouth tipped up even higher. "I told you last night you weren't gonna anymore."

This man. Good lord. I wasn't sure whether to be annoyed or amused. My gut was going with amusement. "Yeah, I'm pretty sure that's not how it works."

"Yeah, it is."

I blinked at him. "No, it's not, but thank you for hanging in there with me last night." By last night, I meant almost all night.

After the longest hug in the history of the world, he'd turned on the television and we watched what was left of Stargate in silence. Right next to each other, thigh to thigh.

"Whatever, babe," he shrugged, like it wasn't a big deal at all.

But to me it was. To me, what he'd done had been what had kept me up all night. It wasn't the newfound knowledge of my father's indiscretions, or my brother's lies, but Dex. Dex who'd been the complete opposite of The Dick at the bar. How the hell one man could change his colors so quickly was incomprehensible.

That was just Charlie Dex Locke though, I guess. One contradiction after another.

"Whatever," I mocked him in a husky voice, winking before I even realized I'd done it. What the hell had gotten into me?

His gaze was impenetrable. All that cool, gem-like blue zeroed in on me, making me just a little breathless.

I forced a smile onto my face. "Thank you anyway. It was really nice."

Still, he didn't flutter an eyelash as I widened my smile. The only thing he did was lower the coffee mug onto the kitchen countertop, his head tilting to the side. "Baby, just 'cuz you're cute doesn't mean I wasn't bein' serious about spankin' your tight little ass for doin' dumb shit, Ritz. You do it again, and you're gonna get it."

And… my smile came crashing down. *Do not think about him referring to your butt as tight, Ris. Focus!*

"Just because I've never hit another person in my life doesn't mean I won't make you the first." I blinked coolly. "Charlie."

What did the man do? He laughed.

"I'm serious," I insisted, earning another laugh from him.

"I know, babe," Dex chuckled. "I heard all about you sellin' off the rights to my kneecaps."

Oh crap. There may have been a gulp that was processed in my throat. "About that..."

He leaned forward over the counter, elbows propped up on the edge. "Sooner or later you'll figure out that eventually I find out everythin', Ritz."

That suddenly sounded like way more of a threat that I hope he'd intended it to.

"Get that ugly shit out of my face," Blake snapped at Slim.

I—who had a hummus sandwich an inch away from my face—choked on air, right before gasping, "That's what she said," like there was a fire beneath my ass.

Slim tipped his head back and laughed, loud, pulling the sheet of paper he'd been shoving into Blake's face away. "Ah, shit."

"Sorry," I apologized, looking over at Blake. He was shaking his head, still tearing away at the baked potato he'd been eating. "You asked for it."

He waved his fork-less hand in my direction. "Sure, smart ass."

I waggled my eyebrows over at Slim, referring to the ugly shit Blake had been cawing at. "Not that my opinion matters, but I think it's awesome."

The piece of paper he'd been holding up against Blake's face was a design he'd finished last night. The artwork was of a bright blue dragon with huge black wings, firing out a spray of rainbow colors. I mean, considering my name meant rainbow, I had a fondness of them. Plus, it was epic.

"You want me to save this one for you?" he asked a little too quickly.

Like I wouldn't remember he tried at least once a week to get me to agree to a tattoo. It wasn't like I hadn't thought about it regularly. I did. I loved the tattoos that the guys and Blue did, but there was only one place on my body that I could instantly think of where I'd want one at. That one place was the only location I couldn't have done.

The inside of my arm.

But I didn't want to hurt Slim's feelings and have him think that I didn't want his work since I'd kept shooting him down each time he brought it up.

"If you could tattoo over some scar tissue I have, I'd tell you let's do it right now. You can't though, right?"

The redhead nodded slowly, frowning. "Not a good idea." He tipped his head in question. "Where at?"

That wouldn't give away too much, would it? "My inner bicep." Well, what was left of it.

"Is it a lot?" Blake asked, narrowing his eyes.

Crap, I forgot how observant he was. "Yeah."

He pursed his lips. "Is that why you're always wearing long sleeves?"

Of course he'd notice. Of course. I mean, I did happen to be the only person I could think of that wore long-sleeved clothing every day. Sure most of the material was light, but the fact was, in Texas heat, I'd stick out like a sore thumb. Someone was bound to notice it at some point.

Most girls my age were usually trying to take clothes off instead of putting more on. That seemed to be the story of my life. When some people my age were worrying about certain things, I'd be stuck tackling a whole different type of monster. Oh well.

I wanted to touch my arm but I had to fight the urge so that I wouldn't draw more attention to it. "Yeah. It's pretty big."

Blake glanced down at the wrong arm before shaking his head, smiling just a bit. "Girl, we all have stuff wrong with us. You see these ears?" He pointed at them and for the first time, I noticed that they looked just a little bit larger than they should have been ideally proportional. "Kids used to call me Dumbo."

Slim snorted really loud. "I can see that."

I elbowed him in the side. "That's so mean."

The redhead shrugged. "They used to call me Gingervitis." He paused. "Cinnamon dick." He looked up at the ceiling as if in deep thought. "Once, some shit-nuggets pulled down my pants in gym class to see if—," he sent me a sidelong glance, "the carpet matched the drapes."

"Holy crap," I started laughing, not able to help it.

Slim nodded, grinning. "Yeah. I was a late bloomer, so you can only imagine."

Blake covered his face with his hands, his shoulders shaking. "You had a little tonsil tickler, didn't you?"

"I hadn't hit puberty yet!"

"Be honest, that really happened like last week, didn't it?" Blake snorted.

By some miracle, right before I face-planted the desk from how hard I was laughing, I caught Slim shooting the middle finger in the bald man's direction.

"Fuck you, Dumbo. I was just trying to make Iris feel better." He cocked his head to look at me with an expression that showed how hard it was for him to not bust an amused gut. "Did my Little Red make you feel better about your arm?"

I didn't even have to think about it before nodding. Most of my life, my mom and *yia-yia* had told me that the imperfection gave me character, that it wasn't a big deal. And it wasn't. Really. It was ugly, but I'd managed to hide it as well as I could because frankly, more than the looks of disgust, the pity faces I got were what truly bothered me.

Most people thought that the cancer made me into some weak, broken thing. The only thing I'd sacrificed along the journey of four different surgeries was physical strength. My left arm would never be as strong as my right for obvious reasons. I'd lost most of the muscle over a decade. But that was it. The doctors had worried that I'd lose mobility but thankfully—*thankfully*—I didn't. It was just a little smaller and weaker. Big deal. I couldn't ask for more when the prognosis could have been so glum.

I wasn't built out of glass. I'd been healthy and strong my entire life except for those stages throughout my childhood and teen years. It was me who had kept my family afloat when things had withered. No one needed to feel bad for me because of my arm. I was made of tougher stuff than that.

And in that moment, it struck me that I'd felt bad *for myself.* I didn't need to hide my arm to know what I was capable of, what I was made of.

Because like Blake and Slim had tried to point out, we all had our physical nuances. Blake's ears didn't make him any less friendly or creative. Slim's hair was probably his signature now that he didn't have to deal with a bunch of immature douche-bags.

I felt... renewed and grateful to them.

I couldn't help but smile over at him. "You definitely did," I snorted. "Pippi Longstocking."

To his credit, Slim waited almost a minute before tossing the balled up napkin at my face.

"I think I liked you more when you didn't talk."

I tossed the napkin back at him before collecting my leftovers. I opened up the fridge to put my stuff up and spotted Dex's bottles of Nesquik lined up neatly inside. Snatching one up, I pressed the cold bottom of it to Slims's neck as I walked past him and made my way toward the front. The office door was closed and so was the private room.

Dex was at his station with a client when I walked by. He happened to look up at the right time, so I held the bottle up and gave it a swirl, mouthing, "For you." I tipped my head in the direction of my desk and grinned at him.

The smile that came over his face before he mouthed back, "Thanks," made my chest constrict.

What was happening to me?

"You gonna make it all the way home?" Dex asked as we made our way out of Pins that night.

The last three hours had been painful for me to get through. Having such a fitful night of sleep the day before on top of the two hours I spent at the YMCA when Dex had dropped me off that afternoon, and then working, had paid a toll on my body. I'd caught myself falling asleep once or twice at my desk.

I nodded at him after waving goodbye to Blake. "Yeah, I'll be okay." At least I hoped so.

He gave me a weary glance like he wasn't entirely convinced I wouldn't fall off the back of his bike halfway to his house. It'd be his fault though. After I'd told him that morning that I wanted to have a swim at the Y, he'd insisted on driving me there and picking me up. It made more sense to me to drive myself there, and then work, but the man was relentless.

He had shit to do at Mayhem like always.

That shit to do was why I found myself back on his bike, bordering on delusional. So I'd blame the fact I was delusional on how I ended up in his bedroom just minutes later.

Yes, in his bed.

It'd been hard enough to keep my arms wrapped around him so that I wouldn't fall off the bike. Dex's warm body and the mind numbingly loud roar of his motorcycle were like a potent sleeping pill. It was only an intense fear of falling off and getting run over by a car that kept me hanging onto him for dear life through my drowsiness. The moment he parked in front of his house, my brain stopped working altogether. There weren't any cars to run me over in his driveway, thank goodness.

I remember Dex pulling me by the hand across the circling driveway, into the house and past the living room before swiftly pushing me into his bedroom and closing the door in my face with an insistent, "You get the bed tonight."

I wanted to argue with him, I swear I did, but when I pressed my hand to the corner of the mattress and realized it was a Tempurpedic, that thought went right back out. Just one night. At least that's what I told myself.

Most of my clothes were stripped off, I rinsed out my mouth in his master bath, and stumbled into bed wearing just the tank top I'd worn that day and my panties. Exactly three seconds later, I was dead to the world. Hunger wasn't even a blip on my radar—nothing was.

Until the bed compressed behind me not long after I laid down.

"Dex?" I asked in a sleepy whisper. I was so tired it could have been those masked serial killers I'd been stressing about forever, and I would have stayed in bed regardless.

Something touched my shoulder. A husky voice made a sleepy sigh. "Couch sucks, babe."

Even though I was tired as hell, I knew that there was something completely inappropriate about sleeping in the same bed as my boss regardless of how hot he was. And that I might have a bit of a—nope, I wasn't going to say it was a crush. That would make me feel like I was sixteen again. I liked him, that simple. How could I not?

I wasn't even sure if I could really consider Dex a friend, even if I wanted to justify what was going on by saying that friends could sleep on beds together. It took everything in me to roll onto my back and tilt my head over to where he'd laid down on the other side of the mattress.

Besides the times when I'd had to share a bed with Will as kids, and that one time I messed around with my boyfriend a few years back, I'd never even been on the same bed as another guy. God, that made me feel lame.

It took all the baby scraps of will I'd stashed under my nails and tendons to sit up completely, yawning like it was morning time instead of the middle of the night. "I'll go sleep on the couch then," was what I told him, although I'm sure it sounded like some mutilated version of it.

His hand draped across my waist in a move that I had no doubt had been practiced many times in his life. "Stay. The bed's big enough for the both of us," was his brilliant answer.

It was the truth but still. He was laying in the middle so it defeated the purpose of his comment.

I yawned again. "It's not a good idea." Once again I'm sure it didn't sound anything like that out loud.

Dex grumbled, fingers wiggling at the bend of my hip and waist. "Quit bein' a prude and go to sleep, babe."

If I'd been more awake I would have been offended by being called a prude. Though I kind of was.

I groaned. "Dex."

"Baby, please. Just go back to sleep. That couch is fuckin' uncomfortable."

Dang it!

He made another grumbling noise. "I swear I'm not gonna try to feel you up or anythin', Ritz."

That notice didn't exactly make me feel any better. Of course he wouldn't. I was like his... pet dog or something.

"I can just sleep, I swear," he insisted in a yawn.

Eek. Score two for Dex on the not-making-Iris-feel-better scoreboard.

"Babe, c'mon. I promise."

And it was a Tempurpedic, damn it.

I was a weak sucker. I knew that. Even though I made huffs and puffs as I shuffled back under the covers and rolled further away from Dex, I still didn't think staying on the same mattress was a good idea. But I did it anyway.

CHAPTER TWENTY-TWO

Waking up next to Dex had to be the most awkward experience of my life.

More awkward than the time I'd walked in on *yia-yia* naked.

Because it wasn't like I opened my eyes facing the wall. I woke up on my belly. Normal, right?

With an elbow digging into my shoulder and a heavy leg thrown over one of mine—not so normal.

It wasn't like there was a boner pressed up against me or anything, but the bodily contact was enough. I straightened out as much as I could before trying to slide out from beneath the limbs pinning me down. I'd barely managed to scoot over about two inches before the leg over mine locked me down.

"What'cha doin'?" Dex's incredibly husky voice asked.

I froze. "Trying to get up."

The weight of his leg lessened as his heel slid up from my ankle to my knee. He had to be sleeping on his back, I figured. "Mmm," he grumbled. The elbow on my shoulder shifted off of me at the same time I heard him yawn. His foot shifted again, the sole coming to rest on the back of my knee before sliding down my calf. Holy moly, that was hot. "What are you wearin', honey?"

Aww crap.

"I'm not wearing pants," I told him, not moving an inch while his warm foot rubbed up my leg again.

All of a sudden, a cool breeze swept over my legs and I peeked over my shoulder to see Dex holding the sheet up, his head tipped down while he looked below it.

Wait a second...

I slapped the sheet down with my hand, half shrieking and for some unknown reason, half laughing. "What the hell are you doing?"

Of the ten different ways he could have answered, Dex chose to laugh. But it wasn't a regular laugh, it was the lightest, most genuine sound I'd ever heard from him. "Checkin' out that ass," he answered breezily.

"Jeez," I groaned, rolling onto my side to face away from him. My shirt didn't cover my upper arms at all, so as long as I kept my arm clamped down he wouldn't be able to see it. Which only meant that I needed to quit testing fate and get the heck out of the room. "That's inappropriate, Dex."

"Who says?" he answered from behind me. I could hear the sheets rustling with his movement.

My brother, I wanted to answer him but seriously? What had ever given me the idea that Dex would do something he didn't want to? Oh, please.

I sighed and sat up on the edge of the bed, facing the wall. My clothes were piled on the floor and I carefully slid my pants up my legs without standing up too much.

"You wanna shower before we get goin'?" Dex's voice carried over from the opposite side of the room.

I had no idea what he was doing. Knowing him, probably not getting dressed. I had a terrible feeling he slept in only his underwear. I'd barely survived seeing him in shorts back in Austin. Seeing him in his underwear now that I realized how I—unfortunately—felt for him? Disaster.

"Where are we going?" It was Sunday and the shop was closed.

"My niece's birthday party." It sounded like he'd opened the bathroom door. "I need to stop and get her somethin' or else I'll never hear the end of it."

Now that made me laugh. Dex Locke scared of his niece's wrath? The fact was, I hadn't met his family. I wouldn't know anyone besides him at the party, and just thinking about that made me anxious.

I leaned back to zip up the tab on my pants. "I can just stay here if you don't mind."

His huff was distorted by the distance. "I want you to go."

Crap.

The recommendation just kind of came out. "You sure you don't have anyone else that already knows your family?" The stupid redhead flashed through my brain. Ugh.

"No," he answered too quickly. "You're comin'. So grab your bathin' suit and whatever else you're gonna need at the lake, so we can leave in an hour."

A bathing suit? In front of his family? I'd just come to terms with my arm the day before, but that didn't mean I was ready to have a ton of people I didn't know looking at it weird.

Shit.

"All right." I was such a wuss. Such a big, friggin' coward.

I stood up and slipped my cardigan on over my tank top, grabbing my socks off the floor before rounding the bed. Dex was standing just inside his bathroom, a toothbrush shoved into his mouth, his face still too sleepy.

And the cruel bastard that weaved the fate of people's lives together decided that the beautiful black-haired man with brilliant tattoos all over his upper body, would be standing there in his boxers. The hand on his hip only accentuated the contoured lines of muscle beneath all his tattoos. Damn him.

"You seen my cuts?" he asked through a mouthful of toothpaste.

But of course I was standing there looking at Uriel, the friendly, vibrant octopus that twirled a tentacle around one of his nipple piercings.

I coughed, dragging my eyes up to his bristly beard. "What?"

"My cuts."

"What's that?"

He lowered his chin in disbelief. "My cuts, babe. My MC vest. You seen it?"

The redhead flashed through my memory. Again. I had to fight the urge to call him an idiot for leaving me at his house alone that day. I'm sure my nostrils flared as I plastered a pleasant smile on my face. I'd completely forgotten to tell him about his stupid vest the day before since he'd been so busy with clients. "It's at the shop. Your lady friend dropped it off a couple days ago."

His forehead crinkled. "Who?"

Just how many houses had he gone to that night? You know what? I didn't want to know. God, of all the people in Austin—hell, in the Gulf Coast, that I could have grown feelings for, it'd been Dex. I was a total idiot.

"The redhead," I probably snapped a bit more harshly than I would've liked. "Sky-something."

Dex's lips turned down just a fraction, the lining of his forehead staying in place. "When?"

"That day you were planning on skinning me alive." I might have glanced down at Uriel—not his pierced nipples—again.

He looked at me like he didn't believe me. "Why?"

Why? "She said you left it at her house the night before." Crap, I really did sound a lot more crabby than I would have liked.

At the sound of my tone and the words that had come out of my mouth, Dex pulled the red toothbrush out of his mouth and spit in the sink. He glanced up once before rinsing out his mouth, quirking an eyebrow in my direction. Slowly, he straightened up, those sooty cobalt eyes lingering on me for longer than I was comfortable with.

He narrowed his eyes. "Why do you sound so pissed off?"

"Because you left me alone here all night," I replied just a little too fast. It wasn't because he'd spent the night with a pretty redhead. No, siree. "I kept thinking someone was going to break in and murder me since we're in the middle of nowhere."

"I wouldn't let that happen, Ritz."

I almost rolled my eyes. How would he have stopped that from happening if he hadn't even been around? "All right," I said a little more sarcastically than I intended.

The line of Dex's unshaved jaw twitched. "I wouldn't," he insisted.

"All right," I repeated myself. "It's fine."

I had a sickening feeling that he didn't exactly believe me. "You sure?"

Still, my response of a nod was too instinctual to be played off as cool and distant.

Dex kept that heavy gaze on me as he crossed his darkly tattooed arms over his chest, muscles and colors popping with the movement. He was watching carefully, way too carefully.

Suddenly, I didn't want to keep standing in front of him like I was waiting to go to trial. One foot out of the door, I rolled my eyes at myself for being so dang transparent. "Your thing is at Pins, and I'm going to shower real quick and get dressed."

"Bathing suit, Ritz!" he called out after me.

Like I could forget.

The only positive thing I could think of while Dex drove my car down the dusty road that led toward the lake, was that I was extremely grateful I'd been a Floridian before coming to Texas.

I'd grown up a short drive from the beach. I'd lived most of my life right by the ocean. And when you're broke as a joke, you can always go to the beach for free. So it was inevitable that I had almost as many clothes for sand and water as I did for a normal day. Specifically beach wear that could cover me up.

Dex and I had to make a stop at Sonny's to get my things because I hadn't brought anything to his house that was water-friendly. I found a really thin long-sleeved beach dress—plus shorts—to cover my royal purple two-piece.

I'd come up with my game plan somewhere between Sonny's and the toy store for going undetected. I could either simply not get into the water, or I'd just make sure to keep my arms down constantly. I'd only done that a few times while at the local beach back home but that was because the strangers that saw my scar were just that—people I'd never see again.

But Dex? And his family?

My secret was better off safe for a while.

"Chill out," Dex murmured as he maneuvered the car toward a grouping of cars the furthest away from the entrance to the state park.

"I'm fine." Lie.

He chuckled low, turning the wheel into the first spot he found by his family's collection of cars. "Babe, you're all tense. Quit worryin'. My sisters are all right, and my ma's been houndin' me to bring you around since she found out you worked for me." He flashed a little grin over. "The worst you gotta worry about is Han not likin' her present."

"I think you should be worried about your sister when she finds out you got her a karaoke machine." I'd gotten Hannah, Dex's youngest niece, an alarm clock of that kitty character that she supposedly really liked. The big brute had spent an arm and a leg on a pink karaoke machine with two microphones that he swore the little girl would love.

Obviously this man had never been around children for longer than a couple of hours if that was the kind of present he liked to buy.

"She won't do shit," he murmured, waving me out of the car.

I grabbed the two gift bags from the backseat while Dex dug around in the trunk for the stuff he'd thrown in there. Even though we were parked quite a way down from the concentration of the cars—and motorcycles I noticed a little late—the loud laughs and screaming children could be heard pretty darn clearly.

Something jabbed me in the side. "Ya ready?" he asked, pulling his elbow away from my ribs. He'd traded in his black and navy blue t-shirts for a plain white one. But those friggin' light jeans that were perfectly molded to his butt hadn't been replaced.

"Did you bring a bathing suit?" I asked him, looking down at the new pair of Nike's he had on instead of boots.

"Nope." He elbowed my side again, raising both of those pure black eyebrows. "I'm on babysittin' duty."

"You? Why?"

Dex tipped his chin up. "I brought you along, didn't I, babe?"

Asshole.

"Waah." I rolled my eyes and reached to pinch the back of his arm. "You get on my nerves, you know that, right?"

He ducked out of the way, his mouth splitting into a wide smile, all pretty white teeth, before laughing. "Nobody's tried to do that shit to me since back in the day when I'd piss off my ma."

"It's overdue then," I told him, aiming for his arm again before he wrapped his hot palm around my fingers.

He squeezed his grip gently for a moment before dropping his hold, still grinning. "C'mon, you little shit."

It should probably bother me that he called me a little shit but with the big grin on his face and the loud burst of his laugh, I kind of thought that he was using it as a pet name. He let out another lower, huskier laugh and I was completely convinced it was like his way of calling me... what? Whatever you'd call a pet baby rabbit.

"How many nieces and nephews do you have total?"

"Lisa has three girls, and Marie has a girl and a boy."

The noises from the group in the tree-lined area ahead of us got louder each step we took. "Lisa's your oldest sister?"

Dex nodded. "She's Hannah's mom." The birthday girl, he meant.

I tried my best to mentally prepare myself to face three women that were potentially female versions of Dex, and I couldn't help but feel just a little intimidated. From what I've learned over the course of my stay in Austin, there was probably a big chance that Dex's mom knew my mom back when she was going to college here. Who knew how that could go. If her father was a member of the Widows' Original 12, then she was more heavily invested in the club than just about anyone else.

More than likely, it also didn't help that my crap-ass father left the MC for my mom.

Hmm.

Slowly, the group came clearly into view. What looked like two dozen adults and at least a dozen kids scrambled around a circle of four picnic tables, while a thick column of smoke spiraled in the background. From the looks of it, most of the men wore WMC vests.

You know, besides Dex.

My stomach couldn't help but clench up at the reminder.

I didn't recognize hardly anyone beside a couple of the women I'd met at Mayhem weeks back, but I couldn't remember their names to save my life. No one paid us any attention as we walked up to the group until we stopped alongside the picnic table furthest away from the lake shore.

"I'll leave our shit right here—" Dex started to say, dropping our two bags onto the bench.

"It's about time you got here," a woman's voice suddenly said. "We've been waiting for you to start grilling, Dex."

Holy crap.

The woman standing just to the side of Dex had to be his mom. The hair color, that square jaw line, the eye color—it was all the same. Well, minus the boobs and the gray hairs that peppered her blue-black mane. She even had the same smirk as she looked at what had to be her son.

"I'm not even late, Ma," Dex confirmed it, turning around with a matching sneer on his full, pink mouth. Holding out his arms, the woman stepped into them, slapping him on the back, hard.

"You're never late." She laughed. Her dark blue gaze moved from the ground and zeroed in on me just standing there. Her eyes went up, up, up, before they stopped on my face, and she frowned. "Oh dear."

I wanted to say something but I didn't because my stomach dropped nervously. Why hadn't I stayed at his house?

"You look just like Delia," she choked out.

My mom? Suddenly my voice seemed to find its way back to my throat. "Hi, Mrs. Locke." Shit. I hope she still went by Locke or this was going to be incredibly awkward.

Before I even realized what the hell was going on, Mrs. Locke—I hoped—was pushing Dex out of the way to stand right in front of me. Nearly eye to eye if it wasn't for the inch or two she had on me. Her fingertips moved to my face, prodding at my cheekbones. "Girl, you could pass for your mama," she breathed.

Of course, I started smiling like a fool, all overwhelmed nerves. "Thank you. You're really pretty." How lame was that?

It must not have been that lame because Mrs. Locke laughed right in my face. "I know."

Dear God, this woman really was a female Dex.

But just as quickly as she laughed, her face sobered, and *no.* I knew that face. I knew the words that were going to come out her mouth before they actually did. "I'm so sorry about your mama," she said in a low voice. Those dark blue eyes turned sad and heavy, and shit, shit, shit this was too soon after my conversation with Sonny to think about her.

"Thanks," I somehow managed to cough out.

"Ma, where's the food?" Dex rudely interrupted.

Those strangely familiar cobalt blue eyes narrowed in the direction of the man that unhinged me half the time. What came out of her mouth next made me laugh because I couldn't help but believe she was one of the select few that could talk to her Dex so crisply. "Open your eyes, dipshit."

"What are you doing out here all alone?" Dex's mom asked just as I'd started pulling my dress over my head.

For the last twenty or so minutes, I'd been sitting on the edge of the sandy shore, watching the group of shrieking little heathens throw sand at each other. After spending the last hour sitting and watching the group of people I barely knew interact with each other, it'd gotten to be too much. Their familiarity, their easiness, made me nostalgic.

It wasn't often that I was really struck by how lonely I was. Well, at least how lonely I'd become since Will left, even while living with Lanie.

Before, I always had someone. After The Greatest Disappointment left, it was Mom, Will, *yia-yia* and me. Then, everyone started getting picked off. We'd always been a tight-knit group. Everything was communal. We all worked in whatever way we could for the other, for the greater good of the family.

And now all I had left was Sonny. My little brother, the same little brother that I'd busted my ass for, couldn't even email me back.

So being around Dex's family, both the biological and the motorcycle club, reminded me of how in-between I was. I was but I wasn't one of them. I was but I wasn't Sonny's sister. I was but I wasn't a lot of things.

After getting introduced to a cousin of Mrs. Locke—or Debra as she'd asked me to call her—I made my way toward the beach where all the kids were. I realized it was rude but it just made me too sad to be around such a close group at least in that moment.

It made me want something that I wasn't sure I'd ever have again.

"I just needed a little break. I have a headache," I told her before throwing my dress onto the towel I'd bunched up on the sand.

She smiled sadly, and I had to wonder whether she had any idea that I was lying. She probably did. My mom had always known and so had *yia-yia*. It had to be some weird mom-instinct that gave them bullshit meters.

Wading out into the murky greenish-brown lake water, I fought back the urge to think it was gross. There's no competition between fresh and salt water. The calm made me miss the waves and the salty air. This room temperature water was just... strange.

"I can never get used to how warm this damn water is," she said once we were about waist deep.

I had to make sure to keep my bad arm down as I nodded at her. "It feels really weird." More like gross but I didn't want to be completely rude.

Dex's mom snorted. "Every time we come out here, I have to pray that the water isn't too hot. I don't feel like getting some flesh-eating virus."

And, I stopped walking. "What?"

"You didn't hear about the cases these last few years?"

"No..." Holy crap, I started walking backward slowly.

Debra laughed and waved me forward. "Don't worry about it. Lisa made sure with the ranger that the water was over eighty degrees before we came."

I was still tempted to get out but I didn't want to seem like a big baby. Crap. I mean, I kind of liked my arms and legs.

"Trust me," she snorted.

I was left with no other choice but to trust her as we swam out to the floating dock not too far away. I was a little glad she wasn't in the mood to talk as I hoisted myself up onto the edge while she treaded water nearby. My head did hurt but I knew it was more because I felt a little disappointed than anything else.

"Are you healthy now?"

The question was like a punch to the gut. "Hmm?"

Her head bobbed just ten feet away from the dock, she tipped it toward me. "Your cancer. Is it all gone now?"

Blood rushed to my face like there was a fire it was trying to get away from, and my mind went reeling right along with it. I shouldn't be surprised that she knew. If I gave myself more than ten seconds to take in her question, I would probably think about the fact that she'd been involved in the Club long enough to remember hearing about me as a kid.

But answering her still didn't seem natural. "Yes. I've been in remission for almost six years now."

"Good." She smiled wide like I'd just told her that I'd bought a new car. "No one's said anything about it, so I figured you were probably one-hundred percent again."

"I'm okay." I returned her smile, even moving my arm a little so that she could see a hint of the scarring. When the hell was the last time I showed it to someone? I couldn't remember. "Thank you for asking though."

Debra winked. "Glad to hear that. Dex been treating you okay?"

Now that made me snort. Why did everyone always ask a variation of the same question? "Except for his little temper tantrums, he's been good." I was tempted to say very good to me but luckily I managed not to. It just sounded dirty in my head.

And I'm surprised to have been disappointed that it wasn't like that at all.

"I'm even more glad to hear that. I love that boy—," like Dex could still be considered a boy. Ha. "But I know how he is. I'm sorry to say he gets that shitty temper from me and his pa."

What do you say to something like that? *It's okay*? No. Absolutely not.

Thankfully she wasn't expecting an answer. "That's just about all he gets from his pa." The tight laugh was so bitter I definitely didn't know what to say afterward. I understood what she meant. I had an idea of what his father was like after Houston and I think Dex needed to hear that even his mom didn't see him in the same light.

"MA!" someone yelled from the shore.

Lisa, Dex's sister, stood on the beach, tossing towels at the kids around her.

"Food's ready!" she yelled again, not bothering to look up.

We both silently agreed to get out of the water. I dropped back in and swam slowly to shore alongside Dex's mom. I was only going to have this one chance to say something. "Debra?"

"Yeah?"

"I don't think Dex knows I was sick, and I haven't exactly got around to telling him." *So please don't say anything*, I begged her with my eyes.

There was no hesitation in her answer. She nodded immediately. "Got it. That's your business, honey."

I smiled at her tightly, giving her a brief nod. "I'm going to tell him, I just haven't yet."

"Okay." She tipped her chin down a millimeter. "Make sure you tell him though, whenever you're ready. He's never been good with surprises, just to warn you."

Her warning felt ominous but her face was open and honest. I mumbled something to her that meant nothing and was easily forgotten.

Lisa stood off to the side, herding the group of kids toward the picnic tables over the sloped terrain. Regardless of whether the oldest Locke knew about my cancer treatment or not, I was conscious to keep my arm straight against me as I walked toward my towel, reaching up only to wring out my wet hair.

"Meet you over there," Debra said. She hadn't brought her towel down when she came up to me, so I figured she needed to grab one. Besides the remaining kids and Lisa, there was no one else on the beach. Not that I blamed anyone for avoiding the lake.

Just as I reached down to grab my towel, I happened to look over in the direction of the picnic tables to see most of the group standing around the two tables in the center. Just off to the side of those standing was Dex.

He faced me, hands shoved into the front pockets of his jeans, facial expression blank.

But he stared—at me.

For what felt like the longest but was more than likely just a few seconds, I watched him back, and then I waved. He didn't wave in return but it didn't matter. He stood there, completely still, watching.

Okay. I grabbed the towel on the sand and shook it out before drying off. I got as dry as I could, pulled the dress on again and shoved my legs into my shorts. When I glanced back up, Dex wasn't there anymore. Thank God.

I rolled my wet towel under my arm and made my way slowly toward the group. There were so many people milling around, trying to get a little of everything from the buffet laid out that there was no rush to sit down. There were too many of us to all fit and since I was one of the youngest besides the kids, and not really family, I figured that I should be one of the people that got stuck standing up to eat, or sitting on the ground.

"What the fu—I mean, hell is this?" I heard one of the Widows ask as he stood over the table, picking at something I couldn't see.

Marie, Dex's other sister that looked like a female replica of her brother, nudged the man over. "Black bean burgers."

"Black bean burgers?" His tone was part disgust, part outrage. "Who the fu—hell eats that?"

Lord. I hadn't heard that in a while.

"Iris doesn't eat meat," Marie answered him.

The Widow scoffed, moving around the table with his plate held high. I was off to the side, behind a couple I recognized from Mayhem, so I knew he couldn't see me. Or maybe he was just one of those people who didn't give a crap. "Who doesn't eat meat?" A dumb question, obviously. "God gave us all these teeth so that we could eat hamburgers, chicken, meat. Not no damn black bean burgers."

The urge to correct him of his ignorance buried itself in my throat, but I was used to it. I was used to people saying things that weren't correct at all. Like this guy. Whatever.

But apparently, just because I kept my mouth shut didn't mean that everyone else did the same.

"How about you just shut up and eat your hamburgers and watch your cholesterol go up, Pete? She can eat whatever she wants to eat without hearin' you babble off your stupid shit."

Oh. Boy. It was Dex. Dex that I hadn't seen sitting at the fourth table.

"Language!" Marie snapped, smiling right before she turned around.

"I'm just saying." The guy I figured was named Pete had his face turn red.

"Nobody cares," Dex cut him off. "Ritz, come eat."

And then, awkwardness descended. The Pete guy finally realized that I was standing pretty much right by him but he had the decency to look a bit ashamed. Not much but something was better than nothing.

I flashed him a jerky smile but made my way toward the table to start putting things on my plate. Sure enough, there were three black bean burger patties piled onto a dish and I took one to put between hamburger buns, adding more things from the multiple dishes on the table. Egg-less potato salad, leafy lettuce, and skewered pineapple.

I started to walk around the three people still serving themselves, heading toward a patch of nearly dead grass to plop down on, but a hand reached out to grab the back of my bare knee.

"Sit right here," the low smooth tone I'd heard so much of over the last few weeks said to me.

Looking over my shoulder, Dex sat on the end of the picnic table bench, straddling it. His legs were wide, his food set on the table, and while he'd taken up more room than one man his size genuinely needed, it still wasn't enough space for two people.

"I can just sit on the ground." I smiled at him.

But he was watching me with those intense eyes. If watching could be considered that simple when there seemed to be a million different things going on in his head. Dex was staring and I didn't understand why. He'd looked at me in that way a few times before but this time was different. It's like he multiplied the look by a hundred. When he dropped his eyes down to my chest—which unfortunately had my dress sticking to my wet bathing suit—I had to gulp.

"I made room." He looked back up at me. "Sit."

Oh sweet mother.

He wasn't going to let it go, and I guess I must have not really wanted to sit on the grass because I sighed. And then set my plate down right next to his. The only way to fit without having an entire butt cheek hanging off the edge was to straddle the bench, too.

My butt pretty much snuggled safely between Dex's thighs, our quads lined up.

We were sitting way too close. If I were to slouch, my back would hit his chest. I'm positive that if I took a deep breath, I'd touch him that way too. The denim of his jeans practically hugging my bare thighs almost made me make some kind of noise.

It was too much.

I breathed a little too deeply and my shoulder blades touched Dex's pecs. Crap.

You can do this, Ris. You can sit with a man like this. It's just Dex.

But that was the problem—it was Dex.

I swear on my life that his hips move forward just an inch. But an inch was an inch that bumped the seam of his pants, the cradle of his groin, smoothly against my rear.

I shivered.

When I looked over my shoulder as I reached for my black bean burger, his face was right there. And it was tight—so damn tight.

I smiled at him nervously, but Dex didn't smile back.

He stared at my face, his food untouched, and I had no clue what the heck was going on with him.

"Do you want me to move?" I whispered. I could see his mom looking at us from across the table. She wasn't even trying to play her gaze off.

He still said nothing.

Okay. "Charlie," I whispered again in a sing-song voice, trying to draw him out of whatever thought he was lost in.

But still, nothing.

All right. His mom kept watching us and I started to feel weird again.

I tried to get up. My butt was maybe just an inch off the bench when his warm hand landed on my outer thigh, the thumb on the inside and all four of his long fingers curled over the outside of my leg, and he pushed me back down gently.

"You're fine there." His voice was way too low.

I finally managed to nod my head and force a bite of black bean burger into my mouth to give me something else to do besides look at him, or focus on the heat of his body.

Because honestly, my stomach was doing flip-flops at our proximity. At the feel of that long, sinewy body practically cocooning mine. Sweet baby lord.

I mean, we'd been pretty close when he hugged me the other night but this was completely different.

"So, Iris, what's your little brother up to?" Dex's mom asked abruptly.

"He's in the Army in Japan."

She lifted up her eyebrows. "Japan? That's fancy. You been up to visit him?"

"Not yet." Especially not when I couldn't even reach him on the phone. "Hopefully one day soon."

"You should, life's short." Debra winked.

I smiled at her and nodded. "I should start saving up for a plane ticket."

One of the women I recognized from Mayhem tisked. "Girl, just find yourself a sugar daddy to pay for that."

Did Dex just grunt?

"Pretty girl like you, I bet you could find a man like that," she snapped her fingers.

Debra barked out a laugh that was eerily similar to her son's. "Don't listen to her. She's always trying to talk everybody into finding sugar daddies."

"That's true," Dex's sister threw in. "But if you listen to Ma, she'll tell you to find a good man that likes you, has good credit and a steady job."

Debra nodded enthusiastically, pointing at two men standing up. "Yeah, and ya listened to me. See how well my advice worked out for you two?"

The Mayhem woman snorted, cutting me a look. "I still think you should find a sugar daddy."

"Would you quit with that mess?" Debra huffed.

Something traced the curve of my shoulder, breaking my attention away from the women.

"Ignore 'em." It was Dex's fingertip running over the strap of my bathing suit top. "Like your bathing suit." He drew a line down my shoulder blade.

And then he shuffled forward another inch, bringing his lower body even closer to mine. The fingers on my leg tightened, his thighs closing in on mine. Was that a grumble?

His finger made a line back up, slowly, and my stomach fluttered in recognition of his touch. "Eat, baby," he muttered.

Oh hell. I was still holding the burger in my hand, mid-air after the last bite. I glanced at him out of the corner of my eye and smiled.

I'd maybe chewed three times before two thoughts hit me simultaneously. I was eating a black bean burger because his sisters had found out I was a vegetarian. And Dex's hand was still on my thigh.

CHAPTER TWENTY-THREE

"You're kind of a nerd."

I shifted on the couch, deepening my cross-legged position on one end to look at Dex better. He was sitting with his ass in the opposite corner in loose basketball shorts, one leg extended straight out so that his bare foot was just a few inches from nudging my knee. His other foot was perpendicular to it, and he had a bottle of water squished between him and the couch.

Had I mentioned how attractive Dex's feet were?

Maybe I'd been expecting athlete's foot or a serious fungal infection and overgrown toenails to explain why I was so entranced by his long feet and neatly trimmed toenails. Even his freaking Morton's toe was kind of endearing.

What was wrong with me?

Everything. That was the truth.

After a long afternoon at the lake, in the sun, I didn't have a doubt my hair was in a million different directions and I might have a slight sunburn on my nose. We'd left after Hannah opened her presents, both of us hugging his mom goodbye while I just waved at his sisters and the other MC members. Neither one of us had talked much after eating—and by eating I meant that I'd thoughtlessly chewed while staring at the ink-stained fingers on my thigh the entire time.

"I don't know if that's a compliment or an insult," I told him.

He tossed his head back. Yeah, he was definitely attractive. Smoking hot, level one million attractive. "Babe, you go to the library, you read romance books with a big ass smile on your face. You still say cool, and I just heard you recitin' each line from the movie."

"It's a good movie," I tried to justify it. I'd seen all of the boy wizard's movies at least three times each.

Dex smiled, his smoky, intent gaze smug. "Babe, you're the cutest fuckin' nerd I've ever met."

My chest did this thing...I don't even know how to describe it, it was like a seizure-type thing...for all of a split second before I squashed it down. The cute-ground was somewhere I didn't need to go. No, siree. No way. "You like Firefly. That's pretty nerdy." I learned this after going through his DVDs while he made tacos. Another major anomaly in his armor. I mean, seriously? He seemed like the type to try and beat up the nerdy kids that liked those types of shows.

"It's good," he shrugged. "But you're still a little dork."

"You have a Captain America shield tattooed on your chest." He didn't need to know I actually found that incredibly hot. I gave him an obnoxious wink. "You win."

Oh bloody hell. I was flirting, wasn't I?

"He's the shit," he answered simply, completely unfazed by my claims to his nerd-dom and the dreamy look I worried had funelled its way onto my heart—and face, unfortunately.

I was full of crap but I wasn't going to do down without at least a fight. "Next thing I know you're going to tell me you have a comic book collection."

"I do." Without any hesitation, he hooked his thumb to his left. "In my spare bedroom."

Was he joking? "You're lying."

Dex shook his head, returning my earlier smile. When this man was in a good mood...God. It was unfair. Totally, completely unfair to be around him. "Wanna see?"

And it was that question, that had me in his underused spare bedroom minutes later.

I'd read too many books where men had that secret bedroom that seconded as a play room for the kinky, or hell, an operations room for some secret society they belonged to. So when Dex opened the closed door to the room I'd yet to see, it wasn't at all what I was expecting.

There were bright, pure white light bulbs in the ceiling fan, lamps in two corners of the room flooding the space with illumination. A drafting desk very similar to the one back at Pins was pushed up against the wall with the windows. There were large bookshelves filled with books and pristine plastic wrapped comic books. Vintage action figures were settled on shelves that dotted all of the walls where there wasn't posters or more framed artwork. Artwork that looked like Dex's heavy-handed style on kohl.

The frame closest to me looked like an original dark superhero. A black cape billowed behind a massive, muscular man with eyes that looked haunted.

"Did you do this one?" I asked him.

"Mmhmm," he answered right before I felt the warm length of his body just behind me. "That's one of my earliest drawings."

"It's so good," I told him honestly, taking in the sweep of heavy lines around the character. I wanted to turn around but he was too close, and it was easier to play opossum than to face Dex Locke. "You should start your own comic book."

"Thanks, babe." He paused. "I used to want to back when I was a kid, but... shit doesn't always work out that way, you know?" There were no truer words that could have been said for me to understand completely.

"Oh, I know." I blew out a breath. "Stuff happens."

"Shit happens," he laughed darkly.

I tried to look at him out of the corner of my eye but I couldn't. "And here you are, a successful business man."

Dex snorted but it wasn't exactly in amusement. "If my juvie parole officer could see me now."

"You got in trouble when you were young, too?" I don't know why I asked. Like so many other things, this was Dex. It made more sense than not.

"'Course I did. Spent six months in boot camp when I was seventeen," he sounded a little too proud of it.

I smiled even though he couldn't see it. "For what?"

"What do you think?"

"Jaywalking?" I laughed.

"No."

I turned my head to look at him over my shoulder. "Indecent exposure?"

All he did was stare at me for the longest moment in history in response. When I snickered, he blinked, one side of his mouth tipping up just barely.

"I don't think I've ever let anybody gimme as much grief as you do."

"Thank you?"

He grunted.

"Okay, no gay prostituting for you. What else then? Were you shanking freshman in school?" I really had no idea. I wouldn't be surprised to hear about him getting into fistfights with a teacher.

The other side of his mouth tipped up high right before he snorted, the sound was so close to my ear I could feel the heat of his lips and skin. "Graffiti."

"Oh." The teenage graffiti artist who turned into a tattoo artist? Perfect. As I did the math in my head, I realized that his dad's crap must have been almost immediately after he'd gotten in trouble. "And then?"

He shrugged. "Nothin' much. I was still a shit when I got out."

Like that wasn't still the case. Ha.

"I got in trouble again almost right after I got out. That's why I got stuck with the whole five year sentence at county."

And at some point between that period of time, the tiger had changed his stripes but it'd been a little too late. From graffiti to assault. I couldn't have been attracted to a man that had gone to jail for unpaid traffic fines—and once I thought about it, that seemed really lame. Who would want to have feelings for a guy like that?

"The good thing is your big behemoth butt hasn't gotten in trouble again, and now you aren't defacing public buildings." At that, I lifted both of my eyebrows quickly.

I could tell his was in a good mood considering the conversation. "I found a better canvas, you know." He touched the back of the hand I had loose at my side with his index finger. "A permanent one."

Oh boy. I suddenly felt like I couldn't breathe deeply. I had to settle for a shaky smile at the small physical contact. "And it all started because of your comics."

His hand moved away as he reached up to put a hand on the side of the frame, caging me in on one side. "If it wasn't for all this shit, I wouldn't have a damn thing."

Which was true. What else would he have done if he hadn't gotten seduced into art by his comic books? It'd brought his gift to life, I figured.

"I wish I was half as talented at anything as you are at art," I sighed. "But I'm not good at anything."

Two hands planted themselves on my shoulders. "I'm sure you're good at somethin', babe."

I snorted. "Nothing useful."

"Babe." He said the nickname in a slithering tone, part admonishing, part sigh.

"It's fine. It's not too late to learn to be good at something, right?"

The heat on my back intensified as he took a step closer to me, his long fingers dug into my tissues. "I was your age when I got out of jail, Ritz. You got time to figure shit out." He didn't say anything else after that little pep talk. He just stood there, massaging my shoulders for long moments until he squeezed them tightly once and stepped back. "Lemme show you somethin'."

I shook off the dreamy haze his hands put me under and tried to focus on something other than his out-of-the-blue affection. Dex opened a creaky closet door while I looked over one of the big bookshelves that had collectible action figures on it still in their packaging.

"Here we go," he murmured, throwing a cardboard lid onto the floor. He smiled up at me as he held out a comic book I didn't recognize. Tightly restrained excitement vibrated through his bones. "Look, this is the first one Ma ever bought me."

I took his offering with the widest smile I could muster when he grinned at me like he'd won the lottery.

And it was that smile that had me plastered on the ground next to him for an hour, going through an impressive selection of comic books that Dex explained he'd collected through his early teen years. He was so painstakingly careful with each item he showed me, so serious explaining the editions and their value, that I ate it all up like a starved woman on the floor with him.

He'd tell me something special about each comic, and then he'd ask me something about myself like it was a second thought. What my favorite superhero movie was. If I'd liked Teenage Mutant Ninja Turtles as a kid. Who my favorite X-Men was.

Never in a million years would I have ever expected Dex to even have a favorite X-Men or Ninja Turtle, much less care about which one was mine.

"What do your friends think of all this?" I asked him.

He looked me dead in the eye. "I don't give a shit what anyone else thinks." Then he'd paused and quirked a cheek up, like he regretted the word choice he'd used. "But nobody else except Shane's seen 'em. I think Sonny and Trip remember I was into 'em when we were kids but...it's my one thing I don't gotta share with anybody."

God. Where was Dex The Dick when I needed him to keep me far away from this charming monster?

I sucked up how tired I was and looked through another couple boxes he had in his closet.

When I started yawning every couple of minutes, he sat back with his hands propped behind his butt. "You want the bed?"

I shook my head. "I'll be fine on the couch.

"I'm not gonna ask you twice," he warned me, smiling wearily.

"Thanks, but I'll survive." What I probably wouldn't survive was another night spent in the same bed with him after our day together. Specifically, after I'd become personal with the hot, heavy touch he was capable of. "I need to get used to sleeping on the couch again if I'm ever going to try and get my own place in the future."

I'd been thinking about my financial situation a lot recently, when I wasn't thinking about all this crap with my dad. Though I liked living with Sonny, I didn't want to take advantage of him. He would never kick me out but I didn't want to mooch. I was too old for that. Most importantly, I didn't want him to think that I would ever use him. He'd done more than enough for me.

So I needed to move out at some point in the sort-of distant future. I'd saved pretty much all of my paychecks except for gas, my Florida medical bills, and other little things, but it still wouldn't be enough to pay a first month and deposit on even the cheapest apartment, and have money left over to buy some furniture. Which meant that I'd probably invest in a couch whenever I got my own place and sleep on that until I could afford a bed.

Then there was the opportunity to go back to school, too. But that was money I didn't have either, dang it. Why exactly couldn't it grow on trees?

Dex's face scrunched up. "Why?"

"I can't live with Son forever." I blinked at him.

His face screwed up even more. "You can't live by yourself."

"Yes I can."

"No, you can't," he snapped back.

Heaven help me. "I can live by myself."

There was no hesitation in his voice when he ground out, "The hell you are."

"Dex." I glared at him. "You already know it was just me and my brother for a while, and then I lived with a roommate for a year. I'm not a little kid, and I'm not an idiot. I can live alone."

He opened his mouth and my poor eyes went straight to those pink lips. Then he shut it so quickly that if I wouldn't have been looking, I would have missed him opening it, period. That gaze swept over my face, boring straight into my eyes in what I couldn't miss as being an act of domination.

And obviously when he refused to break our eye contact, I had to accept that this wasn't a battle I was going to win. Regardless, he didn't have a say with what I did and it wasn't like I was going to be moving anywhere in the near future.

I reached out and poked him with my index finger in the shoulder. "Chill out. I don't have enough money yet anyway. And if I go back to school, it'll take me even longer."

The smug jerk smiled slowly.

I should have known by then that his slow smile wasn't a positive sign.

~ * ~ *

Two days later, in the middle of my lunch break, I found out why Dex had been such a sly jerk in his spare bedroom.

The thick packet slid across the counter slowly, pushed by two tattooed fingers I recognized from the length alone.

Austin Community College: Fall Credit Catalog

"There's info in there about certificates and degrees and shit you can get from 'em," Dex's gruff voice explained. "Classes start next month. I'll help you pay for 'em if you want, you know. You could go early before we open."

I didn't know whether to look at the catalog that sat right next to the bean salad I'd brought from Dex's house, or look at the man himself.

Dex's face won.

But I couldn't find my vocabulary anywhere, and it must have made him feel awkward because he kept going.

"I know you said you think you aren't good at anythin' but I'm sure you can figure somethin' out, babe. You're smart."

My mouth opened and closed at least twice before my throat decided to work. "You went and got this for me?"

He shrugged uneasily. Uneasily! Dex! "I got a prospect from the Club to go get it."

He could have asked Santa Claus to go get it and it wouldn't have mattered. What mattered, because in life there are so few things that really do, was that he'd listened to me. That he hadn't just heard the words "I'm not good at anything," but that he'd heard everything else I'd said afterward.

"Why you frownin'?"

"I'm not frowning." Pouting, maybe.

"Looks like you're frownin'."

"I swear I'm not." My eyes were stinging. "I'm happy right now."

He narrowed those impossible blue eyes. "You got somethin' in your eye?"

I sniffed. "Allergies." Like I was going to tell him he was going to make me cry.

Out of all of the things Dex could have given me, that was the last thing I could have ever expected: a course catalog for the local community college and an offer to help me with my classes. Not that I would ask him to help me pay for them—I wouldn't. But it was the thought. The friggin' thought that was worth ten times its weight in gold.

How could I not like this man? This asshole, bossy man that listened to me?

"Dex." His name came out of my mouth in the form of a sigh.

"What the hell, Ritz? Are you cryin'? I thought you'd be happy," he said, quickly dropping to kneel right next to my chair. He pulled it out and toward him by the legs, making a horrible grating sound on the tile.

Without thinking twice, because I was so wrapped in his gesture, I threw my arms around his neck and pressed my nose to his throat. "Why aren't you this nice all the time?" I asked, but it was so muffled I'm not sure he understood the question.

Two arms wrapped around me, pulling me flat against him. It's a testament to how unfocused I felt that I couldn't find it in me to appreciate the contact he was giving me. To let me even think about what a gesture like this coming from a man like Dex meant.

"Sounds borin' to me." That large palm cupped the back of my neck. "And nobody else gives me hugs like this but you."

The urge to fall to the ground, rip my heart out of my chest and hold it out like a sacred offering was overwhelming. *Take it! Take it all!* I'd cry.

Instead, I just sat there with my arms around him, breathing in that smoky Dex scent. I squeezed him tighter to me, knowing that I should move.

But I couldn't. Not right then when I had my face buried in the nicest smelling place ever. Not when I was confused by the man who defended me, slept with me, and brought me class catalogs. The same man who was the most good-looking male in both hemispheres.

"Is this our secret then?"

His chest puffed against mine. "Yeah, babe, it is."

"Okay." I leaned back and smiled at him. "I won't tell anyone."

"Better not."

I snorted right as this incredibly tender emotion flooded my chest. And it caused this urge… I had to close my eyes as I leaned forward and pecked a kiss on Dex's stubbled cheek. "Fine."

CHAPTER TWENTY-FOUR

There were times when I wondered whether I'd lost most of my common sense the moment I got within the Austin city limits. Several times, in fact.

And one of those moments was right then.

Who in their right mind would turn down a date from a gorgeous guy that also happened to be really nice? The guy was one of Blake's repeat customers. A computer programmer gradually getting a full-sleeve done. I'd met him my first week at the shop. But I mean, *really*, who would do that if they were sane?

Me, I hoped.

"Just one," Trey, who was tall—almost as tall as Dex, the tallest person in my life— had the nicest shade of close cropped light brown hair. Did I mention he was super cute? *One date, just to try it out*, he'd said a minute before.

My answer was a blush and a goofy grin. When was the last time someone had asked me out and been serious about it? Four years ago?

"We'll do whatever you want," he kept going.

"I don't think I'm allowed to go on dates with customers," I told him honestly. While I hadn't seen it written anywhere, it just seemed like normal etiquette in an employee handbook.

Someone from behind me, Blake, snickered loudly. All of these guys were unbelievably nosey. They had superhuman listening skills when they were busy, but when they weren't busy and a walk-in came in asking for a generic type of tattoo—like a girl who had come in asking for the name of her current boyfriend to be crafted onto the back of her neck for the rest of her existence—they were all deaf. It was a miracle, I swear, that their hearing came back on an hourly basis.

"I think all of us but Blue have done it, Iris," Blake called out from his station.

Trey smiled that nearly perfect like smile. "See? Tomorrow night then?" he asked me expectantly.

I wasn't planning on saying yes no matter how cute and tall he was. I had no business dragging someone into the same stagnant pit I had VIP passes to. I didn't have my own place, I'd barely caught up on all of my bills, and I had no clue what I was doing with my life. Realistically what did I have to offer anyone?

Plus, I'd be lying if I said that the first thing that popped into my mind when he first asked wasn't Dex's face. Not that I knew or understood what the heck that meant but I'd leave that thought alone for another day. Or year, whatever.

I'd just been about to tell Trey I wasn't interested but in much simpler terms when two large hands slipped over my shoulders. Two sets of strong fingers spanned down my chest, the tips dangerously close to my nipples, er, boobs.

"Sorry, Trey. It's against policy unless little Miss Iris wants to quit," Dex's cool voice announced, his grip squeezing the tops of my breasts. "And that ain't happenin'."

What. The. Hell?

Trey's eyes darted from Dex to me, and then back again, before he smiled pleasantly and nodded. Why the hell he nodded, I have no clue. "I got'cha, man."

What did he have exactly?

I tipped my head up to look at The Dick standing over me. His face was tight, his hold even tighter.

"Yeah," was the last thing that came out of his mouth.

Trey looked back at me and winked. "Maybe another time."

I had to be the only one who heard Dex mutter, "Over my dead body," under his breath.

What the heck was all that about? That standard annoyance I'd come to associate with being in Dex's company kissed the nape of my neck. Now it was me who was stiffening while The Dick relaxed.

The first chance I got after Trey was out of eavesdropping distance, I looked back up at my hot boss. "What are you doing?" I hissed at him. Well, maybe that wasn't the question I'd been preparing myself to ask, but it had just come out.

Those longer fingers dipped gently into the soft flesh underneath my shirt. "Nothin'."

Nothing? Threatening to fire me if I accepted a date was nothing? I started to shake my shoulders under his hold. "Why are you being like that?" It wasn't like I was planning on accepting the offer but still. I didn't want anyone else making my decisions for me. Especially not when it was something within my control. Something that only affected me. This wasn't a matter for either of my brothers or anybody else to get involved in, dang it.

Dark cobalt blue eyes gazed down at me. His expression switching from distant to pissed by the way he started grinding his teeth.

"Don't be dense," he snapped.

My jaw dropped. "You have no right—"

He snapped his fingers together. "You wanna talk about this? My office, right now."

The look on my face was organic what-the-fuck. In a month, I hadn't had a man approach me at all. You couldn't really count the men who'd come in that were natural born flirts because those kinds of guys flirted with anyone that could possibly have something shaped like a vagina between their legs. And I didn't think Trip counted either. With experience, you learn to smile and shrug off the winks and the flirts. This was exactly what I'd done. What I'd been through in front of a wordless Dex many times. And now he was going to intervene?

Maybe it was a little immature, but I ground my teeth together and attempted not to stomp my way toward his office. I didn't need to turn around to know that he was following after me. Unfortunately, I'd developed this sixth sense of being too aware of him. I kind of thought it was because of how often we rode on his bike together. Kind of like how some women start menstruating around the same time when they were around each other often. It wouldn't surprise me if Charles Dexter Locke had been able to throw my hormones out of whack.

If anyone could, it would be him.

Dex who I'd quickly learn to gravitate around. The Dex who woke me up every day. The same one that every morning made our coffee and poured my orange juice while I made breakfast. Dex who sat at night with me, watching Firefly while we folded our laundry on the sofa. Dex Locke who wished me goodnight before we went to bed.

When exactly I'd started looking forward to spending time with him, I had no idea. When I started eating up those little smiles at Pins and those little secrets we shared… I have no idea either. But I had. I'd grown to accept the fact that I had a massive attraction to someone who might not be capable of liking me in return.

At that moment though, I forgot all about that. The Dick had just cockblocked me.

He closed his office door and leaned against it, palms flat on the wood behind him. Dex's eyes were strangely tight above his flex jawed. He looked mad or annoyed, or maybe a little of both as he stared at me in silence.

"You didn't have to do that." I told him after a minute, trying to ebb away my own annoyance with him for blocking something I would have done on my own in a classier and less embarrassing way.

He looked at the ceiling, discarding my question. His fingers started tapping on the door. "Do what?" he asked sharply.

"You know what." I rolled my eyes. "You told me to stay here and work for you, and then you're going to threaten my job in front of everyone just because some guy asked me out?"

Dex licked his bottom lip but didn't say anything. His silence was a big, fat *yeah* that had me stomping right up to him.

"Are you kidding me?" This guy was out of his friggin' mind.

"No, Ritz. I'm not fuckin' kiddin' you."

My head was going to start hurting in like ten seconds. "Dex, I don't see why that's any of your business. You already tell me what to do half the time, and I know you're stuck with me staying at your place until this mess with my dad gets straightened out—but my dating life has nothing to do with you, okay?"

"Yeah, it does, Ritz," he gritted out.

"No, it doesn't, Charlie." I poked him right between his pecs twice.

"Yeah. It. Does."

It suddenly made complete sense to me that he was the youngest child in his family. He must have never been told "no" in his life. At least not often enough. "I'm pretty sure you're in no place to tell me who I can and can't date." I looked him right in the eye. "Charlie." Pushing him was more than likely a terrible idea but I was too far gone to care.

He narrowed those brilliant eyes. "Why's that?"

"Because I'm not a kid." Then, the stupidity just popped right out from my mouth. "And you've probably slept with half a dozen people since I met you, so trust me. You're not in a position to try and give me advice on who I talk to."

His face changed as he leaned into me. "I know you're not a fuckin' kid. And I *can* tell you who you can and can't talk to." He took a nice long swallow, and I didn't realize until right then that his hands were fisted at his sides. His entire body was tense. "And you can't fuckin' talk to anybody that wants to put their hands down your goddamn pants."

"What?" Oh lord. Oh dear, heavenly lord. "Why are you being like this?"

"'Cuz. I. Don't. Fuckin'. Like. It."

God, grant me strength. "Dex, I don't mean to sound like a complete bitch but...I don't care if you don't like it. He was asking me out on a date, you stubborn idiot. That doesn't mean he's planning on—"

Nostrils flared. "Don't finish that sentence, baby. I'm about *this* fuckin' close to losin' it." He reached up to rub his fingertips along the sides of his mouth, shaking his head with a gruff groan.

I curled my lips behind my teeth and lifted both shoulders. "I'm not trying to piss you off. Honestly, I just really don't understand why you're being like this with me. I thought you didn't mind me working for you."

Something changed in his expression that I couldn't pinpoint in the seconds before he dropped his hand from his mouth. Dex's blink was slow and thorough as his jaw ticked. "I thought I had more time..."

He didn't finish his rant because he was suddenly in my face, breathing out of his nose hard, his body taut.

Two big hands cupped my jaw the instant before his mouth with its deep pink, full lips and day old scruff, descended on me in a hard kiss—all ownership and demand.

Ohmigod.

Once. Twice. His grip on my face was unrelenting even as he pulled his mouth back a square inch then kissed me even harder, pressing and molding possessive lips to me. His tongue shoved its velvet, hot length against mine with a need and intent I couldn't comprehend.

Never in my life, even if I happened to kiss a hundred other people after this, would anything feel like Dex's long, strong fingers cradling my jaw, his teeth nipping my bottom lip.

I shouldn't have just stood there. I also definitely shouldn't have opened my mouth for him, or met him halfway with my own tongue but when someone who looks like Dex—tall, strong, not exactly always on the right side of moral issues, and talented with his mouth—kisses you, you don't say no. I understood at that point why so many women had fallen prey to him but this was so carnal, it didn't feel natural. When someone like Dex makes a noise into your mouth when you slid your tongue against his in a friendly gesture while simultaneously shoving your breasts against his hard chest, you do it again.

Even if you don't really know what you're doing. You just go with it. You move your tongue in a way that only your body understands. You arch your back because that's what feels right in the moment.

You don't question it. You take advantage of that one moment of insanity that you let yourself live for just a taste of something and someone like Dex The Dick Locke.

He kissed me ruthlessly. His right hand shifted from its spot on my cheek, down my neck before ending up on the opposite shoulder.

And I let him because his lips were firm, his tongue was good and his mouth tasted faintly like the chocolate milk he'd drank earlier and the smoke he had when we'd opened up the shop hours before. The rock solid chest smashed against mine might have also been a reason why I didn't even think about shifting away.

It wasn't until his other hand, the one left on my face, started its descent down my neck and grazed over my collarbone, over the side of my breast that I realized what the heck was going on.

Dex The Dick. Dex The Kind Grump was shoving his tongue down my throat. My boss. Dex. Charlie. The guy who signed my paychecks.

I pulled away from him so abruptly, I'm sure it was the only reason why he let me go. He hadn't been expecting me to back away from him out of the blue like that. It was also because he wasn't waiting for me to pull away that I had a chance to take in the flushed look on his face, the heavy set of his eyes. And the massive pipe lining his jeans.

God.

I should have just stayed where I was, but then I'd regret it for sure.

"Holy crap," I gasped out.

His mouth was just slightly parted, and he almost looked a little... dazed. "Shit." Dex thrust both hands through the mess of black hair that just barely swept over his forehead. "Shit, Ritz."

And, cue the awful feeling that crept into the pit of my stomach.

I didn't want to hear him say something about how much of a mistake our kiss had been, because while it was true, I just didn't want to hear it from his mouth. I couldn't handle the rejection.

So I did the only thing I thought could save both of our minds at that moment. I backed out of the office and closed the door behind me.

Slim wheeled his chair over to my section the moment I'd planted my butt on my own, curling my lips behind my teeth in hopes that they'd stopped tingling.

I had a feeling they wouldn't, but a girl could dream.

"You look—," he ran his eyes over my face slowly, "weird."

I glanced at him out of the corner of my eye. If I looked at him dead on, I'd probably turn red or blurt out what had just happened. That was a terrible idea. So I settled for a soft, "Huh."

Slim made a humming noise in his throat, still looking at me a little too closely. "Anything you want to tell me?"

See what I mean? Nosey. Nosey with a capital letter. "Nope."

"Hmm," he hummed again before sitting back in the chair. "We all knew it was going to happen. I'm just kind of surprised it took so long." Slim spun in a circle. "And I'm surprised you don't want to tell me."

"Tell you what?" I asked him carefully. These guys were piranhas for information.

He smiled all slick and casual, spinning in a circle again. "You know what."

"No, I don't, Slim."

He cocked an eyebrow. "Yeah, you do, Ris." That slick smile widened. "He's pissing all over you." He shrugged. "It was about time."

Things went from bad to worse when Blake piped in from behind the divider. "Boy's probably got blue balls by now."

Cue my choke.

"I'm going to poison you both," I started to threaten them.

Luckily—maybe not so luckily—the door to the shop opened before I could finish the growing list of things I was planning on doing to my friends slash coworkers and a man stepped in. It was Dex's next appointment.

Shit.

He must have been looking at the camera in his office because the office door slammed shut not even three seconds after I greeted the man. The music wasn't on yet, so I could hear Dex's heavy footfalls on the tile. Then, I heard him greet his client and point him in the direction of the bathroom so they could start their session afterward.

I kept my eyes trained on the computer in front of me, trying so friggin' hard not to gulp and bring attention to myself when I was confused beyond belief at what Slim had just said and what happened in the office. I mean, I knew Dex cared about me. But... what the hell was that?

You're an idiot, Iris. Of course I was. The second after I asked myself that, I remembered his face at the lake. His face and his touches in half a dozen other circumstances that I didn't understand completely.

I didn't get a chance to think about it anymore because I saw that black-shirted blur move toward me the moment his customer was out of view. He didn't kneel down like he had the day before when he gave me the community college catalog but instead bent over at the waist, his bottom lip so close I could feel it on my earlobe.

"You and me are gonna have a talk later, Ritz," he warned.

CHAPTER TWENTY-FIVE

"I'm really thinking that those douchers won't do anything to me if I stay at your house," I argued with Sonny as I shifted my leg under me on the bumpy couch at Mayhem.

The television was on in the background, and I could hear the sound of an audience laughing even as he sighed. "Not happening, kid."

"It'll be fine." I wasn't above begging. Especially when my lips still tingled from Dex's mouth. Hours later. Pathetic. "I'll lock the doors and everything."

The son of a gun didn't even bother thinking about the suggestion. "No."

"Sonny." I also wasn't above whining a little. I figured it was fine. I'd never whined much as a kid, I could get away with it as an adult.

"Ris, we haven't found him. Do you know what that tells me? That he's in deeper shit than we know. If it was just the Reapers he owed money to, he wouldn't be going through so much trouble to hide from everyone," he explained. He sounded so tired, I immediately felt bad for stressing him out with my stupid begging.

Because he had a point. Why would he be hiding so well? Why had he borrowed so much money to begin with? Plus, there was no reason for me to freak out over the incident at Pins. None.

Dex probably kissed people on a daily basis.

The thought should have been reassuring but all it did was make my stomach hurt—a lot.

I pushed the thought back and tried to focus on Sonny again. "You don't know who?" I asked.

He sighed. "I don't think I want to know. This shit has turned into such a goddamn headache. I'm worried Trip might kill me before we find him."

I wanted to tell him to come back home. That I'd give him the money I had in my account to pay off a small chunk of the debt The Disappointment owed, but I couldn't. I couldn't because the first thing I thought of now every time our dad popped into my head, was what he'd done. The kid he'd had. The way he just plain sucked.

That small part of me that craved blood wanted him to own up to his mess for the first time in his life, so I kept my mouth shut. I only wished that there was something more I could do to find our sperm donor.

"I'm sorry," I told him because it was the only thing I could say that wouldn't bring him down any more.

"It's fine, kid. I'd do this and worse for you," he said in a slightly more upbeat voice. He was probably trying not to give me a guilt trip for being a useless bag of bones. "I met the kid."

Words, language, and the alphabet all melted off my tongue for a split second. "You—did?"

"Yeah. We went back two days ago," Sonny explained.

My little sister. Or little brother. God, I still couldn't fathom having someone else in my life that I could care about the way I felt for Will or Sonny. Not that it would be the same, because even though Sonny and I had grown up in different states, I'd always known him. Always known about him.

And this kid...

"Is it a girl?"

His snicker answered my question. "Nope. He's a little guy."

Another boy. Good gravy.

"Whoa," I breathed out. "Did it go okay?"

"Yeah, but he was confused. I'm old enough to be his dad, you know. His dad is old enough to be his grandpa." The longer Sonny talked, the more pissed off he sounded. "This is so fucked up, Ris. Terry—that's the kid's mom—said he hasn't been by in like two years. Two fucking years, Ris. Can you believe that shit?"

And two years would eventually turn into three. Three into four. Four into five, and before the little boy would know it, it'd be half his life.

Jesus, I was depressing. And negative.

"I think I'd be more surprised if he'd stuck around." A thought nagged at me. "Do you ever want to have kids?"

He let out a sharp laugh. "That's random."

"Well?"

He hummed. "I guess I haven't thought about it. No?" he asked me, the baboon.

"No?"

"Maybe." Sonny paused. "I don't know. I'd be a shitty dad right now, I know that much."

What an idiot. "Son, you'd be as far from a shitty dad as possible."

He made a disapproving noise.

"Shut up. You'd be great, trust me." I had to laugh at a mental picture of him cleaning a diaper. "I think I want a little niece. How about you make it happen?"

"Fuck that," he laughed. "No, Ris. I'll get a dog, but a kid? No way."

"Party pooper."

Sonny laughed again. "Whatever." I could hear Trip talking over the other end of the line. "Are you at Dex's?"

"Nope, I'm at the bar waiting for him."

Ugh. This was even after I expressed to him how much I didn't want to go to Mayhem after he'd embarrassed me in front of the MC men a few days ago.

There was more of Trip's voice on the other end of the line. "You know why no one's answering the phone then?"

That. The reason why Dex had brought us over to Mayhem instead of going back to his place. "They caught the bartender that's been stealing from the Club," I relayed the information Dex had told me before we'd left Pins.

Sonny huffed on the other end of the receiver, repeating what I said to his friend. "Who did it?"

"I think I heard them call him Rocco before they took him upstairs."

Before I'd stood there incapacitated, wondering what in the ever-loving world was going on with my boss.

Dex had calmly looked over at me then, with the thief just a few feet behind him. He'd swept a hand over my hair and, in a voice much louder than he normally used, murmured, "Baby, wait for me upstairs, will you?" And then he ran his hand over my hair again.

I—I just stood there. Shocked, stunned, flabbergasted, whatever. All of those things. Because...I mean, he'd *asked.* And he'd been affectionate in front of the other Widows, who were looking like they'd just discovered the wheel.

By the time I'd absorbed those ten seconds of my life, Dex had disappeared upstairs along with the poor moron that had stolen from the club. The guy hadn't even batted an eyelash when Dex, Luther, and four of the bikers in the bar escorted him to the offices.

I really didn't think that they'd kill him or beat the crap out of him, but maybe I was being naive. As long as no one started screaming from the office, then it was probably fine, right?

"It would be fucking Rocco," Sonny noted. "Look, I'm gonna get going. We want to make it to Sacramento early tomorrow. Call me if you need anything, okay?"

"Okay."

Trip said something on the other end that made Sonny laugh again. "Trip says hi."

"Tell him I said hi back." I sighed. "Love you, Son."

It was impossible not to miss the smile in his voice. "Love you too, kid."

Oh boy. That conversation hadn't exactly gone the way I'd expected it to. Now that I thought about it, the last two conversations I'd had with Sonny had been disturbing. We should probably stick to text messaging from now on.

I wonder if I could get by communicating with Dex by only texting too?

Ugh, I was such a coward.

My half-assed attempt at going back to Sonny's had been the least hearted thing ever. What it came down to was, did I like staying with The Dick? Yes. Did I like him? That was the problem. I liked him too much. He was a member of the Widowmakers, kind of a half-assed one, but a member nonetheless. I was just me. Tattoo-less. Homeless. Poor. Untalented.

Yeah. I was definitely throwing myself a pity party. *Yia-yia* would be rolling in her grave if she knew.

When was the last time I'd felt so little for myself? I'd always been tattoo-less, homeless, poor and untalented, so why did it matter all of a sudden? I was alive and healthy, and most of the time that was all I wanted. Genuinely, it was all I needed. Yet here I was, giving myself pathetic reasons why I should stay away from Dex.

An ex-felon with a temper that owned his own shop. Talented, employed, a homeowner and tatted. My antithesis.

But he was kind, thoughtful and caring when he wanted to be. And he'd never let me down, if you didn't count the night he left me alone at his house, which I wasn't.

I could hear my mom saying, "You could do much worse, Ris."

What was the worst that would happen?

I'd end up like my mom.

Shit.

The stomping of boots on the stairs yanked me out of my thoughts. There were low murmurs accompanying what seemed like a hoard of men clomping their way downstairs.

When a certain black-haired man didn't appear in the doorway, I heaved a sigh and got up, making my way up the stairs in hopes that I'd find Dex there instead of down in the bar. It wasn't like I wanted to have a face-to-face, but I wanted to go to his house. As soon as I cleared the landing, the scent of cigarette drifted through the doorway. He was standing off to the side in the room, his back against the corner of the wall. A faint orange ember dotted a circle right between his fingers.

Dex's face was down as he pulled at the cigarette, a cloud of smoke distorted his face before a breeze carried it away.

"Hey," I called out to him, making my way toward the chairs across from the desk he'd sat at when I'd gotten my butthole ripped for disappearing.

His eyes flicked up, keeping his chin tucked. "Lemme finish this and we can go."

I nodded and plopped my butt onto the couch furthest away from the window he was at, failing at biting back a scowl at the smell he was putting off. He sucked in another breath before blowing it out slowly, narrowing his eyes.

"You don't like the smell?"

"Nope." Eyeing the stub in his hand, I wrinkled my nose. Now the logical part of my brain recognized that I should avoid talking to him. If I did, maybe we could both forget what happened in his office. But if I kept talking to him, it would be like throwing bait into shark infested waters. Even realizing that, I kept talking. "I don't like that whole cancer thing you can get from them either."

He brought the cigarette back up to his mouth, holding it between his index finger and thumb. "You're not gonna nag at me to quit?"

What? "You're a big boy, Dex. And I'm sure you don't like people hounding you." He lifted both eyebrows up like in acknowledgment that I was right. "It'd be nice if you quit so you wouldn't have to worry about getting lung cancer but it's your life. Your body." I smiled at him, the honesty just kind of pouring from my mouth. "I care about you and I hope that you don't ever go through something like that if you can help it."

Dex's mouth didn't form a smile but the way the creases at the corners of his eyes pulled back, it looked like he was trying not to. "Oh yeah?"

And he thought I needed reassurances. "Yes." I confirmed what I'd said. The thought of seeing big, strong Dex with his healthy, bright tattoos, laying withered on a hospital bed physically hurt me.

"I only smoke a couple a day," he argued.

That warm feeling I associated with my mom gripped my chest. "You don't get to choose." For once in a very long time, I wanted to tell him how I knew for a fact that cancer wasn't a bigot or particular about who it went after but the words just wouldn't come out.

One shoulder went up in what wasn't acceptance or denial. "No, I guess ya don't, babe."

Dex looked at me for a long moment, his face pensive and calm under the thick black stubble that had grown on his cheeks over the day. Neither one of us said anything as he took the last pull between his lips. Holding the cigarette between his fingers, he stared at the lit tip with pursed lips before leaning out the window and stubbing it out on the brick building.

He closed the window and leaned against the wall like he had been. Dex swept a finger over his upper lip, trailing his eyes back over in my direction. His head ticked to the side. "You heard what everybody's callin' me now?"

I raised an eyebrow, forgetting that the last thing I needed was to get playful with him. "A nerd?"

"No." It looked like he wanted to smile again but he managed not to. "Your majesty."

Just because he wasn't smiling didn't mean I wouldn't. I snorted, loud. "I like it."

His facial expression didn't change at all. Those blue eyes were too intent, too focused to assure me that I'd get through this day—heck, this week—unscathed. "Know when the last time someone came up with a nickname for me was?"

I shook my head.

"Fifth grade," he explained coolly. "Poindexter."

I had to bite my lip to keep from grinning.

Still, he didn't smile. Dex just kept on looking. "I beat the shit outta the kid that came up with it. Got expelled from school, too."

Also, not a surprise, but I couldn't understand why he was telling me this. Not that I didn't appreciate learning about him but there had to be a message he was trying to put across. "Are you going to beat the crap out of me?"

"Ritz," he sighed. "You trust me?"

I blinked. "Why are you asking?"

"You trust me, or not?"

Did I? It took me less than a heartbeat to decide that after Sonny, I probably trusted Dex the most. And that was even over Will. What that said about the lack of people of in my life, I had no idea, but I didn't care. "Yes," I answered him a little breathless.

"You sure?"

"Yeah," I told him again. I did. "Absolutely."

He rubbed that finger over his lip again. "Absolutely," he muttered under his breath, shaking his head. "You think I trust you?"

There wasn't a need for me to wonder about the answer to his question. It was instinctive. This was the man who told me things about his childhood, his family. He'd shown me his spare bedroom. I couldn't have fought the strain in my chest if I tried. "Yes."

Dex planted both of his hands on the desk in front of him and leaned forward. "I tried all night to think of somebody I trust as much as you and I could only come up with one. One fuckin' person out of everybody in the world, babe," he let me know.

The sudden urge to cry and smile had me make some kind of stupid face.

"My ma," he said. "The only person who knows me better than you do is Ma and that's cheatin'. Not my sisters or my brothers, babe. Just. You."

I couldn't breathe.

"I really didn't wanna like you, honey. A part of me still doesn't," he said, his expression guarded. "You're not the kinda person I had in mind for the shop. But your damn brother begged me to hire you, threatened my future kids if I wasn't nice to his baby sister. And now you're here."

Umm...what?

My neck itched as my throat went dry. His admission explained a lot, and at the same time, it made me feel uncomfortable. "Dex, if you don't want to be my friend that's okay." *You'd just be ripping my heart out and stomping on it but okay.*

His laugh was hard. "Honey, you and me, we're more than just friends."

And… I was dead. I had to be.

Dex scrubbed his fingers over his lips again, his glare violent. "Look at you. I never stood a fuckin' chance."

I blinked at him, refusing to absorb the creamy words that were coming out of his mouth. "I'm pretty sure you've made it known to half of Texas that you're not attracted to me." Then there were the times I thought he looked at me as his pet.

Dex's nostrils flared. "Baby, have I or haven't I, warned you a million times that I say shit I don't mean all the time? You expected me to tell your brother I wanted to fuck his little Ris the first time I saw you in shorts? Or should I have said somethin' to you when I knew you were still pissed at me?"

"Charlie…"

"Babe." He said my nickname like a challenge.

"You told Shane you didn't like me not even three weeks ago!"

"I never said that, babe. Quit puttin' words in my mouth."

Damn this man. I felt like the walls were closing in on me. "You're the most confusing person I've ever met in my life."

He shrugged. "Forgive me for bein' so damn stupid and confusin' you."

"You're not being stupid, I just don't think you're thinking clearly. " I swallowed even as my heart hurt. "Maybe you just need to go...you know...with someone."

"Baby, there's nothing wrong with my judgment. I know exactly what I'm doin', and I know damn well that if I ever see you smile at somebody like you did at Trey today, I'll kill the poor bastard."

"Dex!"

"I'm not jokin'. I don't ever wanna see that shit ever again so unless you want me goin' to jail for murderin' somebody, quit it," he stated, not blinking, not breathing, totally focused.

And I stood there just waiting. For what, I had no idea. Maybe to wake up from this dream.

But the beautiful dark-haired man in front of me wasn't saying anything. His gaze was zeroed in on my face, jaw tight, shoulders pulled back. He must have realized I thought he was on drugs because he kept going. "That shit made my chest burn. *I hated it.* You know what that's like for me? Standin' there thinkin' to myself that I don't wanna share you with anybody?" His neck visibly strained. "I can't ignore this shit between us anymore, and I'm not gonna. Not when it makes so much sense."

Oh. Dear. God.

I wasn't sure whether to have a panic attack or run around fist pumping. But still. That fear crept threw my bones, warning me, preparing me, making me wary. "Why does this make so much sense?" The question was hoarse.

"Nobody's ever made me feel the way you do."

Was that my throat burning? Oh hell, it was. No amount of swallowing made the sensation go away. "But...I'm like your little rabbit. Your pet."

"Oh, you're somethin' of mine all right, Ris. But my pet? Huh uh," he said with more conviction than any man should be capable of.

At least a little bit of fear flooded my system because I thought for a moment about walking out of the room to end the conversation.

"You go and I'm comin' after you, babe." Dex ate up those few feet to loom over me on the couch, his body longer and leaner than it'd seemed hours before as he hovered. "I'm not your daddy. I'm not gonna do the shit he did. You don't need to be scared of me."

At the mention of my dad, my spine stiffened. "I know you're not. I'm not scared of you either, okay?"

"Yeah, you are." He bent at the waist to place his hands on the back of the couch at my sides.

Heat exploded on the back of my neck. "I'm not," I insisted.

He lowered his head even more, cornering me like the bully he was. "You are, but I'm not your pa and you gotta remember that. I told you when you tried to quit that I keep what's mine, and I meant that."

Yeah, I couldn't move. I couldn't breathe. I couldn't do a single friggin' thing as his mouth came to within inches of mine. I should have moved, should have pushed him away, screamed, anything except just sit there. But the closer he got, the more of him and his lulling body heat, the less I wanted to do that. It was like being in a trance.

"I suck at pretendin', babe." He brushed his mouth over my cheekbone, making my spine tingle. "You suck at it, too."

I don't know what it said that the word 'suck' hit me right in the lower stomach.

And really, what is there really to say when Dex Locke brushes his lips against that spot between your jaw and ear?

Nothing. Absolutely nothing.

CHAPTER TWENTY-SIX

Mine.

I keep what's mine.

Mine.

Mine.

Mine.

It was the first thing I thought of when I woke up the next morning alone on the couch.

He hadn't said anything else after he'd kissed my jaw and right off the corner of my mouth. Dex had just thrust out a hand to pull me off the couch, and led me toward the stairs. With a firm hand on my lower back, we walked out of the bar without speaking another word. Rode to his house in silence, and then ate dinner and watched television the same way.

It was only when he got up to go to bed that he leaned in to kiss the corner of my mouth, just a hair off from my lips that he said two sentences. "I know you're confused, Ritz, but there's no reason for you to be." With that, he disappeared into his bedroom, leaving me dazed and on the verge of panting on the couch.

It was a friggin' miracle I'd managed to fall asleep.

I definitely didn't need to think about that right before I went into the shower. Or maybe I did. There was a detachable showerhead...

Yeah, *no*. I grabbed my bag from its spot on the other side of the couch and rifled through it, grabbing clothes for my shower. The clock on the DVD player showed that it was a little after ten. Normally, Dex would be in his garage working out so that gave me more time to wonder what the hell was going on.

Was I being a pushover by letting him assume that I would want to.... to what? Be with him? Date him? Dex didn't seem like the type of man that dated. Or the type of man that had a girlfriend.

Where did that leave us?

If I was smart, as smart as I'd been my entire life, I'd call Sonny and tell him what was happening.

I wasn't though, not today or tomorrow. I could justify not calling by saying that I didn't want to stress him out or piss him off. *Right.* It wasn't at all because the thought of making Dex hard—like he'd been back at Pins—turned me on more than any time I'd spent with my ex-boyfriend times a hundred. No, siree.

Who am I kidding? I was a total, complete liar.

The idea of not seeing Dex nearly every day made me incredibly unhappy.

I was screwed.

Twenty minutes later, I was out of the bathroom, teeth and hair brushed, clean, and slightly more alert. Dex hadn't made an appearance yet, so I wandered into the kitchen to make something for breakfast.

I had just stuck two frozen waffles into the conventional oven before pouring the coffee Dex had already brewed when I felt what had become an all too familiar heat pierce through the thin material of my long-sleeved t-shirt. This was right before arms caged me against the counter, one on each side, biceps touching my triceps.

I froze.

"Sleep good?" the raspy voice asked against my ear. Warm breath wafted over all the skin within centimeters of it.

The instinct to turn my head in his direction was right there, taunting me, calling for me, and that was a bad, bad thing. I couldn't step backward because that would bring us flush together, but there wasn't any space to step forward or to the side either.

"Like your shampoo, babe." More moist breath against me.

Jesus, I needed to get it together.

Luckily I was facing away from Dex, so I was able to keep my wide, alarmed eyes away from his view. "I did," I answered his question a little weakly, ignoring his comment about my hair.

He chuckled right up against me. His chest so close to mine I could feel the vibrations radiating from his laughter onto my skin. I wanted to scowl but instinct told me that something so simple would cause more unnecessary physical contact so I tried to pull my best imitation of a statue for longer.

His nose grazed the skin right behind my ear. "Pour me a cup when you get a chance?" His voice still had that rough edge to it. Paired with the heat of his chest and the breath touching a spot that should be an erogenous zone—if it wasn't already—he was making it so friggin' hard to stay still.

I was going to need to change my underwear if he didn't step away in like a second.

So I nodded with more enthusiasm than I needed. I mean, he usually served our coffee, but still. "Sure."

Then this guy moved the tip of his nose just a little higher, resting it right where skin met my hairline and took a deep, deep inhale. "Goddamn that's good."

New underwear. Oh crap, I was going to need new underwear. Stat.

Dex didn't move away. He took another inhale and if I wouldn't have been floating around in the universe to keep from dissolving into a pool of melted ovaries, I would have noticed that his arms tightened around me.

And I panicked.

When I panic, I either laugh or say things I regret. In this case, it was the latter.

"Is that Rocco guy still alive?"

His chest started to shake with repressed laughter. "You serious?"

"What do you mean am I serious?"

Dex's chest kept shaking. "Babe, you watch too much TV," he snickered.

I tipped my chin to the side so that I could look at him over my shoulder. Yep, he was definitely trying not to laugh but happened to be losing the battle. "What? I didn't see him leave."

The head shake he gave me and little smirk on his face said that he thought I was crazy for making such a question. "Well? I don't know what you guys were planning on doing to him. On TV they'd probably cut him up to pieces to make a lesson out of him."

And then he laughed. Loud. "What the fuck, babe? We've all been to county at one point or another except your bro. None of us wanna go back. Half the guys got kids they worry about. I already told you most of us aren't into doin' real shady shit anymore."

To be fair, he had told me most of those things before but I guess I hadn't really believed him. Even Trip, who seemed like the friendliest guy, didn't give off a friendly neighbor vibe. "Really?" I still asked him a little hesitantly.

"Really. Most of the guys work at the auto parts store or Mayhem, couple of the others work with Lu, and the ones that don't have nonstop shit on their records, work at other places. We're watered down now."

"Oh." Well, now I felt like a huge jackass. What business did I have stereotyping everyone? "So Rocco's fine?"

"He walked out on his own after we were done," he explained. "All we did was have a little talk with him."

"Oh yeah?" I raised both my eyebrows in disbelief.

Friggin' Dex cracked a grin that seemed to crack my chest in half. "We might've told him he wouldn't be intact if we didn't get every single cent back he stole within a week but you know, that's all, babe."

Ahh. Owed money. A story every motorcycle club that I knew of—a whopping two—were familiar with. Well, at least they were giving him a week. "Will you promise me something?"

"Depends."

"If he doesn't pay you guys back, don't do anything to his family," I whispered.

The smile on his face transformed into a stony expression that made his jaw clench. Dex tilted his face downward, reminding me that our position was a terrible idea. Terrible because it made me want to close the distance between us. His forehead touched the edge of mine. "Baby, I won't let anythin' happen to you, you gotta know that." Warm breath wafted over my cheek. "Don't worry about it."

"I know." It was the truth. My bones knew it. "But not everyone has a Sonny or a Dex to keep them safe, Charlie."

He nodded slowly, his eyes understanding. "All right."

Good gracious. Calm, sweet Dex was like a tranquilizer straight to my neck. I shared a little smile with him and dropped my gaze back down to the counter, knowing there was nothing left to tell him. "I wanted to go to the Y before work. Were you planning on going to the bar or should I drive myself?"

I had no idea why I even bothered asking.

His answer was always the same: "I'll take you."

"Okay."

"Finish your food, and then we'll get going. Yeah?" he asked me from somewhere several feet away.

"Sure."

Maybe he was onboard with me and the not-bringing-shit-up game. That would work. It would also work if neither one of us spoke to each other, period, to avoid dipping into an awkward conversation that I wasn't sure I was ready to have. Today or ever.

The sound of my cell phone ringing from the living room had me bolting. No one called me. Ever. Ever. I knew who it was.

I sprinted over the back of the coach like a track champion, reaching for my purse as if touching it would save the world. When the "unavailable" popped up on the screen, I shrieked and pressed the answer button with the strength of Hercules.

I panted. "Will?"

"Ris, it's me," my brother's calm, baritone voice came over the receiver.

A weight I shouldered so often I forgot it was there, levitated off of me. It was one thing to know that my brother was off on the other side of the world in a decently safe area, but it was an altogether different experience to box those worries up and try not to deal with them. It made the worries stew beneath my skin, beneath my heart, under all of the fibers and the tissues that protected me.

"I was worried you were dead."

Will laughed in his own reserved way. "Sorry I haven't called in so long, but you know how it is."

I didn't though. Hearing the sound of his voice kind of made me a little bit mad since it'd been months from the last time I'd heard from him. Months! It wasn't like I emailed him daily, or asked for him to call me weekly, but the length of multiple months crossed the line—and it pissed me off.

"How you been? How's work? Austin okay?" my little brother asked quickly.

My stomach churned in frustration. So he'd read my emails and just decided not to write me back?

I had to hold back the shuddering sigh that had built up in my chest at the realization and calm down. "Pretty good. You got my emails I guess?"

Will paused before making a grumbling noise in his throat. "I read them before I called. I figured I'd get all caught up so we wouldn't waste time."

Maybe I was just being too sensitive but his comment about wasting time scratched at me. Like writing me an email or talking to me for five minutes longer once every other month was a hassle. Like what Sonny was doing—taking time off from work and traveling around the country—wasn't a waste in its own way. I bit back the smart ass comment that floated into my vocal chords and tried to appreciate the fact that I had him on the phone finally.

"Are you still staying with Sonny?"

I needed to quit being a baby. "I was, but he had to take a little vacation so I'm staying with a friend until he comes back," I explained to him vaguely, suddenly not in the mood to really share with him more than I needed to. What was the point? Why had I been fighting Will growing up and moving on with his life, so much?

Will knew even less about the Widows than I did. Growing up, it was as if he'd just cut our dad out of his memory and life.

Existing without him, while I'd been the one stuck with the memories and the wishes.

"Huh. I have leave coming up in a couple of months, are you gonna stay there?"

Where the hell else would I go? "I'll be here."

The awkward silence that followed left me feeling weird. Since when had talking to Will been a strain? Was this what Sonny and I sounded like when we talked on the phone? No way. Speaking of Sonny... "Hey, umm..." I really didn't want to tell him. A part of me genuinely didn't think he'd care but that was the difference between us again. Will liked Sonny enough but then again, did he even like me now? I didn't want to answer that.

The point was, he deserved to know so that it wouldn't the same situation I found myself in with Sonny. "Dad had another kid." Shit. That wasn't exactly the way I wanted to blurt it out.

The disheartened, uninterested "Oh," confirmed that my brother didn't give a crap. "That's... cool."

Yeah, he didn't care. At all.

When he immediately started talking again, I knew I'd messed up. I'd pushed too far. He'd done the same thing when we were younger and I thought he wanted to talk about Mom. Will would bring up something else or suddenly remember that he needed to do something. "I need to go, Ris, but I promise I'll call or email you as soon as I know when I'm going back to the States, and we'll figure it out, all right?" he mumbled out the sentence so quickly it made him sound desperate.

Maybe I wasn't the only chicken in the family. "Deal. Love you."

"Love you too. Be safe and we'll talk soon," Will said right before disconnecting the line.

I sighed and pocketed my phone, immediately sensing Dex's hulking presence behind me for the first time. His lips were a hard slash, eyes deceptively distant on me before he spoke. "Your brother?"

"Yeah."

There was so much about our phone conversation that bothered me. It wasn't that I wanted or needed to have a long conversation with my brother, but it'd been so long since the last time we'd spoken, getting rushed through a five minute conversation didn't seem fair.

Dex narrowed his eyes. "What's wrong?"

"Nothing."

He rolled his eyes. "What is it? Looks like somebody just told you Santa wasn't real."

Oh lord. The man who got pissed off about his property taxes going up wanted to make a statement by comparing us? Please. I snorted. "Nothing," I insisted.

"Somethin's botherin' you. Tell me."

Dex wasn't going to drop it so I groaned. "I haven't talked to him in months. I've emailed him at least a dozen times and he never responds." I rubbed a hand over my forehead. "I mean, I know he's not a kid. He's a grown man, he doesn't need me anymore. I guess I'm just being a girl and getting butt-hurt that he has a life without me."

His nose wrinkled but he didn't comment on my rant.

I took in a deep breath and shrugged, forcing a smile onto my face. "Anyway, let me know when you want to leave, okay?"

If I thought for a second that I'd have the ability to think about something other than my conversations with my brothers and whatever was going on with Dex, I'd have been terribly wrong.

I'd be in the middle of logging the number of hour sessions that one of the artists had done for the week and suddenly, I'd think of the action hero Dex had in his spare bedroom. Or I'd be sitting in the front, uploading pictures onto the shop's website when I'd hear Blake on the phone with his son and I'd start imagining what the little boy in Colorado looked like.

My whole day went like that after the two hours I'd spent in the pool and the aerobics class at the YMCA I took.

Dex, Dex, Sonny, Dex, Will, Brother, Dex, Dex.

And then some more Dex.

My gut told me that I was insane. That constantly thinking about him wasn't normal. Then again, what was normal about Dex?

Nothing.

The only good thing I could come up with was that he'd been giving me a decent amount of distance. That wasn't to say every time he walked past me or stood by the receptionist desk that he wouldn't send a heated look my way or put his hand somewhere on my body when he was close enough. Whether it was the back of my neck, my hip, or the small of my back, his hand was always there in some way or another.

I didn't do a single thing to move away from him.

My brain said "No!" Yet everything else in me screamed "Yes!" obnoxiously.

Yeah, I was a friggin' mess. A mess that had no hope of getting sorted out properly. There was no point in me even trying to fight it or figure it out.

I sighed and got up feeling defeated, to see if Slim and Blue needed anything. I'd been putting off eating something for at least an hour but my stomach had started grumbling so much I figured it was time to quit procrastinating. "I'm going next door before they close, you guys want anything?"

They both shook their heads. Slim had been messing around on his tablet and the last time I'd seen Blue, she was working on a tattoo for her next customer. Even at seven at night, it was way too hot. Definitely too warm for the sweater I'd pulled on before riding to Pins on the back of Dex's bike.

I ordered a Mediterranean wrap from the deli and tried my best not to think about what Sonny had told me. Another brother. Well, shit. A little one at that. I didn't even want to consider what other kind of mess my dad was in that he'd be hiding. What had started as a headache didn't need to become a nightmare.

Especially not if whoever he owed money to decided to come after someone who didn't have Sonny to watch out for them. Someone like my new little brother.

God.

I was so entrenched in the idea of actually having another sibling that I didn't see the silhouette of a man leaning against the stonewashed wall until his heavy black boot hit the top of my thighs.

"Doll," that rumbling low voice I'd only heard once before, greeted me.

My body didn't react immediately to it. It took a second for me to accept what the voice meant.

It meant my friggin' death if any of the Widows saw me.

Shit!

The brown bag I'd been holding with my wrap in it slipped out of my hand, and I'm sure my face went pale. "What are you doing here?" I squawked. Yes, squawked of all friggin' things. I didn't even know I was capable of making such an ugly noise but in the face of my potential death, nothing was impossible.

Liam looked at me coolly, like he wasn't on the wrong side of town. "What do you think I'm doing here?" he asked, straightening up off the wall.

God, he was a big guy.

But that wasn't the point or the time to notice how broad he was. "Trying to get us both killed," I hissed at him, taking a step away.

"Nah," he mumbled, eyeing me with way too much interest.

I looked down both sides of the street to see if anyone I recognized was coming along. The only good thing about the Widows was that I'd hopefully be able to hear the loud roar of a bike before I saw it.

I hoped.

To God.

And maybe even a few other deities.

"Look, I'm sorry for going to bother you before but it won't happen again."

Liam ran a hand over the closely cropped hair on his head. "I'm thinking it's okay if you come bother me again, doll."

Oh, whatever. I had to fight back the urge to roll my eyes and cry bullshit. Something in the pit of my stomach said that this man didn't have the same kind of control—or it might have been fondness—that allowed me to talk crap to Dex and get away with it. For the most part at least.

"Umm, yeah, I don't think that's a great idea." My smile was more creepy-awkward than convincing.

Apparently, Liam either didn't pick up on it or didn't care because he kept going. "I'm also thinking that you and me can work something out with your daddy's debt."

Infinite amounts of the word *shit* flew through my brain in a long rant.

I'd been stupid for going to the strip club on my own, but standing here, talking to the president of the Reapers MC when I had a temperamental Widow less than thirty feet away, was even dumber. Way dumber.

Extraordinarily stupid.

My silence as I thought about how much of an idiot I was being, was taken as a token of a possibility when the rough man in front of me kept going with his proposition.

"You wanted a solution, I got you one, Miss Taylor," he purred easily, taking a step so close to me that he managed to reach out and almost touch my face.

He didn't because I dodged his hand, but when he laughed, I figured it wasn't really a deterrent.

"How bad do you wanna make sure we don't have to go after your bro when your daddy doesn't pay up this week?" Liam asked.

This week? "What do you mean this week?" I asked him carefully.

Liam licked his lips in a move that most women would probably find sexy, but I found overkill. "Your daddy's got till the end of the week to pay up." He grinned. "I'm offering you a chance to help him out. Help your brother out, too."

If I'd screamed "Shit!" out of my mouth at the same volume I screamed it in my head, it would have been heard across two city blocks. Instinctively, I wanted to panic but I didn't. I took a deep breath and made myself calm down. This guy could be bluffing. That wasn't out of the question. He could also be taking advantage of the bout of stupidity that had ganged up on me when I'd gone to visit him last time.

The point was, I realized how dumb I'd been in going to Busty's, the strip club, now. Sonny would probably kick my ass if he found out that I was bargaining with the bald devil in front of me.

The sudden image of Dex's face was my second warning. He'd kill me.

And if he happened to walk out and see me talking to Liam, he'd probably kill us both. Or, at least beat the crap out of the other man, which was something he had no business doing because of his record and his career.

Did I really want to risk him getting in trouble just because I'd been an idiot?

No. I didn't.

I also didn't want to offend Liam more than necessary but I had a feeling that he was the type of person who didn't deal with rejection well. Which meant I was totally screwed. But better to save myself from the devil I knew than the one I didn't.

"How much does he owe you?"

"The same thing he did last time," Liam snickered. "But I'll take you for six months in exchange for some more time."

What. The. Ef.

Any sense I had in handling the biker gently went right out the friggin' window. Six months with me in exchange for an extension? My virginity. My pride. My honor. My friggin' common sense.

No.

Absolutely no.

If I didn't let my ex pop my cherry after we'd dated for four months, then I sure as hell wasn't going to let this manipulative jackass do it.

"No." I told him calmly. There was no, "No, thank you." No, "I appreciate the offer, but no." None of that. Nothing to ease my way out of the situation.

Sonny would never forgive me for doing something so stupid for him, and especially not for the sperm donor. Most importantly, I wouldn't be able to forgive myself. I wasn't a prostitute and I wasn't a pawn in whatever game this psychopath wanted to play.

His eyes flashed in brief anger. "No?" he scoffed, incredulous. "You're telling me no?"

Well, there was no graceful way out of this. "My dad doesn't give a crap about any of his kids." I watched him carefully, seeing that he wasn't taking that as enough of an excuse. There was only one thing left to do: lie. Desperate times call for desperate measures, dang it. "Either way I don't think you'd want sloppy seconds."

"What?"

I needed to end this conversation three minutes ago. "I'm with Dex." That was better than saying I'm Dex's, wasn't it? That sounded too possessive. Too permanent and the situation I was in was neither.

The carefully controlled mask that had graced Liam's face morphed into one that barely contained the irritation lurking behind his eyes. He was pissed. "Locke?"

I nodded.

Liam wasn't just pissed, he was incredibly pissed. He straightened to his full height and visibly ground his teeth. "You're right. I'm not a fan of Widows' seconds." He raked his gaze over me one more time. "Didn't know you messed around with trash like Locke, doll."

Trash? He thought Dex was trash?

If there was a word to describe the facial expression that came over me it had to be described as a sneer. I knew in my gut that I shouldn't say anything back to him. He'd been fine and relatively decent before but did that mean he was harmless? No way.

Trying to diffuse the situation I gave me a shaky smile. "Thank you for the offer. I hope you get your money back soon."

The words had barely gotten out of my mouth before grabbing my bag off the floor like a lifeline and darting into Pins. I may have burst through the door a little too loudly, catching Slim's confused expression over his shoulder while he worked.

"You all right?" he asked before focusing back on the tablet below him.

I looked around to make sure Dex wasn't nearby and let out a deep breath. "I'm fine." I wasn't. At least not completely.

What I needed to do was catch my breath and decide whether or not to tell someone that Liam had been outside propositioning me. I didn't want to. My gut said it was a bad idea but wouldn't it be a worse idea for me to keep my mouth shut? Of that I wasn't positive.

Craaaaap!

I hustled down the hallway toward the break room, briefly glancing into the office to see Dex on the phone. That was okay. That was better than okay. It gave me time to keep thinking through what I was going to do, if I did anything.

Keep your mouth shut, Ris, my logical brain said.

Tell him, Ris, the other half—the emotional half—egged on.

Double friggin' crap.

I forced my wrap down though I'd magically lost my appetite for once. It took me longer than it would have if I'd still been starving but I didn't care. With my trash in the garbage I walked out of the kitchen slowly, still debating whether or not to say something to Dex. As I came to the office doorway, I found him sitting at his desk, drawing.

I wasn't going to lie anymore, I'd told myself months ago. I'd failed that, so at least I'd keep it to a minimum.

Oh lord. My fingers shook a little as I knocked on the door faintly.

"Hey."

Those dark blue eyes flicked up in my direction, Dex ducking his head just a bit. "Come in, babe."

The two steps in felt like I was going to the gallows. I started wringing my hands as I stood awkwardly to the side of the chairs in front of his desk. He'd looked back down at what he was drawing, which was the only way I managed to start talking.

"Liam was just outside," I rushed out. "He offered to give my dad an extension if I went with him."

At the mention of the biker's name, Dex's pencil stopped its movement in midair. His entire body tightened, strained, and shifted in ripples of muscle and stress. It was the fact he kept his face down that worried me.

"I told him no. I told him I was with you," I blabbed out.

Oh boy.

The way he slowly looked up at me could have been creepy, but for some reason it just fell short. Instead, he pushed his chair back roughly, smacking the wall with the back of it. In a growl, he rounded the desk and pointed at the chair I stood in front of. "Wait," he said and stormed out the door.

Fudgsicle sticks.

I should have listened to him and waited, but I didn't. I was out the door and going after him a split second later. If Liam was dumb enough to still be outside in front of Dex's shop, on Widowmaker territory, he was a dead man. Or at least a bloody one.

But it wasn't his being that I cared about.

It was the moron running after him that I didn't want to get in trouble.

I could only imagine what Dex had to look like as he ran out of the shop that had the employees and the clients captivated. The door was barely swinging shut when I jogged up to it.

Dex was stalking toward the end of the block, a phone held up to his ear, and I could hear him barking something ugly and low into the end.

Shit.

I gathered up my guts and followed after him, catching bits and pieces of "Motherfucker—at Pins—lost his fuckin' mind—Ritz!"

Oh boy.

The moment he thrust his cell phone into his pocket and made way to start stomping across the street, I slid my finger through the belt loops at the back of his jeans and tugged. "Charlie."

Miraculously, he paused.

"Hey, he's gone," I told him in the most soothing voice I could come up with. My free hand settled on the small of his back. "Calm down."

Dex turned to look at me over his shoulder before gradually turning around, the tips of his boots pressing against the tips of my flats. For once, that carefully blank expression was missing. In its place, Dex's mouth was pulled back in a tight snarl. His eyes narrowed.

Yeah, he was pissed.

I smiled at him, hoping that it would calm him down, and I tugged at his belt loop again. "Chill out." I used the same words he'd used on me so long ago. "Nothing happened."

"Ritz," he gritted out. "He came here. To my shop. On my territory. And tried to fuckin' get you to go with him." He bared his teeth. "That's not fuckin' nothin'."

Sometimes I just wanted to roll my eyes at him. "But he's gone, and I don't want you to get in trouble."

Okay, he was still pissed.

"And I'm here with you, not him, so it doesn't matter."

He stared at me for a long moment, his gaze hard. Then his hands were cupping my face. He tipped my head back to nip at my upper lip, sucking it between his.

Oh my crap.

Dex moved to do the same to my bottom one before I reacted. Before I tried to kiss him back the same way he was kissing me, with the dull edges of my teeth catching his bottom lip. He tilted my head even further back, arching me against him as he wrapped an arm around my waist.

His hot tongue slipped into my mouth the first chance he got, brushing against mine with more force, more possession, than I knew what to do with. But it didn't matter that I'd only kissed three people before him. That his experience more than likely eclipsed mine by hundreds, because he moaned into my mouth. He pulled me tighter against him, gripped my waist more strongly than he needed to.

The kiss was a claim.

His tongue dueled mine in a way that was completely friggin' inappropriate on a busy public street. His hard body curled over me, consuming me.

And I loved it. I let it happen. I sucked his tongue into my mouth like I knew what I was doing. Like I'd cease to exist if he didn't bite my lip again.

"Iris." He gently bit the soft place between my jaw and throat column.

Holy, holy, holy crap.

I was going to go up in a pile of flames. A burning inferno that rivaled hell, that would be worth every second of pain to have Dex's mouth so aggressively on mine.

He bit down again before nuzzling the line of my jaw. "You're mine." His lower body pressed into my stomach. Hard, he was so hard. "Your mouth, your face, your ass, your pussy, Ritz. You're all mine."

Me, who had never even kissed another person in public, was panting. Ready to give everything and more to the man that scared the crap out of me.

And if it wouldn't have been for the throat clearing that yanked me so abruptly from the sexual daze I was in, I would have gladly stayed there with his tongue in my throat and his teeth at my jaw forever.

"Uhh, Dex?"

He sucked my lip one last time, hard, into his mouth before pulling his mouth away reluctantly.

The sound of that same throat clearing came from behind me again.

"Dex, Luther's on the phone." It was Slim talking. Slim that was clearing his throat.

Slim that had caught us making out. In the middle of the sidewalk. In the middle of the day.

Oh. No.

The ginger had a smug look on his face and I really don't think I imagined him mouthing, "I knew it," at me.

I'm sure my face turned a kaleidoscope of reds and pinks as I tried to take a step back and away from Dex, but when he kept his arm tight around my waist, it was useless.

"Okay," he finally answered in a hoarse voice, not bothering to turn around.

Dex kept his head down, toward me. His arm was stiff on my back. Sucking in a crisp breath through his nose, he let out a shaky exhale out through his mouth. He leaned in and whispered three words that made me break out in goose bumps. "This isn't over."

I really friggin' hoped not.

CHAPTER TWENTY-SEVEN

"Tell us what happened."

Ef me.

Sitting across the office from Dex, Luther, and that cute biker that worked at Mayhem, I sucked in a breath and folded my hands across my lap to hide the fact that I was on the verge of panicking. I mean, it wasn't like I didn't know the question was coming. It had to be.

After our brief make-out session outside of Pins, the subsequent phone call that Dex had with Luther in his office, and then seeing at least two motorcycles drive down the street in the opposite direction of Mayhem—I found myself there. In the office. Under the second Inquisition.

Now, I could lie. Or I could tell him exactly what happened outside with Liam. That's what made me panic.

I'd been a moron and I was scared to admit it.

But I hadn't been a liar before this, except for kind-of, sort-of not telling Sonny about my arm for months. Since then, I'd tried not to lie because keeping things quiet by omission wasn't lying. Right? I think it depended on the circumstances, or at least that's what I liked to think to keep my conscience clear.

"Ritz," Dex spoke up, screwing the Rangers cap on his head from side to side in a gesture I wasn't familiar with.

Well, shit.

I was tougher than that. What did I have to be scared of?

Looking at Dex's pissed off face, I knew exactly what but that didn't mean I was going to cower from his judgment, damn it.

"He saw me outside and he said he had a proposition for me," I started. "He said that he had a solution to save my dad and Sonny from the debt that needed to get paid at the end of the week."

Luther looked over in Dex's direction with a wary glance I didn't miss.

"He said he'd take six months with me in exchange for... I don't know, not going after one of them if it wasn't paid. I just told him no." And then told him I was with Dex.

"He didn't say anything else?" The hot older guy asked.

I shook my head. "Nothing important." He just called Dex trash, but I'd be an idiot to bring that up.

Luther blew out a deep breath that made his lips flutter in exasperation. "That son of a bitch."

Hot biker guy shook his head incredulously. "I heard he just split up with his old lady not too long ago."

"I heard the same," the president of the MC agreed. "But why the hell would he try and take Ris as an exchange? That doesn't sound like their style even if he's trying to piss us off doing it."

Now that question, I had no answer for. And all of a sudden, I felt guilty that I hadn't agreed. That I wouldn't do my part to assure Sonny's safety but...

"I'd do almost anything for Son, but I don't want to go with Liam," I tried to explain to them in a small voice.

"You're not goin' with anybody," Dex interjected quickly. "Not for Son, your dad, for nobody, Ritz. Ever."

I happened to be looking at Luther while Dex spoke and I could see his mouth twitch.

"This is Taylor's shit. You shouldn't have gotten dragged into it," he said.

There went my guilt.

If I kept the truth to myself it would bother me forever.

"I did something stupid," I blabbed, looking up at the ceiling because any balls I had beforehand disappeared.

Just rip it off like a Band-Aid. Quick, quick, quick.

"I went to Busty's last week to talk to the Reapers to see if I could talk them out of going after Sonny. That jerk said it wasn't any of my business." I let out a weird breath continuing to damn myself. "He kissed me and I ran out of there."

Silence.

Complete, mind-numbing silence.

"I know it was stupid but I'm fine." Like that was going to help the situation but something was better than nothing. I hoped. Holding up my hands, I flipped them over. "See? Nothing happened."

The first thing that came out of anyone's mouth was a long, drawn out, "Fuck." It might have been the hot guy or Luther.

The second thing that came out of someone's mouth was, "Get out."

Dex.

"Excuse me?" I asked, still looking up at the patterned ceiling.

"Get out, Ritz," he repeated.

What the hell? I lowered my gaze down, suddenly more confused than scared at his response. Dex had pulled the lid of his cap down tighter on his forehead, his fingertips white and pinched. "Why?"

"Get the fuck out," he snarled.

Ouch!

"Dex—"

"I said get the fuck out!" he yelled.

My heart started pounding so fast, I thought it was going to explode. My face went hot. My chest started to hurt. It was like my skin was being flayed.

I felt awful. So friggin' awful. Why the hell was he yelling at me like that?

So I snapped back for the first time in my life, because here was this stupid dick-brain of a man that I'd slowly started to like, started to feel something for, and he was going to act like a complete friggin' dick? "Go fuck yourself, you...you...mean asshole!" And then I let out a breath that could probably rival a dragon minus the fire and bad breath. "Don't you talk to me like that."

I was embarrassed, so embarrassed that I felt a lump in my throat. I was mortified. No one had ever talked to me like that, and he was out of his mind if he thought he could get away with it.

Getting out of the chair like my joints were those of a senior, pissed and hurt, I shook my head but didn't bother looking at him. I didn't know how I'd feel if I saw his face. Right before pulling the door open with a little more force than was necessary, I muttered, "Dickface," under my breath.

The moment I was out of the office, my heartbeat tripled. The urge to throw up and cry was so overwhelming, I managed to stifle the gag and settle for sucking in a ragged breath that did nothing to keep my eyes from tearing up.

Those damn traitorous tears slipped out in sporadic pairs, streaming weak lines down my face before I wiped them off.

I wasn't going to cry.

You are not going to cry, Iris.

Wiping at my face again, I sucked in a breath that sounded strangled and weak but it worked.

The hallway seemed shorter than normal, and when I immediately spotted Blue, Slim, and a customer sitting on the couch, looking in my direction with pity in their eyes I wanted to bang my face against the nearest wall.

I couldn't catch a friggin' break.

Slapping a shaky smile onto my face I marched straight toward the exit, promising myself that I wouldn't burst into tears before I was out of sight. I wouldn't do it, damn it. I wouldn't.

"Iris!" It was Slim calling out after me as I stopped at the door, hands planted flat on the glass to push.

I looked him in the face, keeping hold of the reins that fisted my smile closely.

"Here," he said right before digging into his pocket and tossing something underhanded at me.

His car keys.

That made me want to cry even more. I gripped them in my hand, ready to toss them back, already shaking my head. "He'll get mad at you."

My sweet friend Slim shrugged, not worried at all. "He'll get over it." Tipping his chin up, he winked. "I can catch a ride home with Blue."

Blue opened her mouth but didn't say anything. Her gaze slid over to me and she nodded, solemnly. "Get outta here, Ris."

Ahh, crap. I had to wipe at my cheeks again to catch the tears that had slipped out like sneaky ninjas.

"Thanks, guys." My voice sounded all wobbly and raspy. I sniffled and gave them the best smile I could pull out of my battered emotions. "You guys are really good friends to me."

Not wanting to waste any more time at Pins, I waved at my two coworkers quickly and rushed out the door. Slim's Scion was parked in the furthest corner of the lot. Taking in a deep breath, I tried to steady my breathing as much as possible before pulling the car out of the lot.

I didn't know where I was going. It took me all of a second to decide that Sonny's was out of the question. My keys were at Dex's and I wasn't fond of the idea of trying to stage a break in. There was also no way in hell I'd go to Dex's. At that moment, the last thing I wanted to do was even think about that asshole.

Well, that was a lie, as soon as I thought of him, my blood pressure went up.

I mean, what the hell was his problem? To yell at me like that. To talk to me like that. Maybe he was used to being able to talk to people in that way. He hadn't exactly been kind to most people I'd seen him interact with but still. His little temper tantrum had gotten the best out of him—out of me, too.

I drove around for a while. I didn't know where I was going and half the time I didn't even know where I was. I'd have to fill up Slim's gas tank before I drove his car back to the shop later, or tomorrow, whatever my mind decided.

That was when I remembered that I'd left my purse and phone at Pins. That's how pissed—err, upset—I'd been. I never even went to the bathroom without my phone.

The only money I had on me was the twelve dollars and change I had left over from the deli in my back pocket. Well, that kind of screwed me over.

I finally found my way back to the side of town I was familiar with, closer to Sonny's house. With only a quarter of a tank left, I pulled into the parking lot of the mall and theater I'd been to before. There was no point in me driving around or sitting in the car, moping. I didn't want to replay The Dick's tone any more than I already had on the drive.

Friggin' asshole.

I'd finally, *finally*, gotten into the acting after staring at the big screen for two hours when I saw the figure standing at the foot of the stairs that led up the row. I'd snuck into the second movie after I'd seen that it was only nine, and there was no way in hell I was heading back to Pins earlier than I needed to.

Because I still hadn't come up with a plan.

If my car hadn't been at Dex's house, then I would have had more options. But it was. I didn't have my cell on me so I couldn't even try to call Sonny and explain to him the situation, because I'm sure he'd hear about it eventually and I didn't want to lie to him. If anyone was going to tell him I'd done something stupid I hoped it'd be me.

Then at some point during the movie that I watched without paying attention, I'd started crying. Just silent tears that burned on their way out. Treacherous little things that embarrassed me even more than I'd already been.

The figure at the foot of the theater took two steps up. I could tell it was a man in the dark. Tall and muscular, but that was all I managed to recognize. Frankly, I didn't care so I looked back at the projection of the two onscreen actors laughing instead.

It was probably my desire to lose myself in the movie that made me blind to the figure that took the steps two at a time before shimmying down the empty row I was in and taking an elegant seat next to me.

I tensed up but I didn't turn to look at the man—at Dex.

The movie played on for what seemed like ten or fifteen more minutes. He didn't say anything though I could feel the weight of his gaze on me. Only he could look at me in such a physical way.

And then he sighed, loud and clear.

"Ritz," he murmured for no reason. There were only three other people in the theater and we were scattered.

That didn't mean I was going to pay attention to him.

Two minutes later, he whispered again. "Ritz."

Nope, still wasn't going to pay him any attention.

"Ritz."

"*Ritz*."

He must have repeated my name at least five times total. A mix of a whisper that eventually blended into a weak hiss.

Still nothing.

I kept my eyes on the screen even though I'd stopped listening to the dialogue after the second time he said my name.

Me ignoring him was nothing to him. He lifted the arm rest between our seats, and I shifted over, away.

Long fingers crept up over my knee before I tried to jerk it away uselessly. He clamped his grip down to stop me, not necessarily rough but it wasn't gentle either. "Quit," he ordered to deaf ears.

I just went back to keeping my eyes forward, ignoring him again.

He lengthened his palm to hold as much of my thigh as he could, his fingers curling over the rest of my muscle. He leaned forward, across the gap of our seats, and dipped his head close to mine. I froze but kept looking straight ahead like he wasn't there.

"Babe," Dex cooed, his nose to my temple. "Don't ever do that shit to me again."

Ha!

Neither one of us said anything else for a while. He didn't move and I kept pretending like he wasn't there until finally, he sighed again, exasperated. "Ritz."

Dick.

He brushed a line from my temple down to my jaw with the tip of his nose. What I really wanted to do was ignore him and pretend that he wasn't there but I knew this guy. He didn't understand subtle. "Leave me alone, Dex," I said as calmly and detached as possible.

He answered the same way I should have expected him to. "No."

Tipping my face away, I pushed my left hand against the center of his chest. "Leave me alone."

Dex let out a long breath of air from his nose that whispered down my throat. "No, honey."

Screw him and his honey. Dick.

"Stop," I ground out.

He gripped my thigh harder, pushing his nose against my jaw. "We need to talk," he whispered.

"No, we don't," I hissed back at him.

"Yeah, we do," he insisted.

This friggin' man was the devil. "Would you please just leave me alone? I think we've done enough to each other."

Another drawn out sigh escaped him. "Babe," he said again in a low coo.

There was nothing for us to talk about. Nothing that I wanted to hear him say. Well maybe with the exception of explaining to me how he'd found where I was at. That would be nice. But no.

We were both quiet again. I watched the movie screen only because I didn't want to see him while he watched me.

It felt like a quarter of the movie went by before he spoke again. "I'm not so good at this," he whispered. "It was bad enough that that asshole shows up and was tryin' to take you away from me.

"Then you tell me that you went to fuckin' Busty's to talk to 'em? You know what could've happened to you? What those worthless pieces of shit do to pretty things like you? They eat 'em for lunch. They would've taken you and hurt you just because of who your daddy is, because of who Son is, Ritz," he growled.

Dex tightened his fingers once more for just a second before loosening them. "It's a fuckin' miracle that they let you get outta there."

Well, he had a point but regardless, I was still pissed.

And when I didn't say anything in response to his explanation, I realized that he was still pissed off as well. "Ritz, quit trippin'."

Yup, still not saying a word.

The rest of the movie went by in a blur. It was words and actors, meaningless on top of mindless. If anyone had asked me what happened, I couldn't tell them anything.

The lights in the theater lightened as the credits rolled and I stood up, glancing down at him for just a second. Was that a bruise on his chin? That wasn't the moment to feel bad for him, if it was. I had more important things to focus on. Like him being a total jerk.

"I get that you're mad because I did something stupid—really stupid, but you were an asshole, Dex. Maybe other people are used to you yelling at them and talking crap, but I'm not and I'm never going to be. I've put up with too much to put up with you making me feel like crap. So I'm gonna go to Pins and give Slim back his car, and go back to your house. If you don't mind, I'll stay there tonight, and then figure out something else to do."

"The hell you will." His eyes went wide in disbelief and filtered frustration. "You can be pissed off all you want, babe, but you aren't goin' anywhere."

This friggin' guy. I was going to end up in jail if Sonny didn't get back soon. Why couldn't he just say that he was sorry? Maybe I'd still be mad even if he apologized but the fact that he wouldn't say the one word in the English language that I wanted, bothered me more than anything.

"Whatever, Dex."

It was his turn to give me that impenetrable silence. The only difference was, I didn't wait around like he had. I slipped past him and left.

CHAPTER TWENTY-EIGHT

Two days.

For two friggin' days I didn't speak to him. To the biggest pain in the butt I'd ever met.

That first day, after I'd driven back to Pins, I hadn't spared another word in his direction. Even after he stopped me outside and asked, "Are you fuckin' serious?" when I wouldn't look at him. After all, it wasn't like I wanted to be around him at that moment or for any other moment in the near future. If I didn't care about pissing Sonny off even more, then the situation would have been a completely different story. I could have taken a much needed break from The Dick by staying at a hotel.

But that wasn't the way it worked out. I could tell Dex was furious that I hadn't accepted his puny attempt at an apology—that lacked the keyword: sorry—and since I was mad and hurt, I didn't give a crap. Then he'd gotten even more mad that I was serious about it, which made matters worse.

And the silence. *Crap.* The friggin' silence sucked.

It might have been made worse because I wanted to find out why Dex had a purple and blue splattering of blood vessels on his chin. I wanted to know how he got it, but it wasn't like I could ask.

He could stay pissed off for all I cared.

The next day was the same. We'd gotten into such a tight routine that there was no need to communicate. I recognized when he was getting ready to leave every afternoon and we went through the motions quietly, tensely, like clockwork.

At Pins, we'd avoid each other. Anger seeped from his pores, from his gaze, from his body language. I let myself soak in a mixture of embarrassment, frustration and disappointment when I had to face Slim and Blue's pitiful eyes.

Luther had come in for the second time ever—or at least the second time since I'd started working at Pins—and given me a sad little smile before patting my hand.

I got mad all over again. Wasn't that exactly why I hadn't told anyone about my arm? The answer was a blaring yes. Only this time it was because I got yelled at by Dex, the neighborhood schizophrenic that got mad when he wasn't immediately forgiven for his transgressions. Jerk.

The night went by in the same way, except Dex made dinner and we ate on opposite sides of the couch, silently.

Even the guys at the shop were quieter than normal, handling me with kid gloves.

Annoyed didn't even begin to describe how I felt. And I hated it.

On top of that, I'd been dodging Sonny's calls. Getting yelled at by one person I cared about was more than enough. Two would just be overkill. It was probably asking to get the pinch of a lifetime when he got back but I'd take my chances with my brother.

Dex on the other hand...

"Do you think I'm being a bitch?" I asked after completely ignoring Dex when he stood by my desk, talking to a customer a few minutes before.

Slim cocked an eyebrow at me from behind the tablet he was currently pecking at. "A bitch?" He said the word so slowly it immediately made my hackles go up.

"Yeah."

He scrunched up his face. "I wouldn't say a *bitch* exactly."

Oh lord.

For Slim of all people to put it like that...damn it. Guilt brushed at the sides of my mind. Did I have a good reason to stay mad? I thought so. On the other hand, did Dex have a good reason to have lost his shit like that? Not to that extent. To add onto that...he had tried to apologize in his own Dex-way.

Slim glanced up before looking back at the screen. "Do you want me to tell you the truth or do you want me to be nice?"

Double oh lord. Had I really been that much of a bitch?

"The truth, Slimmy," I huffed, already feeling like a jerk before my friend had even started talking.

"Well, Ris, you're kinda being just a wee bit unreasonable," he stated evenly. Slim tapped at his tablet. "If somebody yelled at my sister like he yelled at you, I'd try to beat their ass." I almost snorted at the keyword in his sentence: try. But he kept going so I couldn't make a crack. "But if my sis did the shit you did, I would've yelled at her like that."

Ugh.

"He only got that pissed off because he cares, you know that?" he asked carefully, finally glancing up at me with those bright green eyes.

And that comment deflated me.

"Yeah..." I sighed.

"But," he winked, "That 'go fuck yourself' was pretty dead on, Rainbow Ris."

I had said that, hadn't I? Whoops.

Slim smiled indulgently, erasing the last pieces of anger that had clung to my chest. He had a point. "You ever do that shit again though, and I'll hunt you down myself next time. You got it?"

"Yeah, I got it."

And just like that, I felt a little relieved. Staying angry was too much work. I needed to figure out how to apologize to Dex without completely rolling over in submission. I wouldn't give him that much.

So when the phone rang a little while later, the chance fell onto... my desk.

"Pins and Needles, this is Iris speaking, how can I help you?"

A prerecorded message stated that I was receiving a call from an inmate at Byrd Unit.

The name triggered a memory of my dad. Was that where he'd gone to jail before he'd met my mom? Something steered me toward a yes.

I probably should have hung up, but I stayed on the line while the call connected and my brain ran. Was my dad in jail? I didn't think it'd been long enough from the last time he'd been in town but there was a chance.

"'Lo?" a rough voice on the other end finally answered. It wasn't him. Ten years later, and I know I'd recognize his voice.

"Pins and Needles," I answered in a weird way. Okay then, why would someone be calling the shop from jail?

There was some shuffling before the man spoke again. "I need to speak to Dex."

It hit me right then who was calling. There was only one other person in jail that would be calling Pins—Dex's dad. Crap!

It wasn't my place to guard his calls or any aspect of his life but I made myself forget that. He'd been in such a terrible mood since I'd blown him off at the theater, and this would tip his off-balance scales. There was no way in any dimension of hell that Dex would want to speak to his father.

"He's not available right now. I can take a message." A message that would be written in invisible ink.

"I know that fucker's there," the man—the older Locke—grunted. "Put him on the phone."

Oh. Hell. No. "He's not available right now. Would you like to leave a message?" I ground out in my best imitation of Dex when he was angry.

"He's there. Put him on the goddamn phone."

I pulled the phone away from my face and looked at it. *Don't disrespect your elders, Ris.* "I'm not putting him on the phone. If you want to leave a message, leave it. If you don't, then feel free to call his cell phone." Like he'd answer it. Ha!

I might not be able to talk shit to the younger Locke, but the older man was in jail so he was harmless. At the moment at least.

"What did you say your name was?" His voice had started picking up in pitch the angrier he got.

I might do stupid things every once in a while but I wasn't dumb enough to tell him my name. "Would you like to leave a message, sir?"

"What I'd like to do is talk to my goddamn—"

I hung up with a little flourish, smiling indulgently to myself. Not even three minutes later, the shop phone started ringing again. I picked it up, only to hear the prerecorded message start playing, and I hung up again.

The phone rang twice more but I didn't even bother picking it up those times. The shop was empty with the exception of The Dick in his office and Blue at her station. She wouldn't give a crap about me ignoring the phones.

"Phone!" Dex yelled from his office.

Like he couldn't answer the friggin' phone himself. Which in this case, was a good thing.

"Don't answer it!" I screamed back.

There was a brief pause before he yelled again. "Ritz! Phone!"

Crap. I sighed and saved the work I'd been doing on Pins' website so that I could go talk to The Dick.

I tried to mentally prepare myself to speak with Dex on the short walk into his office. He was sitting at his desk, messing around on the computer when I came up to the door.

Then I thought better of it, took a step back, and peeked my head into the doorway instead. "Your dad was calling."

He didn't jerk, flinch, or even blink at his computer screen. Instead, those intense blue eyes I'd grown so fond of drifted over in my direction almost incredulously. "What?" The question reminded me of verbal stalactite.

"That was your dad calling. Or at least I'm ninety-nine percent positive it was him calling from Byrd Unit." I blinked, inching my feet further away from the door. "He was being rude, and I hung up on him."

When he didn't say anything or give me a high-five for standing up for him, I started to think maybe I'd done something wrong. It was one of the biggest things we had in common: our mutual hate for what our fathers represented. The past and the dread of a similar future.

"I'm sorry, Dex. I figured you probably didn't want to talk to him," I rushed out.

Still, he said nothing and guilt pricked my tummy.

"I'm sorry for doing it. If he calls again I'll—"

"No," he breathed. "No. You did the right thing. I don't wanna talk to him."

I nodded while we looked at each other. God, I really hated the awkwardness between us. Hated it. Dex had been my friend—*was* my friend. One of the only people I truly valued and trusted, and my idiocy had messed that up. Then his temper had stomped it down afterward. Why the hell did I hold onto these friggin' grudges with Dex?

Life was too unpredictable to stay pissed off. I'd hate to wake up and not have him anymore and stress that I'd never get to tell him I was sorry. That was something I would never want to live with.

If he didn't like me, then he wouldn't give a shit what happened to me, right? And the fact that he'd gotten so mad...well, it was a compliment I'd just been too stubborn to accept. I'd lived in the shadow of a man who really didn't give a flying crap about me. What the hell was there for me to complain about? What was there for me to be so scared of? Caring and being attracted to a big shit of an asshole that had a barely controlled temper?

I could do so much worse.

So, *shit*. I needed to be an adult and bust out the big girl panties even if it killed my pride a little.

"Look, I'm sorry that I went to Busty's. It was stupid but I was upset. I've been an inconvenience to people most of my life. My grandma went bankrupt paying for—," I hissed. That wasn't where I wanted to go with the conversation. "Things for me and I hated it. I don't ever want to feel that way again and ever since I lost my job in Florida, I feel like I'm reliving that.

"You have no idea how much it sucks to have to rely on other people for everything." I rubbed my forehead and looked down. "I'm sorry that I put you guys in that situation. If it would've gone wrong, then I'm sure the blame would have been on you, especially since Sonny left you in charge of me like I'm a kid."

My hands had started shaking just a little bit as I spoke. "I care about you a lot, you big jerk, and you hurt my feelings. So

I'm sorry that I made you mad and made you worry, but I'm not sorry that I told you to ef yourself, okay? You deserved it."

I didn't expect an answer, and I didn't exactly wait for one either. I shot him an anemic grin that was half-hearted at best and went back to work.

My hands shook the entire time.

"Baby."

"Baby."

I felt myself being moved, being pushed so that my face pressed against the back cushions of the couch I'd been sleeping on for the last week and a half. A big, warm body slowly curled up behind me, sliding an arm around my waist.

"Dex?" I asked him in a hoarse voice, cracking my eyes open in the dark room. I must have been asleep for a long time by how dry my voice sounded.

"Yeah," he muttered against my ear. The hand that had been over my hip slid up to touch my cheek with soft fingertips.

I looked over my shoulder at him, trying to blink back sleep. "What are you doing?"

Because really? What was he doing? Even after I'd apologized for something that wasn't entirely my fault, he'd kept giving me the silent treatment at the shop, on the ride home, and for the thirty minutes we'd been around each other as we ate dinner on the couch. Dick. The last thing I'd expect was for him to crawl onto the couch with me in the middle of the night ready to spoon.

Not that I should complain, but still.

Dex shifted his hips until my bottom sat right against his groin. "Can't sleep," he whispered for some reason. I couldn't be sure but I thought that he might have pressed his lips to my ear. "I've been a shit, babe."

Oh lord, I wanted to answer back sarcastically but I kept myself from doing it. I also had to keep myself from telling him to get off the couch. Which was stupid because the alarms in my head were going off, telling me this closeness was a terrible idea.

Then again, hadn't I left my sanity in Florida? My sanity and my friggin' brain.

"I know I'm an asshole, babe. You know I'm an asshole." Dex punctuated each statement by moving his fingertips from my ear to my chin. "'Specially when I'm pissed." He dotted the ends of his sentences with sighs like the admission was painful or awkward for him, and I'm sure it was. The number of times he'd apologized in his life had to be as small as the number of guys I'd kissed.

He smoothed his finger down the curve of my ear. "I don't know what the hell I'm doin' with you, you know that?"

Oh boy.

I shifted my head to look at him over my shoulder. "Me neither, Dex."

The look on his face was smooth and as open as I'd ever seen. He ran his fingertip around my ear again, pulling goose bumps onto my arms. He repeated the motion a few times, his breath heavy on my neck.

"Baby, you make me wanna kill every fuckin' guy that looks at you. You know what that's like?"

I remembered how awful I felt seeing him with his arm around the redhead. Ugh. I felt honest enough in that moment to nod.

He slipped a hand over my neck, palming it with the full length of his big palm. "My goddamn head hurt when you said that shit-head put his mouth on you. And you know what I couldn't quit thinkin' about? How much that sonuva bitch would've loved to hurt you to get back at the Club and your pa, baby.

"When you told me that you went to Busty's...I lost my damn mind." Dex ran a finger over the corner of my mouth, drawing me into a deep daze that had nothing to do with sleep. "I'm sorry I yelled at you like that. Sorry I hurt you, too. If somebody else would've done the shit I did to you, I'd cut their fuckin' tongue out, Ritz. Thought for sure Lu was gonna do that to me after you walked out," he chuckled darkly.

Dex let out another sigh, settling in so close he was like a human blanket. "I fuck everythin' in my life up. Always have. But I like to learn from my mistakes and fix 'em. Should've said somethin' to you back at Pins tonight when you talked to my pa but I couldn't. I got a hard time gettin' over people lyin' to me, babe, but you doin' that shit and Liam showin' up just about gave me a stroke. Then you go off and watch out for me with my pa, and tell me you think that everybody thinks of you as an inconvenience. It kinda kills me."

Damn it.

It was my turn to sigh into the sofa cushion smashing my face so that I wouldn't make an embarrassing noise. "I get it—but getting yelled at like that was so embarrassing."

He groaned this sound that was pure guilt. "Yeah, I know."

I didn't say anything, earning a low grumble.

"Won't do it again," he added in that silky voice that wasn't accustomed to apologies.

"I think you've said that before."

The same sound made its way out of him. "Babe, I'll try my best as long as you don't lie to me again."

His damn honesty got me every single time. I sighed a little more exaggerated than what was necessary, remembering the callous tone he'd used. "You sounded like you hated me," I admitted, pushing my face deeper into the sofa back.

Dex's hand reached up to pull me back, tipping my face over to see his. His gaze was strong, intent. "Don't ever think that. I might get pissed and I might take shit out on you but that—never. Never fuckin' ever, you hear me?"

His face was solemn and honest. Truth stamped onto the lines of his lips and the placement of his eyelids.

"I looked all over the city for you, Ritz. You think I'd do that for anybody else?"

Him? No. No way. And the reality of that made me happier than it probably should.

The sheer emotion that I felt from Dex, the worry, the need, the repent, was so foreign. And I was so broken in tiny ways that it made me feel small, more needy than I liked. I still didn't understand this, understand him, but maybe I never would.

"Hey...what happened to your face?"

A low little growl curled its way through his throat. Ahh, hell. It was probably something related to me. "Let's just say somebody else thought they could get away with sayin' the same type of shit you do."

It was my whole 'go fuck yourself' spiel. I knew it. "Was it one of the club members?"

His answer was another tiny warning growl.

Yup, it'd been someone in the room with us. Oh well. If Dex thought I was going to change my mind and apologize for saying that to him, he had another thing coming.

"We good?" he whispered into my neck.

"Yeah." I nodded. "We're good."

"Good. Good." His hips moved restlessly behind me, tipping forward in a jerky motion that felt like he was trying to get situated on the couch better.

Only the issue was that we didn't fit. It was too narrow even when we were on our sides. So it came to no surprise when he didn't stop squirming.

"I don't think this is gonna work, Ritz," he finally said after what felt like a shimmy against my butt that drove me face-first into the cushion.

I groaned my response.

He grunted, then he shifted, then he grunted again. "Fuck, this sucks."

With a frustrated huff, the heat of his body disappeared before I felt his fingers sneak into my armpits and pull me back. "C'mon."

"What?" I asked him as he kept pulling, dragging me off the couch. I planted my feet on the floor and pushed up to standing.

"My bed."

My joints locked. "Umm..." Laying down on the couch had seemed okay, but laying on the bed seemed like a whole different league.

And he knew it because he rolled his eyes and tagged my hand with his. "Babe, quit thinkin' about it."

"Ah...."

Dex threaded his fingers through mine, pulling me. "What's botherin' you?"

How about everything? Lying in bed with a shirtless Dex? The way my ovaries had been overheating lately? Holy crap. It wasn't like I could tell him that. It'd be like throwing chum into shark-infested water.

"I've never—" I gulped.

"You never what?" he grumbled out the words.

Lord. I dug a finger into his rib cage, looking up at his tense face. "I've never slept in the same bed with a guy, Charlie. Besides you that other time."

He did one of the last things I could have expected. Dex stared at me for a moment before dropping his head back and huffing at the ceiling. "You're killin' me, babe. You are fuckin' killin' me here."

Dex tugged at my hand as he lowered his chin to look me in the eye. His free hand came up to grasp my chin. His expression was clear and serious. "We won't do anythin' you don't want. Promise. Just sleep."

Oh man. I nodded at him loosely, trusting him implicitly. "Okay." My breathing hitched a little. "I don't do this with all my friends, you know?"

It was the sugary smile he gave me next that had me crawling into bed with him, even with my nerves all over the place. I mean, you only live once. And this was *him*. Someone who cared about me as much as I cared about him. I trusted him.

And in that moment I wasn't scared or worried as I followed him to bed. But as we laid down, with all the anxious nerves in the universe pooling in my belly, he touched my forehead with his fingertips in the dark and murmured, "You gotta get it straight, babe. This ain't just friendship to me."

CHAPTER TWENTY-NINE

There was something most definitely on my ass.

And my back.

And my neck.

It was definitely the thing on my ass that had woken me up. I usually wasn't much of a dreamer when I slept, so when I felt that unfamiliar warmth kneading my bare ass cheek, I knew it wasn't a dream.

One thing I was sure of: I was on Dex's bed and the sheets were down to my waist.

I'd fallen asleep on top of them. I knew that without a doubt. Blinking away what felt like a coma, I looked over my shoulder to see what the hell was on me.

I shouldn't have been surprised.

The lump under the sheet was connected to a ropey forearm, which then connected to a wide bicep with an impressive amount of definition even when it wasn't being flexed.

Dex's friggin' hand was underneath my panties, palming my bare butt cheek.

Just sleep, he said?

I tried to roll over but that something on my back was heavy and solid, telling me that it was Dex's chest, crushing me. So whatever was on my neck had to be part of Dex's anatomy.

Holy moly.

What in the hell had I been thinking agreeing to sleep with him?

You were thinking that you liked him. That you trusted him.

If he wasn't a Widow I probably wouldn't be so scared, right? My gut knew the answer was a loud yes. Was that all really that held me back from him? It wasn't his temper, I could deal with that unless he yelled at me. Dex—Charlie—was so much more than his appearance gave him credit for. He was like aloe vera, rough and prickly on the outside, but the inside held all the gooey goodness.

He'd probably roll his eyes if I ever said that aloud—but it was true.

Which was why I was trying to be cool about his long fingers cupping my butt. And his breath on my neck.

When I tried to slide out from underneath him, the hand on my butt swept over to my side to hold me down. "Where you goin'?" Dex asked through sleep strained vocal chords.

I froze, whispering, "Bathroom."

He yawned, his fingers flexing. "Liar. Go back to sleep," he mumbled, already nuzzling back into that sweet spot of flesh between my hairline and shoulder. More awake now than before, I could clearly feel the warmth of his mouth millimeters away from me.

"Dex," I whispered.

His hand moved across my back to slide completely under the cotton of my panties again, his thumb rubbing a lazy circle on the skin beneath it.

"Dex!" Yeah, that didn't sound convincing at all.

"Please go back to sleep." The heat of his mouth only intensified by a ratio of a thousand to one as he mumbled in reply. My poor body couldn't handle having big, warm Dex cuddling up to me.

"I'll go sleep on the couch."

He growled a response, making me break into goose bumps.

"Dex, c'mon." I tried to plead but didn't budge an inch.

He didn't say anything, his thumb just continued its languid circles right smack in the middle of my cheek. If anything, I think his upper body got even closer to mine. "Relax, babe," he finally mumbled.

Like that was going to happen. My entire body was tense. Telling myself that this wasn't right was like fighting the pull of the ocean's tide. It felt unnatural. "I can't."

"You can." Dex's smooth palm cupped my cheek and I sucked in a breath. Why the hell was I fighting this?

"I don't know what I'm doing," I blurted out, slamming my eyes shut.

His chuckle was smooth and dark. "I know, my sweet baby."

I should have just given up living after that. Living, fighting, existing. All of it.

Before I realized what he was doing, his hand was out of my panties, the weight of his body was peeled off my back. Two large, familiar hands clasped onto my ankles immediately afterward, flipping me onto my back.

And then he was over me.

On his hands and knees, his beautiful, rugged face full of thick, black stubble was right there. Supple lips, Crayola Blue eyes and Uriel all greeted me.

If all that wasn't enough to grip my spine, he was shirtless. His smooth, sunkissed skin was taut over hard, carefully crafted muscles he worked on most of the week in his home gym. But then he loomed over me, without the rust of a new friendship like it'd been in Austin. Hell, it wasn't the same from the week before after his niece's birthday party…

Oh boy. Oh. Boy.

I'd seen him shirtless not too long ago and it didn't matter at all because his upper body was one of those things that got better every time I saw it.

The first thing I noticed again were the small stainless steel hoops through his perfect, dark nipples. Little nipples on a muscular chest and above a flawlessly ridged six-pack. A six-pack that led to the sweet slabs of v-shaped muscles that disappeared beneath black boxers...that did nothing hide to the massive tent his groin was pitching.

And then I remembered he had his dick pierced.

How the hell I didn't pass out would be an unsolved mystery. What wasn't an unsolved mystery was why my mouth went dry. I'm sure that I stopped breathing. Any man or woman would have done the same.

Dex was… better than anything I'd ever seen on print or television. I could even say celestial if he didn't look like he'd work for the devil instead of the good guys. The dark and colorful lines that spanned nearly all of his upper body heightened his hauntingly ethereal beauty. Over the course of the last couple of months, I'd never seen him wearing anything less than jeans and a t-shirt at all times besides our stint in Houston and the other time we slept in bed together.

And in that moment I was thankful it had taken so long for me to see him so up-close. Each of the sleeves I'd seen day in and day out bled up and over his shoulders, traps, and pecs. Only his stomach was left without the thick black, blue, gray, and red ink that painted his skin. Uriel, his tattooed octopus, welcomed me in with his big, beautiful details and classic, striking red flesh.

I dragged my eyes from the sharp colors down to his crotch, and then back up again. I found him watching me with those heavy-lidded bright blue eyes.

"Goddamn." His voice had taken on a husky tone that sounded like it was more than just sleep dragging it in. "In what fuckin' universe did I think I could listen to your brother?"

Holy lord.

Apparently, even though I was able to keep from passing out at the glory caging me in, my voice had died a thousand deaths at the perfection that Dex Locke was. So I had to answer him with a shaky, nervous smile.

"Iris."

Oh dear god.

"I'd never hurt you, baby," Dex murmured.

Jesus. This was unreal.

I wanted him, which was bad, because I knew that I should walk away and act like a decent lady. Like a lady who had seen her mother crumble under the effects that a biker could have on a heart—on an existence. But the man above me wasn't a quitter. He was loyal and caring, and his protection wrapped me up in a cocoon that was all fire and feeling. I could live without it, sure. I could live without it and be perfectly fine, but...that sounded like hell.

I'd take it, damn it. I'd take this Dex with his awful temper that never made me doubt that he worried and cared though he didn't know how to handle himself most of the time. My body decided to compromise and accept the reality of the tattoos and the focus of the blue eyes that were hooking me in.

Dex watched me caught like a deer in the headlights, unmoving and scared. The lines of his body were my siren's song, keeping me in his web as he stayed in place so still. His abs, his biceps, his muscular thighs—which I quickly appreciated in a sweeping gaze—all called to me.

He snagged my wrist with one hand, gripping the back of my neck with his other. The heat from his body radiated through my clothes, through the foot of distance between us. It didn't help that I could smell that distinct Dex scent more closely than ever before.

"Knew the moment I saw you, standin' outside the shop, scared, that you were an innocent little thing. So sweet. So good." He lowered his head to take my chin between his teeth. "You got no idea what it's like for you to give me your trust, Ritz. If I was a good man I'd tell you to find somebody better, somebody that won't lose their shit over an asshole eye fuckin' you."

His tongue traced the oval shape of my chin. "But I'm not a good man, and I'm gonna take everythin' you want to give me and everythin' you don't."

Strike me dead. Dead, dead, dead.

His voice was so gruff and raw, the effect was like having a million Christmas tree lights lit along my nerves. And his words. Holy crap. My brain cells couldn't even process what he was saying without making me lose my breath.

Dex's forehead touched mine gently, as if he could sense the emotion bubbling inside of me. "I want it all, baby."

My breath was shuddered on an exhale, looking up at the rugged beauty of Dex's perfectly shaped mouth just centimeters away from me. "Why?" I had to remind him.

"Why?" he asked in that milky, warm tone.

"I don't get why you like me. I'm not your type." Because that was my only defense. I'd never wanted anything, let alone anyone the way I wanted this tattooed, brusque man. But a huge part of me was really worried about why he'd latched onto me.

He chuckled deep. "Fishin' for compliments again?" His warm breath washed over my lips.

"No."

I could feel him smile against me. "'Course not," he murmured, biting my bottom lip. "Where do you want me to start, baby? You wanna know what I like about you besides that sweet ass? And those legs in your little white shorts?"

His lips touched the corner of my mouth in a brush. "You've got the prettiest face I've ever seen." His lips skimmed my jawline, his breath was hot but it gave me goosebumps. "And that smile you give me when you're givin' me shit? A fuckin' smile's the last thing I'd ever give a shit about before I met you." There was a high possibility that he tapped the tip of his tongue against my jawline because I may have made some sort of weird noise in response. "But you crack me up like nobody else. I like that the most." Dex made a noise in his throat. "Maybe."

I was flailing on the inside. Flailing and dying over and over again. I dropped my head back and looked at the headboard. "You're too much."

A soft laugh made its way out of his throat. "I kinda think you're a treasure."

That was the breaking point.

I didn't care anymore. He was my boss, my brother's friend, a Widow, an ex-felon, and a man that I'd seen casually with other women. But he was everything that gripped me, both the good and the bad. Worst case scenario if things turned awkward between us, I could go somewhere else. I'd gotten over epic heartbreak before, one more wouldn't kill me.

I hoped.

What did I have to lose besides continuing to live my life with carefully constructed walls?

Nothing. Absolutely nothing.

I had to hoard all of my guts and resolve together before pressing my lips to his top one. It was a slow mold, easy. Nerves ate at the lining of my stomach anyway as I pulled my mouth just far back enough to kiss his bottom lip in the same way. Two of mine for each one of his.

I did it again. Kissing his first lip, then his bottom. Easy, chaste kisses that Dex waited patiently through. The kinds of kisses he'd probably outgrown in elementary school. I had just licked my lips with every intention of kissing him again when he pursed his in response, kissing me back with that soft puckered mouth. Soft, soft, soft. His mouth touched my top lip then my bottom. One corner of my mouth, then the other.

Those kisses were everything that our other two weren't. Exploratory in a way that made me feel breathless and restless. They were sweet and patient up until he started sucking one lip and then the other between his. Because after that, they got wet. Slow and sensual. Dex slanted his mouth, slipping his tongue in with so much stealth I didn't realize it until it brushed against mine.

I whimpered as his arm slid around my back. He dropped his weight until we were flush. My breasts to his chest, stomach to stomach, groin to groin. With only the barrier of my thermal shirt, our underwear, and the thin shorts I slept in, I could feel every inch of him. That included the hard nudge of one of his nipple rings against my bra-less breast.

Holy crap.

I'd been kissed before and in between those kisses, I'd put my hand and mouth on one of my two boyfriends. So out of those few times, those few kisses, the porn I'd watched, and the romance novels I'd read, I had a general idea what things were supposed to be like. But with Dex, and his hot insistent mouth, strong, possessive hands, and hard, tattooed, and angelically endowed body, I felt like I'd graduated from high school to college. Better yet, from high school straight to graduate school.

My hands had somehow managed to find their way to Dex's waist as his controlling mouth took over. My fingers curled into the hard muscle that cushioned his hips.

I felt fingers around my waist start to drift lower, slowly gripping the hem of my thermal. I panicked just a little, ready to stop him if he tried to pull my shirt off. I wasn't built spectacularly. I'd always considered myself pretty average by most standards. My stomach was pretty flat, and my skin was dotted with the occasional freckle.

I was okay, my body was okay, but I wasn't ready for him to know about my arm. Not yet.

So even though I knew I wasn't shaped like a model or a bombshell, like I envisioned Dex might have been used to from what I'd seen him with before, I wasn't too insecure. But he tugged my shirt up, up, up. Over my belly-button, over my ribs, and over my breasts until he stopped. *Thank you, thank you, thank you.* He stopped, bunching my shirt just underneath my collarbones. But as Dex's eyes landed on my bare upper body, trailing a hot path over my clavicles and landing specifically and what seemed like permanently on my breasts, I got a little self-conscious but not enough to cover myself.

With a sigh, he grazed the backs of his fingers over my nipples making them pucker immediately. Dex's other hand reached up so that his thumb rested directly beneath a swell. He tested the weight of it by lifting his finger. "Iris," he said, drawing out the consonant in a hiss.

"Mmm?"

The backs of his fingers brushed over my nipple again. "Perfect, baby." He muttered, pinching the tightened peak with his thumb and index finger, making me gasp at the sensation. "Love your pretty tits."

I was on the verge of telling him thank you for a compliment I'm sure he was being too free with, when his head dipped down and his lips pursed around the nipple he'd squeezed. He sucked the little bud softly, tongue laving over it each time.

Dex's mouth opened wider, taking in as much of my soft flesh as he could. With his teeth and lips, he nipped, sucked, and lapped over and over again.

All I could think was *holy friggin' shit.*

Iridescent blue eyes were open and taking my face in with each tug of his hard sucks, and if what he was doing wasn't the hottest thing in the history of the world, then Dex watching me while he did it, was. These whimpering noises deep in the back of his throat vibrated through me, turning me on just as much as what he was doing was.

I was mumbling stuff that made no sense. A mix of "Dex...God...Dex...shit," and words in between that were the opposite of logical.

His breath was hot across my chest as he moved to bite my other nipple gently. I wanted to touch him before I burned to death from the intensity of our contact. My hands moved to cup his head, his shoulders. A back-and-forth trek that had me grazing over the short, silky ends of his messy, sleepy dark hair.

His mouth finally pulled away from my chest after a lazy lap at each wet nipple. Dex's heavy eyes were on me, lips slightly parted before his mouth was on mine again, taking all of me without a second thought as his hand cupped over my shorts. His fingers slipped up one of my legs, pulling my bottoms and underwear to the side, his pads grazing over the seam of my sex.

He made a husky, raw noise in his throat. "Jesus," he murmured over my mouth, fingertips grazing over the moist line of my lower body.

I was too turned on to care that I was, in fact, really wet, and too wrapped up in my own little world to care that I had a damp spot on my underwear to tell that story. And that little—or maybe not so little—spot was held captive by Dex's palm.

All of his fingers except his thumb fell away, leaving his thickest digit to brush lightly along the slit. "You're so hot, baby."

Holy crap. *Holy crap.*

Dex swept his thumb over me again and again. He didn't ask for permission when his index finger spread me wide, his thumb brushing over me once more with a feather-light touch.

Oh my sweet lord. Holy craaaaap.

I dropped my head to the pillow below me, breathing hard as he parted me open, letting the heat of his hand sweep over me. "Iris, Iris, Iris," he chanted, one of his fingers grazing directly between my legs before continuing its path lower until the tip of a long finger dipped into me. Then dipped deeper. Dex's eyes closed before he slid it gradually completely inside, palm flush against my outer flesh.

I panted. There wasn't anything else to do besides call him God, or moan and beg him to do whatever he wanted except stop. What had I been so scared of? Someone please tell me. It felt like drowning and being born at the same time. He pulled his finger out slowly, the crease between his eyebrows furrowing with the movement before he slid it back in completely with a husky groan.

"Fuck," he drawled like he was in pain. Those bright blue eyes made a trek from the center of my body up to my face, heavy and horny, the weight of Dex's gaze was crushing. His normally smooth skin was flushed pink. Fingers massaged the slick channel they'd buried themselves in and I couldn't help but gasp.

Dex's bottom lip dropped just an inch, his breathing hard. "You like that, baby?"

By some friggin miracle, I managed to tip my head down once in agreement, earning a lick across my collarbone from Dex.

His fingers made a slow withdrawal, the pads grazing something incredibly sensitive and so unbelievably amazing. He circled over the same spot again and I might have made some kind of choking noise.

"So fuckin' hot." The relentless beast repeated the motion over and over again, as I squirmed against his hand, some part of me wanting and needing more and more and more. I arched my back and wiggled my hips in reaction. What did Dex do? He groaned, his breathing getting heavier. "You keep doin' that and I'm gonna finger you all day, babe."

Then he started turning his fingers as his mouth latched onto my throat, kissing me, sucking at me, breathing on me. I had my back arched against him when I spread my legs wider. He slowly slid another finger inside right then, creating that same line of dangerous movement that made my thighs shake with anticipation and my insides sting with the invasion of Dex's digits.

He swallowed hard as he pulled his fingers nearly all the way out before easing them back in. Dex shook his head, licked his lip. "You're ruinin' me, babe."

I pushed my hips down greedily, loving the way he felt stretching me. Any desire to be modest just kind of flew out the window. "Dex."

He groaned, tilting his head to look right in my eyes as his movement sped up. His fingers scissored, his palm grinding against the start of my slit with each sinking thrust of his digits. Dex's eyes were dark, his shoulders tense as he fingered me.

"You gonna come on my hand, baby?" he asked in a rough voice. His body was tight and coiled over me, and I think he might have started sweating but I was too selfish to be sure.

I swallowed and nodded, dragging my eyes down the colorful slope of his detailed chest to land on the bulge beneath his boxers that had gotten bigger in no time. Some deeply possessive, sexual part of me wanted to touch him. My skills might not be anything to brag about, but how hard could it be? My boyfriend in high school had come in his pants just from dry-humping each other.

Okay, well, it was completely different but still. I'd seen enough porn even if my one-on-one experience wasn't something confident-worthy. My hands shook just a little from nerves.

So I told that part of my brain to go to sleep a second before reaching forward to dip my fingers into the band of his boxers and tugging the elastic down low enough so that the broad, blunt head of his cock peeped out. The plum-shaped, deep pink head that was missing a piercing.

Yeah, I didn't care, and I wasn't exactly disappointed. Dex shucked his boxers the rest of the way down his hips and long legs, watching my face as his—*holy-mother-of-all-that-is-magnificent.*

He did have a piercing. Dear sweet lord, he had a pubic piercing.

A surface bar was threaded through the root of his long shaft, two tiny studs dotting the base like the most elegant and erotic jewelry *ever*.

I could hear angels setting off beautiful bells in my head at the sight. There was a chance I whispered, "Wow," but I really hoped not.

Because strike me dead, I had seen the light. And that light was eight inches, veiny, and the cutest shade of pink. You know, if a monster of a pink dick could be considered cute.

Some tricky part of my brain chanted, "Grab it, grab it!" While the other half, the logical one, stayed silent, egging me on its quietness to wrap my hand around the thick girth. My fingers just barely closed around him, but his dick jumped when I squeezed the hard flesh lightly. He was so much heavier and hotter than I ever could have imagined.

I should have known right then, when my mouth started watering with anticipation, that there was something special, something different with Dex. What the hell had come over me? I felt unprepared for what I wanted to do—and I didn't want to disappoint him by sucking at it—literally. But what did it matter? I could figure it out. If I did something wrong, he wouldn't hesitate to correct me and I wasn't planning on asking him beforehand. As it was, I already had 'virgin moron' tattooed on my forehead.

His fingers slipped out of me as I tried to push him onto his back. Moving onto my hands and knees in the same position he'd been in before, I chanced a glance up at his face, angling my body perpendicular to his. His expression was tight, ruthless, and so heavy with lust it choked me. The urge to remind him I was relatively inexperienced clutched at me but I flicked it away and took a deep breath.

I could do this, damn it.

I could do it.

It was with that motivation in mind that I lowered my mouth over the hot, mushroomed tip of his cock, sucking the head leisurely. *Just like a lollipop, Ris.*

A big, thick lollipop. Well, that thought made me way too excited, as I dragged my tongue down the thick vein of his dick. The rumbling groan that escaped Dex's chest had me licking faster, curling my lips over the swollen head. *Watch the teeth, watch the teeth, and suck.*

"Fuck!" He rolled his hips, shoving himself deeper into my mouth on instinct. I gagged for a second and slid him back out, pressing my tongue against the bulging vein on the underside of his thick tip like I'd read about other women doing. I mean, he seemed really into it so I couldn't be doing that bad of a job, right?

I sensed a brush of his hand against the place between my legs as I gave him a long, experimental lick that had him bucking his hips again.

There was no way in hell I could think, much less talk, as two fingers sank inside me, pressing into me even deeper than before. It was rough, and just a little bit painful for a moment as he pushed in and out, slowly at first but gaining speed with each pass. The uncomfortable sensation was replaced by pleasure too quickly. The rougher the movement, the more of him I tried to swallow down, sucking hard around him.

"Fuck!" he yelled, fingering me so quickly I could hear the wet slapping of his movements.

Holy, holy, holy crap. A tingle started in my lower stomach, bursting hot over every inch of my stomach and legs. His palm ground against my clit before his scissoring fingers sped up. A moment later, the sensation deep in the pit of my belly exploded, and a climax that I never would have been able to anticipate, took over my body. My insides were clenching, my thighs trembled, and I cried out Dex's name like an inadequate thank you on my hand and knees, his dick slapping against his flat stomach after slipping out of my mouth.

His free hand was on my cheek as he sat up, stroking it gently, kissing the corners of my mouth as I came back to Earth when he leaned in. Dex's fingers were still in me, their pump languid and fluid while I quivered around him.

Part of me expected Dex to have a smirk on his face, or something equally arrogant, but when I finally had the strength to look, his expression was dark and untethered. I smiled at him, drunk off my high and more sated than I ever could have asked for.

Yeah, I definitely didn't give a crap about being proper or hiding what I felt for him, and he knew it when I grinned at him, kissing just to the side of his mouth right before I reached for his cock and wrapped my fingers around it.

He brushed some of my hair back with loose fingers that kneaded my scalp. I pumped the long length and added a squeeze, squeezing on the pull down to the base. Dex made a sort of whimpering noise in his throat, his hips flexing just an inch when he leaned back into his hands. "You're doin' so fuckin' good, baby—squeeze—*shit*, squeeze me a little harder, honey. Just like that—*yeah*."

Dex's mouth dropped open, his eyes taking their fill of my fingers wrapped around his shaft. But I was busy looking at those two gold studs to the side of my palm.

"Can I touch it?" I asked him, eyeing the bar of his piercing.

Dex groaned, tilting his hips up with a huff. "Please."

I laughed just a little at his politeness. I smiled at him at the same time I lowered my head and licked the two small studs nestled in the neatly trimmed dark hair, the imposing length of his erection right by my face. I took my time exploring the studs of his piercing, timidly. "It doesn't hurt?"

His eyes flashed something that could have been amusement but centered on something more gentle than that. Dex's hand cupped my cheek again, the thumb sweeping over my bottom lip. "No, baby, it feels great." I licked his thumb and he rolled his eyes. Those thick black eyelashes fanned down with a grunt.

I landed a kiss to the webbing between his index finger and thumb, and then dropped back down to his lap, letting the anxiety of what I was doing slip away, my mouth full of him. To my surprise, he didn't buck his hips too much, instead letting me do what I wanted and settling for grinding his teeth together and fisting the sheets when he dropped down to his elbows.

I started sucking on him in a steady rhythm, pumping on the half of his cock I couldn't take in. Dex's grunts grew louder until he was panting and jerking his hips, causing his piercing to hit the sides of my fingers.

"I'm gonna come," he moaned. "Baby, squeeze me real hard. Oh yeah...*fuck me...* baby, jack me off on those pretty titties... please..."

Oh hell. Who was I to tell him no? I gripped him harder and slipped him out of my mouth with a sloppy suck, pumping the rock hard muscle and silky skin until he cried out and long white ribbons shot onto my chest over and over again.

Dex laid back on the bed, panting, his mouth parted while I kneeled in front of him trying to catch my own breath. "Fuckin' hell," he grumbled, sitting up after a moment.

His fingers reached out to touch the mess on my breasts. He was gentle and deliberate with his ring and middle finger, smothering the warm, sticky liquid in circles over my nipples.

"Christ, baby, you're the hottest thing I've ever seen," he murmured, glancing up at me through those long lashes as he finally dropped his hand away from my chest. He smiled almost shyly, threading his clean hand through my hair before slanting his mouth over mine. He kissed me and kissed me, his tongue stroking mine, over my teeth, everywhere.

He pulled away grudgingly after a long time with a deep breath. He sat back on his heels and reached for the boxers he'd thrown off the edge of the bed, using them to wipe off my chest, pulling down the hem of my shirt when he was done. Those bright blue eyes caught mine and Dex smiled again, that carefree, pleased grin that made the center of my chest ache. He reached out, wrapping an arm around my waist to bring our bellies together.

He was naked. His skin was warm and damp as he settled me up against his chest. Dex's free hand brushed the hair back from my face right before he kissed my temple and forehead with a hum and a promise of familiarity. "You okay?"

Shyness overcame me and I nodded. "Oh yeah." I wasn't going to panic. Not at all. "Are you okay?"

"I think I busted three loads on you, honey, I'm more than okay," he said, kissing my cheek with a snicker. "Way more than okay."

It'd be a lie if I said that his admission didn't make me smile. "I—"

He moved his hand up so fluidly that I almost failed to see the red smears on his fingers. I wasn't so much of an idiot to not know that the red was blood. My blood. And then I blushed, feeling incredibly mortified. "Umm... you might want to wash your hands," I whispered.

Dex frowned and looked at the hand I wasn't talking about, quickly lifting the other one to inspect it. His eyebrows went up at a tortoise's pace as he flipped his palm up and down to look at what was on them. His lower lip dropped open. "Ah, Ritz, I...." His lips slammed shut, nostrils flaring as he swallowed loudly. "Baby, I popped your cherry?"

It was my turn to gulp. "I told you that I'd never slept with a guy." God, how mortifying. I shouldn't have said anything and just let him think I'd started my period or something. "You have really big fingers."

Oh lord. I was lame.

He blinked, once, twice, three times. "I guess I—fuck, babe. I wasn't thinkin' about it, I guess." His eyes went back to his bloodstained fingers. "I really popped your cherry?"

What a way to make me feel like a loser. What was a hymen supposed to be? Indestructible? "It isn't my period."

Dex groaned, long and low. He wiggled his fingers for a moment before crushing our bodies together. He placed a warm, wet kiss on my jaw. "You okay with that?"

He smelled so good. I nodded, letting the rough feel of his stubble scrape my cheek. I wasn't going to go back on my decision. I'd take all of this with open arms. "Yeah."

The content rumble that flowed from his chest made me smile. "Good."

He sat across the kitchen bar with a bowl of cereal in one hand, spoon in the other, and those brilliant blue eyes on me constantly. It made me feel really self-conscious despite the fact I was fully dressed. He'd already seen me practically naked. Already had his fingers in places that made my neck hot. I shouldn't feel self-conscious with clothes on, but I did.

"Why are you looking at me like that?" I asked him carefully with my bowl covering the lower half of my face.

Dex's gaze didn't loosen in the slightest. "Because I'm wonderin' what you taste like."

It was a miracle I didn't drop my spoon.

I don't think that I took a single breath either, even after he gave me a devilish grin.

"I bet you're delicious."

Holy moly.

Dex was a dangerous guy, and it had nothing to do with his profession. Or his motorcycle hobbies, his criminal record, or the tattoos that marked half of his body. For all of his talents with his hands, he was a smart, observant guy who knew exactly what his words were capable of. And he had no issues wielding those powers viciously.

"And I bet when you come on my cock later, your pretty little pussy is going to suck me dry."

The spoon clattered to the countertop in an apparent suicide.

Shit!

Why in the world had I talked him out of letting us shower together? Oh, right. Right. My arm. I hadn't told him about my stupid arm yet.

My face flamed up about ten degrees at the same time all the air left my lungs. Dex chuckled, reaching across the counter to pick up my spoon. He handed it over with a smile that was as dangerous as a snake in tall grass. "We either need to get goin' or you're gonna need to hop up on the counter and give me a taste."

I take it back, if any miracle had recently occurred, it was when I didn't fall off the stool after that comment.

My brain scrambled. "Uh…"

Dex flashed me another wicked, slow grin, showing me those even white teeth. "Whatever you want, babe. I'm partial to stayin' here, though."

So was I, and I had no idea where these thoughts and needs came from. Hadn't I been fighting all this a day ago?

"We.... I should get a swim in." What I needed to do was exhaust myself. Definitely. Alone.

He shrugged after a minute, blue eyes narrowing. "That works. I like the idea of waitin' a few hours."

I swallowed the obscene amount of saliva that had pooled in my mouth. Wait a few hours for what? I wasn't positive but I knew it was something good. "Yeah... Yeah. "

Dex slid off the stool, balancing his empty bowl in one hand and taking mine in his other.

I needed to get my head straight and quit remembering how his cock had the slightest upward arch to it. Ahh.

I coughed, trying to clear my thoughts. "Do you know what your dad wanted yesterday?"

"Hell if I know. Nothin' good if he's callin' me. I'll call Lisa or Marie while you swim and see if they know."

Lisa and Marie... why hadn't I thought of that before? "Was your mom an Elvis fan or did she come up with the names on her own?"

Dex locked at me for a moment before chuckling. "Pa wouldn't let her name 'em Priscilla or Lisa Marie so she screwed him like that."

From the little I knew about her, and the significant amount I did know her son, that didn't surprise me one bit. "And you?"

"Named after my great grandpa, C.D. Dyson."

I lifted both my eyebrows. "Fancy. Can I call you C.D.?"

He shook his head. The corners of his eyes tilted up in that mocking little smile that didn't always reach his serious mouth. "Nah. I like you callin' me Charlie."

This friggin' guy.

I'd call him Princess Dex if he wanted me to.

He pulled back and smiled with his mouth that time, twisting me into knots with each millimeter it grew. "You ready?"

"One sec." I flashed him a little smile and darted into the living room, grabbing my stuff for the day.

He waited for me by the door, waving me out of the house and locking the door afterward. With a cool smile, he helped me onto his bike and dropped me off at the front of the center. Dex thread his fingers through mine and bit my knuckles before shooing me inside and taking off after I'd gotten in the building.

I swam and just let myself relax. I wasn't going to worry about whatever precarious relationship I found myself in with Dex, what Sonny would say when I finally called after avoiding him for two days, any of the mess with the Reapers, or who else my dad owed money to. It was one of those things that was completely out of my control.

Dex picked me up afterward, patting my thigh as I threw my leg over the back of his bike. The ride to Pins was broken into pieces when he'd palm my leg at every stop light. As soon as he'd parked his Dyna in his usual spot in front of the shop, he held out a hand to help me off—though he knew I didn't need it—and didn't let go.

I spotted the note on the door first. Dex's eyes had been on the street, inspecting it up and down like he was looking for something, and I figured he'd crossed that path so many times he could have done it blindfolded. I tugged on his hand, earning those glowing blue embers in return.

"I swear I paid all the bills on time." I shifted my eyes in the direction of the door with a tilt of my chin.

Dex's attention shifted to the envelope that had been taped up. His strides got longer, making him pull me just a little as we closed the distance to his shop. He didn't bother opening the door before tearing the blank white envelope across the top, yanking out an index sized card from inside.

The first sign I had that something was wrong was the flexing of a vein in his temple, then the corners of his eyes wrinkled, and finally his jaw clenched. He looked up and turned around, sweeping up and down the street in one glance. His grip tightened before unlocking the door and shoving me not so gently inside, locking it behind us.

"What happened?"

His eyes cut over to me, wide and battling some unknown war I had no clue of. I kind of expected him not to say anything, to keep me from worrying or something equally chauvinistic-like, but Dex shot me a hard look instead. "Shit's up with The Reapers. I need to go talk to Luther, babe." His hand tugged on mine. "Lock the door after me, and don't open it unless it's me or one of the guys."

Oh crap. I nodded at him. "What if you're late?" It wasn't unheard of for Blake to get to work fifteen or twenty minutes after opening.

Dex shrugged. "Don't open it, Ritz. It's nothin' bad but I need to go see Lu." He trailed his fingers over my knuckles. "I'll be back as soon as I can."

He left, leaving me to think about what Liam had said about the deadline for the revised debt. Friggin' crap. Why the heck were so many things out of my control? I wasn't a control freak but the complete absence of it was alarming and frustrating. Everything would hopefully work itself out once Sonny found our dad.

In hindsight, I should have known better than to ever assume that.

CHAPTER THIRTY

There were very few things that ranked higher than calling Sonny on my list of things I didn't want to do.

Like getting my yearly pap.

Or having a root canal.

I'd even go as far as to say that I'd rather get an enema while stuck in a room with a flying roach.

For a few minutes in the break room, I'd even considered having a drink to relax me a little bit before facing the firing squad also known as my brother. But... yeah, no. *No.* I'd put it off for enough time. Now, with the note that had appeared on Pins' door, my time had run out.

The first thing out of his mouth after he picked up was, "I know your phone's not broken, kid."

I sighed. Of course this wasn't going to be easy. "I'm a big ol' chicken."

Sonny huffed. His tone was rough and straight to the point. "No shit."

"I'm sorry," I moaned pitifully. He had more than enough reasons to be mad at me for ignoring his calls but still. When Sonny was mad it was like having your guardian angel disappointed in you. It hurt. "I know I suck."

He huffed again. "The only thing that sucks is that you couldn't just call and tell me what you did. I had to hear it from Luther. Not you."

This conversation sounded remarkably like one I had with my mom when I forgot to take my medicine. *Do you want to end up like me, Rissy?* Obviously it was completely different subjects but the point was the same. I seemed to disappoint the people I loved the most sometimes.

And that...

Guilt and pain ripped at the cavern of my ribs.

"What pisses me off is that you lied to me, and then ignored me when I called to talk about it." Ugh, I felt even worse because what he said was mostly true. He would have been mad but maybe not as much?

Maybe. It was too late to even think about it though. The fact was, I'd been a coward and an asshole.

My head hung. "I really am sorry, Son. I just wanted to help, and I realized too late how stupid it was."

Sonny paused and the silence felt suffocating. "Kid, I get that you'd do something stupid if you thought it'd help. Trust me, I'd do dumber shit than that for you but you know, *you know*, how much it pisses me off when you keep shit from me."

"I know." There was no way my voice sounded as pitiful and crappy as I felt. Because he was right. We'd been through this before.

"Yeah, I know you know," he answered back gruffly.

The urge to say sorry again was right on my tongue but it wouldn't come out. I knew my brother. I knew my brother enough to not be surprised he was mad at me for keeping things from him, and I was well aware of the fact that the word 'sorry' meant nothing to him. Actions spoke louder than words, he'd probably say.

And I'd blown it, and then blown it again by fielding his calls.

"Did they tell you everything?" I asked him slowly. If there was something no one had mentioned before then there might be hope for the big pile of shit I'd dug myself into.

"I hope so. You went to Busty's, and that mother—Liam showed up, wanting you to go with him," he said. "Anything else?"

Was there a trace of a challenge in his voice?

Crap. I bit my lip and took a deep breath. If all my cards were on the line, I might as well drop the bomb too. There was a chance someone had already mentioned to him a part of whatever the heck was going on with Dex but if they hadn't....

Double crap.

"I don't really know for sure what's going on with me and Dex but—," but what? What exactly do you tell your older half-brother about having irrational feelings toward his friend? His friend that was your boss. His friend that he'd left you with. "I really like him and I'm pretty positive he feels the same... in his own way."

Just like a Band-Aid right?

Except there was more stunted silence on Sonny's end. At least a minute passed before he spoke again.

"Yeah, I know, kid. You're not the only one ignoring my calls." That didn't exactly surprise me. "I had a feeling it was headed in that direction but Dex knows what's coming to him as soon as we get back."

What was coming to him?

"Sonny, he's good to me—"

My brother laughed. "Oh, I'm sure he is."

Mortified. I was absolutely mortified. "Not like that!" Well, sort of like that after today.

"I know what you meant, Ris. I'm not blind," he bit back sharply. "I'm sure he's good to you, that's why I haven't driven back to beat his ass just yet. I'm saving it for after we get your dad. I'll give Dex that much until then. If he was Wheels or Buck, then that'd be a different story but I know him. Dex has more than enough phone numbers if he was just interested in playing around."

Ouch. Well. The truth wasn't always made with stuffing and fur. "Don't be mad about that. It's not a big deal."

"He knows it's a big deal, and he knows what the consequences are. You're a big girl, Ris, so I'm not gonna tell you what to do. You might not trust me, but I trust you."

Shit. I was the second biggest piece of crap on the planet after my dad with that one line. But what could I say to make the situation better? Nothing. Absolutely nothing and I needed to live with that. "I do trust you, I promise. I don't trust anyone more than you."

He sighed. "I'm sure, kid."

I banged my forehead on the edge of the table. "All right."

Sonny didn't say anything else.

"Oh, and there was a note on Pins' door when we got here today." I went on to tell him what Dex had said, and then reminded him in case no one had told him about the deadline on the debt coming up.

"I got some intel on a few more places he could be staying at. Trip and I are heading up to northern Cali tomorrow to look. I'll call you if I find anything out," he promised.

"Okay."

He grunted. "See ya, Ris." Then, he hung up. Just like that.

And just like that, I felt like the biggest douche on the planet.

When was the last time Sonny had ever gotten off the phone with me in that way? Years? When he'd found out that the doctors had found more cells in my arm and I hadn't told him until my treatment was nearly over? In trying to spare him, wasn't I doing the same thing he'd done by not telling me about our secret little brother?

Eh. Kind of.

Okay, it was exactly the same. I'd thought I'd learned my lesson at nineteen but apparently not. The reality of it made me feel not just crappy but useless. All these people went through so much for me and I just sat at work or at Dex's house and betrayed them with my lies and bullshit. What kind of crap was that?

What could I do? This whole feeling helpless crap didn't sit well in my stomach. I'd never relied on other people, and I'd done what I needed to do to keep going for as long as I could remember.

It may have only been a few minutes that I sat there, staring at the table while I tried to figure out what I could do, when it hit me. Where this all stemmed from. What could fix the biggest issue. What I could do after doing nothing. If Dad wasn't where he'd lived for the past fourteen years, then why wouldn't he be where he'd lived before then?

Florida.

God. I'd been so stuck in my own world I hadn't even thought of it.

The clock on the wall said it was only a little after seven. If I got my work done fast, I could probably squeeze in a few phone calls to motels that were by where we used to live, or even by *yia-yia's* old house. It sounded a little too easy but then again, Curt Taylor had done a ton of dumb crap in his life. He wasn't exactly the brightest guy.

I went back up front and finished off a supply order, added the newest figures to Quickbooks, and made exactly two calls to motels that came up within ten miles of Tamarac when Dex pulled his bike into his usual parking spot.

The chances of my plan working were pretty slim but I figured it was worth the effort.

"I'm trying to get in contact with my dad," I told the employee. *Liar!* "He's staying at your hotel and isn't answering his cell phone. He's a diabetic and I'm really worried." I was going to hell for this. "Is there any way you can patch me through to his room?" I asked the lady on the other end of the line.

Luckily for me, the woman didn't hesitate as much as the man at the other motel had. "Sure. What's his room number, sweetie?"

I watched Dex through the door. Good lord, he was hot. "I don't remember what room he mentioned. I'm sorry. The reservation is under Curt Taylor."

There was no pause. No hesitation. She made a humming noise before making a squeaky noise that almost took away from Dex pulling the door to the shop open and coming in, giving me a tired but somehow beautiful smile. "Sorry honey. I don't have anything under that name. Is your mom with him?"

Ha. I wished. "That's weird. He might be with his friend. Let me try calling his cell again. I appreciate your help."

The lady bid me a good day, and I set the phone down on the cradle. Dex made his way around the desk, settling both palms on my shoulders

I tipped my head back and smiled. "Hi."

This slow, small smile crept across Dex's square jaw. God, he was so good-looking it sucked. "Hey babe. What are you doin'?"

"Calling motels around where I used to live to see if I can find my dad," I explained to him. "I don't know why I didn't think about it earlier. He doesn't seem to be where Sonny's at, so maybe he went back there."

A small line creased his eyebrows as he wound my ponytail around his fist. "Good thinkin'. Might take a while to call a bunch of places, Ritz." He tugged on my hair just enough so that I felt it at the roots. "Lemme talk to Lu and see if he knows anybody in Florida that might help us out."

Us. The us didn't escape me for a second. My heart relished it and might have even tap-danced.

Focus! "You don't need to bother him. I don't mind calling."

Those dark blue eyes rolled back. "Babe, if I thought I'd be botherin' him—"

"You wouldn't ask?" I offered.

He snickered. "No, I'd still ask but I wouldn't have told ya in case he said no. For you and Son, he'd do it."

"Well, remind me to thank him even if he doesn't know anyone."

Dex nodded. His other hand left my shoulder to palm the back of my neck as he ducked low. "You feelin' okay?"

Oh my. How stupid was it that his question made me blush from my belly button all the way up? The worst part was that he could see it. I'd taken a painkiller earlier, and besides just a little bit of soreness that was way less bothersome than my period cramps, I was good. Real good.

"I'm okay." Real, real okay. "Is everything fine with the Reapers?"

His expression didn't flicker or cloud over with worry, which was a good thing. He settled for a confident nod that was only distracted by what seemed like an intense thought. "Got it all sorted out, babe. Don't need to worry about 'em anymore."

My eyes narrowed on their own, suspiciously. "What did you do?"

"You don't need to worry about 'em anymore. We dealt with 'em," he answered with complete seriousness.

"Please tell me you didn't do anything to get in trouble, Dex." I wrapped my hand around his wrist. "Please, please, please tell me that you didn't do anything stupid." A certain amount of dread settled on my shoulders. If he'd done something that would land him back in jail, I couldn't forgive myself. I definitely wouldn't be able to ever forgive my dad for it either.

That little smile stayed on his lips. "Nothin' like that, Ritz. I promise."

I wanted to doubt him but when had he ever given me a reason to? Never. But the dread stayed in place. "Dex," I pleaded with him.

He squeezed my shoulder. "Promise. Nothin' like that."

My expression must have said that I wasn't completely convinced because he snickered again, squeezing my shoulder.

"Ritz, trust me. Nobody's gettin' into trouble except your pa. You and Son are off the hook, but we still gotta find him and get him so he can deal with the fucks he's gotten wrapped up with."

"Okay." I couldn't say I was relieved exactly but as long as Sonny would be fine, then that's all that mattered. "Thank you for taking care of it for us. You didn't need to but it means a lot to me." And the words just poured out of my mouth, leaving me vulnerable. "You're kind of a blessing."

His smile turned weary and gentle, those bright blue eyes searching, searching, searching. Dex disentangled his fingers from their fist and pinched my chin. "Sure, babe."

I grinned at him again and pulled on his two middle fingers. "You have an appointment coming in soon."

He flipped his grip, rubbing my fingers between his fingertips. "I didn't forget." He looked around. "Blake here?"

"In the back." He'd gotten to Pins an hour late but that was our secret.

The poor guy had left his sunglasses on when he came in, only bothering to wave a greeting. There was something wrong but I didn't want to push him when he seemed like he needed space. And his sunglasses said exactly that.

Dex ran his fingers through my ponytail before disappearing down the hallway a minute later.

I worked the rest of the day setting up new accounts on a couple of social media websites that I thought would be a good idea to branch into. When I had the chance, I called one or two more places that had come up in the motel search. Regardless of whether Luther knew people who could help or not, I didn't want to rely on that. Anything was better than sitting around waiting for things to fix themselves.

It wasn't until a few hours later that Dex came and sat on the edge of my desk that he confirmed the offer of help. "Lu knows a couple of guys in a riding club close to Dade county. He says he'll call 'em tonight."

I held up my hand for a high-five. Dex looked from my outstretched hand to my face and back again. I wiggled my fingers. "Don't leave me hanging."

He shook his head, and friggin' finally slapped his palm against mine weakly.

Jerk. "I owe him big time," I said.

He gave me a small, amused smile. "Don't worry about it."

"I do. That's nice of him. He doesn't have to help us."

Dex raised both of his eyebrows. "He's sweet on you, and everybody knows he wishes Son was his kid instead of Trip."

It felt like half the ceiling came crashing down. "Uh, *what*?" Trip was his son? Trip was Luther's son?

No, no, no, no, *no, no.* Hadn't I been making faces and saying mean things about Luther at the bar when I'd been sitting with Trip? I had. Oh god, I had. Remorse flooded my stomach, making it bottom out. I rarely spoke badly about people and the one time I did, I did it in front of his son. *Why?*

"What? You didn't know that was his pa?"

"No!" Oh boy, I couldn't face Trip again. Ever. "I talked shit about how gross it was that Luther messed around with younger girls with Trip, Dex. I feel terrible."

What did he do? Assure me that it was fine? No, he laughed. Dex tossed his head back and laughed.

"And he even said that Luther messed around with girls younger than his son. Ugh." I moaned. "I'm such an idiot."

He laughed even harder, reaching out to pull on my hair. "It's fine, Ritz. Trip wouldn't say shit. It's not like he's crazy about his pa doin' that anyway, but that is funny as hell."

"They don't even look alike." They didn't. Trip was blonde and tall, and Luther wasn't as tall and he definitely wasn't blonde. And, *and*, Trip had these really strong, handsome features that his dad just... didn't.

"Nah. He looks more like his ma," Dex explained slowly. "Why do you think that Lu's lettin' them both be gone so long?"

It all made complete sense now, and I felt like a major jackass. Never again would I say anything mean about another person out loud, damn it.

Well, unless it was my dad.

I groaned at the realization. "I wish I would've figured that out before opening my big mouth."

Dex smiled, both of his eyes widening as he nodded. "Sometimes it takes everybody a long time to figure out what's in front of 'em, babe."

Ain't that the truth.

"Did you find out what your dad was calling for?" I asked Dex from over a bowl of veggie pad-thai.

He was digging a cut of chicken from his own bowl, a small crease lining his forehead at the question. "Yeah." He chewed thoughtfully until finally looking at me. We'd originally started sitting on opposite ends of the couch but over time, he'd scooted over to end up on the cushion next to mine. "Ma finally served him with divorce papers."

I almost spit out the noodles in my mouth. "Hasn't it been a really long time?"

Dex nodded, the look on his face as incredulous as the one on mine I could only assume. "Fourteen years. I've been tellin' her for fourteen years to lay his ass out but she kept blowin' it off."

"Why?" It took all of a split second to realize how much of a hypocrite I sounded asking that. Hadn't my own mom stayed married to a man that left her? Yeah, she had.

He shrugged but it wasn't casual. By the lines of his shoulders, it seemed like there was something about what Debra was doing that genuinely bothered him. "I've been tellin' her since I was a kid to divorce his worthless ass. And all this time she kept spewin' this ridiculous shit about marryin' under the eyes of God and promisin' to stick by him forever." He snorted at his bowl. "Bull fuckin' shit."

Oh lord. That sounded exactly like my own mom.

It felt so personal to admit that to him but then again, wasn't he telling me this out of trust? Didn't I owe him the same and more? "My mom used to say the same thing. It drove me crazy. I mean, anybody would've been lucky to be with her, but she was so hung up on my dad. I didn't see a problem with it at first but after a while...after I saw how much it pained her...I didn't get why she wouldn't let go of him. Maybe I've blown it out of proportion but I don't think you leave someone you love because you don't like having responsibilities."

Dex nodded slowly, his eyes still down on his plate. "I know, babe. Trust me. I know. If my pa cared about anybody else half as much as he cared about himself, then all of our lives could've been a lot easier. Ma knows that but she kept holdin' on to those dumbass beliefs." He snorted. "And she doesn't even go to fuckin' church unless it's Easter or Christmas. It's stupid as shit."

I wasn't going to disagree with him.

"I used to think that if my mom would've gotten over my dad maybe she would've... I don't know. I always just thought that her being hung-up on him made her even sicker. But I'm glad your mom is at least doing something about it."

His face softened just a bit and he sighed. "Me too, babe. Pa's losin' his mind but he doesn't fuckin' get it. He's never gonna get it."

Another moron member of the Widowmakers. Go figure. Maybe it was just something with the older members?

I poked Dex in the hard muscle of his thigh. "Let me know if there's anything I can do for her. I can screen her phone calls if she wants." I smiled at him.

He snorted. "And hang up on my pa? I'd be all about that, honey."

I poked him again but this time he caught my finger in his fist. "I'm sure you would."

He grinned. "Don't think anybody's ever hung up on him before but me."

"And you? Has anyone ever hung up on you?" I asked.

"Nope," Dex answered a little too proudly.

"There's always a first for everything."

When his grin grew a little too wide, a hint of lewdness crossing his eyes, I realized the interpretation he chose to pick up on my words and groaned.

"I know all about that, babe."

I made a face. "Shut up."

His laugh was louder than the movie playing on the television, and way more entertaining. "You gonna sleep with me tonight?"

The thought both scared and excited me, but it probably scared me more. "I don't know." I paused. "I talked to Sonny earlier and he wasn't exactly happy or mad when I told him that I...uhh...you know."

The jerk raised both his eyebrows. "No clue. What?" he egged on.

I rolled my eyes. "Are you ignoring his calls, too?"

Dex shrugged. "I don't need to talk to him to know what he's gonna say. I don't really give a shit what he wants."

That wasn't exactly surprising and it wasn't the first time he'd said the same thing.

"We'll deal with it when he gets back," he said. "You gonna sleep in my bed?"

Relentless. The man was relentless. That weird mix of excitement and fear flooded my stomach again. "I don't know. I kind of feel like I'm in over my head with you. Like I just learned how to swim and you want me to compete in the Olympics, and I don't want to disappoint you. Does that make sense?"

That handsome face turned serious. "Ritz, I might know what I'm doin' with you when you're in my bed or my office—"

Oh god. The mental picture of him with someone else in his friggin' office made my heart constrict. At the same time I had the urge to gag.

"But the rest of this is completely fuckin' new to me. I don't wanna run you off," he admitted.

I sighed and nodded, but there was something about his words that really stuck for the first time. "Why don't you know what you're doing? I figured you," my heart did that stupid clenching thing again, "get around. And you don't exactly seem like the long-term relationship kind of guy." I wanted to puke at the end of each of my sentences and by some miracle, I didn't. "You're kind of old, Dex. It doesn't make sense."

"Old?" he coughed. I swear it seemed like his eyebrows managed to climb all the way up to his hairline in indignation.

I shrugged.

"I'm not *old*."

Oh boy. Of all the things for him to get hung up on, he got held up by the mention of his age. "Okay, you're not old. You're a spring chicken, whatever. The point is, why don't you have a girlfriend?" After the conversation we'd just had, wondering about a wife would seem preposterous.

He blinked. It took him so long to answer I thought he'd just ignore the question. He braced a hand on my knee, his skin hot. "I haven't exactly been lonely, honey."

I'd gotten stabbed. Stabbed by an invisible blade. I'm sure I made a noise that said just that. How immature was that? How pathetic?

The hand on my knee tightened, and I suddenly had the urge to whack it away. "Well. It's not like I didn't know that." But the verbal confirmation wasn't easy to swallow.

"Baby," he purred. "I could ask you the same thing."

I shrugged. "I didn't have time."

He didn't believe me. "Bullshit."

"I didn't." And I didn't care. In the last fourteen years, I'd only had a brief six month period when I didn't have something or someone to worry about. It was fourteen years that I was grateful for, but… a break would have been nice. The one and only post-high school boyfriend I had consisted of a handful of last minute dates over the course of a few months. It wasn't a surprise it didn't work out between us.

"Keep tellin' yourself that but you know that I know the truth. We're the same, we're both closed off. I only give a shit about very few things, and you don't let anybody in because you're scared. I have shit to do, honey. Why would I wanna waste more than a couple hours of my time?"

It annoyed the living crap out of me that I wanted to argue that point with him but I couldn't. Deep down, he had a point. But I wasn't about to acknowledge it or *how* he wasted hours of his time. Gag, gag, gag. I grit my teeth instead. "I get it, Dex, the point is, I don't get why me. We're like oil and water."

He made a tisking sound with his tongue. "You haven't been payin' any attention, have you?"

I groaned my response, earning a low chuckle.

He set the bowl in his hands aside and shifted over to drop a knee between my legs, straddling my thigh. Dex plucked the bowl from my hands and set it alongside his. He loomed over me, his gaze and face intent, taking my hand and placing it on his chest. "You gotta open those pretty eyes, baby. You're the only one here." He slipped his hand down the center of my chest, straight down to cup the zipper of my jeans. "And I'm sure your romance books will tell you exactly how I feel about me bein' here."

I'm pretty sure I wheezed.

"You understand me?" he purred.

The only thing I understood was that I was on the verge of having a heart attack.

His mouth touched the side of my neck. "Iris? You understand what I'm sayin'?"

No. No, I didn't. Not in any way.

Dex's teeth nipped at the same spot he'd kissed a moment before, making me gasp. "Iris."

I nodded, shaky and quickly. "Yeah, I hear you."

He hummed. "But do you understand?" Ohmigod. I could feel that hum all the way to my underwear. "You get it?"

I had to shake my head because the words wouldn't come.

His nostrils flared. "First time in my life, I think I hate the fact you knew how to suck my dick," he breathed. "Got this urge to kill whatever guy taught you how to give a blowjob. The fuckin' idea of you *kissin'* somebody else makes me wanna dig a knife into my eye. Let me tell you, babe, never in my life have a given a single fuck about any of that. You get it?" His palm pressed into my jeans harder. Then he laid the atomic bomb on my very existence. "You are not a waste of time to me."

Holy shit. Holy friggin' shit.

"Say it," he murmured into my neck.

"Say what?"

"Say you get it."

I said it. Without a second thought even though a huge part of me was terrified. I said the three words because nothing and no one in the world had ever made me feel so grounded, so assured that I wouldn't be forgotten or left behind. I mean, I know most things were out of a person's control, but Dex happened to be the most controlling and overbearing man I'd ever met.

And a part of me recognized that I should run. That if I gave this man an inch, he'd take a mile. That if I agreed to this, it'd be the beginning of the end.

In his words, I didn't give a single shit. I said them anyway.

"I get it."

He looked at me with those dark blue eyes as if he was waiting for me to admit something more. Something incriminating, vulnerable and maybe even painful, but I couldn't come up with anything that could be more of any of those things. It wasn't until later, after he promised that he really wouldn't do anything if I slept next to him, that I thought more about it.

I didn't really let anyone in. Ever. After my dad left, and I got sick, and my mom got sick, and... there was always something, something bigger that snowballed from the size of a raindrop into the size of a softball that made me more and more reserved around others. Even with Lanie, I still didn't fully embrace our friendship. How long had it been since I'd spoken to her? Months? If we were best friends, that shouldn't have happened, right?

Yet the idea of not talking to Sonny on a regular basis, or laughing at Slim and Blake's antics, or just anything relating to Dex made me sad. It made me yearn for that easy familiarity. I finally had people that I trusted. So couldn't that be the same thing with the man that shared so many of the same hang-ups I did?

I rolled onto my back in bed next to Dex and looked at him.

He was face-up, one hand tucked under his head and the other was on his bare chest, just to the side of one of the loops that pierced his nipple. He was so damn good looking with all that ink that darkened those sinewy muscles and skin, it was unreal. If I'd seen him on the street back in Florida, I probably would have kept to the edge of the sidewalk. Well, I would have done that while eye-screwing the crap out of him.

I'd never been a big fan of that saying, "Everything happens for a reason," but maybe, sometimes, every once in a while, things coalesced into a complex, intangible reason. With tattoos and piercings and bad words and unfailing loyalty topped with a temper.

And in its own imperfect way, it couldn't have been any better.

CHAPTER THIRTY-ONE

"I think one of us needs to stage an intervention."

I looked over at Slim as I wiped off the frames by the reception desk and tipped my chin up. "For who?"

The soulless ginger—Blake's words, not mine—widened his eyes like I was dumb not to know. "Blake, Ris."

"Oh." I went up on my tip-toes and looked around the shop.

The bald man wasn't in the main room, luckily. He had been acting weird. Extremely weird. The day before, he'd spoken maybe five words to all of us, which was completely unlike him. Today had been even worse. He was remote and even someone who didn't know him could sense the desperation pouring out from him.

We'd all tried to give him his space but earlier in the evening, Slim had walked over to me and said he was pretty positive he'd heard Blake crying in the restroom. "I think something's going on with his son," he claimed. "There's nothing else that would make him sour up so much."

His son. The same son that had been in and out of the hospital since before Houston. I had a terrible feeling that it was Seth, also known as Blake Junior, giving his dad so much anxiety. The poor kid was too young to get into real trouble. There was only one thing that would make a grown adult—a parent, a loved one—cry.

Illness.

Shit.

I hoped more than anything that it wasn't the case but it'd be naive to think otherwise. Or maybe I was just that pessimistic.

I blew out a breath. "What do you think we should do?"

He looked pensive for a moment before scrunching up his nose in a way that made his lightning bolt tattoo move. "Let's take him out. You think Dex will be up for it?"

"Maybe." How the heck should I know for sure?

It turned out that Dex was up for it. Right before setting the alarm to the shop, I heard him invite Blake out to Mayhem.

"Not tonight, man. I'm not up for it," was Dumbo's creaky, hoarse answer.

Blake saying no to a drink? Unheard of.

"C'mon," Dex argued back. "My treat."

It took a little more coaxing but eventually, like the freeloader he was, Blake finally agreed. We met up at Mayhem a few minutes later, piling into the same booth we'd used on our last trip to the bar what seemed like forever ago. This time, there were more people—Widows, men who weren't members of the MC, and other random clients. I waved at the handful I recognized and slid into the booth beside Slim, with Dex following after, slinging an arm over the back of the seat.

The guys and Blue blasted through two beers each, with Slim and I carrying the majority of the conversation as he tried to convince me—again—to get a tattoo.

"Just a little thing," he insisted.

I lifted a shoulder. "I don't know."

"Tiny." He pinched his fingers together so that there was only about an inch between them. "Smaller than that heart you did for me."

I grimaced. "I don't know about a heart though."

A huge grin swept his face. "I can make you a mini dragon."

He was talking about the electric blue dragon with rainbow fire. "Where?"

"Anywhere but your lower stomach," he said confidently. "If you have kids that thing'll end up looking like a life sized one."

I burst out laughing, watching as a small smile crossed Blake's features. "With my luck, it'll look like it's trying to eat my baby."

Dex nudged me with his shoulder. His facial expression careful. Did he look jealous? Jealous that I hadn't told him I'd started considering it? Jesus. There was enough I needed to tell him, but I'd been too much of a coward to. "You wanna get some work done, babe?"

"I think so, but Gingervitis over here wants it more than me." That earned me an elbow from Slim that I returned with a laugh. "Maybe though. Just maybe."

"Don't know where?" Dex asked.

I glanced over at my favorite redhead and smirked. "I know where I don't want it."

Slim elbowed me again. "Sucks we can't do it by your scar."

My stomach felt the equivalent of a plate shattering on concrete. The blood drained from my face and I lost my breath. The urge to squeak was right there, slithering its way up my vocal chords.

The arm over my shoulders tightened a fraction. "What scar?"

Oh crap. Crap, crap, crap!

I forced a smile onto my face, and there was no doubt in my mind it was shaky and weak.

I could lie. It would be easy enough to change the conversation. The only problem was, the instant I thought about lying again and having to divert the topic to something else, guilt pinched me right in the kidneys. Maybe it was because I knew Sonny was still mad at me, but maybe it was because these were people that I cared for more than I had others in a long, long time.

But the answer, the realization, was right there.

I didn't want to. I shouldn't have to keep hiding something that was as essential a part of me as my name.

It was bound to happen, I knew that. Otherwise, it'd only be a matter of time before they found out. Keeping my cancer a secret hadn't been a permanent plan.

When I looked over at Blake, sensing the deep sadness and wariness in his features, it reinforced my vertebrae and reminded me that I had guts. That I'd used my guts throughout my life. And if Blake really was suffering because of something going on with his little boy, I could do this. It wasn't that big of a deal.

There were worse things in life than having people I cared about babying me. Feeling sorry for me. And I needed to quit being a sneaky jackass that kept things to herself. Would I have ever kept things from *yia-yia*? No way.

I looked over at Dex and pointed at my arm, my fingers shaking as I did it. There was nothing to be nervous about. Nothing to be scared of. "I have this gnarly scar on my arm." Easy, right?

His eyes hooded over as a frown crossed his features. "From what?" he asked carefully.

You can do this, Ris.

It wasn't a big deal. It really wasn't.

I reached for the hem of my sweater and started pulling it up and over my head, careful to keep my arms perpendicular to my body so that I wouldn't give an impromptu arm-flash. I heard Slim chuckle, "Strip show? I need change for a ten."

A snicker escaped me as I peeled it off my arms before balling the material on my lap. I took a deep breath and planted another shaky smile on my lips as I raised my bad arm in a way that made it look like I was going to flex my muscles. Not that there was much left there anymore, more than half of my bicep had been removed.

I watched Dex as I did it. Watched him as he shifted in place, dropping his arm from around the back of the seat and settled his gaze on the silvery white twisted tissue that laced the inside of my bicep. That familiar nerve under his eye started popping instantly.

"I had cancer when I was little," I told them, looking at Blake as I said it. Maybe my story wasn't the best one to try and relate to him. If Junior was sick, hearing that I'd gone through four different surgeries wasn't a fairy tale. But I was alive and I was here. Alive and here were much better words than the simple word—not. Not here. Inexistent.

Back when I'd been sick, I'd always dreaded hearing other words. Spread. Lymph nodes. Amputation. Those words, those possibilities, make you grow up quick. They made me remember to prioritize correctly, to value and appreciate. But mainly the branches of those words scared me so much, I wanted to *live* even if it wasn't always going to be fun and games.

I'd forgotten that along the way somewhere. There was a difference between living and surviving. And this place, these people, reminded me of that.

After a second I dropped my thinner limb, and let out a breath. Dex watched me with a blank expression while Slim's eyes went wide.

"No shit?" he asked, reaching out to grab me. He lifted my arm up and touched the desensitized skin there with gentle fingertips. "What kind?"

"A form of soft tissue sarcoma," I explained. "Cancer in my muscle, pretty much."

Slim's wide expression drooped before a frown crossed his lips. "Why didn't you say something?"

That wasn't exactly what I was expecting. "I'm telling you now."

"But you could've said something before," he shot back solidly. "*Hey, Slim, I used to have friggin' cancer. Just thought you should know.*"

I opened my mouth to argue back with him when Blake made a noise I hoped to never hear from him again. Ever. "JR has acute lymphoblastic leukemia."

Any argument in my mouth or Slim's died quickly.

It was Blue that spoke first. "Sorry, B," she said, throwing her arms around the much bigger man.

"Dude," was the one thing Slim muttered harshly.

Oh shit. I slipped my knees onto the seat and leaned across the table, careful not to knock over any of the bottles, and put my hands on Blake's arm. "I'm sorry."

He let out a weak, worried exhale. "The doctors called to say his red blood cell count was off. They ran a few tests to figure out what was wrong," he explained from Blue's shoulder. "I'm scared outta my mind."

"They have all kinds of treatment for cancer now," Slim piped up.

Blake nodded just a little bit. "Yeah, that's what the doctors said. They told us his kind is one of the most treatable, but it still scares the shit out of me."

Of course it would. We sat around, trying to offer our best words of comfort and reassurance that Junior would get better. No one drank anything else while we talked to him but by the time we left over an hour later, it seemed like he was a little more calm.

I didn't have the heart to say that he'd probably freak out a hundred more times over the course of the next few months, but I hoped he'd turn to one of us for moral support.

What did get me was that Dex didn't say anything on the walk to his bike, his hand on my hip. When we got home, I'd barely sat on the couch when he came to stand in front of me. Four fingers flicked up. He growled, "Take it off, babe."

I raised an eyebrow slowly. "Excuse me?"

"Your shirt," he said like he was telling me to get on the back of his bike.

"Why?"

Dex ducked enough to grab the bottom of my sweater, slipping it up and over my head while I squirmed.

"What the hell, Dex?" I swung my hand out toward him, catching him on the stomach.

He wasn't fazed at all by my pathetic swing. Dex dropped to his knees in front of me, lifting my arm without another word. A crease lined his eyebrows, his mouth set into a grim line. He brushed a tapered, neatly groomed finger over the inside of my arm. One, two, three times. I couldn't feel it well but the act itself seemed more intimate than what we'd done on his bed the day before.

When was the last time I'd let anyone look at my scarring so closely, let alone touched it? Never.

His breathing grew labored, the pressure of his pad increasing before he finally spoke in a low grumble. "You didn't think to tell me about this?" he asked, eyeing the knotted skin. "You didn't think to tell me you're sick?"

"I *was* sick, Dex." I tried jerking my arm away but he held it too tight. "I haven't been sick in a long time."

"How long?" His voice was low, hot and seeking.

"I've been in remission for five years."

Dex's body jerked. "A long time is ten years ago, twenty years ago. Not five, Ritz." He shuffled forward on his knees, ducking his head closer to mine. "*Not five fuckin' years ago.*"

"I'm fine, I promise." The assurance fell on deaf ears based on the look he gave me. "My chances of getting it again are pretty slim."

"I don't care," he rasped. The words sounded ripped from his throat. "You had cancer, not the goddamn flu."

"Dex, it's nothing."

"Baby, it's not fuckin' nothin'. You wouldn't be missin' half your bicep if it was nothin'. You wouldn't have been hidin' this if it wasn't a big deal. *This shit is not nothin' to me.*"

Leaning forward, I grabbed his shoulder and pressed my forehead to his nose. "I'm sorry for not telling you before but it's not that big of a deal. I'm okay, and hopefully I'll be okay the rest of my life."

He repeated the last sentence so low I missed half the words. His breath washed over my face, minty with just a hint of cigarette smoke. "Babe, is there somethin' else you haven't told me?"

"No. Nothing important."

Dex shook his head. "You're gonna give me a fuckin' heart attack. You sure?"

I reached up to place my hands on his cheeks. "I'm positive. I promise. That's all."

The tip of his nose drew a line from my forehead to my temple. "Don't do that shit to me again," he pleaded. "Swear to me, Ritz. Tell me you won't drop some shit like that on me again."

His tone. Christ. The tremble in his voice pulled at the threads of tissues in my spine.

My body started shaking. "I swear."

Dex's hands went for my ribs, kneading the skin and bones. "You'll tell me if you start to feel bad? Anything, babe. Any time you start to feel sick, you swear you'll say somethin'?"

I didn't know where this was all coming from. His need for me to tell him something so simple, but I could feel the tension under his skin. He wouldn't take anything but yes from me. Dex wouldn't accept anything less than a promise. "I swear."

He nodded so slowly it seemed painful for him. The breath that left his mouth was a wisp and a flutter, shaky and emotional. "I'll put you on the insurance plan first chance I get tomorrow. It ain't that great but I'll see if I can get you a better policy. You know, in case..." he trailed off, nostrils flaring, face tight.

It made every blood cell in my body redirect itself to my heart, filling it with so much blood, so much life-giving sustenance, that I thought it was going to burst out in a bloody explosion. I wanted to tell him right then everything. About my surgeries, about the timeline of my loved ones' lives, about the sacrifices made that had shaped the outcome of my life.

Tell him everything that had led me here. To him.

But instead of remembering how to string along the twenty-six letters in an alphabet that suddenly didn't seem so important, I tipped my mouth up to brush my lips against his. He let out a long, shuddering exhale that wafted across my mouth, dragging me in deeper to the vortex that was Dex Locke.

To have this man care about me, not just a little bit, but enough that it tipped the axis of his temperament, calmed me. It was an anchoring acknowledgment. Because I cared about him too and I wished in that moment that I would have had the opportunities to show him that I felt the same way. But all I'd done was keep things from him.

Just like I kept things from Sonny. My beloved half-brother that was so mad he hung up on me—not that I could blame him but still.

I didn't want to push people that I loved and valued away because I made decisions that were well-meaning but stupid.

"I'm sorry," I whispered just a millimeter from those firm, full lips that graced his beautiful mouth. "I don't want to keep things from you, but it's a bad habit to break." I kissed his top lip for just a moment, closing my eyes as the reality of what my bullshit could lead me to set in. "Please don't give up on me, I won't do it again."

Two large hands cupped my cheeks. "Iris," he purred in that silky voice that made me lose my breath all over again. "I already told you I don't give up what's mine." Dex kissed my bottom lip like I'd done his. "Ever."

It was me who closed the distance between us, pressing my mouth to his. The kiss was sweet and slow. His mouth opened mine with a gradual slide of his tongue, hot and insistent.

I palmed the flat, muscled plane of his pectorals. The heel of one of my hands rested just above one of his ringed nipples.

We kissed and kissed like there was no rush in the world. There was no nipping like there had been in his bed, no teeth, or roughness. So when his hands swept their way down my throat, over my collarbones to land directly over the neckline of my tank top, I didn't hesitate when his fingers curled into the material. He pulled it down with a light ripping sound, bringing my bra cups along with it.

I must have made a startled noise that told Dex I was on the verge of freaking out because he didn't let me. He pulled his mouth away from mine and immediately dipped down to draw a nipple into his mouth with a soft suck. Those highly capable fingers shoved the bottom hem of my shirt up to a tight bunch beneath my breasts.

How the hell had I gone my entire life without this?

I couldn't think, I couldn't move, I couldn't do a damn thing but moan and arch myself against his suckling. Holy moly. The draws and pulls were too good, way too friggin' good. He moved his mouth over to lick at the other peak and I swear my nervous system shut down.

In no time, he'd pushed me to lay against the back of the couch, his hands holding my ribs as he hovered his lips and tongue over the vulnerable place between my rib cage. "Goddamn, baby."

Slow, slow, slow he went, ghosting those hot lips and hotter breath down the center of my stomach before stopping at my bellybutton. Dex licked the gold jewelry before sweeping his tongue in a circle around my navel, making me squirm and arch beneath him.

I made some kind of noise that was mostly a moan but had a squeal mixed into it.

"You know this is the first piercing I've done in three years?" He rimmed the piercing with the tip of his tongue again.

I didn't even know the fifth letter in the alphabet in that moment.

Dex replaced his mouth with his nose, making the contact even more intimate for some reason before humming low. "All this sweet skin just for me." He kissed right below my belly button. His fingers slipped into the band of my khaki pants. In a quick move, he undid their button and slid a hand inside over the cotton of my underwear.

Ohmigod!

"Dex!" I gasped and sat up, pulling Dex to me in a hard kiss that was all warm tongue and soft lips.

He moaned and slipped his hand deeper into my pants, his fingertips resting over the start of my slit.

We kissed and kissed and kissed. Dex laid me against the back of the couch, his mouth was possessive, nipping my lips while his fingers redrew soft lines over my underwear. His mouth went straight to my neck, biting the column just hard enough to make me cry out once.

"Fuck, baby," he whispered against my throat. "So sorry." Then he bit me again just a little to the left of where he'd done it before, this time pressing the flat of his tongue against the skin as he did it.

Holy crap, I was going to die.

I tilted my chin back to give him more room and smiled like a drunk prostitute. "You're not sorry."

Dex chuckled. "No, I'm really not."

I didn't realize my hips were wriggling beneath him, searching for his weight. My legs spread to let Dex's slim hips between them. And my hands...they'd managed to work their way beneath the black t-shirt that stretched over Dex's form. His skin was smooth and firm. The defined muscles contracted under my touch. His belly button tensed and his abs contracted as I spread my fingers wide, touching as much of him as I possibly could.

The fingers over my underwear slid a little lower, dipping beneath the band to outline one of my bare lips with a single finger. He ran it up and down just once before groaning.

Should I be embarrassed? Maybe. More than likely, but I wasn't. Not even a little bit.

Dex pulled away again, sitting straight up on his knees. In a quick move, he pulled his t-shirt over his head, and then went for my pants and underwear tugging both down my legs. He tossed them over his shoulder when he was done, shooting me a smile that was more reassuring and pleased than smug.

He grabbed the back of my knees and pulled me forward so that I was on the edge of the couch. His gaze was direct and intense. He looked down at me, my legs just slightly spread, my breasts hanging out of my bra and shirt. And I just laid there, a big pile of need and want. That big hand slid from my knee, making a slow trek across the inside of my thigh, his knee, his palm going up, up—holy crap—over the outlined ridge of his jeans inches from the apex of my thighs.

"I wanna fuck you so bad," he murmured, palming his hard cock roughly. He plucked at the zipper of his jeans, shaking his head simultaneously. "But not tonight. I'm just gonna lick your pussy tonight, baby. I wanna make sure you get this isn't a one-time thing."

That was probably my cue to pass out, and I'm not sure what it said about me, but subconsciously I spread my legs even wider. Dex must have seen it because a smile spread over his mouth. He glanced up and fell over me, arms straight, kissing my lips once.

I'm not sure what was hotter. Whether Dex's immaculate body in general, or the smooth muscles beneath his colorful skin, or the way he slid down to his haunches before he lifted one of my feet up from the floor and draped it over his shoulder. Then his tongue was there, dipping between my legs to flick and lick at the moist skin. He sucked on my lips, on my clit, and then slid the tip of his tongue inside. In and out, circling, flicking, time after time.

I thought I was going to pass out. Or cry tears of joy.

It took all of no time before an electric tingling started at the base of my spine, expanding like a supernova, and an orgasm swarmed throughout my entire body, making my legs shake and my insides clench in satisfaction.

The sound of his zipper making its way down broke through the daze I was in. Sweat beaded on the back of my neck, my lower back, everywhere for all I knew. Dex dropped to his hands over me, caging me in. But it wasn't the tattoos or the piercings that caught my eye at first, it was his stiff cock bobbing that I couldn't help but stare at. The tip bobbed just short of my belly button as Dex flexed his hips.

Was he going to...?

He lifted a hand and wrapped it around the base of the thick shaft, angling it down so that I thought for a second that he was going to slide it in me but instead, he touched the tip to my slit and *holy friggin' crap*. The mushroomed crown tapped that needy little button of nerves that screamed for this man, sliding the smooth head up and down the wet lips. Dex shuffled his body so that the length of his long, hard dick rested against me.

Was that me panting?

And then he moved, his hips and length going up and down. The underside of his broad tip brushed over my clit with each stroke. It was so thick, so unbelievably hot, I wiggled my hips for more. My body knew, it knew what to do even when my brain wasn't functioning, searching for memories of things I'd seen in the past. I tipped my hips up and watched him glide his shaft over me, coated in my juices, faster and faster. The tip hitting my clit every single time.

I couldn't stop watching.

"That feels so good," I whimpered as the thick reddened head peeked out from between my legs.

His breathing got heavier. A slow nod worked his neck. He thrust forward, those dark, tattooed fingertips gripping my thighs tightly. All that ink on his fingers shouldn't have been so hot up against my plain bare skin, but it was. Holy crap, it was. My insides clenched and wept when the meaty underside spread me around him.

I wanted him. Wanted him in me. Filling me. Helping me live. But the words wouldn't come out of my mouth.

Startling blue eyes flicked up to mine, lazy and unfocused. "Iris." He kissed me, closed lips on closed lips, lingering as he whispered into me, "Love this."

I came again with a cry. Hoarse and so loud I was just a little embarrassed, but the sensation was so friggin' fantastic it wasn't enough to regret it.

Dex yelled—yelled!—a split second later as long, white shots exploded in milky streams over my stomach and breasts. His hips pumped the air mindlessly, thick drops falling from the crown of his cock.

I'm not sure which one of us was panting more afterward. Those dark blue eyes slowly slid up my stomach and chest until settling on my face in a lazy smile. I couldn't help but smile back at him.

"You're amazing." The words just came out of nowhere and I felt silly.

But then he smiled even wider and the brief moment of awkwardness I felt was worth every second to get that in return. Dex lowered his face to kiss me gently, his breath washing over my cheeks and mouth unevenly.

He pulled away, reaching for the t-shirt he'd torn off and used it to clean off my upper body. I tucked everything back in and pulled my shirt down. After handing me my underwear and pants, I put them on while watching him clean himself off, too.

We ended up laying on the couch in the only way we managed to fit—me half on top of him. Like he needed to talk me into it. Ha. I laid my head down on his chest, over his Captain America tattoo and just a couple inches from the loops through his nipples. His skin was damp with sweat, his heartbeat pounding quickly into his ribs.

I traced my fingers along the lines of his abs, watching as the muscles there convulsed at the same time Dex let out a pleased little sigh. This friggin' guy...

If someone would have told me two months ago that he would be one of the most caring people I'd ever meet, I would have laughed in their faces. Yet, here I was. My virginity technically intact, my stomach a sticky mess, sprawled happy and warm over Dex Locke.

"I'm sorry I didn't tell you before that I'd been sick," I told him, trailing my fingers over the smooth skin of his abs. "I'm not embarrassed by it or anything—"

He rolled onto his side so fast it made me mutter, "Whoa" under my breath.

A deep furrow cut between his dark eyebrows, his mouth twisted down into displeasure. "Why the hell would you have anythin' to be embarrassed about, Ritz?" he asked.

I blinked. "Well, no reason, I guess. It's just an ugly scar."

It was Dex's turn to blink. "You had cancer," he hissed angrily. "And you're here. There's nothin' ugly about that."

The man who detailed his already beautiful body with even more gorgeous tattoos said that to me? I was torn in that split second between wanting to cry and accepting the fact that realistically, I was well on my way to being more than halfway in love with him. With him and his harsh words, and possessive touches, and quick temper.

Holy shit.

I was in love with The Dick.

I blinked again. Don't cry, don't cry, don't cry.

Don't cry, Iris!

I nodded to myself; I could do this. I could keep it together.

"I know. I know, trust me. I know that I'm one of the lucky ones." I slid my hand from his stomach up to his neck, touching the silky flesh there with nervous fingers. "But I've lived most of my life being 'that cancer kid'. I didn't want to be that person here too. I wanted you guys to like me for me not because of this."

It was Dex's turn to blink a slow draw of ink colored eyelashes that were too long for such a masculine face. "Babe, I think you got some of the worst luck I've ever heard of." He touched the tip of my nose with his index finger. "When I first saw ya, I saw a pretty little girl who got her bro to find her a job. A little girl who didn't grow up a Widow like the rest of us. Now, I know you. I know that you've gone through just as much shit, if not more, than the rest of us. You've survived a hell of a lot, Ritz. Your pa, your ma, your nana, and raisin' your bro on top of this," his thumb touched the edge of my scarring.

And then he blinked again. Once, twice, three times, and I swear, I swear, I swear that his eyes looked glassy between those eyelash flutters.

"And here you are. Life bein' unfair and all. I respect you, babe. Not just because you break my goddamn heart every single fuckin' time I see you smile but because..." He blew out a long breath of air from his lips, blinking blue eyes again and again and again. "I just do. You got me?"

I didn't. Not really. This feeling in my chest swelled and swelled to a size that made it painful to breathe. But I nodded anyway.

"I fuckin' wish you would've told me before you told everybody though," he admitted in a low voice. "Thought I was gonna throw up on the fuckin' table."

I cringed and ducked my face under his chin, nose to the raspy column of his throat. Slim's hurt face at the bar flashed through my brain. I didn't piss people off that often but when I did, I pissed everyone around me off. Ugh.

"Hopefully there won't be anything else for me to tell you anytime soon. I've told you more than I've told anybody else ever. Even Sonny." I sighed. Another person I pissed off. The one person who rarely ever got mad at me. "The last time I had to get radiation, I didn't tell him until I was almost done with treatment. He was so mad at me, Charlie. I thought for sure I wouldn't hear from him again."

Fingers tapped across my hip. "Was that right after his ma's car wreck?"

"Yeah. That's part of the reason why I didn't tell him. He was already so stressed about her accident, and he'd taken off so much time from work. I didn't want to make things worse for him," I explained.

Dex hummed deep in his throat. Those long, artistic fingers tap danced across my pelvis. "Makes sense now. I remember him losin' his shit a few years ago. Trashed his place, got into a fight with half the Club. He was a fuckin' dick 'til he took off. Didn't tell any of us where he was goin'."

Whoa. I had no idea he'd done all that. He'd shown up to *yia-yia's* house with bruised knuckles but I'd been so worried about our relationship, it just hadn't seemed like the time to push. "He came to stay with us for about a month. Now he's mad because I didn't tell him about going to Busty's."

"He'll get over it," Dex said, squeezing my hip.

"Eventually."

He hummed again. "He's mad but he'll get over it. You just gotta quit keepin' shit to yourself."

"I know." I sighed. "I know. I won't. Not to any of you again."

Those familiar fingers, tipped in black ink, threaded through mine and he growled, "You better not."

CHAPTER THIRTY-TWO

I was torn between wanting to kill Luther and giving him a hug.

The only thing keeping me from figuring out a way to overflow his toilet was the fact that there had been quinoa patties waiting for me on his kitchen island. Because I mean, they were *quinoa patties*. Someone, somewhere had made these and I doubted that the Club had any other vegetarians in their crew besides me from the stink old Pete had made with the black bean burgers.

So for that, he'd live and his toilet would survive to see another day.

But for inviting that Becky girl and a handful of other women that gave Dex the googley eyes when their dates weren't looking—Luther would suffer imaginary torture.

Repeatedly.

When the heck had I become this person? This girl that had to grit her teeth because jealousy threatened to make her pop a few blood vessels. The smile on my face felt forced, fake, unnatural.

And the worst part was that we'd only been at his house for fifteen minutes tops.

Why hadn't I pushed harder to stay at Dex's house instead? I'd told Dex I didn't want to go. It wasn't necessarily that I never wanted to see Luther or other Widowmakers again. I just didn't want to see them any time soon. The whole crap in Dex's office had been mortifying. The last thing I wanted was for them to look at me with "Poor Ris" on their faces.

I hated that damn look.

Dex had simply looked at me with those thoughtful eyes and stroked the line of my nose. "You told me to go fuck myself in front of club members. You, who says friggin' and ef, babe." He blinked. "Think you called me a dickface, too. Didn't ya?"

Whoops. That was a positive.

The tip of his finger tapped my nose as he exhaled loudly. "Trust me, honey. I'm sorry I said that to you but the only thing anybody is gonna remember from that day is what you called me, not the other way around."

I had supposed in that moment that Dex had a point. Hadn't he gotten into a fight after that?

I finally relented and agreed to go to Luther's place. The possibility that there might be people there that knew Dex more intimately than I did never even occurred to me.

Based on the number of bodies at his house, the "get together" Dex had told me about that morning, was going to be an all day event. It wasn't like I could complain. I didn't have any right to judge him for the people he'd been with...I couldn't even finish the thought without nausea clawing its way up my throat.

I was *that* jealous bitch.

I bumped into a short blonde as I shuffled out of the kitchen with my friggin' quinoa patty and fruit salad in hand. The girl looked in my direction and gave me a slow, apprising smile. In jeans that looked painted on and a tank top that barely held in her huge boobs, she was all confidence. And gigantic boobies.

"Sorry," she said in a soft voice that wasn't entirely convincing.

Oh boy. Had Dex slept with her too?

You don't want to know.

Oh hell.

I flashed her a strained smile. "Sorry about that."

And then I fled.

Wuss.

Luther's massive backyard was packed with Widowmakers and their families. There was a pretty big pool right smack in the middle of the property with quite a bit of kids splashing around, screaming. Adults littered the folding tables and chairs that had been set up around the perimeter as classic rock blasted through the speakers mounted on the back patio.

It was nice. Really friggin' nice.

But just like at Dex's niece's party, I felt out of place without my brother and the black-haired man I'd slept under last night. The only way to change that was by making friends, right?

But I could make friends later. When I wasn't standing awkwardly by the door like my freshman year of high school in the cafeteria.

There was a cluster of black vests and different shades of white and black t-shirts by one of the tables all the way in the back. Of friggin' course. I side-stepped my way through the screaming kids running around their moms, and spotted Dex's dark hair. He was sitting down, elbows to his knees, watching one of the other members with a disinterested expression on his face.

One of the men, an older one I hadn't seen much of during my stay in Austin, hit him with the back of his hand, tilting his chin up. Immediately, those pure blue eyes shot up and around the chairs surrounding him. He gaze shifted and drifted past the men, past the women, until finally landing on me.

I waggled my eyebrows, circling the chairs the Widows had grouped together. The side of Dex's full, pink mouth quirked up at my gesture.

"Hi guys," I said loudly enough for the dozen other members to hear me.

Ten different variations of "What's goin' on, Ris," came back to me as I came to stand in front of Dex, waving at the Club members in return.

I lifted up my plate. "Can I sit with you?" I asked him. The idea that he would say no wasn't even a figment of a possibility in my brain.

Dex sat back in his chair spreading his legs wide, his bright white t-shirt popped even more against the colorful figures of his sleeves. The corner of his lips stayed tipped up. "'Course you can, honey."

The obvious choice was probably to sit in his lap but instead, I turned around and crossed my legs before sinking to the ground between Dex's feet. I felt him shift behind me, his thighs closing in around my arms. Fingers sifted through my hair, pulling the strands over one of my shoulders.

"What'cha got?" he murmured into my ear. He twisted my hair around his fingers in tight, messy knots.

I showed him my plate.

Dex plucked a piece of watermelon off of it with his other hand. A low rumble of approval resonated through his throat after licking his fingertips clean.

I think I shuddered a little when he picked up a grape afterward with those long graceful fingers.

We ate silently. I finished the quinoa patty in three bites while Dex picked pieces of fruit off, wrapping and unwrapping my hair from his fist over and over again. His chest was warm on my back while we sat there huddled. The rest of the Widows talked about a trip some of them were thinking about taking along the west coast.

"It sounds longer than it is," Luther agreed to whatever specific aspect they were talking about.

I choked on the piece of apple I'd been in the middle of eating. The joke bit at my tongue. Wrong people to say that in front of.

"I've done it. It's not hard, but it's long," an older man I'd only seen in passing, agreed.

Yep. I choked again. The *that's what she said* stuck in my throat right alongside that same damn piece of apple.

"Bunch of pussies. It's doable."

Dex slapped my back as he dipped his face down, his cheek nuzzling my own as I swallowed the fruit with a savage gulp. His breathing sounded strangled, and it took me a second to realize that he was trying his hardest not to burst out laughing.

"Knock it off," he snickered, digging a finger into my ribs with a puff of air against my ear.

I snorted loud and clear.

Dex jabbed me in the rib even harder, his chest rumbling loud, loud, loud. I had to face away from him and shove my nose and mouth into his thigh to stifle the laugh that wanted to desperately come out.

"What's so damn funny?" Luther asked.

"Nothin'," Dex answered a little too quickly.

I buried my entire face tighter against the thick muscle of his quadriceps.

Someone made a noise like they didn't entirely believe him but whatever. It took me a lot longer than it should have to get it under control but by the time I did, there were a couple of women sitting on some of the guys' laps.

But I only zeroed in on one. That damn Becky.

If I had hackles I'm sure they'd be up to the stars when I spotted her. I must have stiffened because Dex squeezed my shoulders.

"What's wrong?" he whispered into my ear.

It was immature, I knew it, but I couldn't help but want to pull away from him. It wasn't fair, I know that. But seriously? *Seriously?*

"Nothing important," I managed to mumble, my fingers suddenly feeling a little less than stable holding the plate.

"I'm askin' for the truth, babe."

Hadn't I just told him the night before that I promised to tell him the truth? I looked over to see her looking at Luther with dreamy eyes. Oh lord. Sonny's words about her lack of intelligence rang through my brain. "You've been with her, right?" I didn't need to be specific about who I was talking about, he'd know.

Dex didn't miss a beat. "Yeah."

Well. Hell. He'd answered that without even thinking about it.

I wanted to puke.

"Why?" he asked in a low voice so that only I could hear.

Why? It was only the urge to punch him in the face that kept me from throwing up. "And the blonde inside?" I was an immature asshole. I knew that and yet, I didn't give a crap in that moment.

"Which one?"

Holy shit. My entire body tensed up.

"Never mind, Dex," I hissed. I didn't want to hiss but it came so naturally, it didn't matter.

"Ritz." The tip of his nose touched my cheek. "Jealous?"

He was out of his mind if I was going to answer that question when he sounded way too pleased.

"Most these girls have been around the Club for a while," he explained like that was a reasonable excuse I'd want to friggin' hear. "It's nothin'."

Nothing. It was nothing.

It probably wasn't. That tiny logical part of me accepted that as the truth, but the other part—the hormonal one—craved castration.

God, I hoped my period wasn't coming sooner than it should.

I didn't need to sit there and stew over the fact that I'd probably be stuck facing women that he'd slept with at these sort of gatherings. I was nauseous. And an idiot. What else would I expect? I needed to get away from the reminder of where Dex's pubic piercing had been, and as I looked down at my lap, where it hadn't been.

Forcing a nod, I came to my feet slowly so that I wouldn't accidentally hit him in the face. It wasn't his fault that he had a history while I practically had a negative one. But wouldn't he at least understand that I wouldn't want to face stuff like that? Even if the girl seemed to hang on to whatever man gave her any attention.

Okay, that was rude. For all I knew she was probably a nice girl that had daddy issues I couldn't hold a flame to. I needed to quit being a jerk.

"I think I'm gonna take a dip for a little bit," I said, averting my gaze to the kids around the oval shaped pool. If I looked at Dex, he'd be able to tell that something was bothering me.

With my luck, he already did.

He grabbed onto my wrist, tugging at it. "Iris." My name came out as a grumble.

I touched the top of his head with my other hand, still unable to look at him. "It's fine. I'll be back."

Dex would make a scene if he wanted, but luckily he didn't. His grip loosened enough until I was able to slip out of it, plate in one hand, my pride wounded and clinging to the other. I threw my trash into the nearest can and went to grab my bag from the pile of stuff on one of the tables closest to the back door.

With my towel in one hand, I made my way to the pool, smiling at some of the women that I recognized with enough enthusiasm that I hopefully didn't look like a raging, jealous bitch in a bad mood.

I needed to calm down.

Chill out.

Relax—

Someone smacked my ass.

I didn't even have to turn around to see the little boy, probably around five, zipping passed me like there was no tomorrow. "Booty!" he shrieked.

I must have stood there for at least a couple minutes digesting the fact that I'd just gotten fondled by a kid who more than likely still peed in his bed at night.

And the laugh that burst out of me kind of hurt.

It was only natural that I took off running after the little turd.

"Uncle! Uncle! UNCLE!" Dean wailed at the top of his lungs, thrashing carefully enough not to kick me. Well, kick me again. He'd already got me in the stomach at least three other times but that was the risk you took when you were tickling the crap out of a little kid. Getting smacked and peed on. I'd take a smack over pee any day.

I dug my fingers into his sides even harder. "What'd you say?"

"RIS! Ris is the master!" he gasped.

"Who's the master?" I laughed, tickling him even more.

Dean thrust his head back, his blonde hair going everywhere. "You! You!"

"Are you sure?"

"Yes!" he shrieked.

"All right," I laughed, loosening my grip on his sides.

The poor little guy's face was all red but when he managed to get his breathing somewhat under control, he shot me a big, goofy smile. After chasing him around for a couple of minutes, I'd finally grabbed him and spent the next hour playing with him in the pool. I learned after dunking him in once that apparently, he had an obsession with booties in general.

What the hell do you say to that?

Nothing, that's what.

We'd gone diving for pennies in the shallow end, played Marco Polo with two other girls around his age, and then started the tickling game.

"Again?" he asked, panting.

"Boy, your mom already told you that you needed to get out." I had no clue who his dad was. I didn't even recognize his mom either but the woman kept mouthing out her thanks to me each time she'd walked by to check on Dean.

He blew out a fart. "Okay."

I squeezed his sides before leading him over to the steps. Dean stopped on the lowest one and took a quick look around. There were still about ten other people scattered throughout the pool but he didn't find whatever he was looking for because a second later, he'd thrown his arms around my neck in a hug.

"Can we play again another day?" he asked in a quiet voice.

Oh hell, he was going to make me cry. "Any time you want, buddy."

Dean squeezed me for a split second before dropping his arms. "Okay." He looked around again and took a step back, whispering, "Bye, booty girl." And then he was out of the pool and heading toward his mom while I stood there in water that reached my chest where I kneeled, smirking in his direction.

I needed to find out who was his daddy. I'm sure that would explain a lot.

Finding myself alone for the first time in an hour, I dog-paddled toward the deeper end where there were less people. But there was someone there, sitting at the edge of the pool, cross-legged and with a look on his face that was the child of amusement and affection.

Oh hell.

How could I stay mad at him for things that had been before me? Okay, well, I could if I were a complete jerk but I wasn't. My heart and brain knew that things between us were different and scary. Yet there he was, waiting for me. Brave and sure like always when I happened to run away from him.

"Hi."

"Hi, baby," he greeted me, planting both hands on the edge of the pool.

I clung to the side, holding just my head above the water. "Did you eat?"

He nodded solemnly, touching the tip of his finger to my cheek. "Looked like you were havin' fun."

"I was. Dean's funny."

"Saw him slap your ass." His finger trailed down to outline my jaw. "Think we all saw you runnin' around after him, babe." Dex kept the trail going down the column of my throat. "Everybody heard you two laughin' your asses off."

I gulped.

"Is this thing even a bikini?"

I nodded.

He didn't look like he believed me. "I like it, a lot. But maybe not so much in front of all these damn perverts." Dex scowled for a moment. "And fuckin' Amy walkin' around tellin' people you should be lookin' for a sugar daddy. I thought I was gonna have to beat the shit outta Wheels when he overheard her."

"Leave that poor man alone. Why are you always getting into fights with him?"

"Always been like that between us." A deep line formed between his brows. "Why are you defendin' him? If you saw the way he looks at you, you wouldn't be thinkin' he deserves it."

I couldn't help but roll my eyes and groan. What a drama queen. "Oh please. I didn't think you were old enough to need to get your eyes checked."

Dex's eyebrows shot up in glorified indignation. So sensitive! As always, he chose to pick up on the least important thing. "You have no fuckin' clue do you?" Dex licked his bottom lip. "You get me hard as a fuckin' rock, honey. 'Specially watchin' you with the kids for so long," he whispered. "Couldn't keep my eyes off you, neither could he."

Bloody hell.

I tipped my head into him, feeling his fingers stretch to span the side of my neck in a possessive grip. "You ready to get outta there?"

Uh, heck yeah.

"Let me get out from the stairs," I told him, tipping my head in the direction where I'd come from.

Dex frowned. "Just get out from here."

"I can't really..." I sighed, thinking of the hundreds of times I'd gotten out at the YMCA. "Because of my arm."

The frown that had been on his face was wiped clean off. Dex got into a crouch, slipping his hands under my arm pits. "I've got you, babe."

He had me up and out of the water before I could argue with him about it, both of us on our knees for a moment before he was helping me to my feet. Dex grabbed my hand and led us toward where he'd been sitting before. There were less Widows in the circle by then, a few of them drifting around the yard with their families or eating.

He must have grabbed my bag at some point when I was with Dean because he bent down to pull out my towel. "Gotta get dried off before you get sick," Dex said in a deceptively soft voice.

I looked at the sky. "It's sunny."

He stood up, holding the pale gray towel wide. "Humor me, babe."

It wasn't like I was planning on getting back into the water anyway, so I nodded and let him wrap the towel around my shoulders so tightly it made me feel like a human burrito.

In the blink of an eye, he'd snatched me up before settling onto the chair he'd been sitting in before. Dex nestled me sideways onto his lap, his arms circling me tightly. His lips pressed into my temple. It seemed normal enough to anyone looking at us, but not me. I knew Dex too well. I recognized the possessiveness of his gesture and it'd be a lie if I said that I didn't get a thrill from it.

Luther was sitting in his chair, looking around the yard. Alone.

I let my head rest against Dex's shoulder. "Sorry about earlier."

He hummed, his strong arms tightening. "I get it."

"You do?"

"Oh yeah," he said in what sounded like a growl. Was it a growl? I kind of hoped so. Rawr. "Those boys better pray I never seen 'em in the flesh."

"Don't get your panties in a wad." I snickered. "I didn't sleep with either one of them, Dex."

His breath hitched at the same time his grip jerked. "The thought of you...you with...holy fuck, I can't...I can't say it."

Dex was jealous? Jealous? Holy crap, I think my ovaries started going into overdrive as he stuttered.

"Thinkin' about you..." he cleared his throat roughly. "You don't gotta worry. I don't like shittin' where I eat."

The blank look I gave him must have been enough for him to understand that I didn't get what exactly he meant.

"Becky was a mistake, Ritz."

I watched him out of the corner of my eye. "Right."

He sighed, his hold becoming more possessive. "You were there that mornin', babe. I had too much to drink the night before."

I had been there the day afterward. The words just kind of flowed out before I could catch them. "Yeah, and you slapped her ass like it wasn't that big of a mistake."

Dex had the decency to wince. "Can't say I don't wish I could take it back. What's done is done, Ritz. I don't get shit-faced often for that reason, babe. Learned my lesson with my pa."

Uh huh. I knew he had a point though. In all the time that I'd known him, and all the nights we'd spent together, he rarely drank more than a few beers. It was definitely never enough that I thought for a second he wasn't completely in total control. The guy was usually more sober than me.

And he was right about his dad. From what I figured, the older Locke was an alcoholic and if Dex knew that... well, he wouldn't want to go down that same road. At all. For a man that seemed to value his control, falling for that stuff must have been hard to swallow.

"And that redhead? Sky?"

He groaned, bouncing his legs beneath me. Dex nipped at my earlobe. "Nothin' happened with her that night you're thinkin' about, babe. Or any other night since you walked into my shop with your sorority girl clothes."

The question that came out of my mouth wasn't intentional. I swear, but all these fears that lurked in the recesses of my brain hadn't gone off to die overnight. A part of me still needed their protection, I guess. "So why did she bring your cut to the shop and say you left it with her?"

"Who the hell knows. My best guess, she was just tryin' to be a bitch and wanted an excuse to check you out since you were stayin' with me."

This sneaky, creepy sensation flooded my stomach with some form of dread…

"You're the only girl I've ever taken home, Ritz. Guess she was jealous I shot her down the times she brought it up."

I was going to throw up and Dex's face was my target.

That's it? That's what I was going to get? A stinking confirmation of the *times* in his past that she'd wanted him to take her to his place but he hadn't?

I guess that's all I genuinely needed and wanted. Did I want details? Hell no.

Hell. No.

Okay, maybe a tiny, sadistic part of me wanted something but that was stupid. Whatever I learned could not be unlearned. No thanks.

I was strong enough to accept the role Dex had carved out for me. He'd told me more than enough times his feelings in a vague but powerful way. I needed to quit being a baby and embrace that. Accept that I knew him better than any other person. Could that be enough for me?

It had to be.

He squeezed me to him, tight. "But you don't gotta worry about anything. There's only a few things I've ever given a shit about. Everything else...is seasonal, as Ma would say." He pressed his mouth to my temple, whispering, "Then there's you."

Swallow, Iris. Breathe, Iris.

I was swallowed whole by emotion. By this terrifying thing that had to be love because it hurt as much as it soothed.

Lifting my knees up higher, I shifted on his lap until I could look him in the face better. His expression was tight. Wary. Maybe even a little worried? So, he wasn't a virgin. Not anywhere close to it, but that was a fact. Dex was who he was and I got a small part of him just for me. I wasn't going to ruin this by hanging on to the past. I didn't want it to win.

I bet no one else got to see his spare bedroom of comic stuff. Iris 1, Hookers Pre-Iris 0.

I bopped the tip of his nose with my finger. "Okay."

He blinked those dark gem colored eyes. "Yeah?"

"Yeah."

The grin that crept up over his mouth was better than Christmas morning, and the kiss he gave me afterward somehow topped that.

"I guess I should be grateful you don't have three ex-wives running around trying to take you back, huh?"

He rolled his eyes, the creases in the corners of his eyes getting more pronounced as he smiled wider. "Ya think?"

"Yeah, I don't know how to fight. If it came down to it, I'd have to use my keys on their faces or bite off a chunk of somebody's ear," I told him with a grimace.

The laugh that erupted out of him had the remaining Widows turning around to look at us like the sight of Dex laughing so loud was a UFO sighting. I swear one of the younger ones, a prospect, looked a strange mixture of scared and baffled. But I was so amused by Dex's response, I just sat there watching him with a huge, stupid smile on my face. What else would I want to look at?

Once he finally got himself under control, Dex pulled back just enough to roam his gaze over my face. I probably looked like a wet rat taco but I didn't care when the expression on his face was so calm and focused. And when the corner of his mouth did that sneaky little tip up. "You're the cutest thing I've ever seen, you know that?"

"Hey lovebird, you want a smoke?"

One of the older Widows sitting opposite of us chuckled, holding a pack of cigarettes in his weathered outstretched hand.

Dex shook his head, and the what-the-hell expression on the older man's face was priceless.

"No?" the Widowmaker asked incredulously.

"She doesn't need to be smellin' that shit."

The man frowned, his eyes switching back and forth between me and Dex. "You allergic or somethin', Rissy?"

Rissy. Ha.

I shook my head, smiling at him. "No. You can smoke here, I'll go find Dean or something."

The legs beneath me bounced again. "She had cancer, Lee. She doesn't need to be around that secondhand smoke and shit, makin' things worse."

What the hell?

I turned my gaze over to Dex slowly. He was waiting for it though. He looked like he was ready for me to challenge him, to get upset with him for spilling the beans he'd just found out about.

And it wasn't like I hadn't already caught him looking at my arm each time he had the chance, teeth gritted and all.

"What? It's true. Everybody's seen those commercials about how many people die from secondhand smoke a year. You aren't gonna be riskin' yourself," he stated solidly. Dex tipped his face closer to mine, whispering, "This is family now, Ritz. You don't have to hide shit from anybody."

Lee, the older man, choked before I had a chance to process Dex's comment. "You had cancer?" He sat back in his chair, his thin legs falling open. "Fuck me. You're a goddamn kid."

"It was a long time ago," I clarified, giving Dex a nasty look.

My comment didn't help whatever was going through Lee's head because he ended up running both hands through his hair with a huff. "Well, shit." With a quick glance over at me, he shoved the pack of cigarettes into the front pocket of his vest. "Nobody smokes around you. You hear me, Dexter? No smokin' around Rissy."

This was my family? This wiry old biker that I'd spoken to maybe one other time in my life, was making demands on my behalf?

I had to curl my lips behind my teeth to stop myself from smiling like a total idiot.

Dex let out a sharp laugh. "Got it, old man."

"Old man my ass," he snipped back mindlessly. Lee dragged his hands through his hair again with a groan. "Fuck. *Cancer?* My sister died from cancer in her ass. That shit runs in my family." He turned his attention toward me, eyes wide. "Can you get tested for that or somethin'?"

I caught Dex giving me wide, amused look out of the corner of my eyes. "Well..."

Thirty minutes later, Lee had got off his chair looking way too frazzled. I think I'd scared him. But when he promised to visit his doctor for the first time in five years, I didn't feel so bad about it. Prevention, prevention, prevention.

"You ready to head home soon?" Dex asked.

I nodded. "Yeah. Let me get dressed, and then I want to tell Luther bye."

He squeezed my shoulder and let me up, passing me the shorts and shirt I'd had on earlier.

I said goodbye to a few people that were around, especially Lee, but didn't see Dean raising hell anywhere. Damn it. I liked that kid.

Luther was standing in his kitchen with a few others when we made our way out. I wasn't that affectionate with people I didn't know well, and Luther was one of those. But I couldn't help but give him a quick side-hug when we were close enough.

"I just wanted to tell you thanks for helping to look for my dad," I told him discreetly, taking a step back into Dex's space.

He didn't seem like the type that smiled often. The rough lines of his face told a story about a man that had been in a biker club before it had gone legal. A man that had lost someone he loved because of a collective of mistakes.

But this man was also Trip's father. He had to have some of that idiot's heart.

The crinkle in his eyes confirmed that for me. "Sweetheart, I did better than that for you. My buddy spotted him yesterday."

CHAPTER THIRTY-THREE

"I don't think it's going to fit."

I wheezed, way too eager from having to keep it together at Luther's house two days before. "That's what she said!"

"Goddamn it, Ris." Slim shook his head and laughed, almost dropping the new thermal fax we'd put together just a minute before. "These arms weren't made for heavy labor, you can't be making me laugh when I'm carrying stuff."

Eyeing him out of the corner of my eye, I grabbed the other side of the machine. "Doesn't it only weigh about ten pounds?"

"Don't worry about it," he huffed. "Move that kit over a little more and it'll fit."

I pushed over the set of inks on the counter he'd been referring to and watched as he slid the thermal fax into place. It'd gotten to be a pain running back and forth to the kitchen when one of the guys needed a stencil done, so I might have been a little too excited about ordering a new machine with the intention of putting it in the front when the old one pooped out.

"You wanna break in the new machine?" Slim asked, his back to me.

"I still don't know what I'd want," I explained, referring to the tattoo.

He looked over his shoulder, fluttering those ginger-blonde eyelashes. "The dragon is waiting for you when you're ready."

He meant the dragon that blew rainbow.

"Would it hurt?" I asked him like a wimp, taking a seat on the nearest chair.

Slim bit his lip and made a face that said *yeah, it's gonna friggin' hurt.* "Well, yeah. A little." Ef me. "But you're tough. You can handle it."

The story of my life. Shit.

I found my voice. "I'm still thinking about it, Michaelangelo."

He let out a resigned sigh. "All right there, grandma."

Blake's head popped up over the divider of my reception desk and his station. There was nothing scheduled for the next hour and at the last minute, I'd asked Blake to man the desk while we set up the new equipment. His head wrinkled as he narrowed his eyes at what we were doing.

"Does Dex know you want to get a tattoo?" he asked carefully.

"He heard us talk about it the other day," I answered him vaguely. The day they all found out about my arm.

Blake barked out a laugh. It might have been the first laugh I'd heard from him in a week. He still seemed stressed out of his mind about Seth, but now that he'd told us, it had hopefully taken a weight off his shoulders.

"I don't know why the hell you're bothering, Slim. You know he's not gonna let any of us pop her cherry."

I almost, *almost* wheezed at his offhand comment as a memory of the night before—when Dex had stripped my clothes off, laid down flat on his back and pulled me over to straddle his face—swamped me. That was probably the greatest fifteen minutes of my life. And the fifteen or thirty minutes that followed after that, when he'd turned me around and made me appreciate a certain number with a six and a nine in it...well, let's just say that I was racking up fun new experiences really quickly.

Hallelujah!

"Whatever," Slim drawled. "Maybe he'll let me do this on him instead. You know I've been bugging him about letting me finish up his other side."

"The other side of his chest?" I asked.

Both of them raised their eyebrows in mock amusement but it was the damn redhead that cracked a smile. "Oh, you know all about his ink now, huh?"

Any resemblance of a smile on my face disappeared. "Shut up."

"What happened to Miss Nothing-is-Going-to-Happen?"

"I hope you forget to put sunscreen on the next time you spend any time outside," I deadpanned.

Slim shook his head with a laugh. "Uh huh. I bet you know all about those piercings now too, don't ya, Ris?"

I made a face. "Keep it up."

"Next thing you know, you're gonna have 'Property of Dex' tattooed on your back," he mused.

There was no way in hell I'd ever get a man's name tattooed on me. "Dream on, sucker."

Blake held up his hands in surrender. "I wouldn't hold it past him."

Yeah, I wouldn't either once I thought about it. That sneaky dick would do it to me in secret the first chance he got.

And yet...

Strangely, I was only about ninety percent against it.

Not that it would ever happen, especially if I couldn't even decide on a small tattoo to get first.

The swing of the door opening didn't alarm me. Blake was free and he'd help whoever came in. Being a Tuesday night, we were definitely going to be slow. Hence the reason why Dex had taken off after finishing up his three hour session to go talk to his mom about her possible divorce.

Except the first thing out of Blake's mouth was a loud and alarmed, "What the fuck?" followed by the sharp sound of something very hard hitting something equally as dense but much more frail. And then the unmistakable sound of a body dropping to the floor had us both straightening up and looking over in Blake's direction

But it wasn't my bald friend standing there. There were three men in black ski masks standing directly over where Blake had just stood. Average height men with average body builds in ski masks with angry curls to their barely visible lips.

And one had a gun raised in his hand.

And that gun was pointed in my direction.

The urge to ask what the hell was going on was right on my tongue, but I held the question back, remembering what happened to Blake just a second before.

"Take whatever is in the desk, man," Slim piped in, wrapping a hand around the edge of the chair in a white-knuckled grip.

I sucked in a breath and nodded in agreement to what he suggested, losing the words in my brain to the trembling that had taken over my hands. Where the hell was my cell phone?

The man with the gun snickered this loud, deceiving noise. "You." He pointed at me, his accent think and sounding Russian—maybe. "You are his?"

Me? Who's?

I was about to open my mouth when another ski masked man just to the right of the one holding the gun, nodded. "It's her. Fast, Fyo."

Holy fuck! Holy fuck! Holy fuck!

I looked over at Slim, thinking that we were going to fucking die. This guy was going to shoot us. My heart rate sped up about a million beats per second, shaking not just my fingers but my forearms and even my biceps at the possibility of what was about to happen. Was this because of my dad? It had to be. It had to be, damn it.

The Reapers? Oh my god. Were these some of the members? Dex had said he'd handled it but… shit!

"Please, leave my friends alone. Whatever this is about, it's only my fault," I found myself stuttering out as two of the three men advanced around the divider.

But neither of them said anything as one of the armed men reached out and grabbed the end of my ponytail in a flash, yanking it back so hard that my head snapped brutally. He yanked even harder the second time, pulling my body over the edge of the chair before repeating the pull once more. I cried out loudly, falling to the floor in a painful lump of hip bones meeting hard tile when the masked man jerked his grip.

The man pulled on my ponytail one last time, lowering himself into a squat with the Glock in hand. His lips peeled back as he brought his face to mine. "Tell your father if we don't have our money back by midnight tomorrow, we're gonna finish the job we started tonight," the man said ominously a moment before his free hand whipped out and slapped me straight across the face so hard my vision exploded in multicolored stars.

"Tell him that, you understand?" the man asked.

I was blinking, unable to really see where the hell he was at because my face felt like it'd gotten beaten with a kaleidoscope made of bricks.

The man slapped me again just as hard if not harder. "You understand me, bitch?" The cool barrel of the gun pressed straight into the middle of my forehead and it took everything in me to suppress a whimper. "Answer me!"

The one and only thing I understood clearly was that I was going to kill my father. I was going to slice him up into little pieces, serial killer style, and drop him into the ocean where his remains would never be found.

Somehow in between the quick murder plan I concocted, I muttered out a "Yes." I managed not to cry as my face throbbed in time with my heartbeat while the men backed out of the shop as quickly as they'd come in.

The slamming of the front door was what made me look up, ignoring the nipping discomfort radiating from my sides, I locked eyes with Slim. "You okay?" he asked me, eyes wide.

I nodded but I really wasn't. My head throbbed and my side hurt really friggin' bad but right then it didn't matter. I was alive and—

"Blake!" we both yelled out at the same time.

Slim vaulted across the chair while I scrambled up to my knees, my hands and body aching in protest. Blake was lying on the floor, blood pooling around his head.

Don't freak out, Iris!

Slim kneeled over Blake shaking him. The men hadn't shot him, I knew that much, but they'd probably hit him with the gun or something along those lines.

I dropped to my knees on the other side of his immobile frame, shaking his shoulder lightly. Dark eyes blinked into focus as his hands weakly reached up to start smacking Slim's persistent hands away.

"Quit it, asshole," he muttered, reaching to cover his head.

Pulling away, Slim yanked his phone out of his pocket, dialing on it so quickly I didn't get a chance to wonder if he'd be calling the cops or Dex first.

"Dex, some men were just here," he spoke a minute later. That answered my question.

I leaned over Blake, watching as he got his bearings together, face screwing up in pain. "Fuck," he moaned.

"It wasn't them. We'll wait for you at the bar. Blake needs to get sewn up," Slim said into the receiver, his eyes flashing up to mine. I could hear Dex speaking on the other end. "She's—she's—they left a message for her pops." A second later, Slim was pulling the phone away from his face, looking down at the screen, worry etching his features.

With great reluctance, he looked over at Blake and me and sighed. "Let's get over to Mayhem, bro," he instructed, hands reaching for his elbow to help him to his feet. I got up and tried my best to help Blake too, my eyes darting over to Slim.

"Are you calling the cops?"

Slim's eyes went wide as he pressed a wad of napkins he kept at his station to Blake's head. "No."

"You want me to call?" I asked him as we cautiously made our way across the street with Blake between us.

He shook his head. "We don't need the cops, Iris."

Blake didn't look over at either one of us during this time, focusing solely on holding the napkins to the cut right above his eyebrow.

"We don't need the cops?" Jesus. This was mafia stuff. Stuff that happened on television, not in my friggin' life.

"You really want to call the cops when there's a Croatian gang threatening to kill you?" he asked in a matter-of-fact voice.

I looked over at Blake who was still completely tuned out of the conversation, and I swallowed. If they had the balls to come into the shop with guns... I didn't want to know what else they were capable of.

"All right." It wasn't all right though. My face hurt a whole friggin' lot and my heart was going to burst out of my chest from how scared I still was. But Slim's observation got to me. "They were Croatian?"

He nodded wearily. "I recognized the tattoo on their hands. I had an old customer that had me cover up that gang symbol a while back."

Jesus. This was a friggin' nightmare.

And this was exactly what Sonny had said he didn't want to know—who our father owed money to besides the Reapers.

The moment we crossed the second block over to get to Mayhem, three men were already waiting for us outside. One was the guy a little older than Dex that was really attractive, and the other two I'd never seen before. One of the guys went directly for Blake, only casting me a sidelong look before he pulled bloody Blake inside the building.

"Oh, fuck," the good-looking man named Wheels muttered when he stopped right in front of me. His eyes went on a search. "They did this?"

Slim had the grace to repeat what the men had told me in a voice much more balanced than mine could have been at that moment.

Wheels groaned in response, shaking his head. "I'm so sorry, doll."

I was too. "It's all right. It could've been worse," I tried to tell him but my voice was wobbly and unpaved. Weak, weak, weak. I was fine. Totally fine. I needed to get myself together when Blake was bleeding all over the place and I ran the risk of peeing my pants in fear. When I lowered my eyes to the ground, I caught a flat black piece of metal tucked into the waistband of Wheels's jeans.

A gun. Holy shit. He had a gun. Why was I even surprised?

"Let's get you some ice," he somehow managed to suggest through gritted teeth.

The three of us headed up the stairs while Blake had gone off with the other men toward the kitchen on the first floor. Wheels and Slim seemed to be having a telepathic conversation over my head. I didn't have it in me to care enough to pay attention to what was being communicated. The throbbing of my face multiplied tenfold with any muscle twitch.

With a Ziplock bag pressed to my cheek and a bottle of water between my thighs on the couch, Wheels planted himself next to me with Slim on my other side. None of us said anything. What was there to say? Wheels didn't ask what happened or ask if I was okay. He simply sat there breathing in through his nose and out through his mouth.

"Is Blake okay?" I finally asked after grabbing another wad of paper towels to cover the bag of ice.

"Jesse'll be stitching him up now. He's fine," Wheels answered.

I sucked in a ragged breath, looking around the dimly lit room with its pool tables and bar. This mess was eating at me little by little. They didn't want to get cops involved. My dad owed those assholes enough money that they drove all the way to Austin to make a point, and I'd gotten dragged into the middle of a mess by a man that didn't love me. And they'd just held a gun to my friggin' face after hurting Blake. It was one thing to deal with Liam but a completely different one to get held up by gangsters.

Gangsters. Jesus. Two months ago my biggest worries had been paying my cell phone bill.

"Is this normal?" I asked the man weakly.

Wheels glanced at me out of the corner of his eyes, sighing. "It ain't totally uncommon."

I didn't know how I felt about his answer.

"Do you think they'll come back if they aren't paid?"

The door burst open, cracking against the wall in a loud pop of cracked sheetrock that signaled Dex's arrival. His tall, fit outline filled the doorframe. He scanned the room before landing on the three of us huddled together.

And I felt it. Everyone felt it.

The snap of his mood plummeting was like a blanketing sheet of ice—it might have even been hell freezing over from how chilling and powerful his anger was. It signified the coming of the second Ice Age. Then his eyes narrowed in on the

Ziplock bag I had pressed to my cheek. And if possible, the taut line of control in the air pulled to the point of unraveling strand by strand.

In the span of two seconds, Dex had stormed over and dropped to his knees in front of me, one hand burying itself in my hair, the other one planted on the couch cushion just to the side of my thigh.

"Iris." His tone was wild and low.

I blinked at him. "It's okay."

The hand on the couch moved up to pluck the ice pack from my grasp. Dex's face shuttered down. Something indescribable flickered in his bright blue eyes, something that was related to fury and a distant cousin to murder.

That added in with his tone, scared me. "Tell me."

"Those guys came in and hurt Blake. Then they told me that if my dad doesn't pay them back by tomorrow they'll return." And finish the job, whatever the job was—me dying or something equally brutal. Not that I would ever say that to him.

Dex's head dipped toward mine, his eyes not losing an ounce of that dark emotion that swam behind them. "What did they do?" he asked me in a whisper.

I was torn between giving him a shortened version and the truth. I figured both would somehow blow up in my face. The expression I must have made was a sign to Dex that I wasn't telling him something because his hand reached up to trace my jaw, his eyes locked on what I could imagine was the swelling red mark on my cheek.

I didn't want to worry him, but I knew if I didn't tell him what happened, he'd be more pissed about it later.

"He grabbed my hair when I was on the chair and he yanked me off of it," I told him honestly. I could see by his bulging Adam's apple that he swallowed hard. "Then he slapped me." I sucked in a breath, letting that wild fear creep over my shoulders. He pressed a gun to my face, I wanted to tell him but I couldn't convince myself to say the words out loud.

Dex's mood shot through the room like a live current. His face hardened, his posture stiffened, and I swear he even stopped breathing. Molecules in the air paused in deference to him.

But instead of saying or doing anything, he dipped his mouth to mine in a press of a gentle kiss. A lingering kiss that made me forget my head hurt because it made everything else feel better.

"I'll get one of the guys to bring you some Advil," Dex whispered, kissing my jaw with a tenderness he so rarely possessed.

It was right then that I noticed his hand was shaking—trembling. He kissed me once more right next to my eye, careful not to hurt me.

Dex took his time getting to his feet, his movement was steady and level but there was something off about him.

"Where are you going?" I asked, scanning his face. That look in his eyes wasn't right. It was savage and unruly, and it made my heart clench even harder.

"I'm gonna go take care of this," he said, eyes flashing up to the ceiling.

Oh crap. Panic nudged at me. Worry over what in the world this man was going to do if he left. In that split second, I couldn't have cared any less about what happened back at the parlor. Not if Dex was going to go do something stupid. "Charlie."

"Babe," he growled. "I need you to feel better. Sit down."

I reached out and grabbed his hand, threading my fingers through his in a tight squeeze. "Don't do anything." I tugged on his hand. "It's fine. I'm fine. Really. I'll figure something out so that they can't find me."

"You're not goin' anywhere." It was stated. Demanded. His Adam's apple bobbed with hard swallows, his muscles tightened and loosened twice.

"Dex, please," I begged him. "*Please.* If you get in trouble with the cops again..." A sob was lodged deep in my chest. "Don't go." My heart was going to shatter. It was getting julienned by what-ifs.

He ground his teeth together, a vein in his neck bulging. "Don't ask me to do nothin', Ritz." His neck tipped up in barely controlled anger. "You want me to sit back and let them get away with this shit?"

"Dex—"

"Look what they did to you!" he snapped. His eyes flashed bright. "They hurt you. They put their hands on you. I can't sit here and look at you with a clear conscience. I should've never let this happen."

Oh my God. My heart did this dumb pitter-patter-clench thing in reaction to his words, to his conviction, his loyalty...everything. I really was in love with this man. It was horrifying and amazing at the same time. I squeezed my fingers around his. "This wasn't your fault, Dex. "

He scrunched his eyes together, blowing out a breath that made his lips flutter. Ticking his neck from side to side, he rolled his shoulders. "You're my responsibility. You're mine. And I won't stay here like some punk. I think I'd do anythin' for you, believe me. But I won't do this." He pressed his lips to my forehead, his breath hot. "I gotta do this."

I could have let him go. I could have just sat back and let him seek vengeance on my behalf, but I wouldn't. Not that day, not the next or any month or year after that. Because the situation wasn't worth the possibility of losing him, and I wasn't above playing dirty. Saying what I needed to. Doing what I needed to.

"Please. Don't leave me, too," I whispered.

That statement must have hit home in his thick, stubborn skull. He blinked those brilliant blue eyes repeatedly before finally nodding slowly, as if it pained him. He lifted a hand to rest on my bad arm, pressed his lips to my forehead and let out a shuddered breath. It was a low move to say those words to him but I didn't care when he finally spoke. "Lemme get you some Advil."

I looked up at him as I sat down. Dex's eyes were fierce on Wheels's, his mouth curled cruelly. That fierce tension pumping through his veins returned with every second he communicated wordlessly with Wheels before he retreated. It wasn't until he had turned to walk out of the room that that static he seemed to radiate expanded, tripled and quadrupled.

The next thing any of us knew, he'd grabbed one of the stools at the bar and thrown it across the room, where it met a loud, messy death with the wall. Dex roared. He friggin' roared this guttural, primal noise that could have caused earthquakes. Dex tipped his face up, hands clenched at his sides. "Goddamn it!" he yelled, raking his hands through his hair.

Holy crap.

He grabbed another stool by the legs and launched it in the same direction. "Fuck!" exploded from his lungs.

With one final burst of noise, he disappeared through the door. Just like that.

And for some not so strange reason, I trusted him enough to not assume he'd lied to me.

"That went better than I expected," Slim sighed.

I pressed the ice pack to my face again and reached out with my free hand to grab his fingers. "I'm sorry about all of this."

I was sorry. But more than anything, in that moment, I was mainly really pissed off.

What in the hell was wrong with my dad? What kind of a selfish asshole would put other people at risk for his mess? And why in the universe would I have to be related to him? I knew it was unfair and maybe even a little mean but what he was doing eclipsed any of my thoughts. There was no way he didn't know what the friggin' Russians or Romanians or Croatians were capable of. This gang and mafia crap was on a level reserved for the books I read and movies I watched.

I was pissed. And now that even more people that I cared about had gotten involved, this felt all the more like my own personal battle. My own mess to fix. Obviously there was no way in hell those jerks would get their money the next day but if I left, nothing would happen, right?

It was a long shot but it was the only hope I had.

Slim tugged at my hand, squeezing the fingers he held. "It's not your fault."

"It is." I told him with a sigh. I felt terrible.

I needed to fix this.

It was Wheels that told me exactly what I needed to do. "You still don't know where Curt is?" he asked.

I did—now, at least. Luther's friend had found him blocks from the house we lived in back... back before everything had gone to hell when I was a kid.

And I knew what I needed to do, regardless of whether or not I'd told both Luther and Dex that I'd let them handle it. Handle bringing him in, that is. The moment those assholes had come into Pins, this had become my problem. Not anyone else's.

Not even Sonny's.

Sonny. *Crap.* My fingers flexed nervously as I reached into my back pocket to pull out my phone. Later on, I wouldn't even remember tapping on his speed dial button. All I was aware of in that moment was that I had to be the one to call my brother and tell him. This wouldn't fix the trust issues between us but it was a start, I hoped.

I didn't even let him finish greeting me before I cut him off. The event and my recent decision taking the front of my thoughts by storm. He had to know. "Son, I have to go back home."

"We're here, baby."

I felt the hand on my thigh pressuring me back to life, and I yawned. It had to have been close to three in the morning by the time Dex was pulling Luther's pick-up into the driveway. Despite the nap I took at Mayhem, I was exhausted—absolutely exhausted. I also had a feeling that they'd given me some sort of sleep aid instead of Advil, but I wasn't sure and I didn't care.

After Dex's meltdown, I'd only seen him in passing twice at the bar. He'd come back up the stairs with Blake in tow. Poor Blake who had to get a handful of stitches in his eyebrow. I apologized to him about a dozen times but he waved me off, and left the bar after giving me a hug that hopefully said he wasn't holding the incident at Pins against me. Dex, on the other hand, had watched me with a tight jaw, his fists clenched at his sides until he'd bowed over to kiss the top of my head. His nostrils had flared and the corded veins in his neck had been the only sign that he was on the edge.

The second time I saw him had been when he'd been heading down the stairs of the bar. I knew he was mad and even though all I really wanted was to climb onto him and ask for a hug, the distance was probably good for both of us. I needed to figure out how the hell I was getting to Florida, and he needed to chill out.

Worry and fear had burrowed itself into me, and I was trying my best to talk myself out of it. I wasn't completely successful either. As long as I could leave Austin until this mess got sorted out, no one that I cared about would get hurt.

At least that's what I hoped more than anything.

And it was that argument that finally lassoed my half-brother into agreeing with me that I should try to find our dad. With supervision, he'd insisted, but I'd never agreed. Sonny realized, just like I did, that this mess had just turned into a disaster. A disaster that he'd tried to contain, but now that he was so far away, it fell on my shoulders.

It wouldn't be the first time responsibility was on me, and it certainly wouldn't be the last. The fifteen minute conversation had worn me down to the bone. If anything, it'd also made me just that much more angry, too.

Drained, pissed, and sore, I'd napped on the couch and eaten the food that one of the younger guys had brought me. Someone kept me supplied with ice packs for the first couple of hours. Even after that, I kept having people I'd met briefly in the past ask if I needed anything. My new friend Lee had come up at some point and rubbed the top of my head before sitting on the couch next to me and going straight into a story about how weird it was going to be getting his "goods" fondled at the doctor's office.

But what I needed the most was for my fingers to quit shaking. The pain on my face I could deal with, but that hard printed memory of the gun on my forehead was semi-permanent by then.

Slim and Blake left about an hour after the incident with plans on going home. Dex had decided to close down shop for the time being. Not that I could blame him though I felt even worse that they needed to reschedule appointments because of my mess. I didn't want to have a repeat of that afternoon anytime soon.

Or ever.

I hadn't even woken up from my nap until Dex had carried me halfway out of Mayhem. He'd brought the familiar big truck around and carried me into the passenger seat, going as far as to buckle me in. Later on, I could worry about where he'd left his bike, and remember to thank Luther for loaning out his truck again. Riding on the back of his Dyna hadn't exactly sounded like an appealing idea in that moment. No sooner had he slipped into the driver seat than he was fishing my hand off my lap and pulling it onto his, linking our fingers together.

He opened the passenger door once we parked outside out of his house. Big hands undid the seatbelt before pulling me into his broad build.

"I can walk, Dex," I told him, pressing my forehead to his shoulder.

He made a noise in his throat. "Give me this, Ritz," he said hoarsely before I was up in his arms with my head nestled right into his neck as we went inside.

He didn't stop in the living room or in the kitchen. Dex didn't drop me off at the bathroom to get cleaned up. Instead, he weaved our way into the master bedroom, setting me down on my feet as he toed off his boots and I did the same to my own shoes.

He was wordless, unsteady. His hands reached for the hem of my blouse, slowly tugging it upward until it was thrown into a corner. Dex's breathing got heavier as he paused, hands at his sides.

In a bold move, I did the same with his shirt, watching his eyes closely. "What's wrong?" I whispered.

"Nothin'." He shook his head, those blue eyes screwed shut. "Just...goddamn it, Ritz!" He slammed the palms of his hands against the wall on the sides of me. Those thick, muscled arms bunched and strained with an emotion I doubted that he completely understood. "Fuck," he choked out, dipping his forehead to mine. "You have no clue...no clue..."

He was right. I didn't have any idea what he was thinking, what was turning a knife into his spine; but if it was fear, anger, disappointment, or one of a million other emotions, they were all rooted back to me. And it was only me that could help him.

I glanced down at the column of his throat, at the tip of Uriel's red tentacle following the curve down to the multicolored body circling the ring through Dex's nipple. Hard abs and a trail of dark hair disappeared into the band of his underwear, which then melted into his jeans.

My hands shook as they planted themselves on his ribs, on Uriel, and slid down all that soft skin, rippled muscles and obliques, before pausing at the button of his jeans. I plucked at it like an old pro, my heart beating a quick nervous beat. I tagged the zipper, and slipped my fingers into the band of his underwear. Down, down, down they went. Everything. Jeans and boxers went over hard thighs. I dropped to my knees and kissed the Widowmakers tattoo inked on his thigh, ignoring the long bobbing muscle aimed right at me.

I could do this. I could do it.

The moment he kicked his clothes to the side, I tipped my face up to kiss the diagonal line of muscle over his hip after helping him take off his thick socks. The tiny round studs at the base of his pink cock were right there, right next to my face, as the sleek muscle pointed straight at the wall.

"Babe," Dex hissed.

My shaky hand wrapped around his meaty shaft, squeezing the hard length. I watched his face as I licked a circle around the broad tip of his crown just like he'd shown me days before. He tasted salty, musky, and so, so good. The groan that tore out of his throat when I wrapped my lips around the thick head was like an aphrodisiac, reaching right between my legs.

God, he was thick. My hand could barely wrap around him completely as I licked a circle in the deep ridge between his head and shaft. Over and over, I dragged my tongue into the crevice, letting the low sounds coming from Dex's throat fuel me.

His hand slipped around the back of my head, holding me in place. Those blue eyes were hard and heavy above a tight mouth. "Wrap your mouth...oh...*oh*...fuck, just...*ah*...just like that...suck it...suck...*mother fuck...*"

He only gave me the chance to suck the pink tip with all the pressure my lips could vacuum twice before he jerked out of my mouth abruptly and pulled me to stand.

"Baby," he murmured, slanting his mouth over mine immediately afterward.

The kiss was emotion and ownership all wrapped into one. His tongue was raspy and warm. I was so involved in his lips and the heat of his hands on the middle of my back, I barely noticed when he undid my bra, or when his thumbs flicked at the button of my pants and shoved my underwear down to my knees. His bare feet brushed my legs as he helped me get my bottoms completely off.

He didn't stop for a second while pulling my bra off my arms, and I didn't let myself stew on the monumental steps we were taking. He didn't hesitate when his fingertips found the peaks of my breasts, circling his thumbs until they pebbled. Dex's groin pressed against my stomach, a thick pipe of warmth that wrote erotic dreams into my skin.

"Need you," he panted against my mouth. Not *this.* He didn't need *this*, he needed *me.* And that's what made a world of difference.

This was it.

This was it.

I raised my leg without any suggestion, hooking it over his hip in a move that made me feel incredibly vulnerable. What if this didn't live up to his expectations?

The worry was forgotten a second later when Dex grabbed the back of my thigh in a firm hold. With his other hand, he slid it from my breast down, down, down until he slipped those long, artistic fingers over my slit. Fingertips dipped between my damp lips, stroking the tiny little button hidden between them.

I cried out.

The cry spurred those miraculous fingertips to move from my clit until they were sinking inside me, slowly. Two thick fingers stretched the tight tissues, earning a stifled breath from Dex.

"Shit, Ritz," he hissed.

He pulled his fingers nearly all the way out before pushing back in. Dex thrust in and out, over and over again, scissoring then plunging until I was soaking wet, until his hand was drenched with my excitement, my lips spread tight around his digits

"Never wanted anything the way I want you," he groaned into my skin. "Feels like I'm gonna die if I don't have your hot little pussy wrapped around my cock, baby."

Then, he stopped. Just like that, he stopped. Dex pulled his fingers out slowly, trailing over to the back of my thigh. He hoisted me up to brace my back to the wall. Dex's grip flexed over my ass as he brought his pelvis against mine. The long column of his erection rest between my slit.

God, he was so warm, and his muscles were so firm...

Dex edged his hand from my ass up my spine as he laid a soft kiss on my shoulder. He rolled his hips so that the tip of his cock nudged up my stomach, all hard and hot and insistent. The breath that fanned my neck was choppy.

"Honey." He ground his pelvis into me, the smooth globes of his balls brushed my cleft. "I can't—"

I kissed him to cut him off. My arms wound their way around Dex's neck, fusing our mouths together. "Dex."

He pulled away only to bite my chin, his breathing so heavy I worried that he'd pass out, or in his case, spontaneously combust from whatever dozens of emotions were hammering through his system. "Please. I need—"

Me.

I snuck my hand between our bodies to grasp his thick erection. Adrenaline and nerves pumped through my veins as I tried to line him up where he belonged, the thick tip nudging too high, then too low until finally, *finally*, he was there. The big mushroom head dipped the barest inch inside, more like a friendly kiss than anything.

Dex slid an arm under my ass to hold my weight, the other one crossing my back diagonally so that his palm cupped my shoulder, bringing our chests flush. "Here, Ritz?" he asked in a husky voice, sinking an inch deeper into me. The fingers on my shoulder tightened.

The choice was mine.

He could do this, here in his bathroom—not even in the shower—or... somewhere else. His bedroom. Wherever. I knew Dex well enough that I was sure if I told him I wanted to have him taking my virginity officially in a different place, that he'd do it.

But I didn't care. Not at all. It—me—I was his. Here. In his bedroom. On the couch. It didn't matter.

My answer was crafted into a nip at the column of his throat right by Uriel.

Dex groaned, thrusting what felt like half of his stiff cock into me so slowly, so precisely, it only felt uncomfortable as he went where no man had gone before. "Jesus fuckin' Christ," he hissed, loud, kissing my neck with more than just his tongue and lips.

"Okay?" I asked him, which seemed ridiculous when he looked up at me with a pained expression.

His dark blue eyes were heavy, the rough line of his jaw locked. He flexed his hips, letting himself sink in another inch. "You're perfect, honey. So goddamn perfect." His hips withdrew almost completely before he pushed back in with a care and a patience he usually didn't possess. It was only a small, breathless huff that gave away the battle going on beneath his skin.

Breathing in and out of my mouth, I tried to relax around him, feeling that huge, blunt dick split me around its solid shape. With two more planned, short thrusts, Dex had filled me to the hilt. I could feel the cool metal of his piercing grazing me. It wasn't painful exactly, more strange than anything as he stood there completely still while I flexed my inner muscles around him, experimentally, earning a rough grunt.

"Don't," he hissed through clenched teeth.

I stopped and kissed his throat. "Tell me if I do something wrong," I whispered, keeping myself still.

Dex sighed, tilting his mouth down to kiss me sweetly. "It feels like you're wringin' the cum right outta my cock when you do that."

I guess that sounded like a good thing. Right?

Instinct struck and I did it again. Dex let out a low noise that went straight to the bundle of nerves between my legs. "Baby," he moaned, hiking me up higher in his arms.

Dex tilted away from me just a few inches, letting my shoulders settle back against the wall as he thrust in and out, one inch, two inches, three... That pretty pink cock impaling me each time.

A slow, steady withdrawal and push between my legs that left me achy and needy, the tight discomfort dissipating with each thrust. He bit at my lips, alternating between sucking one and then the other as he moved. Soon, too soon, the awkward feeling had practically disappeared until something hot and wonderful clenched my belly.

"Dex," I gasped. "Please."

The hand on my shoulder squeezed as he bit my earlobe, tilting his hips at even more of an angle. The movement was more of a low bounce, picking me up and down over him, never more than a couple inches at a time. But the angle, holy crap.

Holy friggin' crap.

The angle made the tiny studs at the base of his cock grind against my clit. Every. Single. Time. Rub, rub, rub.

I threw my head back against the wall and gasped out his name.

"Fuck...fuck...baby..." he hissed through clenched teeth. His hips pumped faster, still an inch, two inches, three inches. The long shaft stayed buried in me, stretching me around his thick cock. "Too good."

Heat burst between my legs, shooting up my spine, down my legs as his piercing hit my clit roughly over and over again.

Then, all of my nerves went galactic. My entire body exploded with electricity and fireworks that couldn't be described, blood pounded through my ears and I went deaf.

I didn't hear the loud choke that squeezed from Dex's throat, or the grunts that he pitched as his thrusts turned frantic, jerky. I didn't see his wild eyes turn down to look at where we were joined, to see him lose his mind as he watched his length disappear. I didn't hear the sound of pleasure that poured from him as he came, warmth and wetness flooding me.

Dex pumped his hips slowly, his breaths hard and gasping as he shifted our combined weight again to press my back securely against the wall. His chest was flat to mine, all sweaty and panting. I squeezed my legs around his hips, his cock jerking inside of me. I rested my face to the side of his as I caught my breath.

The hand on my shoulder made a slippery slide up and down my ribs, coming to rest on the nape of my neck. From the waist up, we were wrapped up in each other, and if I could, I'm sure I could have felt the pounding of his heart on my own skin.

I took a deep breath and pressed my lips to his Adam's apple. "Can we do that again soon?"

A chuckle rose up from him, loose and happy, as he rubbed the side of his stubbled face against mine. "You've gotta be the best thing I never knew I wanted."

Oh man.

I was suddenly way too glad that he couldn't see the huge smile that overwhelmed my face. Telling him that he was sweet didn't seem like something he'd like to hear, so I kept my mouth shut and kissed the line of his jaw instead. I wanted to tell him that he was the best thing I never thought I'd have but I kept that to myself. It felt like too much right then.

Too much emotion for one day.

"That wasn't the way I planned for this to go," he panted.

"It's okay." I kissed his chin. "I'm not going anywhere." Permanently at least, my brain chose to remind me.

"Fuck yeah." Dex nipped at my ear once more. "Gotta put you down," he said in a way that sounded apologetic. "You made me cum like a freight train, baby. It's a miracle I haven't dropped you yet."

He was right, at least I expected he was after he'd put me down on my feet and pulled out, a gush of liquid seeped out, wetting my inner thighs. Realization slammed into me.

Shit. Shit!

Sweat beaded on my forehead, my temples. "Dex, I'm not on any birth control."

He made a humming noise as he brought his hands up to cup my face with those darkened, tattooed hands. He stroked the top of my head. "I'm fuckin' up all kinds of shit tonight. I'm sorry, baby. Didn't even think about it." He wrapped my hair around his fist, bright blue eyes intent on my own. "I've always been careful. You don't got anything to worry about," Dex promised.

Nothing to worry about. Oh bloody hell.

There were very few things I remembered about the semester of health class that I took, but the safe sex class was recorded in there. *Safe sex,* they'd stressed. *You don't want to end up pregnant or taking meds the rest of your life.*

"Baby." He pulled on my hair. "Nothin' to worry about. I've never…" Dex looked awkward for a moment, because *yeah*, I definitely wanted to hear about him having sex with other people right after he was with me. Not. "You're the only one. Ever. We'll figure out the rest, all right?"

Well, it was done and over with. My period was coming in no time, so my chances of ovulating...I should be fine. Plus, I was 'the only one.' He wouldn't lie to me about something so personal. The calm look on Dex's face was my reassurance that things would be okay. At least this something would be okay, maybe not everything in general.

I nodded into his throat. "I know."

He nodded right back, smiling just a little as he swept a palm down my ass to cup it. "Good." With a soft sigh, Dex kissed my chin. "Shower time."

I rubbed my thighs together, the sticky fluid coating skin. "Good idea."

Dex was silent as he turned on the water, leading me into the large tub. Wide, suspecting eyes glanced over the deep, colorful bruises on the hip I'd landed on.

He mumbled something in a harsh voice but didn't say anything else, and he didn't touch the injured parts of my body. Dex washed my hair and back with slow, gentle, sudsy hands. His palm skimmed over the scarring of my arm, but he didn't pay too much attention to it. The only indication he gave that there was something wrong was the nerve that popped continuously under his eye.

I waited next to him while he rinsed off, running my eyes over the parts of Uriel that looped on his back. So much even, smooth skin everywhere. I couldn't stop looking him over. His wide, muscled back. Narrow hips. The meaty shaft of his dick laying semi-hard on his thigh. I took the soap from him and lathered my hands, rubbing over the colorful and not so colorful parts of his chest. Over the dark and not-so-dark colors of both his arms.

Dex just stood there, outstretched limbs letting me get to him. Thighs. Knees. Calves. Even his feet. I flashed him smiles every time I got to a different body part, smiles he returned to me genuinely.

I didn't have any words left by that point, or even after he helped me dry off.

A few moments later, he'd led me back to his bedroom and deposited himself on the edge of his bed—naked—draping me over his lap casually. One arm went around my back and the other faced palm down on my thigh. Up and down he stroked the bare skin.

Dex didn't talk as he kissed my forehead and my nose so gently it worried me. He didn't say anything when I winced after he'd accidentally grabbed my bad hip. And he didn't say a vowel or a consonant when he tried to brush a hand through my hair.

But when he tilted my face up to his, eyes intense on mine, my strength screamed its end.

"You okay, babe?" he whispered, and I knew he wasn't talking about what we'd just done in the bathroom.

My nod was reluctant.

Dex pressed his cheek to my forehead. "That's my girl." His voice was a quiver.

That undesirable fear from earlier crept over my bare skin. I'd been told my entire life that I was worth something. That I mattered. Between *yia-yia* and Sonny, the two had never let me feel like I was worth anything less than gold. And I valued myself, I did. While I wasn't talented, a genius, or really good at anything, I was smart enough and hard-working enough to make up for my other weaknesses.

But in that moment, with the weight of the mess my father had brought down into my life, and the acceptance that it had all cascaded into other people's lives, I suddenly felt unsure. I'd known people who had left others for less.

All Dex had done was help me from... well, nearly from the beginning. And everyone else before Dex that had cared about me had done the same and more.

Something that resembled fear gripped my neck in an intangible hold. "I'm so sorry." The words were choked from a place in me that I usually stashed all of my regrets and worries. All I did was cause Dex headaches. Make him lose money. Time. Patience and credibility. He was under no obligation to put up with my shit. "I'm such a pain in the ass."

His entire body tensed. "Iris."

I shifted to set my cheek against his. "You know my mom knew she had growths before she went to the doctor? She waited because we were always broke. Because I was sick and she had to pay my medical bills."

It was a miracle I wasn't sobbing as I spilled these things I shoved deep in me. "And my poor *yia-yia* had to sell her house so that we wouldn't go bankrupt when I got sick again. I had to come move in with Sonny because I was broke. And now you and the guys are suffering through all of this shit because of me."

Guilt, guilt, guilty, guilt, guilt.

"I'm so friggin' sorry, Dex. I never wanted any of this. I don't want any of you guys to get hurt. I don't even want to see my friggin' dad. Or get a fucking gun put up to my face. I don't—I don't—" It took every single inch of determination I had inside of my gut to keep from letting the broken words turn into a fractured cry. "I need to go back home to look for my dad."

The hand on top of my thigh stiffened, squeezing the lean muscle so hard it hurt. In a flash, Dex had flipped us over so that I was on my back and he was on his hands and knees above me, looking pretty murderous. Those cobalt colored eyes flashed angrily. "No."

"I have to."

He shook his head, staring hard. "No." He blinked. "Fuck no."

"Dex," I whispered, my voice sounding so much more pathetic than I wanted it to. "It's my responsibility. This needs to be over."

"He's there, Ritz, you heard Lu, but you're not goin' back." he insisted. "'Specially not without me."

It was my turn to blink in disbelief. "You'll go with me?"

"Yeah." Dex dropped his face down to catch my bottom lip in his, and if it wouldn't have been for that touch, I wouldn't have felt the way his hands trembled on my cheeks. The way his entire body shook.

I nodded at him, pulled between the urge to burst into tears at feeling so overwhelmed and the need to throw myself at him to feel the warm reassurance only he was capable of. Could I do it by myself? Yes. But did I want to? No.

I was in love with this guy. Completely, terrifyingly in love with him. And life suddenly seemed so short again. Would I want to live the rest of my life hiding behind my dad's shadow? Living out his mistakes? No. Absolutely not.

Dex must have seen something on my face that had him dropping his weight down on me. That warm naked body spread over my own nude one, his legs bracketed on either sides of mine, his arms caging me in. *Ohmigod,* Dexter Locke was naked on top of me. His nice, clean groin was resting on my stomach.

Brain dead. I was brain dead.

"You aren't leavin' alone," Dex demanded.

Oh hell. "I won't."

Holding his weight on one bent arm, he cupped the side of my face. "You took ten years off my life today, baby," Dex said.

Oh man.

"Thought I was gonna have to go to jail for the rest of my life, babe," he whispered. His hand cupped my calf, demanding and hot. "We're gonna find that piece of shit you and Son got cursed with and we're gonna get this taken care of. You and me. Understand?"

Did I understand? Oh yes. I nodded.

Those brilliant blue eyes locked on mine. He breathed, "I don't know what the fuck I'd do if somethin' happened to you." Dex squeezed my kneecaps. "Scared the livin' shit outta me, and I'm gonna make sure your pa knows what that feels like."

A tremble engulfed every inch of my skin. It was slow but powerful, eating up my muscles and nerves like it was famished. The moment, his proclamation, all seemed like a dream. Like something that would have happened to the Iris Taylor I could have been in an alternate universe, if life had gone the way it was supposed to.

Did I care he was threatening my dad? In that moment, not really. I chose to ignore it because I wanted to be the one to hurt that selfish jerk.

Dex's hands held me firmly. One hand slipped up to cup my cheek tenderly as he pressed his forehead to my temple. "I don't ever wanna feel that way again."

I think my heart cracked a little right then.

"I'm okay," I whispered, placing my hand over the one he had high on my thigh. I wanted to tell him that I'd never been that scared either but I couldn't. Not when Dex was opening up and telling me about his own fear. He wasn't scared of anything. Not roaches, the dark, clowns, scary movies, the possibility of getting hurt. Nothing.

The fact that he'd been scared for me speared right through my gut.

He tipped his head to touch his lips to mine. "I'll never let anything happen to you," he murmured as his thumb brushed over my cheekbone. When I didn't say anything in response, mainly because I was so wrapped up in his touch, he kissed the side of my mouth.

I, better than anyone, knew how unsteady life could be, but that was the beauty of it if you recognized the potential ahead of you. I had to appreciate the best things, the good man who intended to protect me, because it was real and present. Feminism be damned. I'd shouldered enough burdens alone, and let me tell you, it's not easy.

Every nerve in my body was prepped for tears and choking emotions but I wrangled them in. I'd always considered myself strong, but on Dex's lap with his arms around me despite the day I had, I felt invincible. I didn't need tears. So I told him the truth that had grown roots right into the untilled section of my chest. Clear, concise, precise. "I know. I trust you."

The movement of his hand faltered on my back. "Iris," he whispered to my temple, his voice sounding like a croak.

This man. My heart swelled in a way that wasn't natural.

I squeezed my arms around the warmth cage of his ribs and mouthed the words I wouldn't let out of my mouth into his shirt.

Three little words that held all the power in the world.

CHAPTER THIRTY-FOUR

"You want me to drive?"

I glanced at Dex sitting there, his wrist thrown loosely over the steering wheel. We'd been in Luther's truck for the last six hours and besides three pit stops, the old man—he wasn't amused when I called him that out loud—had been driving straight. He was like a man on a mission, insulting my slow driving skills the first time I'd asked him if he wanted to trade positions. His answer now, like it'd been before was the same. "I'm good."

I could rattle off plenty of things that were more than good about him but him driving for so long wasn't one of them.

The ache between my legs was a friendly reminder of one of them. As was the memory of his colored skin, and those little round studs on his Little Dexter, against me.

Ugh. It was all so hot, everything about him. My neck went warm.

"You all right over there?" he asked.

The jerk had a knowing little smile on his face. When he woke me up that morning, nearly spread out over my back, a hairy thigh tangled with mine, he'd been all hooded eyes and smug smiles. He'd ground his stiff erection against my butt in a slow circle.

And what did I do? I let him. So sue me. Even a recently former virgin knew when she was in the presence of a pretty penis. A long, perfectly thick penis.

Hell. What in the world was wrong with me? I'd gone from thinking about sex and having raging hormones right around the time of my period, to being unable to think about anything else besides all things naked-Dex related.

He'd drugged me. That had to be it.

Okay, not really, but still. That *thing* was practically magical.

Unfortunately, the slow morning had come crashing down too quickly when his cell phone started ringing the moment he'd eased himself over me on his hands and knees. It was Luther. And it was Luther's offer to let us borrow his truck that had Dex and I packing up our stuff to head out.

Which was how we ended up halfway to Dade county with Dex hogging the steering wheel and being an all-knowing jerk.

"I'm fine," I answered, resting my back into the corner of the truck's seat and door. "You're sure you're not too tired to drive?"

He flicked those blue eyes over, his mouth flat. "I'm ready to get outta here."

In ten hours. "Okay," I told him with a shrug.

Dex let out a long deep breath, reaching across the console to grip my thigh. "Wanna get this shit over with, Ritz."

I'd tried my best not to worry about this mess over the course of the last few hours. Going to bed after crying all over Dex had been distracting, and I'd managed to fall asleep pretty quickly but that hadn't meant that I'd been in the clear. I'd woken up at least four times over the night, sweating, nervous, battling nightmare after nightmare of what had happened at the shop. Two out of those times, I'd looked over my shoulder to find Dex wide awake, too.

Whether he'd been asleep or if I'd tossed and turned and made enough noises to wake him up, I didn't know for sure. I didn't ask either. I had slipped my fingers close to his once, and he'd rubbed my back until I fell asleep again the second time. Chances were, he'd probably slept less than me.

And I could only imagine what his own thoughts had been.

Because I knew what I'd been thinking of when I gave myself the chance to. What if...

What if my dad didn't have the money?

We were driving out to Florida to find him, but what then? What would we do if he only had ten bucks to his name?

The reality of it was...I'd make him figure it out. The possibilities were endless, and my ruthlessness was as well. I sure as heck wasn't going back to Austin until this crap was resolved. When I accepted the possibility that he was broke, I thought of Blake passed out and bleeding on Pins' floor. And that's what kept me going. But...

I would always be a worry-wart at heart.

"What do you think the chances are that he has any money?" I asked Dex without even thinking about it.

The sigh he responded with wasn't exactly reassuring. "Pretty slim more than likely, babe."

Not what I wanted to hear. "What should I do if that's the case?"

"We'll figure it out," he said putting emphasis on the first word. "Depends on the situation."

Well. While that wasn't exactly reassuring, at least I could mentally prepare myself for the truth. I wondered if we dragged Curt Taylor back, whether the gang would call it even. Or maybe… "Know anyone in the black market? I'm sure he could live without a kidney, gallbladder, or lung if he needs to," I said, scared to investigate whether or not I was serious. Something told me I was.

Dex chuckled, squeezing my thigh. "Like the way you think, Ritz."

"You think that makes me a bad person? That I'm not completely opposed to doing something extreme to get this mess straightened out?" It suddenly worried me how nonchalant I was being about the whole thing. Could I really let my dad do something like that? I didn't feel guilty. Not in the least.

"No." He paused for a moment, clearing his throat. "You can't expect to care about somebody that hasn't cared about you, babe. It's only natural. Doesn't help that he's a fuckin' moron on top of bein' a piece of shit. I think you've wasted enough of yourself on him."

I didn't say anything as I thought over his words. Because he was right. Every time the old man made an appearance, he was like a harbinger of doom. The man was a human wrecking ball with no regard for others. And it was about time that I let him go completely. "You're right."

"Sure am," Dex agreed with a small snort.

I groaned and leaned back into the seat, trying to relax. To ease myself out of this unholy grip that strained my emotions. "After he sells a few organs, maybe I can finally have a nice, normal life."

Dex shot me a long side glance, his mouth twitching. "Baby, I don't know what you think normal is but you're gonna have a nice, safe life as soon as we get him. All right? You can bet on it." His tone was low, gravelly. He was mad, mad for me—in my honor, and my insides recognized it and thrived on his emotion.

I nodded. "All I want is just to not worry about things for a while." For as long as I could remember it'd been my health, my mom, my health again, *yia-yia*, raising Will, bills, my lack of employment, and now all of this. I'd skipped the part where some people went to school and focused on that. Where kids got to be kids instead of having to sit through radiation treatments and funeral services.

I wasn't complaining. I wouldn't. But... something so little wasn't much to ask for, right?

"Right now, I'd give my left bicep for my only worry to be whether or not to tell you that I ordered the wrong ink." I sighed.

He groaned, a smile cracking one side of his cheek and mouth. "Shit like that's under appreciated, ain't it?" he asked, letting his fingers drift a little higher up my thigh.

"Everyone takes things for granted, little things, big things—everything."

Dex made a humming noise of agreement. "I learned my lesson in jail. You have any idea how much I missed my smokes when I was locked up? Drivin' around? Takin' a fuckin' shower without worryin' about gettin' jumped?"

And if by 'jumped' he meant...

Not going there. No, siree. Especially not when I was pretty positive he was trying to connect with me and not scar me for life.

"Learned some patience in there, so I guess I shouldn't complain."

And...it was a miracle I wasn't drinking, otherwise I would have spit liquid all over the dash. "You? *Patient?*"

Dex huffed. "Yeah."

Cue my snort. A snort that ripped the serious silence we'd wrapped ourselves in. "I don't even want to know what you were like before twenty-five if you think you can say the 'p' word with a straight face."

The sideways look he gave me was a guilty one. He'd definitely been a huge pain in the ass in his younger days. D-e-f-i-n-i-t-e-l-y.

I put up both my hands in praise. "Thank heavens I met you as an old man." I winked at him.

Weird.

Driving through the part of town I'd grown up in was just plain...weird. Strange. I'd driven down these streets a million times throughout my life. The very last time had been three months ago when I had accepted the fact that my unemployed butt was out of options—I was going to have to move in with Sonny since I'd been so adamant about not going with Lanie to Ohio. Driving to the cemetery where Mom and yia-yia were buried had been my official goodbye. At that time, I hadn't thought I'd ever make it back to Florida. What would be the point? I had no ties left there besides memories that were as good as they were bad.

Yet, here I was, in a vehicle with a man I would have never been capable of fabricating even in my dreams. In a place where I should have felt at home, but didn't any longer.

"This is all too weird," I whispered as we passed the convenience store I used to always pump gas at.

He watched me wearily. After the last half a million hours in the car, of which he drove all, I couldn't blame him for being darn near exhausted. I hadn't napped either but adrenaline and nerves had kept me going. My dad was here somewhere. Some seedy little place with the words Motor Inn at the end.

But we'd agreed to get some sleep before going hunting for the cause of all the recent hell.

"You all right?" he asked in a rough, tired voice.

"Yeah." We passed by the daycare I'd worked at immediately after finishing my last round of radiation. God, this place depressed me. "This is all just messing with my head. I should be excited to be here, but I'm not. I just want to go back to Austin."

Dex nodded severely. "Nothin' wrong with that, babe. Kinda relieved I'm not gonna have to drag you back home with me."

I narrowed my eyes. "Drag me?"

"Yeah. Drag you." He huffed. "You ain't stayin' here even if you wanted." Dex paused and glanced over in my direction, those dark blue orbs intent. "I lived in Dallas and I missed Austin every day, even if I didn't miss all the Club bullshit and drama. Don't wanna give you a reason to miss this dump."

This wasn't a dump but I wasn't going to argue that point with him. I knew what he was trying to do. Talk me out of any residual love I had for Tamarac and Ft. Lauderdale. The sneaky son of a gun.

I couldn't help but laugh more to myself than at him. I'd let him slide, so instead I focused in on what he said about the Widows. "Dex? Why are you even in the club if you don't really care about it? I mean, I know you do all their accounting crap and other stuff with them but I don't think you really...how can I say this? Enjoy being in it, I guess?"

He lifted a hand and tapped his fingers over his lips in a thoughtful gesture. "Tradition, babe. I'm a legacy. And by the time I got out of county, Lu had already cleaned shit up. Half the Widows were gone, and..." he paused and dropped his hand. His lips pursed in what I'd later on figure was a disbelieving and possibly embarrassed gesture. "Luther had been the only one to offer to help me out once I got back from Dallas, so I kinda owed it to him, ya know?"

There it was. That fierce loyalty. He didn't have a clue how that was the most attractive thing about him. It trumped his face, his ink, his body, everything. Dex Locke was true. He was grounded.

And, I really was in love with him.

"He signed Pins' first lease and loaned me the money without even thinkin' about it. Nobody else even offered besides Blake helpin' with the shop's license. I help out the Club mainly because of Lu."

"That was really nice of him."

"He's the best man I've ever known. Most people don't see all the good in him because he's so serious, you know. But Lu's got his shit together and most of the time, he knows what he's talkin' about. Can't help but listen to him when he says somethin'. *Keep your shop separate from the club. Keep your nose clean. Lock that sweet girl down before you regret that shit.* So I pay attention. "

I couldn't help but grin to myself when he touched the side of my thigh with his last statement. I reached out to touch the side of his thigh in return. The corner of his mouth tipped up at the contact.

"As long as he's in, I'm in. I like mindin' my own business and he gets that. I'm there when I'm there, and they got enough members to do whatever else I don't wanna. Works out all right every way around."

Even imagining someone trying to get him to do something that he didn't want to, seemed ridiculous. Preposterous. And that thought made me smile. He was who he was and you either accepted it or not.

And then I dropped the smile as soon as I thought of how much of a dick he'd been when we'd first met, any thought of loving him temporarily slipped away.

Well, I guess it wasn't always so cute, but we'd gotten past that and I wouldn't bring it up.

Knowing he'd lose his mind if I unbuckled my seatbelt, I kissed my fingertips and reached over to press them to his cheek, grinning like a moron because Dex would be amused with the gesture. He didn't let me down, a goofy half grin covered his mouth. "You're one of the best people I know."

He didn't say anything in return, but each time I looked over at him afterward, the pensive look on his face was stained with pure smugness.

We passed by the hospital my mom used to work at, and I was suddenly slammed with the reminder that I'd hopefully be seeing my dad in a few hours. I wondered what he looked like for some reason. Would he still have the same beard? Would he recognize me immediately? Would he think that I looked like my mom?

"Babe, what the hell is that sigh for?" Dex asked.

I groaned low enough that he might have not heard. "I think I'm nervous about seeing my dad for the first time in forever." I sighed. "It feels like the first day of school or something. It might be almost as bad as my first day at Pins."

He flicked both dark eyebrows up. "Nothin' to be worried about," he assured me.

Nothing at all.

Not if he didn't have the money.

Not if he'd skipped town.

If, if, if, if, and more friggin' if.

Had I mentioned before how much I hated relying on another people?

Especially when that person was the least reliable individual I'd possibly ever met.

"Charlie..."

He chuckled, flicking those bright blue eyes in my direction. "Don't worry about it."

I mashed my lips together and kept my worries to myself. There wasn't a point in stressing until we knew for sure if he really was in town. Sure Luther wouldn't have a reason to lie, and I'd hope his friend wouldn't either, but I wasn't going to put all my eggs into one basket. I'd worry when I knew for sure Curt Taylor was around.

I spotted a few more places I'd seen a hundred times before. The family owned hardware store, the grocery store, the salons that had been around since mullets had been in style.

And it was all way too déjà-vu like.

Reminders of some of the best times of my life and the worst.

The hotel we pulled into was a member of a big chain, something I'd found for cheap on my phone when we'd entered Florida. I'd paid for it before telling Dex anything because he'd try to talk me into grabbing his credit card. I sleepwalked through check-in, filling out paperwork with the worst handwriting ever.

"Here you go," the hotel employee said as she handed me two key cards, her eyes straying from the tattoo on Dex's neck, and then back over to the nasty bruise on my cheek.

Oh hell. Whatever.

I wrapped my arm around Dex's and leaned into him, the side of my face pressed to his bicep like it was the most natural thing in the world. Those blue eyes glanced down at me, lined and circled in purplish blue, and one side of his mouth tipped up. His free hand went up to smooth over the top of my head. "C'mon, lazy bones."

There's no doubt in my mind I resembled an adoring puppy on the walk to our room.

"Shower first, honey, I gotta call Son and Lu to check up with 'em," Dex said as we dropped our bags just inside the door.

I nodded at him before fishing through the duffel bag, eyeing the king sized bed that took up the majority of the room. I poked him in the arm as I passed by, rushing through my shower, and getting dressed in an old threadbare sweatshirt and plain bikini panties before I somehow managed to fall asleep standing.

Just as I was about to open the door, I heard Dex on the other side.

"—better than that. Quit bein' a dumb fuck about it," he bit off.

Well. I don't think he'd be talking to Luther like that, and if it was Sonny he was talking to...then, I'd like to hear that conversation.

"She told me everything." He paused. "Yeah, that too. Look, Son—"

Five guesses as to what my traitor-ass brother could be finally spilling.

"I want this shit over with...Yeah...I wanna go back home, and she's comin' with me. How fuckin' hard is that for you to understand? She's mine, my brother, and I don't give a single fuck if you're mad about it or not. It is what it is and you gotta remember how well you know me....You think I'd be here if I didn't?"

Crap. At that moment, I would've given my first born to know what Sonny was saying on the other line instead of settling for guesses. Sometimes I hated how curious I was. I should have just gone into the bedroom like a normal person. Oh, who am I kidding? Anybody would be standing on the other side of the door eavesdropping.

Dex made a noise that sounded like a snarl. "This isn't gonna be a goddamn waste of her time or mine. I'm a grown ass man, Son. You're not gonna tell me what I can and can't do. I know exactly what I'm doin'. You wanna try to beat the shit out of me when we get back? 'Kay. I don't give a shit. You're not changin' my mind. Piss your little pants—"

Sonny must have cut him off because the next thing he did was laugh bitterly. "Not a single fuck. Not half of one. Not a quarter of one. Nothin'. You can kiss my fuckin' ass and so can Trip. I'll call you when I find your pa, ya stubborn fuck."

Then there was nothing.

I waited a few minutes on the other side of the door, waiting to see if Dex said anything else but that was a negative. There was only some rustling and creaking as he moved around the room.

Well. Okay. Wiping off my what-the-hell expression, I opened the door casually. Dex was sitting on the edge of the bed when I came out, stripped down to his boxers and yawning with his mouth wide open. Totally comfortable. Completely relaxed like he hadn't just gotten into an argument with my brother.

Once again, Charles Dexter Locke, with his solid, bulging six pack, full ink sleeves, pierced nipples, and the darn cutest tattooed red octopus, was sitting there nearly naked.

My mouth fluttered wordlessly.

Would this ever get old? I sure as heck hoped not.

"You're so hot." The statement was out of my mouth before I could withhold it.

Now, the smile that crept over his tired, still yawning features, was absolutely not withheld. He leaned back on his hands, watching me with those tired eyes. "Come here," he murmured.

Like I was going to hesitate when I had the chance to stand so close to him and all that glorious warm skin. I stopped between his widespread legs.

Dex sat up, gripping the back of my thighs loosely before starting a trail up over the curve of my ass, beneath the thin and stretched out material of my sweater. It was second nature to still wear long-sleeved stuff, regardless of whether he knew about my arm or not. Luckily, he didn't point it out as his hot hands circled most of my waist, his thumbs making these tiny circles just above my belly button ring. My shirt bunched over his arms.

"Seen a lot of things in my life—"

Don't vomit, Iris.

By a lot of things, he didn't necessarily mean people.

Okay, who am I kidding, he probably did.

I wasn't going to puke. I wasn't.

"But you," his nostrils flared, "my sweet, sweet baby, have gotta be my favorite by far. I think you win first through one-hundredth place." His head dipped forward to bite at the loose cotton draped over his forearms. He slowly edged the material up with his teeth and tongue until he finagled his head beneath my sweatshirt, a solid lump above my tummy.

The tip of his tongue tapped the stud of my belly button ring briefly. His breath warmed the skin above it before he pressed his lips to the same spot, damp and gentle. Dex touched his tongue to the same place, more of a wet kiss than a lick.

"Smell so good," he murmured as his hands kneaded my hips, making me arch into him.

Looking down at him, with his face up my shirt, kissing and licking at me, I didn't think there was anything hotter in the world.

Dex kissed each side of my ribs with slow, chaste pecks. "Wish I wasn't so tired," he said, tongue tracing a line up my stomach.

Oh boy.

That wet, raspy tip stopped right between my breasts. I could see his head turn to the right, brushing a small line on the underside of my breast. His lips latched on to that inside swell, sucking it gently. Holy friggin' crap. He switched his mouth over to the other little globe and did the same.

I made noises that weren't entirely human as heat bloomed at my core.

And that's when he pulled his head out from under my shirt, planting one last quick kiss on my piercing. "Gotta shower, babe."

I choked. *Was he serious?*

My expression must have conveyed the what-the-friggin'-hell look on my face because he smothered a laugh by pressing his lips to my now-clothed hip. "I'm so damn tired. You don't need to stay up if you don't wanna," he said, coming to stand with his hands still beneath my shirt.

Dex flashed me another tired grin, kissing the top of my head right before he side-stepped me with a smack to my ass.

"Get some sleep," he said as if that was even an option when it felt like Niagara Falls was between my legs.

By the time I realized that he wasn't kidding, leaving me there standing like a complete moron, he'd already turned on the shower.

That dick.

I climbed into bed trying my best not to think about Dex's pleasured face the night before—all loose and relaxed with happiness mixed in there. Which then got me *not* thinking of how he'd looked days before that with his mouth...

Stop it.

The bed was surprisingly a lot more comfortable than my bed at Sonny's, and definitely way more than Dex's couch. I wasn't surprised when I fell asleep almost immediately after putting my head on the pillow.

And it felt like I'd barely done that when I was rolled onto my stomach, my cheek against the sheets. Warm lips and cool air tickled my spine. Two sets of fingers swept over my shoulder blades, down the twin sections of my back.

I was still half asleep as his forearm slipped between my belly and the mattress. His mouth traced over the notches of my spine. Warmth curled from the nape of my neck down to my tail bone, and instinctively, I arched my back like a cat into his touch.

Blinking sleepily, I noticed it was pitch black in the room. We must have only been asleep for a few hours at the most. The only noise came from the low hum of the air conditioner against the wall and the creaking of the bed under Dex's shifting weight as he inched his way down the mattress, arm still locked around me.

"Not tired anymore?" I whispered the question in a hoarse voice.

His low chuckle filled the room, tongue swirling a circle at the lowest point of my back. "All I needed was a little nap," he breathed right before nipping my butt cheek.

Oh man.

I may have stretched into a deeper arch, which earned me another nip on the other cheek.

Dex's free hand cupped my bottom, his long fingers spanning from the crease to nearly my hip. "This ass..." he groaned, kissing each cheek simultaneously. "Do I gotta thank all that time you spend swimmin' for it or your ma, that you got blessed with it?"

I wiggled my butt a little. "I don't know."

There was no warning for the hard crush of his arm hiking my hips up high before the tip of his tongue streaked its way down my cleft, slipping into my slit with a wet thrust.

Holy crap. Holy times a million craps.

Dex's flat tongue licked over my seam, once, twice—not enough—careful and controlled when he'd make a quick detour to dip his pointed tongue inside.

Dead, dead, dead. He was going to kill me with his mouth. And his lips.

Oh lord, especially his lips when he started sucking gently on the each soft fold.

Mother. Blooming. Heavenonearth.

I probably should have been embarrassed by the cries and the moans that wormed their way out of my throat as I tried to push my hips back against him. My cheek was still flat on the mattress, fingers curled into the hotel room's bed sheets, and it must have been the lack of vision that heightened every wet touch, every low little groan he made of approval when he'd slip his tongue where I wanted—needed—something bigger.

Almost as if he'd read my mind, his hand gave my ass a little squeeze before I choked out a cry in time with the deep press of long fingers inching into my channel, replacing that brutal, raspy tongue. Dex's mouth kissed my cheeks, fingers sinking deep in me. Curling. Moving in and out as I whined into the bed.

"Perfect, baby. So fuckin' perfect..." I barely heard him pant into the skin of my bottom.

I was so wet I could feel it. Hear it. The sloppy sounds of his fingers going in and out of me, making me desperate for that tingle that had blossomed in my lower stomach the moment he'd rolled me onto my stomach.

The speed of his movements doubled then tripled. That burn grew and grew as he kissed and nipped at my cheeks, biting harder and harder the more wet I got. Between the frenzy of his fingers, and that blessed heat radiating off of his body, it was paradise.

Until he suddenly pulled away.

I turned to look over my shoulder, not caring at all that I could barely see the outline of his frame in the darkness, but the hot presence of his arm around my waist confirmed he was still there.

Then, he was there. The fat tip of his cock was suddenly between my lower lips as he dropped his weight down to cover me. Thighs on the outside of mine. Groin over my back. Chest on my back. Dex was a human blanket that slowly pushed his broad, beefy shaft into me inch by delicious inch.

Even now, after barely twenty-four hours, it was the tightest fit. Not painful exactly but there was no way in hell I could ever forget, even after just having that bulbous head in me, that he was there. Filling me. Stretching me. Grinding himself into my cleft once he'd worked that long length in me.

And holy shit. Holy. Shit.

I pulsed around him before he even had the chance to withdraw for the first time.

Dex's mouth came down on the curve of my shoulder and neck, biting down hard, we both groaned for completely different reasons. "Fuck, Ritz," he whispered but there was no power behind it. No real need or desire for me to stop.

So I squeezed my inner muscles again, and got a circling of his hips in response along with another deep, guttural groan. It felt like I was filled to the max. One more inch, one more millimeter in girth and there's no way in hell I could have taken him without being in pain, I figured.

But this... this was perfect.

I arched my back even deeper, appreciating the years I'd spent practicing yoga and stretching after swimming, and that settled the ridge of his cock even deeper. "Oh!"

Dex groaned, long and low against my back. "Goddamn it, baby," he hissed. Damp lips moved across the line of my shoulder. Never withdrawing an inch, he slipped his knees between my legs, spreading my thighs so wide if I had on clothes, it would've looked like I was crawling under barbed wire in the military.

The arm around my waist tightened when he finally withdrew the barest inch, and then thrust forward. Hard. He withdrew two inches the second time, and then slammed home. Slow and steady, Dex built up the push and pull, one inch on top of another inch until just the very tip of his engorged head stretched home.

Then, he thrust.

And I choked sounds and wild gasps as his warm balls slapped against me on splitting pushes in. The sounds of Dex panting on each measured slide broke the steady panting out of my mouth, the sound of flesh meeting flesh. His hard cock burying itself into me with powerful thrusts that made me push back for more.

I groaned into the bed when he tipped his hips a certain way that hit something magical in me.

He growled his agreement before biting my shoulder again. "Good." He nipped the other side. "Fuckin'...good."

Oh hell.

With a quick shift of our bodies, he gripped me hard to him and flipped us over, keeping the wet, filled connection between us until he was on his back with my back and hips settled perfectly on top of him. Dex planted his feet on the bed and spread my legs so that they went over his, knee to knee, leaving me open and vulnerable.

At least until he bucked his hips.

I cried out his name and got another pump of his pelvis.

It was instinct that had me reaching both arms up on either side of his face to brace myself on the headboard. Dex's face was right next to mine when I tipped it to the side. I couldn't see more than just the easy shape of his features, so hard and strong even in the dark that I knew where his mouth was, finding it where I shouldn't have been able to.

His tongue searched mine out, clashing with it completely off rhythm from the way he thrust that long shaft in and out. His arm snaked around my upper chest and the other directly beneath my breasts like steel bands. The position made his thrusts more shallow but the angle...

"Please don't stop," I gasped, curling my feet around his calves to anchor me down as his hips pumped harder each second.

"Not happenin'," he said hoarsely, slipping a hand down to press his fingers to the top of my cleft. Dex jerked his hips, spearing me hard. I tipped my head back, locking my elbows to keep me in place when his thrusts got rougher and quicker.

I'm not sure whether it was him or me that started to sweat first but my back was damp. My inner thighs trembled as they stretched wide over Dex's bent knees. "Dex, Dex, Dex," I chanted his name.

Gently, he drew circles over my clit as I squirmed on top of him, desperate for more of his cock, more of his fingers. More, more, more.

His teeth nipped at my jaw. "Love you like this," he murmured. "All soft and wet for me, baby." Dex thrust hard, making me cry out. "My own sweet little pussy… all mine… isn't that right, honey?"

What? What the heck was he talking about?

"Say it," he insisted when all I did was moan in response to a circling of fingertips over my clit. "Say it."

Oh boy.

I squirmed my hips over him, squeezing my core around his thick erection. "It's yours, Charlie."

"Always," he made clear with a sharp thrust.

Oh friggin' hell. I could feel it. Feel that magical explosion of fireworks and rainbows in my toes. "Always."

The way he pistoned his hips at my confirmation said that he was a pleased man. Thrusting clear off the surface of the mattress, the arm around my chest clamped down.

Dex was like a man possessed, ripping an orgasm straight out of a pot of gold from me. I could have screamed, cried tears of joy, or started speaking in tongues as my release came over me, and I wouldn't have remembered. Fireworks zipped up my spine for so long I thought I'd melt into him, or at least melt around his girth.

In the quickest movement ever, he pulled out of me, closing my thighs around his cock as he thrust into them. One time, two times, sprouting out a rough shout as he came, splashing hot streams over my stomach and chest with languid pumps in the aftermath.

I panted in time with Dex's own harsh breathing filling my ear, making me deaf and dumb to everything else.

It was only the hot sweep of his hands over the swells of my breasts, shoulders, and up my arms that pulled me back to reality. His thumb brushed over the scarring of my arm. Lazily, slowly, Dex lowered our legs flat to the bed before rolling us to our sides.

Looking over my shoulder, I flashed him a tired smile and tipped my face up for a kiss. And what a kiss it was. Silky, gentle, more lips than tongue. More affection than possession.

Well, almost.

"Wake me up like that any time you want."

A smile broke out over Dex's face. All he did was palm the side of my face and kiss the corner of my mouth with a soft murmur, "Plannin' on it."

CHAPTER THIRTY-FIVE

I had the terrible urge to throw up when I woke up the next morning.

The first thought in my head, before I accepted that I was laying in bed naked with Dex, involved my dad. My friggin' dad. The man I was probably—hopefully—seeing today for the first time in eight years.

Shit.

Not crap, *shit*.

Whether it was nerves, anger, or a sickening sense of anticipation that filled my belly, I wasn't sure and it made me uneasy.

So uneasy that Dex caught onto it before we'd even left the hotel room. He was standing in the doorway to the bathroom, buttoning his jeans, when he frowned at me. "What's wrong?"

I wanted to say "Nothing" but I didn't. No more lies and all, right? I had to settle for giving him a sheepish smile at the same time I stole a glance at Uriel. Who am I kidding? I was looking at his nipple piercings, remembering briefly how they'd felt on my back hours before.

Snap out of it!

I tried to hide my awkward cough. "I think I'm a little nervous."

"Why?" he asked like my admission was absolutely stupid.

"I don't know. I think I'm nervous to see my dad since it's been so long, but I also kind of feel like we should be on a bounty hunter show or something. Does that make sense?" I scratched at my throat.

Dex narrowed his eyes, pulling his toothbrush out of his mouth slowly. "No."

Well.

"Don't be nervous, babe. What you got to be nervous about? We're gonna find your pa, and then we're gonna figure out a way to get this shit handled before I get sent to jail for murder," he said so nonchalantly, I almost could have dismissed the fact that he even brought up the possibility of going back to jail.

For murder. Because of me.

Oh lord.

I'd shank him before he did something that stupid, so I chose to ignore that part of his comment. "I don't think it's that easy."

He gave me a hard look, shoving his toothbrush back into his mouth. "It is."

I left it at that because in reality, how the heck could I explain to Dex why I was so nervous to see my dad? It wasn't like I didn't already accept the way things were.

He'd left me and my family. Check.

He'd left me at sixteen in the middle of radiation with a dead mother. Check.

And then he'd left me again to deal with his mess at twenty-four, obviously knowing what kind of people he was dealing with. Check.

It hit me right smack in the face. A hard smack that might have knocked a few teeth loose.

He sucked. Plain and simple.

He was no Sonny. He wasn't even a Will because I knew that if I told my brother people had been showing up to my job threatening my life, he'd do whatever he could to fix it. Literally, he would have done anything. I just hadn't wanted to drag him into this mess.

Curt Taylor was no Luther even. Lu had gone as far as to let Dex and I borrow his car to come look for my dad. He'd helped me look for his crappy ass. And he barely knew me.

Curt Taylor was absolutely no Dex either. No Charlie. There was no fierce possessiveness or loyalty. Nothing. Besides both being males and members of the Widowmakers MC, that was it. There was no other trace of similarity between the man standing in front of me and the one who had walked out on me.

This was a man that had left people who needed him hanging a million and a half times. What in the friggin' hell did I have to be nervous about? If anything, he needed to be nervous about meeting me. There wasn't a single thing that I owed him. This wasn't about reconnecting with him or seeking the love and guidance he'd ripped from me when I was too young to understand it.

He should be scared of me.

At least his organs needed to be. Because I swore to myself right then, sitting on the edge of the hotel bed, that I'd make sure he paid the damn Croatians back somehow.

The old bastard owed me that much.

"He's a sneaky son of a bitch," Sonny sighed on his end of the line.

Bracing my feet on the bottom rung of the stool, I glanced around the diner like my dad could be hiding in a booth. That friggin' asswipe. "The guy at the front desk told me he checked out yesterday. Yesterday, Sonny. It was like he knew what happened or something."

"Maybe he did, Ris. Wouldn't hold it past the old bastard."

"It's bull crap." I cast another glance around the diner, this time looking for Dex. He'd left for the bathroom a few minutes before but he hadn't come back yet. "We're going to try to go to a few different motels around the area and see if we can find him."

Yeah, the chances were slim, and Dex and I had both acknowledged that my dad would have to be a complete moron to move hotels within a few miles distance but...I'd never said he wasn't a total moron. I could hope for the best, it was all I had.

Sonny hummed in response, the tension awkward between us still. I almost hadn't called him, but after the phone conversation I'd overheard the night before between him and my tattooed behemoth, I figured it was the best option. The truth was, it pained me that Sonny was still mad at me. Even after I'd told him all about the incident at Pins, he'd sounded angry but still so distant. It wasn't the way I felt he would have responded if things had been fine between us.

And it was my fault, which was the hardest thing to swallow but probably the most important. Actions always have consequences, right?

I looked over my shoulder while I waited to hear if Sonny said anything else, to see Dex standing just outside the bathroom with a waitress crowding his space. Not our waitress, just a cute one that had smiled at us when we walked in. Whore.

Okay, that was rude.

"Keep me posted on whether you guys need me to drive down there or not, I should be getting to Austin in a day or two depending on how many times Trip wants to stop," my brother said.

Still looking at Dex as he shook his head at whatever the waitress was saying to him, I swallowed back the weird feeling in my throat and focused on my conversation with Sonny. There was no way I wanted to spend minutes of my life worried about whether or not Dex was doing something suspicious behind my back. I mean, he was right there. He'd never given me a reason not to trust him.

I closed my eyes and tried to imagine the many, many times Sonny had eaten something he didn't like all because I wouldn't eat meat. Or the hundreds of times he'd worried about my health and well-being. Sonny mattered to me. And I needed to try and fix what was wrong with us. That mattered.

"Son, I love you. A lot. And I'm sorry I've been such a lying shit and I know that my promises probably don't mean anything to you anymore but I swear I won't lie to you again. At least not over anything so stupid. I mean, if you ask me if I finished the last PopTart, I might lie but that's it. Nothing else important."

And then I waited. And waited. And waited.

Jesus, Mary, and Joseph, he really was that pissed off at me. Holy crap. I'd finally done it.

"Kid," he finally spoke after what felt like a year. "You pissed me the hell off but I love you anyway. Nothing will ever change that. Not even that dumb monkey you got playing bodyguard."

"I like my dumb monkey." Like hell was I going to bring up him being mad at me again. I was going to focus on something other than that.

Sonny sighed again, this long, suffering sigh. "That's unfortunate."

"He's really nice to me," I whispered into the phone, turning around in the stool to look for said dumb monkey. He was still standing by the bathrooms with the waitress talking to him. "I'd like to keep him, so I hope you aren't planning on murdering him."

"Kinda ruining my plans there, kid," he said, and I wasn't sure whether he was joking or not. More than likely, he wasn't. "He didn't exactly keep to the truce between the Club, of leaving family alone. He knows that's not cool."

"Eh." I glanced around to see the tall, black-haired jerk making his way around the booths toward where he'd left me. "At least leave his face alone." I paused before adding, "And his hands."

My half-brother groaned. "Getting off the phone now."

I was torn between laughing and being ridiculously embarrassed by the way I'd made the comment sound. "That wasn't what I meant!"

"Don't care, kid. The damage is done."

Warm fingers drew a line from my bare shoulder down to my wrist before Dex sat down next to me, his chest a solid wall of muscle and heat on my side. I glanced at his face, seeing it calm and passive. So handsome. Yet, I still cringed when I thought about the mental picture Sonny was probably having. "Yeah, okay."

"Call me later?" he asked.

I kept my eyes on Dex as his own gaze dragged its way from the low cut half of my shirt, and then up over my face. The corner of his mouth went up in a soft smile. "Sure will. Drive safe." Then, I added for good measure, watching Charlie as I said, "Love you."

Sonny must have mumbled the response to me but I missed it. The only thing I captured was the dial tone after he hung up. Because the man sitting next to me was watching me with those curious blue eyes.

As soon as I set the phone flat on the counter, I nudged my shoulder into his arm. "Just checking in with Son."

That hot gaze ran over my face, my mouth, my cheeks, before making its way to stare straight into my eyes. "Got all y'alls shit straightened out?" he asked in a lower voice.

"Mmmhmm. I had to let him call you a dumb monkey to get his forgiveness but I doubt you care."

Dex slid those long fingers over my wrist, circling the bones gently. "You happy he's finally talkin' to you again?" I nodded, earning a shrug. "Then I don't give a fuck what he thinks, you know that."

I did know that. Like I knew plenty of other crazy things. Like the fact that I'd offer up one of my dad's body parts to ensure Dex's safety. Leaning into him again, I pressed my mouth into his biceps. "Yeah, I know you don't."

"One stack of blueberry pancakes, and a double stack with a side of sausage," our waitress appeared then, dropping each of our plates in front of us.

I thanked her and watched her disappear, looking around for the younger one I'd spotted talking to Dex just a few minutes before. But she wasn't anywhere.

"I think I pissed her off," Dex said abruptly, making me drag my eyes back to him.

He was busy cutting into the huge mound of pancakes in front of him, his tone casual.

"The waitress you were talking to?"

He lifted a single shoulder in a shrug. "She was annoyin' the shit outta me. Don't know why she'd think I'd care whether she likes my ink or not."

My first thought was that the girl had run to the kitchen and spit in our food. Oh hell.

Dex cut into another thick triangle, eyeing me out of the corner of his eye. "Wouldn't quit ramblin' about how she wants to get tatted up, even after I told her my girl was waitin' on me."

It'd be the biggest lie in the universe if I said I didn't get a thrill out of him calling me his girl. Was that a little barbaric? Maybe, but who cared? I didn't. "You can't blame her, you're pretty cute, Charlie. I'm sure plenty of women wouldn't care that you're with someone else." As much as the thought bothered me, it was the truth.

An exasperated sigh made its way out of his pretty mouth. "Cute?" he said the word like he was torn between being disgusted and amused, ignoring my other comment.

All right, I could pretend too. "Excuse me, you're a hot, virile, stud-muffin."

He pinned me with a flat look that made me laugh.

"What? You are." When his facial expression didn't change for a long minute, I laughed again and poked him in the side. I wasn't going to let my dad and his disappearance plummet my mood. He wouldn't have that much power over me. And I definitely wasn't going to take it out on the one person that was here trying to help me, no siree. "Fine, you're just hot. Smoking hot. Not cute. Definitely not cute at all."

Dex gave me that signature little smile before returning his attention to his plate. We took a few bites of our food before he finally spoke again. "You know there's nothin' and nobody you gotta worry about, Ritz."

Here we go. I nodded but didn't look at him. "I believe you." I just didn't want to carry around this fear that Dex would eventually get bored. He wasn't my father, and every day I knew him better and better, that fact was cemented in place more firmly.

He plucked the fork from my hand before pulling it beneath the counter of the diner, setting it palm down right next to his groin. "Babe, you got me as much as I got you, and that shit's not changin', you understand? Not today, tomorrow, not ever." He slid his hand over mine, cupping it firmly to the shape of his thigh. "Got it?"

"Dex," I sighed.

"Ritz."

"You can't say stuff like that. You might get tired of me at some point."

"No." He shook his head. "I know exactly what I'm sayin'. I know exactly what I mean. Yeah?"

He wasn't really asking, I knew that. So I also knew it was pointless to argue with him, and at the same time, it was pointless to make excuses as to why he couldn't care for me like that. I'd never know unless I let him. I squeezed his thigh and nodded. "Yeah, I got it." For good measure, I smiled. "Cutie."

"Ritz," he groaned, but I could tell by the look in his eye he didn't care.

"Just kidding." Taking my hand off his leg, I cut a neat triangle out of my blueberry pancakes before muttering under my breath, "Not really."

That got a snort out of him.

The younger waitress that had been harassing Dex before made an appearance right then at a table on the opposite side of the diner. So I took the opportunity to make Dex laugh again. I think I enjoyed the sound way too much. "Dex?"

"Yeah, baby?"

"She's back," I whispered, and then paused. "I think I'm going to need your keys."

And as always, he didn't disappoint me with the loud, loud laugh that burst out of my reserved, broody man.

Three days passed and nothing.

No trace of him.

That son of a friggin' gun had disappeared and my irritation had reached a level never before seen courtesy of my short-lived period. That's how pissed off and stressed I was—my period had lasted half the time it normally did.

"We'll find him," Dex had assured me about a dozen times a day.

The problem was that it was incredibly hard to hold out hope of finding a man that excelled at disappearing. We'd met with Luther's friend the day before but the older man hadn't seen him either. Luckily for me and everyone else, the normally moody man that drove us from Delray to Boca to Deerfield Beach, was optimistic enough for the both of us.

There's no way he knew we were in Florida, of that I was certain. Luther's friend had promised us he'd been discreet, so it just had to be a coincidence he'd gone somewhere else.

At least that's what I really hoped.

"Never heard of 'im," the older biker drawled from over the rim of his highball glass, drinking something that was all amber and no ice.

I felt like a balloon that had gotten stabbed with a needle. Deflated. Completely deflated.

Dex shot me a look before extending his hand out to the crazy bearded man. "Thanks, brother."

Another bust. Again. How many was that today? Eight different bars in and around Hollywood? Who the hell even knew there was that many kind of bars here?

I shook the man's hand just like Dex had, and followed him back out. The man had been the last of the three we'd made an effort to zero in on at the bar. Follow his lead, he'd said, and I had. But we were coming up with nothing. Four days in my home state and nothing.

This sucked.

The moment I'd climbed into the truck and shut the door, Dex cut me a glance before reaching over to grab my hand. "You feel like doin' somethin' else?"

I was too old to pout and cry about how unfair this crap was, so instead, I threaded my fingers through Dex's and sighed. I want to find my dad. But that wasn't happening. This entire trip had so far been a dead end. No dad. Painful memories. And food from places I'd gone to with Will hundreds of times that suddenly didn't seem anywhere near as delicious as they had months before.

All this driving around did was make me miss my mom and *yia-yia* more. That was probably what led me to open my mouth and suggest something for the first time since we'd started our search.

It was still early in the day. Only about six, so there should have been an hour of sunlight left...

"Do you mind if we go to the cemetery?" I asked Dex hesitantly.

"Why the hell would I mind, babe?" he asked, already putting the truck into reverse. "Tell me how to get there."

The cemetery was pretty close to where we were at. It seemed like I'd just been there yesterday. I didn't need a map or directions to instruct Dex on where to go. In no time, he was pulling into the long, winding drive through the grounds.

Until he wasn't.

He parked the truck along the ultra familiar drive. I could recognize the slight slope of the grounds even if I were blind. I got out and looked around, watching as Dex climbed out as well, his eyes wary and uncomfortable as they flitted over tombstone and tombstone.

"Are you okay?" I asked him after he'd taken a long gulp. He didn't look well.

"Yeah," was his simple answer.

Was he...uncomfortable? From what I could remember, his grandfather had died when he was a baby. All of his family members seemed to still be kicking, so the only thing I could come up with was that cemeteries freaked him out. There was nothing wrong with that.

But I kept my mouth shut and appreciated the gesture instead. "You can stay if you want, I won't be long," I told him,

Those dark eyes narrowed in suspicion. "You sure?"

I could see it on his face. *Please be sure.*

"Yeah, it's fine. Fifteen minutes tops."

It took him a second to agree but once he'd fed me a nod, I blew him a smile and started making my way toward the large tree that served as a marker to where my mom and *yia-yia* were buried together.

Months had done nothing to the lush grasses or the classy tombstones that my grandmother had paid for years in advance of her death. She had never found anything ironic about planning for her passing before she was even close to the day. I found the spot almost immediately, taking in the side by side headstones beckoning me forward.

In some sweet, romantic movie, there would be flowers from my dad on the grave with promises of love that could survive an apocalypse. Of a love that had no value for time and no understanding of death.

But there wasn't.

Not a weed. Not a live flower. Not even a dead flower. Or an old love note.

Nothing. Nada. Zilch. Grass and more perfectly manicured grass.

To say that it was disappointing would be the understatement of the week. Then again, what did I expect from a reigning disappointment of a human being?

I should know better.

It was almost an afterthought lowering myself to my knees when I came up to my mom and *yia-yia's* grave. Sweet but incredibly bitter. How many times had I sat here in the years after *yia-yia* had died asking for her moral and mental help with Will? Dozens?

Raising a brother was hard. It had always been hard, but after *yia-yia* died, it got even more difficult. Yet, somehow we'd found a way.

My hands brushed over the sticky green blades, feeling how closely cropped they were. Immaculate and untrodden. I suddenly wished, more than the hope of finding my dad, that I'd have either one of them around to tell me what I should do with this situation.

I wanted their guidance. Their suggestions. Their support.

And all I had was this damn grass.

I wasn't nervous or afraid. I was desperate. What should I do? Give up? Sell my car? Try to get a loan? Start a murder-for-hire business?

Quitting wasn't a part of my DNA. Being forced to submit was but it was also a last resort. I'd always thought of myself as being practical.

I had no idea how long I sat there, looking at the etched names with a heavy soul. It couldn't have been that long if the sun was still out—low but it was there. Tired emotionally rather than physically, I got up and made my way back to the car to find Dex sitting in the bed with an unlit cigarette in his mouth. His eyes made a slow path over me as I got closer, checking and inspecting.

Dex stood up, throwing a long leg over the tail bed. With a graceful hop, he dropped to the ground, tucking his cigarette behind his ear.

Neither one of us said anything as I walked over to him and slipped my arms around his waist. Dex wrapped an arm over the top of my shoulders, his free hand finding its way into my hair. I took a hesitant sniff of his shirt, but all he did was smell faintly like soap and laundry detergent.

"You don't have to quit smoking because of me," I told him though obviously I'd rather he did, but I wouldn't ask him to.

He twisted my hair around his fingers. "'Kay."

"I'm serious."

He kept twisting knots at the end of my ponytail. "Went five years without a smoke, babe," he whispered into my ear, his lower lip brushing the shell. "There's shit I want and shit I need. A smoke's not one of 'em, 'specially not when I'm around you."

Was it wrong that his words made me swoon a little? And that I wasn't even going to bother arguing with him more about it?

Going up to the tips of my toes, I pressed my lips against the underside of his chin. "In that case, thank you." I pressed my face to his chest for a moment, savoring the hug.

"You doin' all right?"

I nodded enough so that the top of my head brushed his chin. "Yeah. I just miss them."

Dex hummed in his throat, his arms tightening around me in response to my comment. His body, his heat, his comfort, and safety, saturated me. The feel of him fed the parts of me that were needy and that grounded me. It wasn't that anyone or anything could ever replace the two women who had raised me, but Dex was so much man and personality, that I realized I wasn't alone anymore.

And as selfish as it was, I hoped I wouldn't be alone ever again.

I squeezed his waist. "Since we're here and all, want to go to my favorite pizza place? Sonny used to say they made the best pepperoni."

"I like pizza." A hand slid down the curve of my spine until I felt a strong pinch on my bottom. "What are you gonna eat? Cheese?" he snickered.

"Spinach alfredo, smart ass." I snorted and took a step away from him, rubbing where he'd gotten me.

Dex wrinkled his nose but made his way around me, swatting my rear when he had the chance. "Spinach alfredo it is, babe," he said.

I got into the truck after him, smiling like a moron. I was in the middle of thinking all about magical thin crust delicacies as Dex steered us out of the cemetery. For some reason, just as we were stopping at the gates, I happened to look across the street. There was one of those pay-per-hour motels on the corner.

"Left or right?" Dex asked.

It was supposed to be a left but something had me zeroing in on the hooker hostel. "Right." Worse case was, we could circle around and head back in the same direction, right?

Dex turned right.

I craned my head to look into the parking lot. What would I really find? Nothing, more than likely.

And I didn't, at first at least. Cars and trucks. Then I saw the handlebar. It could have been anyone's but what if it wasn't? It couldn't be that obvious...

I reached over to slap Dex's arm. "Pull in there, please."

That wonderful man didn't even bother asking why I wanted him to turn into the lot. Swinging the truck to a hard left, he drove the pickup into the two-story motel's parking lot. Up close now, the bike was like a kick to the sternum.

It was still shiny, black with a coil of red shot through the body. Almost a decade later, I still recognized it like the back of my hand. Torn between the memories of being a kid and climbing all over it when it'd been parked in the driveway, and the last memory I had of my dad riding away immediately after Mom's funeral, a frog curled in my throat.

"It's him."

The tires squealed as he slammed down on the brakes. Dex didn't even bother pulling into a spot before parking behind two cars in the lot. I was out of the truck before him, looking at all of the doors like I had some type of internal radar that let me know which room he was in.

"Lemme go find out where he's at," Dex murmured with a squeeze to my forearm.

Uhh...

Yeah, maybe I didn't want to know how he was planning on getting that information.

I stood there as he walked in the direction of the tiny office by the parking lot's entrance. Looking, looking, looking. In less than five minutes Dex's loose gait had him standing next to me.

I took a deep breath to steady my nerves and tipped my head up, trying to be confident. "Is the employee still alive?"

He smirked, the corner of his mouth arching up so high those pretty white teeth flashed at me. He tugged on the hem of my shirt. "Alive and fingers intact, babe."

"Smart ass." Not laughing was impossible. I held up my hand for a high-five. Dex shook his head with a chuckle and slapped it, linking our fingers together afterward.

"Let's go."

I wrapped my free hand around the inside of his elbow, taking confidence in the dark tattoos on his arms. They reminded me of Pins, and my friends there. Safety. Familiarity. Tattoos were Dex. My friend. My protector.

"Let's do this," I agreed.

Up the stairs we went. Down the hallway. A turn to the right.

And we stopped.

Dex held up a hand to knock on the door but I stopped him by grabbing his wrist. I ducked my head and pressed my lips to his thumb, sucking a breath to steady myself. Dex was watching me with those dark, steady eyes—curious.

"Thank you for coming with me," I whispered.

His nostrils flared, and he nodded briskly.

I knocked but no one answered immediately.

I knocked again, this time harder.

Still nothing.

I knocked even harder, faster, more annoyingly persistent.

Still, nothing.

Dex leaned over me, pounding his fist against the door. "Open the fuckin' door," he growled.

Oh hell.

Six foot three and bossy? As long as it wasn't directed at me, it made my ovaries sing an opera.

The lock turning was the only thing that pulled me from my Dex-fantasies. For some reason, I suddenly wondered whether my dad still had facial hair or not.

It was just like a movie in slow motion.

The door opening.

The dark hotel room.

The expectation.

At the door, a woman stood in a t-shirt three sizes too large. A woman that was possibly only a decade older than me.

"Uh, can I help you?"

If he was in there, I was going to kill him. I decided that immediately.

I ignored the woman in front of me and looked over my shoulder at my dark-haired Dex. I wasn't going to have a panic attack or turn into a rabid raccoon with him behind me, that was for sure. "Are you sure this is his room?"

All he needed to do was nod before a confidence and a rage I wasn't extremely familiar with, flooded my stomach.

Fuck this.

With balls that I didn't even know I had, I leaned forward and spoke louder than I probably ever had. "I know you're in there, and I'm not leaving until you get out here."

Where the hell had meek little Iris gone?

"The fuck?" the woman spat, frowning.

Classy. "The man in there with you needs to come talk to his daughter."

"Daughter?" Baloney. This woman was absolutely baloney.

There was a noise coming from the recesses of the hotel room, a voice talking so low I'm surprised the person in front of me could hear. My ears were ringing so loud with adrenaline and frankly anger that I couldn't hear anything clearly.

I had my eyes locked on the lady in front of me, taking in her dark hair, olive skin, light eyes. She was a poor replica of my mother, I thought, as mean as I would have normally assumed the thought was. But I didn't care then. I sized her up. I watched her take a step back and turn around to talk to the man in there.

I had to swallow hard to keep from making some awful noise. If it wouldn't have been for the warm heat on my back that radiated from Dex's chest, I'm not sure what I would have done as I waited for my father to come to the door.

My father. The thought was so immediately detached it should have alarmed me, but I'm surprised by how freeing it was. Not my dad. My father. My sperm donor in Sonny's words.

"Iris."

He was there.

Shorter than what I remembered, or maybe the careful balloon I'd inflated with his memory had been too exaggerated. Or maybe I'd just been around Dex's long bones for too long.

Curt Taylor stood there. With his heavily tattooed forearms void of any past Widowmaker insignia. A salt and pepper mustache curling his upper lip. Hair still short. And so much older than I remembered.

My heart churned in recognition—in need. But only for a split second. For a millisecond I allowed myself to miss him. To miss the times he'd made me feel like I was the most important person in the world to him.

But that time had been decades ago. A faded photograph. It was broken and corrupted.

And most specifically and fortunately for me, I'd been patched up along the way.

I let my hand reach backward until I grasped Dex's thigh, using it to center me as I stared at the man I'd denied myself loving for so long.

But the love I knew, the form of love I remember as a child was completely different than the version I recognized as an adult. There's no chemistry to it. You can't break apart love's properties and make it something it's not. I knew that now.

A small, stupid part of me might always feel something my father, but that didn't mean that I respected him. That I truly valued him. Not when it had suddenly occurred to me how obvious it was that he didn't feel the same toward me. And love without respect and appreciation isn't actually anything. It's worthless.

I knew what it was like to be valued. To be cared for. To be a priority. And I wasn't going to settle for less from the man that should have shown me all of those things throughout my life.

Fuck. That.

I wasn't a little girl anymore. I wouldn't fall for his tricks or his foolish, meaningless words.

If I had a baby, a little tiny boy or girl that had grown up in my arms, there was no way I could ever leave them willingly. There was no way I couldn't think about him or her daily and wonder if they were fine, when I did that for my own little brother. Hell, I even worried about Slim and Blake all the time. What did that say?

It said I wasn't my father, and I never would be.

"We need to talk."

"Iris?" His voice cracked.

I'm not sure what it said about me that I was able to look at his face steadily without feeling a thing besides resentment. "We really do need to talk."

He blinked those hazel eyes. The Taylor eyes he'd given Sonny and me. "Rissy," he said my nickname slowly, "I haven't seen you—"

Dex's growl cut him off. "I don't wanna hear it. She don't wanna hear it. Get your shit, 'cuz we're goin'."

My father, Curt, blinked rapidly. His eyes widened like he had barely seen Dex standing behind me, well, more like towering behind me. My own personal eclipse of ink and ego.

The angry frown that curled over his mouth was the predecessor for those hazel eyes flicking back and forth between me and Dex. Slowly, his eyes moved over the multicolored bruises on my cheek that still hadn't exactly faded. "You son of a bitch," my father boomed. "Did you do that to her?"

My bruise?

Dex? Dex who'd been ready to tear apart the universe because of what those morons had done?

"Old man," Dex hissed, bringing his body so close to mine that I could feel him settle himself around the curves of my back and bottom. "You should shut the fuck up before you say somethin' I'll make you regret."

Oh hell. *Diffuse the situation, Iris!*

I had to take a calming breath. This wasn't just about me. This was about Dex, Sonny, Slim, Blake, and the little boy in Colorado that shared my bloodline. As much as my subconscious would love seeing Dex stand up to this man, my brain said that this wasn't the right time.

This visit was about preventing something terrible from happening to all of them.

I could do this for them. I could keep it together.

"This is because of the Croatians. Because of you," I stated evenly, watching the color drain from his face. "And I don't care what you have to do, but you're paying them back."

"The...they...found you?" he blabbered.

Stupid, stupid, stupid.

The wicked laugh that snaked its way out of Dex let me know he thought my dad was just as full of shit as I did. "You wanna play stupid? I'll play stupid with you. What'd you think? You'd take their money and nothin' would happen?"

My father's eyes slashed over in Dex's direction, his mouth pulled tight in aggression. "Shut your trap, kid."

"Kid?" He was outraged.

Kid? Dex? Did he need glasses?

"Yeah, kid. I been bustin' people up longer than you been alive, don't come up to me, trying to be a bad ass. I'll beat it out of you," Curt snapped.

Dex barked out a laugh. "Old man, you might have been doin' it for longer than me but that don't mean I won't wipe the floor with you. At least I fight my battles with my own two hands instead of lettin' my blood get it beat out of 'em for me."

"You piece of trash—"

And... I was done.

Done.

What did it say about me that I was willing to throw away the thread-like connection with my father for a man I loved? Nothing. Because ultimately, it didn't matter. I'd throw away more.

My stretched out palm met with my father's chest as I pushed him back with more force than was necessary.

His hazel eyes flared, more in response to the moment and the conversation with Dex than with me. At least that's what I could assume. I pointed a finger at my father and shook my head, watching as his eyes drifted the length of my arm until they came in contact with the silver-white scarring my sleeveless racerback left open for everyone to see. See it, he did, and it only reinforced my words and my mood.

"Don't say a word to him. Not a single friggin' word. In the last month, Sonny's gotten the crap beat out of him. I got assaulted at my job, and I've been asked to become some douche bag's mistress. All because of you. You owe me, and trust me, you don't want me to start with the million and one things I've dealt with because of you before this year."

He opened his mouth to argue with me. His eyes going from my arm to Dex's face above mine.

"Don't," I insisted. "Just don't."

"He's a Widow, Rissy!" my dad yelled, completely oblivious to the fact we were standing outside of a cheap motel with dozens of other people.

That's where he was going with this?

"He's mine," I enunciated slowly. "And my business stopped being your business when you left."

I couldn't have slapped him any harder. And my inner jerk couldn't have been more pleased by the stripe of pain and humiliation that blazed across his face.

"Yeah," I taunted him. "Exactly."

Where had all of this ugliness bubbled up from?

"I didn't think..." he stammered. "They came after you?"

I didn't even bother with an answer, settling for a brisk nod.

My dad lifted both of his hands up, running them over the short trimmed hair on his head. "Jesus." He shook his head. "I never thought—"

Dex's body heat seared my back as he stepped forward, into me. He braced his hands on the doorframe, caging me. "You never cared. Don't mistake bein' a dick for bein' an idiot."

He bristled, his mouth poised to argue or talk shit back to the younger man.

Them arguing wasn't the point. It wasn't necessary. "It doesn't matter anymore. I need to know if you have the money."

The face he made wasn't a good sign. "Rissy."

"Yes or no?"

My father blew out a breath that made his lips flutter. "Not all of it."

I guess that could be worse, unless he considered twenty bucks to be a significant chunk. "How much?"

"Fuck." His lips fluttered again. "You wanna come in and talk about this?"

Dex and I answered at the same time. "No." Especially not when that woman was still in there. Gross.

"You got five minutes to meet us downstairs," Dex said. "Gimme your keys."

My father took a step back, frowning fiercely. "Excuse me?"

"Your keys. Give 'em to me."

"Why the fuck would I do that?"

Maybe he didn't know, but I did. I held my hand out. "We can't risk you leaving."

"I'm not leaving," he argued and for a split second I felt rude agreeing with Dex's request.

This wasn't anyone else's battle but mine. I held out my hand and waited. He didn't hand them over immediately. My father's face made a dozen expressions until he finally turned around and went into the room. Whispers stacked on top of each other before he returned, dropping a set of keys into my palm.

"Five minutes," Dex spoke from behind me as I eyed the woman in the room moving around.

The woman dressed in my father's clothes. The woman that looked like my mom if I closed my eyes, squinted, and made my vision blurry.

I sighed. All I could focus on right then, was how disappointed I was in this man I used to call my dad.

Awkward wouldn't even begin to describe the atmosphere in Luther's truck, or the tension across the table at the pizza parlor.

Tense also wouldn't be an appropriate adjective.

"Rissy—," he'd started to say about a dozen times before Dex shut him down.

"Don't," my dark-haired man snarled.

I didn't make an effort to assure Dex that it was fine, that I wanted to talk to my father, because honestly, I didn't.

"Rissy," he'd start again on deaf ears.

My mom. My poor, beautiful, sweet mom had been in love with this man. She'd thought the world of him even after he abandoned her with two small kids. She loved him even though he never called, never helped financially, never did a single damn thing.

Rage boiled beneath my veins.

If I'd known everything that I knew now...

That I was related to a self-centered man-whore...

I reached out to grab Dex's hand, threading my fingers over the top of his. The look he gave me was tight. He was seething beneath his skin and I had no idea what directly fueled him, but it wasn't like he didn't have a dozen possible sources.

Dex wasn't my father. Not in any way, shape or form. And I loved him.

"I owe 'em twenty but I got eighteen on hand."

Okay, that wasn't so horrific. A two thousand dollar difference wasn't as bad as I'd been expecting. Then again, I wasn't expecting him to owe people twenty friggin' thousand dollars either. Holy crap.

How much money did I have in my savings account? I tried to do the math in my head.

Twelve hundred for sure, maybe fifteen hundred...

Fingers gripped my forearm. Dex made a grunting noise in his throat that caught my attention more than his grasp. "Don't even think about it," he warned in a stern voice.

How the heck did he know what I was thinking? "What?"

"We aren't usin' your money." He squeezed my arm. "We talked about this, Ris. We'll figure it out, right?"

That's exactly what we'd agreed on. I nodded at him, ignoring the inquisitive look on my father's face as he watched us.

Dex tilted his face back over to him, eyes narrowed. "You like that, big man? Your daughter offerin' to pay for your shit? Her cleanin' up your mess? Seems to be somethin' you're used to. Leavin' your shit layin' around for other people to clean up."

It was impossible not to hear the grinding of Curt Taylor's teeth, or miss the way he leaned across the greasy table. "You don't know shit about me—"

"I know enough."

"You don't know a damn thing—"

"You think I don't know everythin' there is to know about you? I know what I need to, and lemme tell you, I'm not impressed. You're a grade A pussy, Taylor, and you're a fuckin' moron," Dex rolled the words out of his mouth.

Oh hell. They were talking so loud people at the tables surrounding us started to turn around. I palmed the inside of Dex's thigh to try and calm him down. Not that it was an easy task to begin with when he was pissed off.

He was defending me though, not picking a fight just for the heck of it.

"What are we going to do?" I asked them both.

The sperm donor reclined back in the booth, crossing his arms over his chest. The resemblance between him and Sonny was shocking. The eyes, the build, the freaking attitude. "I can come up with the other two but it'll take a little while," he explained in a low voice.

It was too much to ask for that he'd be embarrassed by the situation, much less have him admit that he was guilty of being a Grade A Jackass.

Dex snickered, slipping his hand over mine. "Not two. Twenty-one."

I think we both turned to look at him like he was crazy.

All Dex did was raise a lazy, defiant eyebrow. "You forgettin' about the money you owed the Reapers?"

"Goddamn," my dad muttered, scrubbing his hands over his hair again.

Hadn't he told me just days before that that had been sorted out? Wait, what the hell had he meant by sorting things out? And what the hell had I been thinking assuming that the debt had magically disappeared? Like that kind of crap actually happened.

"Twenty-one?" he choked out.

Dex tapped his fingers on the counter, his fingers kneading my thigh. "There's somethin' called interest, ya know." He tipped his chin up. "But don't worry about that right now. You and me can work out a payment plan once my girl is off the choppin' block."

Payment plan?

Say what?

I wanted to ask him for clarification but this wasn't the time, at least not while the sperm donor sat three feet from us. He could see the question on my face. *You paid it off?*

Curt opened his mouth like he wanted to say something else. He mouthed, my girl, but said nothing. He rubbed his hands over his scalp again, exasperated. "I can make back the money in a few days if I drop by Mississippi and Louisiana, and hit up the casinos."

I looked at Dex, and he looked at me, and I didn't even think twice about dropping my forehead to the table and banging it on there a couple of times.

What had I said before? About how you can't change people's natures?

It was right then that the buzzer on the table went off, signaling that our food was ready. Dex smoothed a hand over my thigh before sliding out of the booth with the contraption in hand.

Out of the corner of my eye, I saw my dad reach across the table, fingers outstretched. "Rissy," he whispered.

I watched him, watched those long fingers try and make a trek toward me but I stayed still.

"Talk to me."

I flicked my eyes up to his. There was no effort on my half to forget the memories I had of him as a kid. The memories that had kept me from bulldozing him into being a complete asshole but now... nothing. I felt nothing toward him. "We're talking."

He ground his teeth again. "Without the asshole."

Oh. Hell. No. "I love that asshole. He stays."

The expression he made gave the impression that I'd slapped him. He was outraged. "You're kidding me."

"I'm not."

"I never wanted that for you," he hissed. "Don't you get that? You think me and Delia moved all the way out here for no reason? We didn't want you around the MC, and especially not fuckin' around with one of them."

Anger prickled my neck. Resentment. Bitterness. "Things don't always work out the way you want them to." I could have explained to him the line of events that led me to Austin but I wasn't going to. I was happy there, and I didn't regret my move for a second. And this man didn't deserve an explanation.

It wasn't like he'd explained anything to me. Ever.

"You don't get it..."

"There's nothing to get," I cut him off, sharply.

"Your mom—"

The more he mentioned her, the angrier I got because it made me think of the woman in his hotel room, and the little boy in Denver. "Don't bring her up."

His light colored eyes flashed. Indecision and who knows what else tore through him. "She was the love of my life."

Now, he was just asking for Dex to kick his ass. Better yet, I'd kick his ass. My hands clenched into fists in my lap. "Is that why you left? Because you loved her so much? You loved her so much you cheated on her and had a kid with someone else?"

He rocked back in his seat. "You don't get it," he repeated.

"No, I do get it. I get that you loved her in your own messed up way, but what were me and Will? Collateral damage? Accidents?" My chin tipped up on its own as my jaw clenched. "Nothing, right? We were nothing to you?"

"Goddamnit, that's not it at all. Why won't you stop being so fuckin' hostile and let me talk?" he snapped.

Yeah, I was done with this. Done with this man and this bull crap.

I swallowed hard and took a deep breath. "I'm here because you need to fix this mess with those Europeans before they kill me or someone I care about. This isn't a social visit to talk about how much you've sucked being a human being, much less a father."

"Quit being such a bi—"

The drop of two pizza trays on the table droned out the end of his sentence. Dex's imposing figure loomed over the table, his hands gripping the edge. "You finish that fuckin' sentence, and I'll skin you alive."

Was he going to call me a bitch? Me?

My throat knotted up at the same time tears managed to find their way into the backs of my eyes. I ducked my head to keep either of them from seeing my reaction. I had to take a deep breath to center myself.

Of all the people in the universe, why did I have to be related to such a douche bag?

Unfortunately, you don't get to choose family, Sonny had told me once. But you do get to choose everyone else. In this case, I was cherry picking who I was going to spend the gift of my life with. Now *that* I deserved. Even without the cancer, without losing my mom and *yia-yia*, I would have wanted more. Not this sloppy excuse of a man.

I blinked and blinked again until I got myself under control.

Looking up, I caught the murderous look on Dex's face. The way his shoulders stiffened. He knew. He knew exactly what I was battling.

I couldn't glance at my father as I spoke. I kept my gaze steady on the tip of Uriel's tentacle peeping out from the black lip of his collar. This was right. Being there with him, that was fate. That was me taking control of my life and paving a new path. "I never want to see you again."

It was only the straightening of Dex's back that gave a warning he had processed my words and come to a conclusion.

That conclusion was in the shape of his fist nailing my father in the chin.

Maybe in a few years, or heck, maybe even months from then, I might feel guilty about what we did after that.

Then again, maybe I wouldn't feel a thing. Maybe, just maybe, I would never think about that visit to the pizza place or the man we left bleeding there. Who knows.

But what I did know, without a doubt in my heart, was that we did the right thing. The only thing. Maybe not the ethical or the nice thing, but when you're left to fend for yourself and for the ones you love, being proper and good-hearted goes straight out of the window.

We left.

My dad's keys in Dex's pocket, Dex and I walked out hand in hand.

A ruthlessness I didn't think I was capable of reinforced my veins and determination filled me as I spoke for the first time after Dex had stood up for me. "How much do you think we can get for his bike?"

The slow way in which he turned his head, brow up and lips pursed, was a mixture of shock and something else. But the smile that took over his features after that was the most stunning thing I'd ever seen. He reached across the console to palm my cheek. Those tattooed fingers, with the words LOYAL DREAM etched on them permanently, filled my chest with so much love and assurance I would have gone through the incident moments before all over again a hundred times for the same result.

Dex's nostrils flared as his thumb swiped over the yellowing bruise along my cheekbone. "Not sure but I know somebody who will."

Thirty minutes later, our plan had been hatched, a motel room had been broken into, and a motorcycle had disappeared from the parking lot it'd been parked in.

CHAPTER THIRTY-SIX

Linking our fingers together, Dex led me toward the elevators that night. In a matter of hours, we'd committed at least four crimes between the two of us. Battery, assault, breaking and entering, theft and who knows what the heck else.

Who would have ever thought I'd consider myself a criminal? Normally, I sweat going five miles over the speed limit.

I wrapped both my arms around his, resting my forehead on his shoulder while we rode up silently. What was there to say? We'd taken fifteen thousand from the vent my dad had hidden it in—I didn't ask how Dex knew to look there—and taken his bike to Luther's friend, who assured us he could find a buyer for the Harley Davidson Classic. For a fee, of course.

Paperwork? Tax, title, and license?

Don't worry about it, he'd said. So I wasn't going to worry about it.

The only thing I was going to worry about were the remaining thousands my dad would still owe him if we got what was expected from the bike. The Reaper money.

"So...is there something you want to tell me?"

His fingers loosened around mine letting his fingernails scrape my palm. "I tell you everythin', honey."

"Not exactly," I said in a sing-song voice as we walked toward the hotel room. He slid the keycard in. "Dex, did you pay off the Reapers?"

He grunted, holding the door open for me to go through first.

I stopped in the middle of the room and waited for him to come in, setting the deadbolt. Gosh, he was so good-looking.

His body was lean and long, his arms looked fantastic under his white shirt. Well, white with a couple small red dots on the chest. My sperm donor's blood. Dex stopped just a few feet away from me, sliding his hands into his front pockets.

"Yeah." So simple. So honest.

"Why?" I cut the distance between us, stopping close enough so that I could slip my fingers beneath the band of his jeans. Warm skin greeted the backs of my fingers.

Dex reached up and pulled the elastic out of my messy bun. "'Cuz." He twisted the hair around his fingers, not watching my eyes. "I didn't want anybody botherin' you."

How the heck was I still standing?

"You think I want that douche-bag comin' around for you when your pa didn't pay up? Fuckin' asshole wasn't even plannin' on payin' them back, babe."

I thought it was a little less him not remembering and a little more him just not choosing to remember. Dick head.

Dex's fingers made their way to my temple, the tips sliding down, down, down behind my ears and the column of my throat. "Don't like thinkin' about him wantin' you."

Him as in Liam.

Oh boy.

Everything in me that had been crushed and stomped on by my father's careless words and stupid actions, regenerated itself with Dex's touch and words. Slipping my fingers out of his jeans, I reached for the hem of his shirt and pulled it up enough to bare the lower half of his abs.

"I'll pay you back the rest of the money," I promised, slipping my hand up his shirt to palm the space between his pecs. "It'll take me a while but—"

Dex's hands cupped the top of my head, stroking me tenderly. "No."

"I'm serious. I promise I'll pay you back—"

"No," he repeated. "You aren't payin' me back a cent."

Discomfort tingled the back of my neck. I owed him for a lot of things, but almost ten thousand was too much. The last thing I wanted was for him to think that I wanted to take advantage of him. "I am."

"No. You won't. Ritz, look at me." I tipped my eyes up to meet his blue ones. "I don't give a shit about the money. I'll make more."

A groan vibrated through my throat. "It's too much."

His lips pulled into a grim line, eyes searching mine. He wanted to argue with me, I could tell. But he didn't. That beautiful face was tight. "You wanna pay me back? Enroll in school and take over all the accountin' for the Club and the shop, yeah?"

My mouth drooped. "That's not the same."

"I'm not sayin' for a few months or somethin', baby. I'm sayin' you take it over from now on," he clarified.

From now on.

Oh friggin' hell.

"Take it or leave it," he murmured, his mouth losing that tight vector. "Don't care one way or another."

This man. "It's too much money. Way too much money, Charlie. I don't want to take advantage of you."

"You're not, babe. I know you and you know me. Either take the offer or leave it, but I'm not takin' any of your money. You got the rest of your life to pay me back by doin' shit I don't like."

My rib cage clenched all of the organs and muscles within it. It pulsed, full of life and warmth and gummy bears and glitter. This was... I don't know how to explain it—it was like Christmas morning when you were a kid. It was everything I'd wanted since my dad first left, in a way.

And there was nothing better than that.

"It's a deal," I agreed with him in a breathless whisper.

Each of his thumbs curved over the shells of my ears. "That's my girl."

His girl.

After all the crap that I'd gone through today, there couldn't have been three better words to hear.

Well, there were three other words I'd like to hear but I'd take these from him. That didn't mean that he was the only one who knew how to give. He'd given enough. My bones and heart knew that there was nothing for me to fear. I loved him and sometimes there were consequences of it that were scary, but it—the emotion itself—wasn't. I knew that now.

What kind of life was I living if I let my fears steer me? This was a gift I'd forgotten to appreciate lately. For so long I'd been happy to just be alive but now...now I had Dex. I had my entire life ahead of me, and I needed to quit being a wuss and grab life by the balls. In this case, I'd take his nipple piercings.

"What'cha thinkin', Ritz?"

I held my hands out for him to see how badly they were shaking. "I'm thinking that I love you so much it scares me. See?"

Dex's thumbs tipped my chin back so that I could look at his face—at his beautiful, scruffy face. "Baby." He said my name like a purr that reached the vertebrae of my spine.

I curled my lips behind my teeth and took a deep breath, overwhelmed by the good things that nipped at my nervous system. "And even though it really scares the living crap out of me, I love you, and I want you to know that. Everything you've done for me..." Oh hell. I had to let out a long gust of breath. "Thank you. You're the best thing that ever yelled at me."

He murmured my name again, low and smooth. The pads of his thumbs dug a little deeper into the soft tissue on the underside of my jaw. "If all the shit I do for you, and all the shit I'd be willin' to do for you doesn't tell you how deep you've snuck into me, honey, then I'll tell you."

He lowered his mouth right next to my ear, his teeth nipping at my lobe before he whispered, "Love you."

The feeling that swamped me was indescribable.

He gave me hope. This big, ex-felon with a temper, reminded me of how strong I was, and then made me stronger on top of it.

"Dex," I exhaled his name.

He nipped my ear again. "I love you, Ritz." The scruff of his jaw scraped my own before he bit it gently. "Love your fuckin' face, your *that's what she said* jokes, your dorky ass high-fives and your arm, but I really fuckin' love how much of a little shit you are. You got nuts bigger than your brother, baby."

I choked out a laugh.

Dex tipped my head back even further, holding the weight on his long fingers as he bit the curve of my chin. "And those are gonna be my nuts, you little bad ass."

Fire shot straight through my chest. "Yeah?" I panted.

"Yeah." He nodded, biting my chin even harder. "I already told you I keep what's mine."

EPILOGUE

I was going to puke.

Literally.

"You're gonna have to pull over."

Sonny turned to look at me over his shoulder, eyes wide in exasperation. "Again?"

This was only the third time.

Well, the third time in the last hour.

The overly enthusiastic nod I gave him must have been enough for him to jerk the rental car over to the side of the road. The uneven payment made my stomach roll even harder. We'd barely come to a rolling stop when I threw the back passenger door open and jumped out, throwing up things that shouldn't have even been in my stomach after puking my guts out twice before.

To think that Dex's mom had told me I'd be suffering through this for the next two months.

Two months. If I was lucky.

Why? *Why?*

It wasn't as often anymore that I missed my mom but when the morning sickness had finally kicked in—just weeks after that friggin' test came back positive—it had hit me like a battering ram. Who would I go to for advice? I didn't know the first thing about....that. So even though I'd been excited—and terrified out of my mind—missing her, needing her, had dampened all of that those first few days.

Until I'd gone to the doctor and known for sure that my life would be changed forever.

Then again, I guess it'd only been a matter of time. I'd swear on my life that Dex had been working toward this goal from the moment...well, knowing that smug dick, probably from the moment he'd decided to tell his two best friends to—in his words—"Go fuck themselves."

"You okay, babe?" Two hands landed on my shoulders, kneading them as I stood hunched over the overgrown weeds.

I probably had puke on the edges of my mouth. Great.

Nodding, I straightened up, pulling one of the many paper towels I'd stuffed into my back pocket to wipe at my mouth. "I'm okay."

Dex's chuckle filled my ears as he wrapped his arms around my chest from behind, his chin resting on the top of my head. "Just okay?"

He was taunting me, I knew it.

I hadn't told him the news yet, but in that same preternatural way he was always aware of what I was feeling or thinking, he could smell my lies a mile away. He was just giving me time to come to him.

To tell him I'd be baking his bun for the next seven and a half months.

I'd just wanted the insanity of these last two weeks to be over. My semester's finals had ended three days before, Dex had been busier than ever with the Widows opening up a new bar, and then there'd been this trip. The trip that had originally been planned for Sonny, Will, and I.

Yet, not so surprisingly, Will had flaked out two weeks before, and Dex had suddenly 'decided' he wanted to come along. It just so happened that I'd taken the pregnancy test the day before he bought his plane ticket.

Right.

This man never did anything without a reason. And this reason had him resembling a mama bear. A really aggressive, possessive mama bear. Which said something because Dex was normally that way. I couldn't even sit around Mayhem without him or Sonny within ten feet.

I leaned my head back against his chest and laughed. "Yeah, just okay."

He made a humming noise deep in his throat. "Ritz," he drawled in that low voice that reached the darkest parts of my organs. "You're killin' me, honey."

Oh boy.

Did I want to officially break the news on the side of the road with chunks of puke possibly still on my face? Nah. So I went with the truth. "I have it all planned out in my head. I already ordered the cutest little toy motorcycle to tell you, so don't ruin it."

A loud laugh burst out of his chest, so strong it rocked my body alongside his. I friggin' loved this guy. Every single time he laughed, I swear it multiplied. At this rate, I loved him more than my own life cubed, and then cubed again.

"All right," he murmured between these low chuckles once he'd calmed down a bit. His fingers trailed over the skin of the back of my hand until he stopped at my ring finger and squeezed the slender bone. "I can be patient."

That earned him a laugh from me. Patience? Dex? Even after more than three years, that would still never be a term I'd use to describe him. And it probably never would. He'd started to lose his shit during our layover when Trip had called for instructions on how to set the alarm at the new bar.

"Dex, Ris, and Baby Locke, you done?" Sonny yelled, peeping out from over the top of the car door.

"Are you friggin' kidding me?" I yelled back. Did everyone know?

The bulging eyes my half-brother gave me weren't apologetic in the least. I wasn't even going to bother asking how he knew. These two jerks knew me better than anyone, including the flake I called my little brother. The same little brother I'd only seen twice. The wuss that had been too scared to come meet his little brother.

Not that it said much considering it'd taken me three years to finally get out to Colorado but Carson, my thirteen-year-old half brother, had been more than okay with our gradual progression into getting to know each other. We'd gone from me sending him a birthday present, to a single phone call as a thank you. Then monthly phone conversations for a year, to weekly emails, and finally, Skype video calls.

Even then, it had taken me a couple months to finally getting around to calling him once life had gotten back to normal after the crap with the man who shall never be named.

It had taken Dex and I another week and a half to get my father's motorcycle sold. That money had been enough to cover the remaining amount he owed the Croatians. Then, getting the money to them had been another tedious process to ensure that the matter was closed and we'd be safe afterward.

Just that easily, after those assholes got their money back, there was never another issue.

With the mafia, with the Reapers, or with my father.

The same father that had never made another appearance in my life, or any of my brothers'.

And I could easily say I hadn't felt an ounce of guilt over what we'd done on that trip even years later. It also helped that we never did find out what the money had been for. By the end of it all, I didn't care. At all.

"Ready?" Sonny called out again, tapping the roof of the car with his palm.

"Chill the fuck out," Dex yelled back. Well, their friendship had taken a few months to get back on track but they were fine now.

You know, *after* they got into a fist fight at Mayhem. And *then* got into a second fight in Luther's backyard . *Yeah.* I missed witnessing both, but I didn't miss the swollen noses, black eyes and busted lips afterward. Yet I couldn't help but feel a sense of completion that these two caveman-esque idiots were mine. *My* proud, loyal morons.

I pulled away from him and slowly turned around, tipping my head back to look at his face. God, he was so good looking. So incredibly perfect. I could see the tip of Uriel's tentacle on one side of his neck, and the multicolored burst of a rainbow on the other side of his neck. The rainbow was my tattoo. The blue dragon Slim had been hounding me about getting for weeks.

Only Dex had beat me to it, weaving my name through the colors in violet, in a way that only Slim was capable of.

My own little blue dragon, a fraction of the size of his, had finally found a home on the inside of my wrist shortly afterward.

Going up to my tippy toes, I kissed the underside of the neatly trimmed beard he'd been growing in over the last few months. "Love you."

That slow, seductive smile crawled over his features. Brilliant and more affectionate than it was possible for me to handle, it sucked the breath out of me. When he palmed my cheeks and kissed each of my cheeks and nose and forehead, slowly like he was savoring the pecks and the contact, I ate it all up. Like always, and just like I always would.

"Fuckin' love you," he breathed against my ear, an arm slinking around my lower back to press us together. "More than anything."

The damn car horn honked, long and low. Friggin' Sonny.

I smiled up at Dex and threaded my fingers through his. "You ready?" I asked him. The question was broad and reached in a dozen different directions.

And he answered the way I knew he would every single time I asked him from them on, the way that told me he would never let me down. That he was an immovable object. That he'd always be there for me to battle the demons we could see and the invisible ones we couldn't. "*Iris.*"

ABOUT THE AUTHOR

Mariana Zapata lives in Texas with her longtime boyfriend and two oversized children—her beloved Great Danes, Dorian and Kaiser. When she's not writing, she's reading, cursing the gym or pretending to write. Or burning experiments in the kitchen.

www.twitter.com/marianazapata_

www.facebook.com/marianazapatawrites

Printed in Great Britain
by Amazon

31552396R00281